SHE BLINKED, AND HER lips parted once more. The pink tip of her tongue darted out. Heated need shot to his groin, and he forced himself to loosen his grip.

She must have sensed his hesitance, for she moved closer. "Please."

Oh, damn. If she planned on begging him in that cracked little voice, he was well and truly buggered. "Isabelle—"

"Please, I need . . ."

He touched his fingers to her lips to stop her from completing that thought. "It's not a good idea. I should leave."

But he couldn't very well rise with her nearly in his lap, couldn't dump her onto the floor.

"I cannot bear to be alone." She formed the words around his fingertips, and his resolve slipped a bit further.

"There's a difference between keeping company and asking for trouble."

"Please." That word again. It burned through him.

And then she took away his choice along with his chance to protest. Seizing him by the lapels, she covered his lips with hers.

By Ashlyn Macnamara

A Most Scandalous Proposal
A Most Devilish Rogue

A Most Devilish Rogue

ASHLYN MACNAMARA

BALLANTINE BOOKS • NEW YORK

A Ballantine Books Mass Market Original

Copyright © 2013 by Ashlyn Macnamara
Excerpt from *A Most Scandalous Proposal* by Ashlyn Macnamara
copyright © 2013 by Ashlyn Macnamara

Published in the United States by Ballantine Books, an imprint of The Random House Publishing Group, a division of Random House, Inc., New York.

BALLANTINE and the HOUSE colophon are registered trademarks of Random House, Inc.

ISBN 978-0-345-53476-7
eBook ISBN 978-0-345-53477-4

Cover design: Lynn Andreozzi
Cover illustration: Alan Ayers

Printed in the United States of America

www.ballantinebooks.com

9 8 7 6 5 4 3 2 1

Ballantine Books mass market edition: September 2013

To Kathleen—
you helped me out of a jam on this one
in more ways than one.

A Most
Devilish
Rogue

CHAPTER ONE

London, 1820

Iｆ ｔｈｅ key to announcing bad news lay in the timing, George Upperton's mistress knew when to deliver.

"What's that?" Some odd emotion invaded the haze of post-coital bliss, and he rolled to his side. "For a moment there, I could have sworn you told me you were with child."

Lucy Padgett closed long-lashed eyelids. Strawberry-blond hair tumbled over bare shoulders and breasts as she ducked her head. "I did."

Like a fist to the gut, her affirmation sent the air rushing from his lungs. He frowned and pushed himself up on one elbow. "Are you certain? This could make for a very bad joke."

She shifted to her back, arms crossed, and her eyes snapped open, sparkling with blue fire. "Joke?" Her usual melodic tones hardened to ice. "This isn't a joke. How could you be so coldhearted as to question me?"

"I only . . ." The fist was still planted in his gut. It settled into the pit of his stomach, hard and leaden, yet managed to expand until breathing became a chore. He pulled in a lungful of air through his nose and tried again. "I thought it took a while before a woman knew."

"It's been two months since I last had my courses. They've never been late before."

George counted back the days in his head. Two months . . . eight weeks . . . A lot could happen to a man in that time. In his particular case, a lot *had* happened. Quite enough to drive thoughts of Lucy claiming she was indisposed from his mind.

"I thought . . ."

She wasn't going to like his next comment, but damn it, he had to say it. They weren't likely to pass the rest of the evening in a more agreeable fashion. Not after her announcement. The mere thought of engaging in additional bed sport now made that weight in his gut twist until he rather felt like casting up his accounts.

"I thought you'd taken the usual precautions."

"Precautions?" She yanked the sheet free of the mattress and wrapped herself in it, the same way she draped herself in indignation. "Precautions?" She squeaked a high note on the final syllable. "You know very well the usual precautions are no guarantee. Last I looked, I didn't create a brat all on my own. I had help."

George had no clue how to reply to this. She was right, of course, but truth was, he'd never considered the matter. He'd assumed she'd protected herself because that's what wise women of her standing did—ensured no unpleasant consequences might cost them their protector.

The heavy sensation intensified until beads of sweat broke out on his brow. How coldhearted he'd become. How cynical. He thrust aside an image of Lucy cradling a tiny, gray-eyed boy with waves of light brown hair. His son. Who'd have thought? Of course, he couldn't cast the poor woman off at a time like this. Bitter experience had taught him just how rejection felt.

"No sense in arguing over the matter now that it's too late." He was amazed at how reasonable he sounded, voice low, steady, almost comforting. It nearly set *him* at ease.

Nearly.

The thought of raising a child made him want to carve out a neat hiding spot in his liquor cabinet and remain there for the next few decades.

Blast it all, he couldn't afford this. He could barely afford Lucy, especially since she'd revealed quite extravagant taste where her wardrobe was concerned. The latest bill from her modiste had sent him straight to his club.

She glared at him. "What do you plan on doing about this?"

"Doing?" Damned if he knew. The bottle of brandy in the sitting room was calling at the moment. A deuced siren it was, just as seductive as the Lorelei.

"You . . . you don't want me to raise it, do you?" She sniffed. "I shall require some form of compensation. How else will I live? I certainly won't find another gentleman once I'm fat with your get."

"No, no, of course not." He swung his legs over the side of the bed and plucked his dressing gown from the heap of clothing on the floor. How blithely he'd shed it an hour before. How blindly. "When you mention compensation, what did you have in mind?"

He paid close attention to his dressing gown as he awaited her reply. He slipped his arms through heavy velvet sleeves. Easier to concentrate on the weight of the fabric on his shoulders than to witness her calculated assessment of what she might gain from him.

But he owed her now, didn't he? He'd taken his pleasure in her body and now he must pay a much heftier price than he'd ever imagined.

"I'll need the house, of course."

"Of course," he echoed. He was already behind on rent.

"And I'll need to keep on the cook and my maid. Oh, and a new wardrobe." He imagined her ticking items off on her fingers. He couldn't bring himself to look. "In a few months, I won't possibly be able to wear my gowns."

The weight in his stomach plummeted, and he sank to the mattress. He covered his mouth with one hand until he was certain his dinner would stay where it belonged before sliding his fingers down his chin. "Lucy, my dear, I meant to tell you . . . I mean, I really ought to have said something before now. That's entirely my fault. But honestly . . ."

The words wouldn't come. George Upperton was known among his circle of cronies as a prime wit, but now, when it mattered most, he couldn't summon the means to reveal the truth.

"How dare you!" She leapt from the bed, dragging the sheet along with her. "You utter, utter scoundrel. How could you possibly?"

He glanced sideways at her. Her face had gone a deep crimson that clashed horribly with her red-gold hair. "How dare I what?"

"I've just announced to you that I'm in a delicate condition and you have the colossal nerve to hand me my *congé*?"

At delicate, he almost snorted. The notes she'd just hit with that shriek were nearly pure enough to shatter crystal or set nearby dogs to howling. Lucy was anything but delicate. But then the rest of her accusation struck him in the gut. "*Congé*? I'm not as coldhearted as all that. What I was trying to tell you—"

A pounding on the bedroom door cut him off. "What the deuce?"

Lucy stared at him, round-eyed, and drew the sheet more firmly about her breasts. The pounding increased until the heavy oak plank rattled on its hinges.

George tightened his belt, rose, and strode across the room. "Here now. What is the meaning—"

He whipped the door open and found himself face-to-face with a tall, dark-haired man. A ratty topcoat covered a rough linen waistcoat and loose trousers.

Behind the intruder, Lucy's maid cowered. "Beggin' yer pardon, sir, but he insisted."

George narrowed his eyes and glanced over his shoulder at Lucy. "Might I ask what this man is doing, demanding entrance to your private chambers?"

"I didn't come here looking for her," the newcomer growled. He grabbed George by the front of his dressing gown and whipped him about. "I came here looking for you."

Him? What the devil? George forced a grin to his lips. "You could just as easily have found me at my townhouse during regular calling hours. Now you've caught me completely unprepared for company. Suppose we might persuade the maid to put the kettle on, but I'm afraid we've finished the biscuits."

As he clattered on, he sized up the stranger—an old strategy of his that had extricated him from any number of tight situations. The man's face was squarish, topped by a slash of dark brows with a firm line of a mouth at its base. Nothing familiar about it. Certainly not one of his creditors. His creditors had a better sense of style.

The stranger gave George a shake. "I didn't come to pay my respects."

"Yes, I'm getting that impression." He allowed nonchalance to infuse his tone. It was too difficult to inspect one's nails when a great oaf had one by the lapels. "But suppose, before you beat the stuffing out of me, you tell me who you are and explain why. Then I may or may not take it like a man, depending on whether or not I agree with you."

Another shake, this one hard enough to rattle his back teeth. "You talk too much."

"So I've been told." He grinned—winningly, he

hoped—while balling his hand into a fist. He'd learned the trick as a schoolboy. Make the opponent think he'd try to charm his way out of a fight until said opponent succumbed to a false sense of security. That strategy, combined with an innate sense of when to duck, had saved his nose on more than one occasion. "Can't seem to help myself, though. I have a tendency to natter on when threatened. See? There I go again."

"Shut your gob and listen. You've put my sister in a delicate condition, and I'm here to see you pay."

"Sister?" In spite of himself, he tossed another glance in Lucy's direction. "You never once intimated you had any family." A very large-boned family to judge by her brother's appearance. Lucy must be an exception. "My dear, you've been holding out on me."

The instant the words were out, something akin to a sledgehammer slammed into his jaw. His head snapped back. Pain exploded from the point of contact and rattled through his body. The floor tilted, and he stumbled back to land in a heap at the foot of the bed.

Right. Lucy could wait. Time to concentrate on the danger at hand.

Ignoring the ringing in his ears, he scrambled to his feet and waded in, but his opponent was clearly in better practice when it came to fisticuffs. Despite his size, Lucy's brother danced lightly on the balls of his feet, left fist raised to block, while the right hovered menacingly at chin height.

George feinted left before jabbing with his right, but his opponent anticipated the move and weaved out of range. The blow met with mere air, and George staggered once more, off balance, his guard dropping. Another punch whizzed past his ear, but the second jab caught him squarely on the chin.

Stars danced before his eyes, and the room reeled. He stumbled sideways into something soft and yielding.

Lucy steadied him, but he wouldn't allow her to distract him again. He kept his gaze pinned on his opponent, who stood back for the moment, red in the face, perhaps, but his breathing steady and even.

The arrogant bastard.

With a roar, George lunged.

"Roger!" Lucy screamed.

George ignored the ungrateful wench and went for Roger's throat. The ape dodged, but George anticipated as much and mirrored the move, grasping his enemy about the waist and hauling him to the floor. He applied his weight to the other man's belly, planted a hand on his throat, and pulled back his fist.

"George! Stop it! Now!"

Lucy's terrified cry made him hesitate a moment too long. Roger heaved his bulk and George's hand slipped. The next thing he knew, the back of his head struck unforgiving oak floorboards. Roger's weight bore him down and forced the air from his lungs. He gasped but pulled in nothing. Blackness shrouded the edges of his vision.

"Stop," he croaked. The weight on his chest eased just enough. "What do you want from me?"

"That's simple enough," Roger growled. Not even winded, the scoundrel. "You're to do right by my sister."

A raw jolt of panic speared his gut. Roger couldn't possibly insist on a marriage, not when any number of protectors had preceded him in Lucy's bed. "What's that supposed to mean?"

"Simple. You got her into trouble. You're going to get her out. The proper compensation ought to hush things up."

"That's blackmail."

Roger smiled, an evil sort of leer that disrupted the square lines of his face. "That's good business. And you might have avoided the matter entirely if you'd kept your prick in your pocket."

"If *I'd* kept . . . What about all . . ."

Roger tightened his grip on George's throat and gave him a shake. "The others didn't get caught, now, did they?"

"She can have the house, and I'll settle a sum on her to see to her upkeep. Beyond that . . ." He couldn't admit to his true financial situation. Not with an ape sitting on his chest.

"Beyond that, you'll cough up a tidy sum. My sister deserves a decent life."

"CHIN up, dear, we've almost arrived."

George suppressed the urge to roll his eyes at his mother. Gads, how could the woman beam so after hours of jostling in a carriage through the Kentish countryside, crammed in with his sisters?

He exchanged a glance with Henrietta. "And not a moment too soon," he said. "I can barely stand the excitement. We'll go from being packed into this carriage to being packed into a house with entirely too many people."

How he dreaded the thought of a house party, even if the host was his oldest friend. Worse than a ball, because the blasted things lasted days rather than mere hours. He could only escape to the card room in the evenings, while the rest of the day he'd have to find more creative means of avoiding his mother's attempts at matchmaking.

Mama's smile wavered not at all. "Sarcasm does not become you. How many times must I say it? You'd do better to put on a bright outlook. I imagine you'd attract a bride if you did that."

His left eye twitched, as it always did when his mother

brought up the topic of matrimony. "I'll keep that in mind, should I wish to attract one. What do you recommend? Something like this?"

He pulled an exaggerated face that doubtless exposed his back teeth. God knew his cheeks would ache soon enough if he maintained the expression. It didn't help matters that he'd tweaked a few bruises in the process.

"Stop this instant," Mama scolded, but the woman, Lord help her, could never manage to sound stern. "Pity you had to turn up with your face all beaten. Why you men insist on pounding each other is beyond me."

"It's sport." He'd explained the state of his face away with a minor lie about an incident at his boxing club. The truth would only give Mama the vapors.

"Be that as it may, I am certain you will meet your future wife at this party. See if you don't."

"Ah yes, and Henny"—he winked at his sister—"will announce her engagement to the head groom at the same time. Why, I think a double wedding at Christmas will be just the thing."

Mama made a valiant attempt at creasing her brows, but an eruption of laughter quite ruined the effect. "You are completely incorrigible."

"But endlessly diverting."

"And if you turned that charm on a few young ladies . . ."

He held up a hand. "Madam, I believe I'm not the only incorrigible one in this conveyance."

"Nonsense." Mama tossed her head, and the feathers on her bonnet scrubbed across his sister Catherine's face. "I'm simply determined. There's a difference."

Single-minded and obsessed were the terms that immediately leapt to George's tongue, but he swallowed them back. Of course his mother wanted to see him wed. It was what mothers did once their children reached an appropriate age. Unfortunately, his idea of an appropriate age didn't agree with hers by at least ten years. For God's sake, he was only twenty-nine.

He caught Henrietta's eye. Her mouth twitched into a smirk that spoke volumes. *Better you than me.* But Mama would turn her attention back to her oldest daughter soon enough. No doubt the moment they reached the ballroom where Revelstoke housed his pianoforte. Coupled with what Catherine passed off as singing . . .

In spite of himself, he winced. He prayed Revelstoke had laid in a good supply of brandy. He was going to need it in vast quantities if Mama insisted on her daughters being part of the entertainment.

The carriage rumbled to a halt at the head of a sweeping drive. The stone bulk of Shoreford House rose gray against a backdrop of blue sky. Shouts hailed from the yard, followed by a heavy *thunk* as the steps were let down. George leapt from his seat, ready to hand his mother and sisters out of the conveyance.

A gentle breeze bore the salt tang of the Channel, mingled with an earthy heaviness that wafted from the stables. The late August sun beat a gentle warmth on the back of his neck.

"I can't believe you've actually come."

George turned to find Benedict Revelstoke approaching from the main house, a grin across his cheeks. But as he neared the carriage, his gaze glanced over the bruises on George's face, and he frowned. "I was about to ask how far your mother twisted your arm to convince you to come, but I see she's resorted to more drastic means of persuasion."

George clasped his old friend's hand. "Do me a favor and don't call attention to it. If I have to put up with any more cold compresses and female twittering, I may as well take to my bed permanently."

"I don't know how you'll avoid it. Once Julia gets a good look at you . . ."

"I thought I heard my name." Benedict's wife appeared just beyond his shoulder, waddling from the house in the wake of a prominent belly. "Gossiping about me behind my back, are you?"

Revelstoke caught her hand and pulled her close. Their fingers entwined as if they couldn't bear as much as an instant apart. For a moment, they stared into each other's eyes, and in that brief expanse of time, they disappeared into their own realm where only the pair of them existed. It lasted less than two seconds, but an entire conversation seemed to pass between them.

Fighting the urge to roll his eyes, George cleared his throat. God help him if he ever became that love-struck.

Julia stepped forward to inspect him more closely. "My goodness, what have you done to your face?"

Revelstoke raised his brows and shrugged.

George made sure his mother was well occupied in directing the servants with the baggage before responding. "Came out on the wrong end of a rather vigorous discussion, but never fear. It looks worse than it is."

"I shall ask Cook to make you a poultice to draw out the bruising."

He shook his head. "Don't trouble yourself on my account. I'm sure she's got enough to oversee with a houseful of guests for the next week."

"It's no trouble at all. She acquires a special blend of herbs from a woman in the village. One of our yearlings got himself into a scrape a while back, but the herbs worked their magic, and he's back as good as new. Outstrips the rest of them from one end of the pasture to the other, and barely blows at all."

"You want to dose me with a remedy that you use on livestock? I think I'll pass, thank you. Only do me the service of not mentioning your ideas to my mother."

With a laugh, Julia excused herself and trundled off

to greet the Upperton sisters. Soon the air filled with high-pitched chatter.

George tilted his head in the direction of the main house. "You look disgustingly happy."

Revelstoke shook his head. "Ever the one for a flowery turn of phrase, I see." He took a few steps in the direction of the house. "Are you planning on telling me what you're really doing here?"

"I'm attending this house party at your invitation. Why else would I have come except to pass a few days rusticating here with your guests? Can't think of anything I'd rather be doing."

Revelstoke cast him a sidelong look. "Pull the other one. From all appearances, you've got yourself into some scrape or other, so you've either come here to hide or you want me to get you out of it."

"Don't you have some horseflesh you'd like to show off?" George waved a hand in the direction of the stables. "A new broodmare? Perhaps one that's produced the next champion at Ascot?"

Revelstoke clapped him on the shoulder. "That bad, is it? Perhaps you'd rather we have a drink in my study while the ladies settle in. And if you've got any particular sins you'd like to confess, I'll have a listen."

"I never held much with religion. Too many diversions count against you, you know. But if the vicar offered brandy to his parishioners, he might find he had a more faithful flock." They tramped up the front steps in the wake of two footmen juggling a trunk. The sight reminded him of his sisters and their mother's advice to pack their entire wardrobe. "I say, who have you invited to this gathering?"

"Entirely too many, but Julia thought we ought to show a bit of hospitality. If I can interest a few of the men in acquiring some horseflesh while they're here, it may all be worth it. She's invited her sister, of course, and my brother, and since we'll be entertaining an earl and a marquess, naturally half of polite society saw fit to beg an invitation whether we wished to see them or not."

George suppressed a groan. "That means my mother will insist on putting my sisters on display. Tell me your pianoforte's out of tune. They might actually sound decent for once."

"As a matter of fact, Julia just had someone look at it."

"Better order another case of brandy, one I can reserve for my own personal use."

Revelstoke closed the door to his study and strode to a side table where a cut crystal decanter stood full of rich amber liquid. He poured two healthy measures and handed George a glass. George stared into the swirling depths and considered downing the alcohol in one go. No, best not to over-imbibe or else he might confess more than necessary.

Revelstoke clinked glasses and raised his drink. "Come now. What's brought you here and in this state?"

"Seems my mistress forgot to tell me a thing or two. Like the fact she has a brother who doesn't quite appreciate his sister being a kept woman."

"It's not as if you're the man who ruined her." Revelstoke raised a brow. "Are you?"

"Of course not, and you shouldn't even have to ask. I draw the line at leading innocents astray." He stared out the window to the greenery beyond the crosshatch of the mullions. Along a whitewashed fence, mares grazed surrounded by their cavorting foals. "I'm not Lucy's first protector, and I certainly won't be her last."

"Then why would her brother have a problem with you in particular?"

George sipped at his brandy to play for time. "I didn't come here to discuss my problems with my mistress."

The look Revelstoke gave him clearly communicated his skepticism. "Then why are you here?"

"I can't visit an old school chum, especially considering you never come into Town?" He set his glass on a burnished oak table. "Why, you practically forced me to make the trek out to this godforsaken corner of Kent."

"The last thing I'd expect of you is to attend something so respectable as a house party, especially considering chances are quite high your sisters will torture us with their musical talent. So what is it?"

Revelstoke knew him too well, damn the man. "How's the horse-breeding business going?"

"It's flourishing." He nodded toward the pastoral scene just beyond the window. "Ask Julia to show you about the place later, and you'll see all the improvements we've made with the profits. But you're no more interested in acquiring a horse than you are in attending a house party."

George snatched up his glass for a fortifying drink. "I was wondering, since you're doing so well, if it was possible to spot me a loan."

Revelstoke tore his attention away from the window. "How much do you need?"

Another mouthful. His last. "Five thousand pounds."

Revelstoke spit out his brandy. "Five thousand? Good God, man. What makes you think I can afford to hand you that sort of blunt?"

"Could you see your way clear to lending me a thousand, say, or five hundred?"

"I daresay you stand a better chance, yes." He marched back to the sideboard in search of the cut-glass decanter. "But what on earth have you been up to that you need those kinds of funds?"

George studied the pattern in the Axminster carpeting. "This and that. I may have got myself in a bit too deep at cards, on top of everything else."

Revelstoke eyed his freshly poured glass before slowly setting it aside. "Dare I ask what everything else comprises?"

George shrugged. "A mistress whose tastes run to the expensive, mostly. She insisted on a fairly fashionable address, and I've fallen behind on the rent."

Revelstoke fixed his gaze on George. "Don't you think it's time you gave up that sort of living and settled down?"

George stared at the ceiling beams. Dark and heavy, like the rest of the room. "Oh no. Don't you start, too. Bad enough my mother's planning on throwing every eligible young miss in attendance in my direction, I don't need you waxing poetic on the virtues of married life. Besides, you can't tell me keeping a wife and child isn't any less expensive than keeping a mistress."

"But it is. No need to maintain separate addresses, for one thing. No need to staff two houses."

George wagged his head from side to side. "You've come over all practical since you became leg-shackled. It's downright boring."

"With the right woman—"

"There you go, sounding like my mother again. I will be the first to commend you on your excellent taste in brides. At least you had the foresight to choose one with wit and cleverness. I'm afraid there aren't many others like your Julia, though. You'll have to understand this mere mortal doesn't possess your luck in that department."

Revelstoke rolled his eyes. "Now you're just being absurd."

"Absurd or not, a betrothal is not going to solve my financial problems. Not unless you've invited an heiress or two who might be willing to overlook my long list of shortcomings." He paused just long enough to allow Revelstoke to reply, knowing full well his friend didn't maintain the proper social connections to attract such an heiress.

In the face of Revelstoke's silence, he went on. "Since no heiresses seem to be in the offing, you might tell me which gentlemen among your guests might be persuaded to play a few hands of whist."

"Have you learned nothing at all from your current predicament?" Revelstoke pushed his glass away. "You're in trouble because you played a few hands too many. Another game isn't going to get you out. It may even put you in deeper."

"Then how do you propose I get my hands on five thousand? I need blunt and soon."

A line etched itself between Revelstoke's brows. "This is about more than a demanding mistress."

"What makes you say that?"

"Because if that were your only problem, you'd hand her her *congé* and be done with it. So perhaps you tell me the real reason you need so much money, and I'll consider a small loan."

"You're right." George took the decanter and topped off Revelstoke's glass before pouring himself another measure. Talking about that night inevitably called visions of an old school friend to mind. One who had been in far worse straits than George—straits narrow enough to drive a man to put a pistol in his mouth and pull the trigger. At the memory, George shuddered. "Do you remember Summersby?"

Revelstoke paused, glass halfway to his lips. "I heard. Damned tragedy, that."

"Do you know why he did it?" When Revelstoke shook his head, George went on. "Creditors hounding him. He got in too deep and couldn't pay."

"And him with a wife and young child." Revelstoke shook his head once more, this time in censure. "This is the sort of thing I mean. You get in too far—"

"The debts aren't mine," George cut in. "They're Summersby's. I mean to pay every last one. No reason his family should suffer. They've been through enough."

Revelstoke set his glass aside with a clunk and clapped George on the shoulder. "Commendable of you. Never thought I'd say this, but it's noble."

"Hardly." George let out a harsh bark. Some other man might have thought it laughter, but Revelstoke knew him too well to mistake the sound. It was pain, pure and simple. "I mean to ruin every last one of them, starting with the Earl of Redditch."

Revelstoke let out a low whistle. "Summersby involved himself with that crowd?"

"Unfortunately." While he might be one of the wealthier men of the *ton*, Richard Marshall, the Earl of Redditch, could seemingly never get his hands on enough blunt. If a man fell afoul of him at the card table, the earl called on the entire family's power to ensure repayment of any debt. And that was precisely where Summersby dug his hole too deep.

"You might be aiming a bit too high there. If you came here with the intention of meeting him, I'm afraid that family is too well connected for the likes of us."

George had suspected as much. "No matter. If you can spot me some funds, I can work on turning them into more. That way when I go back to Town, I'll be ready for the bastards."

"I'm afraid you're in for some difficulty there." Revelstoke clapped him on the shoulder once more. "Julia's father, you see. She doesn't want him tempted, so she's asked me to let all the gentlemen know she's prohibited deep play for the duration of the party."

CHAPTER TWO

GEORGE STALKED down the path bisecting beds of trailing flowers and shrubs. No deep play. Ridiculous, but he might have guessed. Julia's father had nearly ruined his family four years ago with his debts. Well, George would find a way around the restriction, if he could interest anybody—preferably someone with deep pockets—in a few hands of piquet. They could retreat to the nearby village.

Pea gravel crunched beneath his Hessians, but not loud enough to drown out the infernal racket coming from the ballroom. Catherine hit yet another off note, and the keening jangled through his brain.

He didn't even bother wincing anymore. The action was fruitless. Once his sisters started rehearsing, the best remedy for the pain was a large bottle of brandy, preferably taken in Wales. If he set off walking now, he might arrive in Cardiff in a week or two, but that wouldn't solve his financial woes.

A carriage hound, white with black spots, ambled toward him for a sniff. George scratched the beast's neck absently while more musical atrocities assaulted his ears. The dog let out a plaintive whine.

Damn it all, was nowhere safe? If he didn't escape soon, his head would begin pounding worse than if he'd drunk several bottles of Whitechapel gin the previous evening. Another false note, and the hound threw back its head and howled.

"I know how you feel, old boy," George muttered.

He raised his fingers to his temples and rubbed. God, he needed to get away. Already the pulse-like current was throbbing in his head, faint for now, but it would not remain so for long. The floral-scented air did nothing to hold off the next twinge. He strode off at a faster pace.

The garden ended abruptly at a high hedge. On its other side, mares grazed in the middle of rolling pastureland while their foals nipped at each other and kicked up their heels in raucous circles. He followed the hedge to the cliff where a path wound its way down to a sheltered cove.

There, at least, the roar and hiss of the surf would cut off the caterwauling from the house. There, he might find a touch of peace for a few hours if he was fast enough to forestall a vicious megrim.

His booted feet had just reached the flat strand of pebbles when he saw them. Sunlight glinted off a pair of golden heads. A child, a small boy of no more than six, ran through the waves, squealing when the cold water lapped at his bare toes. A young woman strolled in his wake. Her watchful eyes belied the ease of her gait.

A sharp gust off the Channel seized her bonnet. With a cry, she grabbed for it, long fingers curling around the brim at the last moment before the wind snatched it. After a fruitless attempt to secure the flimsy bit of straw to her head, she left it to straggle down her back by its ribbons. Her hair blew free of its bindings in long, tattered curls. Like the child, her feet were bare, and the damp hems of her skirts flapped about her ankles.

George caught his breath. He shouldn't stare, but he couldn't help it. When she laughed at the boy's antics, the sound tolled like the pure note of a church bell on a frosty winter morning. The echoes might carry for miles through crisp air. They fell on his beleaguered ears like a healing balm.

The boy trotted into the surf, letting the waves chase him, while his sister—she couldn't be anything else, she was so young—stood back, ever mindful. The set of her shoulders betrayed a readiness to act.

The pair still hadn't noted George's presence, and he held back, sensing he'd somehow crashed in on an unguarded moment. No young lady would want a gentleman to catch her unshod, her hair unpinned and her bonnet dangling. Who was he to spoil the moment by forcing her to adopt the formality a stranger's presence required?

Not only a stranger, but a man, and she was hardly chaperoned.

He really ought to return to the main house, but the prospect of enduring his sisters' performance kept his feet planted on the spot. Here, the air was blessedly free of false notes and the only screeching a child's joyful cries.

A child, hang it all. A child, such as Lucy was carrying. The thought pounded through his head like the cacophony of his sisters' singing. It jangled and clashed. He'd never asked to become a father. He wasn't ready, damn it. What would he do with another soul who looked to him for support, for guidance, for protection? He hadn't the slightest idea how to be a father. He'd never had a proper example.

A shout drew his attention back to the boy—a different kind of shout, infused with fear, rather than joy. The young woman's cry followed, its plaintive note drowned in the surf's roar.

The child's sodden head bobbed on the surface for a moment before disappearing. He'd run too far. A wave had caught him.

George didn't pause to consider. He didn't even bother

with his boots. He pelted across the strand, the pebbles rolling beneath his feet, and plunged into the surf. The water's icy grip numbed his legs on contact. His chest constricted, and he fought to gulp in air. Now was no time to freeze. He must go on. Must reach the child.

There. The boy's head surfaced, blond hair darkened and waterlogged and falling into eyes round with fear.

George dived, reached, grabbed at nothing but cold water. On the second attempt, his fingers brushed something solid—a tiny hand. He grabbed for it and hauled the boy upright. The child took one look at him and clawed at his topcoat.

"Easy there, son. I've got you." Somehow he forced the words between chattering teeth.

The boy put his arms around George's neck and clung as he struggled back toward solid ground. Wave followed wave; each one reached for him in an attempt to drag them both under. The need to keep hold of a quivering body prevented him from using his arms in the fight. The ground melted beneath his feet, threatening to topple him at every footstep and leave him to the mercy of the sea.

The young lady fought her way to his side. They faced each other, waist-deep in the waves, while he gulped in air and she reached for the boy. Her dark eyes stood in stark contrast to the whiteness of her face. They hardened, caught somewhere between a glare and fear.

"Give him here," she said, hard and abrupt. Dismissive.

Well. The least she could do was thank him for ruining a perfectly good pair of trousers in freezing saltwater so he could rescue her brother.

"Certainly . . . miss." A wave crashed into him, thrusting him forward. He lunged to catch his balance and knocked her aside. In another breath, he righted himself. "As soon as we're on shore, I'd be happy to."

On closer view, she was older than she first appeared. Her face gave the illusion of a younger woman—drawn on delicate lines to a pointed chin, it appeared almost fairy-like.

He shook his head. Imagine, such a fanciful idea, especially now that her brows had lowered to a full-on glare that emphasized a twin set of lines above her nose. They were etched deeply enough to put her beyond the age of a schoolroom miss. Her soaked bodice accentuated curves more generous than he'd first thought. Lovely, firm, round curves.

In spite of the danger, she reached again. The tips of her fingers trembled, and she held her lips in a firm line, as if to suppress an echoing vibration there. Hitching the boy higher against his chest, he fought his way free of the waves. She splashed behind him, and wrenched the child from his grasp.

She pulled him to her bosom, her eyes closing, and she drew in a long, shuddering breath. Her hands tightened, until the boy let out a whimper and wriggled in her grasp. He fought his way free and slid to the ground.

"Jack!" she said rather sharply.

"There's no call to shout at the boy." George sat down hard on the beach and gasped for breath. Water slogged inside his Hessians, and a nasty bite of breeze sank its teeth into his sodden garments, chewing through to the skin. Even the spot on his chest where Jack had clung to him had grown cold. "He's had a fright. Give him a chance to recover."

"Jack, we need to go home. Now."

ISABELLE drummed her fingers against her thigh to mask their trembling. So close. She'd come so close to losing him.

"Come, Jack," she tried again, but her tone refused to soften.

It was that blasted man, that stranger. He'd surged out of nowhere to splash into the water and save Jack when her fear took hold. She ought to be grateful; she ought to thank him, but annoyance at having her privacy invaded twined with the old wariness. It kept her blood pumping hard, long after it ought to have subsided.

If only Jack would let her hold him for a moment or an hour, but he'd turned his attention back to the man, staring at him as if he thought to keep him. Obstinate child.

With a sigh, she marched over and held out a hand. "I apologize for the inconvenience, sir. I prefer not to carry it any further."

"It's no trouble at all." The man shifted his weight, leaning back on his elbows. His waterlogged topcoat plastered itself against his chest. His very broad chest topped by wide shoulders.

Isabelle cast her eyes downward, but that wasn't much safer. The surf had wet his trousers until they clung to his thighs. She wrapped her arms about her waist to hold off a bout of shivering. She had no business looking over a man's body. Most especially, she had no business noting his long, tapering fingers or the roguish lock of hair that flopped over his forehead. Its color matched the tan of the damp pebbles that lined the shore. No matter his face was battered, one eye puffy and swollen.

Even worse, he was looking right back, his gaze traveling down the lines of her body in frank appraisal. Doubtless her soaked dress left little to the imagination; it clung to her form the same as his garments. His glance came to rest on her feet. She curled her toes against the pebbles.

Her bare toes. Oh, how could she have forgotten herself to such an extent? Her shoes and stockings lay discarded up the beach where she'd left them in a fit of girlishness. For a few brief moments, she'd wanted to run along the shore as carefree as Jack. For those moments, she'd wished to relive her innocent days.

When would she learn she could never go back?

At last, Jack tore his attention away from the stranger. He turned his face toward her—and grinned. The very devil lit that smile.

"You little scamp," she murmured.

His grin broadened, but he still refused to come to her. His face glowing with admiration, he stepped closer to his rescuer. "What's your name?"

Isabelle gasped. "Jack, where are your manners?"

Laughter rumbled from deep in the stranger's chest, an oddly comforting sound. She pushed the idea aside. She had no business thinking that about him, either.

"You may call me George."

"You most certainly shall not," Isabelle said. Time to nip this in the bud. "It's improper to address one's betters by their Christian names."

The stranger—she refused to think of him as George—winked at her. Winked! "How do you know that's not my family name?"

She pressed her lips together. For some inexplicable reason, they wanted to stretch into a smile. "Even so, it's improper, Mr.—"

"Very well. It's Mr. Upperton to you." He raised himself to a crouch, bringing his face to Jack's level. "But you can call me George when no one's listening. Now, shall I call you Jack or do you prefer something a bit more formal? You wouldn't happen to be Lord Something-or-other, would you?"

"No." The boy's smile showed the gap between his front teeth. "Just Jack."

"Well, Just Jack, suppose you tell me your sister's name, and we shall be properly introduced."

A nasty jolt coursed down Isabelle's spine, and her pounding heart drowned out the roar of the surf. "It's Isabelle."

Oh, why had she blurted her Christian name after her insistence on propriety? For an awful moment, she waited for the protest, the challenge, the contradiction. Jack blinked at her, his forehead wrinkled. The challenge, such as it was, came from a different quarter altogether.

"Am I to presume you wish me to address you by your given name?" Mr. Upperton asked.

"Miss Mears will do." Another hasty reply. If only she'd stopped to think, she might have claimed the title Mrs., but Mr. Upperton seemed to have a strange effect on her mind. It would have made matters so much easier if Mr. Upperton believed her married, or at the very least, widowed. He wouldn't ask difficult questions. He wouldn't make suppositions. He wouldn't question her morals.

Irritation prickled at the back of her neck. Why should she even care what Mr. Upperton thought? She wasn't about to make friends with him. After today, she'd probably never see him again—and so much the better.

The cut of his clothes, their quality, the fine leather of his boots told her all she needed to know. He was a young buck from Town, no doubt staying at the manor up the cliff face, and she knew from bitter experience that made him dangerous.

"I much prefer Isabelle." A smile spread across his face, revealing even, white teeth. "It suits you better. Mears sounds almost common, like you were a mere Isabelle, but I doubt you'd settle for being a mere anything."

Oh yes, he was dangerous, all right, gifted with a quick

and clever tongue. She'd succumbed to a silver-tongued charmer once before and paid the price. Never again.

She raised her chin and tensed her jaw. "I have not given you leave to address me by my Christian name."

He pushed himself slowly to his feet. She recognized the gesture for what it was—an attempt to level the field. He could not tolerate her standing over him. He, on the other hand, towered over her. She'd always been small, but Mr. Upperton's imposing height made her feel as if she were closer to Jack's size.

"Indeed, madam." He infused the words with an aristocratic, officious chill. A dismissal, nearly a cut. Oh, how she remembered that. How happy she'd been living apart from the judgment, the superiority. The utter hypocrisy.

But he continued to stare, and his gaze penetrated until she fancied she felt it burning from inside, the sensation at once familiar and disturbing. Beneath the fire of his scrutiny, she shifted her weight from one foot to the other, keenly aware of her soaked skirts sticking to her legs and the abrasion of small stones against her bare feet. She clenched her teeth to stop them from chattering.

Jack looked from one to the other. "Mama?"

She closed her eyes as blood rushed to her cheeks. Dear God, now she really could not bring herself to face this stranger. Not now that Jack had let the secret slip.

"Mama?" A tug at her skirts forced her to face her young son. "Shouldn't we say thank you for saving me?"

She covered the top of his head with her palm and smoothed his dripping mop of blond hair. "Of course, darling." Gritting her teeth, she bobbed a curtsey. "Your pardon, sir. I've quite forgotten myself. I'm most grateful you fished Jack from the sea."

"Not at all."

Something in his tone drew her gaze. He watched her closely, assessing once more. Reevaluating, just as she'd known he would. His glance flicked from her bare left hand to Jack and back to her face. Calculating her age.

Everyone did, as soon as they worked out the truth. And yet . . .

She didn't feel as if he were judging her. The only impression she got was curiosity. Thank God. Thank God she wouldn't have to put up with more. She didn't think she could handle it, not after the scare she'd just had. Her trembling increased, and she clenched her hands into fists.

"George?" Jack asked brightly. Isabelle opened her mouth to admonish him, but he'd already tripped onward. "It was fun."

"Fun?" She forced the word past her quivering lips. The heart-pounding fear rushed in to replace any worries about propriety. She'd almost lost him. Might have watched his small, blond head disappear under the waves while she stood by, paralyzed. "You nearly drowned."

"You'd best listen to your mama," George said mildly enough. She didn't dare look at him, not now that he'd acknowledged the truth. "She's working very hard not to let it show, but I'm sure you've given her a fright she won't want to relive any time soon."

Her eyes snapped to his. She couldn't help herself. How had he seen? He was a complete stranger. She knew nothing about him or his intentions. She did not want his scrutiny or his perception. And she most certainly did not want him around Jack, not when his gentle admonishment had her son blinking hard at the ground, the back of his neck red. Gracious, the man hadn't shouted, hadn't scolded, hadn't threatened. He'd expressed a simple enough truth, and Jack stood there, quiet and contrite, but, dash it all, if the lesson hadn't sunk in.

"How many children do you have?" The question slipped out before she could stop it.

Mr. Upperton blinked. "What? What makes you ask such a thing?"

"It's just . . ." Oh, why had she given in to her curiosity? The last thing she needed was to encourage him. He might get the wrong impression—that she was looking for a protector. "You're so good with children, I thought you might have a few of your own."

Goodness. Why not come out and ask if he was married? She could hardly have been more blatant.

A muscle twitched in his jaw, and his cheeks darkened slightly. "Me? Good with children? That's a laugh." To prove it, he let out a chuckle. The sound carried just enough of an edge to make her suspect it was forced. "I'm not married, and I haven't any by-blows that I know of."

She flinched. Of course, he'd only been trying to make light and had forgotten himself, but that didn't prevent a prickle of shame from overcoming her. The back of her neck burned with it. "Come, Jack. We've taken enough of this gentleman's time. We ought to head home."

"Might I escort you?"

Escort? As if they'd been exchanging pleasantries on some society matron's terrace and she'd hinted she might like to see a bit more of the garden? Heaven forbid. At any rate, six years had passed since her life resembled anything of the sort. And just such a proposition had placed her in a great deal of difficulty.

Besides, she still retained some measure of pride. She couldn't allow such a fine gentleman to witness what her life had become, whether he paid attention to gossip or no. Whether or not he saw through the sham of her name and worked out her true identity. "I hardly think that's necessary."

"It would be no trouble at all, I assure you."

She eyed him, alert for any sign he might consider her an easy mark. After all, to his mind, she'd lifted her skirts once. In reality she'd been duped, but he wouldn't know that. "We've been managing rather well on our own, thank you."

"Do you live in the village? I thought—at first—you might be a guest of Lord Benedict."

A sharp breeze off the Channel whipped at her skirts, slapping them against her shins. She hugged herself to ward off its sudden chill. "Please, I wouldn't dream of inconveniencing you any further. We ought to be off for home. I would not wish either of us to fall ill."

"MAMA? Mama! You're walking too fast."

Isabelle pressed a hand to her breastbone and came to a halt. Her breath came in shallow pants. She'd practically been running and hadn't realized.

Jack trotted up the rise from the beach, his short legs pumping. She waited until he'd reached her before pulling him into a fierce embrace. All the emotion she dared not show in front of a stranger poured into the strength of her grasp. Once more, her heart thumped a desperate cadence against her ribs, as the terror returned.

"Mama," he protested. All too soon, he pushed her away. Water dripped from his trousers, and his hair hung in lank strings. She'd need to cajole him into sitting still while she combed the knots out before it dried and the situation became hopeless. If Biggles had baked biscuits, she stood a reasonable chance, at least as long as the confections held out.

"Come, we'll put on our shoes and stockings before we get back to the village." She fought the ache in her throat to keep her tone brisk. These days, he'd only tolerate so much mothering. "Quickly now."

He plunked himself down in the middle of the path and scrunched his stockings over dirt-encrusted feet. With a wrinkled nose, he worked the coarse knit over damp ankles and shins. Her throat tightened to watch him perform the most mundane of tasks so soon after—

Too late, she closed her eyes. Too late to shut out the image. In her mind, she relived the terrible moment when the wave engulfed him. All that blond hair, so bright in the sun, gone like a flame being snuffed out. In the blink of an eye. Disappeared. The backs of her eyes stung as if they'd been exposed to seawater.

"Mama?" He tugged at her skirt. "Aren't you going to put your shoes on?"

"Oh . . . Oh, yes."

She could hardly traipse back to the village barefoot like some beggar woman. Their bedraggled clothes were bad enough. But she could dress in the finest silks and the butcher's wife would glare at her. Not that she could afford meat very often, at any rate.

She sat on a rock and eased a stocking along her leg. Her feet were in as bad a state as her son's. The drying grit prickled between her toes.

"We'll need to stay close to the house tomorrow," she said as she pushed her feet into her shoes.

"Aw, Mama."

"You had your holiday today." She took his hand and set off down the path. "Tomorrow we must work."

He poked out his lower lip. The expression boded no good at all.

"You can help Biggles in the garden. I'll wager you can pull more weeds than she can."

"I don't want to pull up weeds."

Well, blast. Normally the prospect of putting both hands into the soil and getting as much dirt as possible ground into his shirt was enough to turn work into play.

"We don't always get to do as we please." How often had she reminded him of that over the years? Half the time, she felt she was reminding herself as much as Jack.

"If you're a good boy and don't complain, I shall tell you a new story. One you haven't heard before."

His lower lip receded somewhat. "Will there be a dragon in it?"

"There might be."

"Will you tell me about the people who live in the big house?"

She glanced over her shoulder. Off to the left, the outline of the manor on the hill etched itself against a cloud-scattered sky. "I don't know if I can manage that and a dragon." The only dragons she associated with country manors were the grand dames of society.

She lengthened her stride. They needed to get home. The cluster of dwellings, each neatly whitewashed with gleaming tiled roofs, lay less than half a mile ahead at the base of a gentle slope. At the far end, a larger building held itself above the rest. The inn, although more often than not it housed locals out for a pint and a bit of gossip at the end of a long day.

She trudged toward her cottage, a lone building at the very edge of town. It stood apart by design.

"George came from the big house, didn't he?"

"Yes, I believe he must have." He couldn't very well have been a guest at the inn. He would have shared the path back to the village with them. "And you are not to refer to him by his given name. It isn't . . . proper."

Good gracious, she'd nearly said good *ton,* and that was the last thing she wanted Jack asking about. Out of necessity—out of her own actions—she'd put that life firmly behind her.

CHAPTER THREE

"Where have ye been? It's nearly tea time." Sleeves rolled up and her arms dusted with flour, Biggles paused over the lump of dough she was kneading. Her eyes widened. "Lawks! Wot's happened to the pair of ye?"

Isabelle entered the kitchen, breathing deep of its aroma—yeast and flour and wood smoke, cut through with the scent of lavender. Bunches of the plant—her livelihood—hung from the ceiling beams to dry. "Jack had an adventure in the sea."

"Heavens!" Biggles circled the table and crouched until her creased face was level with the boy's. "Are ye quite all right? Look at ye, all bedraggled."

Jack puffed out his chest. "I wasn't scared, honest. And George pulled me out."

Biggles glanced up at Isabelle. Both brows disappeared beneath her fringe of straggly gray curls.

"I've told Jack he's not to refer to a gentleman by his given name," Isabelle said.

"But he said I could," Jack insisted. "He gave me leave, he did."

Biggles fiddled with the boy's collar. "Off with ye and put on some dry clothes. When ye come back, I'll have a biscuit ready for ye."

As Jack padded off to change, the old woman heaved herself upright. "Gentleman, is it?"

"I ought to change as well." Isabelle's cheeks burned,

and she ducked her head to hide the reaction, but not quickly enough for Biggles's sharp eye.

"Ye'll dry just fine by the fire. Ye'd best tell me what's happened."

Isabelle turned toward the hearth and let the flames heat her cheeks. If she blushed any more deeply, it wouldn't show. "Simple enough. I took Jack to play along the shore, and a wave caught him. A gentleman happened along and pulled Jack out before he drowned."

She threaded her fingers together to hide their sudden trembling. A surge of renewed terror engulfed her with the reminder of how close she'd come to losing her boy. The image of his small blond head disappearing beneath that icy gray water flashed through her mind.

She'd see it for the rest of her life, for part of her would always question—if she'd been alone, would she have managed to save her son? Her father had never approved of sea bathing. Would she have broken through fear's grip to plunge beneath the waves again and again until she found him? Would her shoulders have possessed the strength to pull him out?

She wrapped her arms about her waist to ward off a sudden chill.

"There, there, miss." Biggles laid a heavy hand on her shoulder and squeezed. "All's well as ends well. No harm's been done, so best not dwell on might-have-beens."

Isabelle nodded. She'd been listening to Biggles's adages for years now. As a young mother struggling with the challenges of learning to care for an infant, then a fast-growing, curious boy, she'd heard Biggles repeat them often. The old saws were as effective as they'd always been at calming Isabelle's racing mind—that is to say, not at all.

Biggles gave her shoulder a few extra pats for good measure before returning to her baking. "Where d'ye suppose this gentleman came from, and in the nick of time, too? I don't know anyone in the village as goes by George."

Isabelle watched her dig the heels of her hands into the dough, turning and pressing in a practiced rhythm. "Only the apothecary."

"But he don't go by George, do he? He puts on airs and wants to be Mr. Putnam, whether or not he ought to be." Biggles punctuated this pronouncement with a nod that set the ruffles on her mobcap aquiver.

Isabelle smiled at the show of loyalty. She suspected the apothecary only insisted on such a level of formality with her. She might be good enough to sell him sachets made with her lavender for a few extra pence, but that was the extent of his good will. Beyond that, she wasn't worth knowing.

She pushed the thought aside. Best she appease Biggles's curiosity before the woman asked too many probing questions. "At any rate, it wasn't the apothecary."

"I should think not. He'd not wet the hems of his trousers for the vicar."

An expectant silence fell. "I think he came from the manor," Isabelle supplied at last.

Biggles's arms stopped their rhythm. "Oh, *that* sort of gentleman."

Isabelle turned her eyes away from Biggles's scrutiny. "His social standing hardly signifies."

"It certainly does if the man's got blunt."

Isabelle gritted her teeth. Biggles had been with her far too long—her only companion through sleepless nights of worry when Jack had been ill, the only voice of experience in her life—for her to become enraged over the implications. "The man may well have blunt, as you put it, but he is far, far beyond me, and therefore it does not matter whether he has ten thousand a year or nothing. I most likely shall never see him again."

* * *

"And where have you been?"

Halfway across the stable yard, George froze. Henrietta stood, arms crossed, eyeing him up and down as if he were a recalcitrant schoolboy and she his tutor.

"I took a walk down to the water," he said. "Didn't think it was forbidden."

"You're running away again. What did you do? Attempt to drown yourself?"

"Now, now." He eyed his sodden garments. Not even his valet could save them, he feared. "Mama hasn't pushed me quite that far."

"Yet."

Although his sisters' musical performances were likely to drive him in that direction sooner than their mother's schemes to marry him off. But he couldn't insult Henrietta with such an observation. Even he knew the limit.

"I wouldn't blame you, you know." She rolled her gaze skyward. "She's pushing me at Marcus Chatham."

"Chatham?" He fell into step beside her, and they ambled toward the servants' entrance. "He's not such a bad fellow."

"He reeks of cheroot and brandy."

"Does he? And how would you know unless you've been standing entirely too close?"

A frown creased her brow. "One does not need to stand closer than propriety demands to take note of it. One smells it the moment he enters a room."

"Well, it's a decent, masculine smell. Can't have a man smelling of roses or lavender or any of that female stuff."

She smacked at his elbow. "And what do you know of it? You're just as bad."

"I beg your pardon." He made a show of breathing

in. "At this very moment, I most certainly do not smell of brandy." A situation he intended to remedy as soon as possible.

She wrinkled her nose. "You smell of seaweed."

"That I do, but you will note that seaweed and cheroot smell nothing alike."

"It doesn't matter. Before the evening is through, you shall reek thoroughly of both."

"If it has the same effect on the other young ladies as it does on you, then perhaps I ought to adopt it as a strategy."

She halted before the door and crossed her arms. "Humph."

"How is it any different to you hanging about the stable yard in order to avoid unwanted attention?"

Her cheeks colored. Hah. He'd caught her out. "I was looking for you, if you must know. Mama missed you. Prudence Wentworth has arrived along with several of her friends, and she wanted to secure an introduction."

George suppressed a groan. "Introduction? I've already met her once, and that was more than enough."

"Not for her, for her cousin. Her younger, unmarried cousin," Henrietta specified.

"This cousin—did she inherit that unfortunate nose?"

Henrietta slapped at him again. "Honestly. There's more to a girl than her looks. You ought to at least talk to her and see if you don't have a thing or two in common."

He stopped short of commenting that at least in the bedroom he could douse the candles so he wouldn't have to look at the creature. "I shouldn't wish to marry a woman who shares my interests. It would be quite indecent."

"Which interests are those?" She raised a single brow, in an excellent imitation of, well, himself. "A penchant for cards?"

"Among other things—which I'm not about to share with an unmarried sister."

She sniffed. "It's quite unfair, you know."

"What is?"

"Unmarried men are rather expected to gain experience in certain matters, while unmarried girls must remain ignorant or risk ruin."

He froze. An unwelcome prickle raised the hairs on the back of his neck. "What do you know of such matters? By God, if some man has made advances, I shall call him out."

She blinked at him, her blue-gray eyes round and guileless. "I know very little, more's the pity, so you can calm yourself. You won't be facing anyone down the end of a pistol. Not on my account."

"Are you certain?" After all, she'd attained an age where certain men might no longer consider her marriageable, but perfectly acceptable as a mistress. Or if the man who had jilted her the year of her debut suddenly returned from India . . .

"Completely."

He pressed his lips together. At five and twenty, his sister was headed firmly for the shelf and quite seemed to prefer matters that way. She never danced with the same partner twice, never encouraged gentlemen to call. In fact, ever since the disastrous breaking of her betrothal, she entertained no suitors at all. "Then why bring the matter up?"

"An observation, nothing more. But you have to admit men are allowed more latitude in their youth."

"You've been reading that harridan again."

The corners of Henrietta's mouth quirked. "Miss Wollstonecraft? And what if I have?"

"People will think you a bluestocking."

"What if I am?" She waved the idea away with one

hand. "It hardly signifies, as I've come to a decision. I do not intend to marry."

"Not marry?" He opened his mouth and closed it again several times until it occurred to him he must resemble a goldfish.

She regarded him coolly. "Are you about to voice an opinion? If so, I caution you to tread carefully, or I might construe any comment you make as hypocritical."

He'd seen many examples of his younger sister's quick mind over the years, but he rather disliked having that wit turned on him, especially when she got the better of him. "Mama ought to stop you reading. It's made you too clever for your own good."

"If you are permitted to swan about unwed, I don't see why I cannot do the same." She nodded once, as if that decided the matter.

"Henny, have pity on your brother. If Mama gets wind of this, she'll be utterly relentless."

She fixed him with a hard gaze. "Yes, well, you *need* to marry and carry on the family name, while I would become nothing but a receptacle for some man's seed."

He let out a breath while turning her words over in his mind. Yes, she *had* just called herself a receptacle. "Good God, Hen, listen to yourself."

"You can't deny it's the truth, now, can you?"

"What . . . what do you plan to do with your days, then?"

"I imagine I can devote myself to any number of good works." She set a finger on her chin. "In fact, I might earn my keep. I hear Lady Epperley is looking for a paid companion."

"Paid companion? I'll not have it. As the head of the family, I forbid it. Paid companion. As if we cannot afford to keep our own."

Henrietta went still, and her face paled except for a red

blotch on each cheek. Never a good sign, that. "What next? You'll oblige me to marry the first suitable man who comes along? No. As long as you remain unwed, you cannot force me along that path. It's only fair, and you can't deny it."

George blew out a breath. "Are you saying I need only choose a bride and you'll stop this nonsense?"

She smiled—a wicked little grin that sent a nasty pang coursing through his stomach. Last time he felt anything like it, he'd just received word his friend Summersby was in grave difficulties, and look how that had turned out. The man was dead by his own hand. "Given your reluctance, I feel I can hardly lose at such a prospect."

"Prospects?" said a new voice. "I'd say prospects are nothing but favorable. What do you say?"

George turned. A man approached—or more accurately, a dandy. His collar was so stiff, his cravat so intricately knotted, his hair so artfully tousled, it must have taken his valet hours to achieve the effect. George searched his memory, but could not recall spotting the fellow at any of his usual haunts. If they'd ever been introduced across a card table, George had been too foxed to recall the other's name.

Beaming, the newcomer came to a halt before Henrietta, and his smile widened. "Prospects are becoming more favorable by the second, I'd say."

Henrietta sent him a stare made all the more withering by long practice at fending off undesired male attention. "Have we been introduced?"

"I daresay, that's a wrong I intend to see righted." He cast George a hopeful glance, while Henrietta turned a fish eye on him.

He allowed himself a sly quirk of his lips, an expression his sister would interpret rightly as his brotherly revenge grin. She'd brought it on herself since she insisted on needling him about his stance on matrimony. "My sister, Miss Henrietta Upperton."

Whatever else George might say about this man, he bowed quite impressively in one smooth motion from the waist, as if they were standing in the midst of a ballroom rather than outside a dusty servants' entrance. The act took up a great deal of space, however, and Henrietta was obliged to retreat a step.

"Reginald Leach at your service."

Thank God the man possessed the foresight to name himself and spare George an awkward moment. Not that they'd ever been introduced. Foxed or sober, George would never have forgotten such a ridiculous name.

Henrietta inclined her head politely enough, but as she straightened, she caught George's eye. One corner of her mouth twitched, the only outward sign of the laugh she was certainly holding in.

"And how is it," Leach went on, "that I've never yet had the occasion to make your acquaintance?"

"I could not say, sir, only I do not go out much in society." Her tone was courteous, but she carefully kept any warmth to herself.

"Not go out in society? Goodness, what a waste. We must remedy that matter this instant." He offered his arm, and when she declined to take it, he hurried on, unperturbed. "I might introduce you to any number of delightful young ladies and gentlemen. I've heard tell a goodly number are in attendance, beginning with the Marquess of Enfield and the Earl of Highgate and right on down to Miss Prudence Wentworth. I've heard tell that Lady Epperley might even remove herself from her estates to put in an appearance. Unheard of occurrence, that."

"Oh, indeed," George deadpanned. "Tell me, have you heard any rumors of Hector Poore planning on attending?"

Leach tore his attention away from Henrietta. "Good Lord, no. He's had to leave the country. Hounded by creditors. If he was lucky, he escaped to the continent with a change of clothing, but of course, without a valet to attend him, he's in a bad way." He jerked his head for emphasis. "Bad way, indeed."

Damn, there went his best chance at winning some badly needed funds. Poore was infamous for his deep play once he'd had his share of brandy—deep and foolhardy.

Henrietta waved a hand in front of her face. If she'd been in the ballroom, she'd have used her fan. "Well, I'm sure this is all very fascinating."

Leach beamed at her. "Isn't it, though?"

"George must find it so, but I daresay he thinks the news of Poore a disappointment."

"Why on earth would you say that?" George attempted to infuse his tone with a measure of boredom equal to Henrietta's.

She studied her nails a moment before swiping them along her shoulder. "I imagine you expected to get in a few hands of piquet while you were here."

George blinked. How in God's name had she known anything about that?

"Do you play, Miss Upperton?"

"Of course not," George interceded before Henrietta could reply. "At least not for any sort of stakes."

His interruption earned him the oddest expression, a glare accompanied by a gleam he knew meant no good at all. His sister was about to make him pay for introducing her to Leach—with interest.

Compounded, no doubt.

"My brother has the right of it." Henrietta tucked her fingers into the crook of Leach's elbow. "I do not play. But I should love the opportunity to learn from someone so knowledgeable."

"I should be delighted." Leach smiled down on her, his expression akin to a child in a sweetshop. "Delighted indeed."

George stepped closer and fixed Leach with a frown worthy of any protective older brother. He'd been on the receiving end of enough of them in his younger days to have mastered the art. "Perhaps such knowledge is best passed on by family."

"Nonsense, George. I said I'd like to learn from someone who knows what he's about."

Blast. Not only compounded interest, but usurious rates. "Here now, what gives you the idea I don't?"

Henrietta allowed a moment to pass before replying. "When's the last time you won?"

"Ah, excellent point, Miss Upperton." Leach smiled so broadly, George had to tamp down an urge to slam the man's teeth down his impeccably cravated throat.

And he would, too, if Leach made any sort of improper advances toward Henrietta. Not that Henny would stand for it. She was clever enough to see past these *ton* nobs. But then she was returning the idiot's grin, and the devil take it, were her cheeks coloring? After the conversation they'd just had, how dare she?

He'd be damned if he saw his sister married to such an overdressed simpleton. Hell, the man would probably compliment Henny's musical talents. "Didn't Mama say she wanted you to keep close watch on Catherine? Make certain she got the right sort of introductions? That kind of thing?"

"Oh, I'm sure Mama wanted you to do that." She didn't even glance in his direction, so riveted was she on Leach.

Leach. And just what sort of name was that? It wasn't one that needed to be passed on by any stretch of the imagination. He ought to have gone into trade, or better, become a doctor. "Now—"

The sound of someone clearing his throat cut him off. He turned to find a footman hovering next to a flower-bed. Poor man, he'd had to come the roundabout way to find his quarry. "Mr. Upperton, this message just arrived addressed to you. It's apparently most urgent."

George eyed the folded scrap of foolscap on the footman's tray. It hardly looked urgent. In fact, it looked rather flimsy. A stiff breeze off the ocean might snatch it away at any moment. He found himself wishing for that very event to occur. Then he could go back to ensuring his sister didn't accept any proposals from idiots with preposterous names.

Then he could cheerfully ignore whatever dire news that innocent little scrap of paper held. For his gut told him it was dire. A good many so-called gentlemen liked to call in their markers with just such notes.

He trudged toward the servant. The liveried man stood, his face expressionless—just carrying out his duty. Of course. The blandness alone weighed even further on George's stomach. If it was good news, the man would have occasion to smile, or at least ease up on his jaw.

Feigning nonchalance, George plucked up the scrap of paper and opened it slowly, as if it mattered not at all what the note contained—certainly not as if he were reluctant to read it.

Ah yes, a marker all right, or one being called in. God, and not one of the lesser ones, either. Did he really owe Barnaby Hoskins five hundred guineas? He must have been thoroughly in his cups that night, for he did not recall it. He did, however, recognize the old bastard's signature, black on white, as clear as the sun sparkling off the Channel. And then his glance drifted further down to a second signature, and the dead weight in his gut ignited.

The unfamiliar scrawl, once he deciphered it, spelled out Roger Padgett.

CHAPTER FOUR

PADGETT. LUCY'S great, hairy ape of a brother. Damn his eyes, how had he found George in the wilds of Kent? And why had he acquired Hoskins's marker?

George's mount, the deuced thing, surged ahead, an attempt to catch up to its fellows, no doubt. He sawed on the reins and shifted his weight back in the saddle, but the blasted horse tossed its head and pawed the ground. Revelstoke had assured him the creature was gentle, but the morning's ride had only proved the master a liar. That, or the nag was an expert at deception. Either way, the beast was most definitely in control.

He squinted along the path ahead. Encroaching trees, their leaves already edged with red and gold, closed in. The rest of the party had already ridden out of sight. So much for healthy companionship. Even his sister had abandoned him to fate—or at least his musings. Worse, if a few of the gentlemen took it into their heads to run races, George wouldn't be on hand to wager on the winner.

"Ho there, you blasted thing." Once more, he pulled on the reins and leaned back. The beast pulled to an abrupt halt, allowing George a breath of cool late summer air, tinged with the tang of salt. "Better. Now at least stand still long enough to let a man think."

But the sea tang called to mind the previous day and images of a secluded beach surmounted by high bluffs.

No, not that. He shook his head. He needed to work out what bloody Roger Padgett was up to, and how he was going to get himself out of this mess.

As if that small movement of his head were some kind of signal understood only by equines, his horse let out a snort and reared. The world tilted. For an instant, George knew a sensation of weightlessness, but then his rump hit the ground with a tooth-cracking jolt. His ungrateful nag wheeled and galloped for the stables, the earth trembling beneath the thunder of its hooves.

George drew in a painful breath. "Goddamned, bloody, foul, bugger of a wretch."

Why he'd ever allowed Revelstoke to convince him to get on the beast in the first place was a complete and utter mystery. He'd have done much better to lie in bed, only then he'd have had to endure his mother's matchmaking when he finally turned up at breakfast. At the moment, sitting in the middle of a bridle path, his tailbone aching and a sharp stone jabbing him in the arse, he reckoned he'd have stood a better chance with his mother.

With at least a mile between him and the manor, he might as well set off on foot. He pushed to his feet and dusted himself off. A perfectly good set of buckskins ruined, and of course, he couldn't afford to replace them until he'd settled the matter of his mistress and her brother.

Damn the wench. No, no. He oughtn't think of her in those terms. She hadn't got herself with child all on her own. But a child. What was he to do with a child? Lucy, at least, ought to see to most of it, but he'd be expected to pay visits and, above all, contribute enough blunt to ensure the child's future.

He tried to call up an image, not of a tiny babe, but of a boy, perhaps about Jack's age. A little blighter, but full of the devil with a quick grin, a sharp tongue, and a glint of mischief in his gray eyes. A streak of fearlessness, as well, enough to send him haring into the ocean even if he couldn't swim—just like Jack.

George recalled the steady weight of the child in his arms, the clinging bite of small fingers tightening their grip against his nape, the suppressed trembling. No, old Jack wasn't about to let on he was afraid. The scamp, he needed a man about to teach him such useful things as swimming and standing up for himself once he got to school.

But then Jack wouldn't go to school, would he? Certainly not away to a place like Eton where he'd have to fend for himself or be consumed by the system. Fortunate for Jack, perhaps, that he'd avoid such an education, but the boy still needed a father.

George shook his head. Why was he even concerning himself? The lad wasn't his child, while in a few short months Lucy would present him with his own little bundle of responsibility. The thought settled heavy on his stomach. Thank God he'd foregone an early breakfast. Eggs, kippers, kidney, and all such were liable to come back up to make room for the weight of impending fatherhood.

"What are you going to do now?"

George started. The voice, familiar and youthful, had come from somewhere above. He peered through the branches of a nearby oak. Jack sat on a limb, his bare feet dangling at least six feet above the path. "I say, how did you manage to get all the way up there?"

"Climbed." Jack swung a smudged foot. "What does bugger mean?"

"Now don't you go repeating that to your—" He looked about him. "Where is Isabelle?"

"You mean Mama? She's at home."

Home? Yesterday, he'd assumed they lived in the village, but that had to be a mile distant. Jack and his mother certainly didn't reside on Revelstoke's estate. "And does she know you're here?"

"Don't reckon she does." Something in the boy's tone—a hard note—gave George pause.

"Why don't you climb out of that tree, and we'll go see her?" He planted his hands on his hips as if the gesture would lend him a measure of authority. "She'll worry if she misses you, and you already gave her enough of a scare yesterday."

"I'm vexed with her." A hint of petulance crept into Jack's words. "She said she won't take me back to the beach after yesterday."

"Ah." He reached for the boy, hoping he'd take the hint and lean down, but Jack simply sat there, arms crossed and brows lowered. "The thing about women, see, is they need time to get over something like that. If you wait a few days, she might come around."

"I don't want to wait. I want to go now." Then his expression softened, and he leaned into George's waiting arms. "You wouldn't take me, would you?"

"That would hardly be sporting of me." George let the boy slip to the ground. Small but sturdy, that one. "I'm afraid we'll have to respect your mama's wishes for now. How about I take you back home? Will you tell me where you live?"

"I bet when you were little, your mama let you do all manner of things."

"She most certainly did not." He stopped himself before adding he'd got away with enough forbidden things on his own. Jack was clever enough to work that much out for himself. He hardly needed any further encouragement.

"Then what did you do for fun?"

"Same as most boys. I teased my sisters."

Jack reached out and plucked a stray branch from the ground. "Don't have any sisters."

"Aren't there any other boys your age in the village?"

Jack shrugged. "Only the vicar's son, and he's not allowed to play with me. Not that I want to. He's too namby-pamby."

ISABELLE ran a forefinger across the bonnet's delicate lining, careful not to let her work-roughened skin damage the fabric. Silk, white and pure and virginal. Costly. Far beyond her means. Like the ball gowns she'd taken when she left home, she might have sold the entire piece for as much as a crown, but the one and only time she'd worn it, she'd caught the outer shell on a branch. The most she could do now was salvage what she could.

She took a needle, pulled in a breath, and began picking the lining from the worn straw, one careful stitch at a time. Some harried milliner had spent hours until her fingers ached and neck cramped from painstaking stitchery in creating this bit of headgear.

All so some young lady making her come-out could wear it for a few fashionable hours in Hyde Park before casting it aside. During her single foreshortened season, Isabelle had spared little thought for the shop girls. Now, as she undid their handiwork, she appreciated their efforts. The fine fabric would turn into a few fancy cases for her herbs.

A knock at the door made her jump. "Blast."

She couldn't afford so much as a pull in the fabric with a slip of her needle. This scrap of a bonnet was the last of the lot. Through careful management, she'd lived on the proceeds of her ball gowns for the past six years, her dwindling funds supplemented by what herbs she might sell. She set the headpiece gently on the floor before pushing herself to her feet.

"Who's there?" Who indeed would pay her a call?

None of the village wives, certainly. As for the men . . . She reached for the shears.

"Mrs. Weston" came the muffled call from beyond the door.

Isabelle let out a breath. The vicar's wife, a relatively safe prospect, that is, as long as Jack had obeyed her latest dictate and stayed away from the woman's son. Despite a similarity in age, the two boys seemed incapable of getting along. Whatever the truth of the matter, any tears and wailing were invariably Jack's fault.

She opened the door to find the other woman standing calm and cool just beyond the threshold. A proper distance. It went with her upright bearing, the respectable poke bonnet that covered her cloud of dark hair, and her very proper morning dress that fell in precise folds to her feet.

Isabelle resisted the urge to smooth her rough skirts. "Your pardon. As you can see, I wasn't expecting callers."

"I've come about Peter."

Isabelle closed her eyes for a moment. "What's Jack done to the boy now?"

"Oh, this has nothing to do with Jack."

Isabelle held in a sigh. Apparently she wasn't about to be treated with a litany of her boy's shortcomings—a result of his mean birth, no doubt. Not that Mrs. Weston would ever be so rude as to make such a bald statement, but the implication always lay behind her words. Her family connections might not be worthy of the *beau monde*, but the woman's tongue could lash just as sweetly and politely as any *doyenne* of the *ton*.

"It's my boy," she rushed on. "He's poorly again."

"Have you sent for the doctor?" The vicar's wife, after all, ought to be able to afford an educated medical opinion.

"Oh, I don't think this warrants the doctor." Mrs.

Weston advanced into the room. "Not when that infusion you gave me last time did the trick."

Last time, she'd offered a bottle of one of Biggles's brews, since she had it to hand. "Is it his stomach again?"

"Yes, it pains him."

"But not enough for the doctor?"

Mrs. Weston paled. "The doctor insists on bleeding him, and I don't think . . ."

Isabelle hesitated. On that count, at least, she agreed. A quick glance at her open cupboard, on the other hand, told her Peter might have to face the lancet after all. "I seem to be out of stomach remedy."

"Oh, would you make another recipe?" Mrs. Weston fished in her pocket. "I can pay."

A few shillings glinted temptingly in her gloved palm. They'd perhaps buy a bone from the butcher's, enough to flavor a watery vegetable stew and remind her how beef tasted. "Of course. I'll bring it over as soon as it's ready."

"Please hurry. I hate to see him all pale and aching."

Mrs. Weston placed the coins on the table and left. Biggles had walked to a neighboring village to visit an old friend, but surely Isabelle had learned enough to brew a simple stomach remedy without supervision. All she needed was some meadowsweet, pennyroyal, and peppermint, but she already knew no peppermint hung from the rafters. They'd used up their supply.

"Jack? Jack, I've got an errand for you."

No answer. She drummed her fingers against her thigh. She might have known the house was too quiet. He'd probably gone outside.

She raised the window that looked over the back garden. A riot of color floated on graceful stems in the morning sunlight. Butterflies floated from flower to flower.

"Jack? Wherever you're hiding, come out at once."

Still nothing. That boy. A cold thread of unease drifted

through her belly. An image of him at breakfast, sullenly spooning gruel into his mouth, flashed through her brain. What if he'd defied her and gone back to the beach alone?

He was fully capable. He was as mischievous as any boy his age, full of the dickens at times and as hard-headed, well, as hard-headed as his own mother. Blast it all, she didn't have time for this. She'd have to give Mrs. Weston her money back. But she couldn't take the chance.

Hoisting her skirts, not bothering with a bonnet, she bolted through the door and pounded down the street toward the path to the shore. Soon her breath shot from her in ragged spurts, her ribs crushed against her stays. The late August sun pressed on her, but despite its heat, a cold trickle of sweat coursed between her shoulder blades.

And what if a wave had taken him again? What if he'd been pulled into the icy grip of the Channel? Tears blurred her vision at the thought of his small body tossed from wave to wave on merciless currents. Her Jack, at once sturdy and fragile, tough enough not to show his fear and yet no match for the power of all that water.

Blindly, she stumbled down the crumbling chalk that led to the strand. When her feet slipped on yielding pebbles, she took a breath to steel herself, opened her eyes.

Nothing, save the mournful cry of a lone seagull. The wind rushed along the empty shoreline, its steady hiss underscored by the relentless rhythm of the surf.

Her knees buckled, and she slumped against the wall of rock at her back. A sob choked her, and she pressed a fist to her mouth to hold back the pitiful wail. She should have kept a closer watch. Should have long since sought an apprenticeship for him. A boy his size might find any number of menial tasks within his capacity that would keep him occupied.

She needed to let go of the notion that the grandson

of an earl was above such things. Her family had cast her out, and rightly so, because of Jack. She'd failed at acting the proper society miss, and now she'd failed at motherhood.

A shout from the pathway above reached her ears. Oh God. Someone was about to discover her shame yet again. Unwilling to face whoever it was, she stared at the broad expanse of pebbles that stretched from the cliff face to the waves lapping at the shore. So deceptively gentle today, so calm. Even the pristine shoreline mocked her in the perfection of its smoothness. Not a single hint of a footprint marred the surface.

Not a footprint?

She clenched her fists. Blast it all, if the boy wasn't here, where on earth had he gone? She turned, and the source of the shouts became clear. Jack and Mr. Upperton picked their way down the slope.

"Jack!" She raced up the path toward her son. The heart-pounding sensation of panic turned hot. "Where on earth have you been?"

He'd begun to trot in her direction but stopped short, his smile fading. His brow puckered in uncertainty. She was so rarely harsh with him. Biggles claimed she wasn't stern enough. She knew she ought to be, but every time she strove to be firmer, part of her wondered if she wasn't being overly hard on the lad.

She hadn't wanted him, after all. Hadn't wanted any of this.

"Did you come looking for me here?" Jack asked.

"I couldn't find you anywhere." Her voice quavered at the memory of the hollowness in her gut when she realized he was gone. "Don't you ever, ever run off like that again."

"You'd best listen to your mother." Mr. Upperton pronounced the words with a quiet authority. "You don't want to give her another fright."

Jack hung his head and drew a line in the ground with one toe. "Yes, sir."

Isabelle forced herself to look Mr. Upperton in the eye. A mistake, that. The laugh lines fanning across his temples had smoothed to seriousness, leaving only shallow furrows to mark their presence. Laughing and good-natured, she'd thought him handsome. Sober and stern, he was devastating. Her mouth went dry, and her lips parted of their own accord.

Dash it all, she couldn't allow herself to react this way. If only she'd shown a bit more self-restraint during her first season, she wouldn't be in this situation. She couldn't afford to succumb yet again to a man's charm, no matter how overwhelming.

"Where did you find him?"

Upperton ran a hand along the back of his neck. A grin pulled at one corner of his mouth. "He was up a tree, actually."

"Up a tree?" The only significant trees close to the village lay on the Revelstoke estate. "What on earth were you doing at the manor?"

Jack looked her in the eye, his gaze guileless. "You said I couldn't go to the beach. You never said I couldn't climb trees."

"You are to stay where I can watch you. You've no business on the property of your betters." Their betters. Yes, the Revelstokes were their betters. Now. At one time, she'd have been their equal. At one time, she might have been invited to the house for tea. She might have met Mr. Upperton under legitimate circumstances. He might have asked her to dance. How she missed that simple pleasure.

Jack stuck out his lower lip. "Bugger!"

She let out a gasp before turning narrowed eyes on Upperton. "And where has he learned such language?"

Upperton had the grace to look away. A flush crept up

the back of his neck, just visible where the breeze stirred his hair. "You oughtn't repeat words you don't understand," he muttered.

Jack raised his chin. "I asked you what it meant. You wouldn't tell me."

"As well I shouldn't. Such isn't meant for young ears." He glanced at Isabelle. "In my defense, I didn't realize he could hear me. A horse unseated me, you see, and I thought myself quite alone. Jack here was hiding up a tree."

"Jack." Isabelle leaned down until her gaze was on a level with her son's. Dark brown eyes, so like her own, blinked back at her. "You are not to repeat such words. Do you understand me? As a matter of fact, I think it best if we stay clear of those who speak that way altogether."

"But Mama—"

"He's a busy man, I'm sure. He's got more to do than chase after the likes of us."

"I say." Upperton cleared his throat. "It was no trouble at all. I reckoned you'd worry where the lad had got to. I only thought to spare you."

She straightened. He stepped closer and reached his hand toward her. She stared at it, and his fingers curled inward, as if that might hide the intent behind the gesture. As if she might render the motion void. Her glance shifted to his eyes, and, as yesterday when he'd looked her over, the intensity behind his gaze slammed into her.

He's interested. He finds me attractive.

If only he wouldn't. It would be so much easier to ignore the heat unfurling in her midsection in response. She couldn't stop the feeling, but nothing required her to act on it. Only . . . the darkening of his eyes was beginning to tug at her—like a demand.

"It was no trouble at all, I assure you." Even his voice

deepened to something gravelly and compelling. "Give over," it seemed to say. But she'd given over once, to her disappointment and ruin.

"I thank you for your assistance." She squared her shoulders, held them stiff to reinforce the formality of her tone. "I do not think we shall require any more."

"Jack, why don't you run along home?" The boy blinked at the request, his eyes alight with curiosity. "There's a good lad. Your mama and I will be along presently. Only I wish a word with her—alone."

"Wait for me, Jack," Isabelle interjected before turning back to Upperton. "I do not have time to chat. I thank you for finding my son and returning him to me. Now if you'll excuse me, I really must be off." Mrs. Weston's stomach remedy wasn't going to wait much longer.

His hand lashed out to clamp on her forearm, firm, solid, not quite a threat, but a demand nonetheless. "I would discuss a certain matter with you."

"What can we possibly have to discuss, sir? We hardly know each other."

"Mama?" Jack looked from one to the other, his brow wrinkled.

"Go on now," Upperton said. "Your mama and I will follow."

Jack, drat the boy, jogged on up the path. She drew in a breath to call him back, but the hand on her arm tightened.

"Unless you'd rather he overhear us discussing him?" Upperton grumbled.

"My son is none of your affair, and I have work to do."

She moved to follow Jack, and Upperton released his grip but fell into step beside her. Gracious, what could he possibly want with her? She'd appear of little enough account to him with her simple dress. No better than a servant or a shop girl. Beneath his notice. She retained no outward sign of what she had been.

"What do you want?" She hated the way her voice sounded, so small and feeble faced with him.

"Where is the boy's father?"

"What?" She quickened her pace, but he lengthened his stride to match.

"His father."

"Jack," she called. "Do you remember that plant I showed you the other day? The one you said smelled so good?"

The boy turned and nodded.

"Do you recall where we found it?" Another nod. "I need you to pick some for me. As much as you can. Hurry along now." She didn't spare Upperton a glance. A steady stride and she'd be home soon enough. She fully intended to close the door in the man's face.

"Thank you," Upperton said. "Best he doesn't have a chance to overhear."

"I've no intention of discussing this with you. It is none of your affair." *Keep walking. Just keep walking. Don't look at him. Don't acknowledge.*

"Did he abandon you?" His voice took on a hard edge of outrage for her sake. But why should he care? To him, she was nothing. He was so far above her, yet at one time that might not have been the case. Six years ago *she* might well have been above *him*.

"It does not signify. He is not here. That is all that matters."

"All that matters? That boy needs a father."

She pulled up short, her hands balled into fists at the memory. "He does not need his true father. His true father was a scoundrel."

Upperton stepped closer until he blocked even the sky. A salt-laden breeze ruffled his hair, standing it on end and giving him a roguish look. "He needs a man in his life nonetheless."

Sudden laughter bubbled in her throat. "Are you volunteering?"

The color drained from his wind-reddened cheeks, and he retreated. "No."

"Then why broach the subject? Why put your nose where it clearly does not belong?" She strode off again. Jack had disappeared down a side lane, after the mint. Ahead, the first cottages loomed closer. Her cottage, up the street from the vicarage, past the inn. Her refuge.

"It's only . . ." He caught up with her once more. "The devil take it. Wouldn't your life be easier with someone else to help you look after him? He's going to be getting into more and more scrapes as he grows older."

"Speaking from experience, are you?" She sent a pointed glance in the direction of the bruises fading about his left eye.

"If you must know, yes. But besides that, he's lonely."

"Did he tell you as much?" An odd burning roiled in her stomach. Could it be jealousy that her son had confided in this stranger rather than his own mother?

"Not in so many words, but I could see it. A boy his age needs companions."

She nodded to a matron emerging from the apothecary. "He has me."

"You're his mother. Someday he'll want a man to tell him about—" He broke off, but the color fast rising to his cheeks filled in the rest of his notion easily enough.

"He'll want to know about seducing innocent girls into ruin?" That stopped him. Bluntness generally did.

He opened his mouth and closed it again. His Adam's apple bobbed as he swallowed. At the same time, a speculative glint in his eye told her he'd taken her point.

"I'd prefer my son not learn such lessons."

"Then he needs some sort of father even more."

"And where do you propose I find such a paragon? He'd have to take me into the bargain, ruined as I am."

His gaze traveled down her body, heating everything it touched, from her face to her breasts to somewhere deep, deep within—somewhere forbidden. And here she was, standing in the middle of a public thoroughfare, letting him ogle her. Time to shut him down here and now.

"That, Mr. Upperton, is precisely the sort of man I intend to avoid."

CHAPTER FIVE

GEORGE STALKED up the dusty road toward a promising-looking establishment. Precisely the sort of man she intended to avoid, indeed. He hadn't intended to imply anything. As if he could take on another woman's problems when he had enough of his own.

He eyed the inn—it must be an inn, given its size. An inn meant refreshment might be had. Lord knew a quaff of ale would go down nicely after the morning he'd had. Rejected by an equine and a female. Not that he wanted anything to do with either. Oh, no.

"I say, you've come a rather roundabout way."

George squinted in the direction of the masculine voice. Leach led his horse from the opposite end of the village. Revelstoke followed, along with several of his male guests, each holding a set of reins.

Revelstoke approached and clapped him on the shoulder. "Do I want to know what you've done with Buttercup?"

"Who's Buttercup?"

The wretch fairly smiled. "I recall lending you a horse this morning."

So the beast was female, too. He might have known. "That was no Buttercup. That was an ungrateful nag that decided to have a lie-in rather than take me on an outing. I'm certain the blasted beast is back at the stables, stuffing itself with oats."

Revelstoke burst out laughing.

"And don't you dare point out the last rider that foul creature threw was a child of six," George added. "I shall have to demand satisfaction."

"You can call Buttercup out if you'd like, but you'll have to ask someone else to stand as your second. We were coming to the inn for a drink, but perhaps you wish to decline the invitation. You'll need the time to walk home."

"That's quite all right. I can use the drink." He glanced at the others. Revelstoke's brother and brother-in-law, the Marquess of Enfield and the Earl of Highgate respectively, flanked Leach. "If one of you happens to have a pack of cards, that wouldn't go amiss, either. What do you say?"

A slow grin spread across Leach's features. He reached into his topcoat and pulled out a small packet. "Thought you'd never ask."

Revelstoke nudged him. "About the card games."

"What's that?"

"My wife's decided she doesn't want any deep play at the house. Too tempting for her father."

Leach frowned. "That's going to leave us with nothing but parlor games for entertainment."

The lines about the marquess's eyes deepened as he laughed. "If you're fortunate, the older ladies will look the other way for Kiss the Candlestick."

"Knowing my mother," George said, "she'll encourage it, and then claim I've compromised some young miss."

"That decides it, then." Leach replaced the pack in his topcoat and patted the pocket. "The morning's exertions have left me decidedly parched. What say we sample the local brew? And perhaps any other delights this village might hold?"

Highgate raised his brows. "What sort of delights might those be in a place this size?"

"Good God, save me from the parson's trap. Has marriage completely coddled you?" Leach let out a bark of laughter. "You can't tell me the inn doesn't house a willing wench or two."

"I can't say that it does," Revelstoke said.

"Yes, another one caught. It only means you haven't looked hard enough, I daresay. I wouldn't want to wager Upperton here has beat us to what pickings there are." He elbowed George in the ribs. "Eh? What about it? Have you been sampling the local talent while the rest of us jounced about working up a thirst?"

George stepped back. Ordinarily, he'd be in the thick of such speculation, if only for a bawdy laugh or two. Not now. For some reason, Isabelle's image floated through his mind. He'd caught a glimpse of her house when she flounced in—tidy, yes, but tiny. Whatever her station had been—and her manner of speaking told him it was high—her circumstances now were far reduced.

And what if, out of sheer desperation, she resorted to the sort of undertakings Leach hinted at? What if she already had sold herself to any who might have a few coins in order to feed her son or maintain the roof over their heads? Such a risk, and if she attracted the wrong man . . .

That, Mr. Upperton, is precisely the sort of man I intend to avoid.

What if she already had?

The notion hit him like a blow to the gut and forced the air from his lungs. Not if he could help it. But what could he do? For now, at any rate, Leach didn't know anything about her. He need only ensure such remained the case.

"It took me half the morning to reach here on foot, I'll have you know." He hoped the others would interpret the edge to his voice as simple injury at having his horse unseat him. Buttercup, indeed. "Now what about that drink?"

Anything to get them out of the street.

Arse aching from his spill, he led the way into the inn. The common room lay dark beneath heavy-beamed ceilings and a few high windows. A fitful fire burned on the hearth, pumping more smoke into the space than heat. Grayish wisps floated through the weak shafts of sunlight slanting down from the eaves. A broad-bosomed woman glowered at them from behind the bar.

George nudged Leach and pointed with his chin. "There's your local talent."

Leach frowned and flopped into the nearest seat. "Let's get on with it."

A few hours later, George was cheerfully willing to overlook any lingering ache in his nether regions in favor of concentrating on heavier pockets, at least sometime in the near future.

"You'll have to accept my marker." Leach pressed a slip of paper into his hand.

"What's this then?"

Leach's cheeks took on a ruddy flush, more so than could be attributed to any ale he'd consumed. He mumbled something too low for George to hear over the chatter in the taproom.

"Come again?"

Leach cleared his throat. "I said unless you'd like to make an arrangement with your sister."

George closed his fist around the marker. "Here now. What's Henrietta got to do with an agreement between gentlemen? You've no call dragging her name into it."

Leach's eyes narrowed, the merest tightening of the muscles above his cheeks, the movement nearly imperceptible in the shadows of the taproom. "She cleaned me out last night, all right?"

Revelstoke burst out in a fit of false coughing, which only served to darken Leach's expression.

"Cleaned you out?" George drummed his fingers on the table. "How did you get those kinds of stakes past Julia?"

Leach shrugged. "Don't suppose she was paying close enough attention."

"That's what you get for letting Henny win."

"I didn't let her win," Leach grated.

George ignored the warning note in Leach's reply. This was just too delicious. He threw back his head and laughed. "In that case, I owe you thanks for teaching her properly. If it weren't for her reputation, I'd have to think of a way to spirit her into my club. I might reverse a few of my own fortunes."

"That's it." Wooden chair legs scraped loudly on planked flooring as Leach unfolded himself. "I'm off."

George studied the other man as he turned and stalked out of the taproom. His pack of cards still lay spread on the table. The tightness about his mouth and the rigid set of his shoulders spoke volumes.

Turning to face the others, George picked up his tankard and swallowed the last of his ale. "And where did he come from? I can't recall ever coming across him before, and you'd think, among friends, I'd know the other guests."

Revelstoke sat up a bit straighter, his gaze panning toward the door. "He's an acquaintance of the Wentworths'. At least, he came out from Town with them. I wasn't about to turn him away, as a friend of invited guests."

"Rather touchy for a hanger-on, don't you think?" George said. "What do you suppose his problem is?"

Highgate leaned across the table. "Did you have to rub it in?"

"The man's clearly an overdressed idiot." George

pushed his tankard aside. "What does it matter?" He smoothed out Leach's crumpled marker to admire the amount. The man's writing was just as flamboyant as his manner of speech and dress. "Soon as he pays me, you'll have your loan back," he added to Revelstoke.

Not only that, he'd be able to pay off that ape Padgett and still have enough left over—to invest in his strategy to bring down Redditch.

Revelstoke leaned forward in his seat. "You don't have to pay me back. Keep what I gave you and apply it to Summersby's debts."

Highgate reached into his topcoat and tossed a leather pouch onto the table. "You can add my contribution."

"And mine." Enfield's coin purse landed next to Highgate's with a *thunk*.

George sat back, unable to respond for a moment. "This really isn't necessary. I never intended to start up a charity."

"Just shut up and take it," Revelstoke said, gathering up the coin.

"But I have Leach's marker." Without a thought, he gathered the cards and put them in his pocket. "It's a start."

"Aren't you assuming a bit much?"

George closed his fingers about the coin purses. "What's that?"

"That he's good for it."

POCKETS jingling, George strode across the lawn, his gaze fixed on the groups of young ladies dotted about the grass. Some of them had set up easels to capture in watercolor the neat ranks of flowers bordering the walkway. Others scribbled on sheaves of paper while their friends exchanged gossip behind their hands. Pastel-colored titmice twittering away, the entire lot of them.

Worse, neither of his sisters was anywhere in sight.

"There you are." Mama's fingers clutched George's wrist in a surprisingly strong grip. "You can't spend the entire week hiding. I won't have it."

"Have you seen Henrietta? I require a word with her." And more than a word. Revelstoke's parting shot at the inn made George question whether Leach had told him the truth about not losing intentionally. If he indebted himself to Henrietta on purpose to lure her into a trap . . .

Mama's grip tightened on his sleeve. "Henrietta is occupied at the moment, and you aren't to disturb her."

The insistence in Mama's tone drew his gaze from the flocks. "Occupied how?"

"I'd never have believed it after all this time. She's attracted a suitor, and she doesn't seem set on turning him away." Mama lowered her voice to a whisper, as if speaking the truth might frighten off said suitor.

Damn, he might have known. "That's why I wish to speak to her. I don't believe the gentleman in question is quite appropriate—"

"Nonsense! Next year, she'll be six and twenty. Between her age and her past, I was beginning to think we'd never marry her off. Best to get the job done before she puts any more notions in Catherine's head. And as for you—"

Her grip changed, putting a decided pressure on his wrist. She practically frog-marched him toward a group of giggling young girls. If they weren't in company, she'd doubtless lead him by the ear like a recalcitrant schoolboy.

One girl stood slightly apart from the others, her hands folded in a perfect display of a demure miss, while another girl made sweeping stabs at a sheaf of sketch paper with a stick of charcoal. Their friends jabbered encouragement. The lot of them looked like they still belonged in the schoolroom. And his mother thought one of them would be a suitable match?

"Mama, really," he muttered.

"I am determined," she said out of the corner of her mouth, giving his wrist a none-too-subtle jerk. If she had him by the ear, she'd have twisted it. "Ah, here we are. Miss Abercrombie, I don't believe you've met my son. George, this is Miss Theodosia Abercrombie."

Theodosia. Good Lord. George felt a stab of pity for the chit, being saddled with such an ungainly name.

Miss Abercrombie looked away from her work and smiled for a fleeting moment before narrowing her eyes into a penetrating glare. The others fell silent while her gaze sketched his face from brows to cheeks to chin. *Interesting subject*, that gaze said.

"A pleasure, I'm sure," she murmured before ducking behind her sheaf of paper once more.

George bowed to the sheaf. "Likewise. Now, if you'll—"

But Mama cut him off. "Who are your friends?"

Clearly the artist did not intend to let herself be disturbed in the midst of such creative energy, for the furrow between her dark brows deepened, and she went on swiping at the page.

Another girl stepped forward and dropped a curtsey. "I believe we were introduced at the Pendleton ball last Season?" Yes, Miss Prudence Wentworth of the unfortunate nose. "You've just met my cousin." She nodded to the artist before rattling off a few more names. "And this is Miss Emily Marshall."

George stiffened.

Mama dropped his arm. "Gracious. Would you be connected to the Earl of Redditch?"

"He is my uncle." The girl's tone was frosty, as if Mama were a servant. Hardly surprising coming from a family whose head thought nothing of ruining a man.

George studied the girl, while his mind whirled with possibilities. She stood, pale, blond, white-skinned, and white-gowned—she might as well be a ghost for all she was nearly translucent in her whiteness. Even her eyes were such a light shade of gray they faded into the blandness of the whole. Little to recommend in the realm of beauty, unless one fancied an untouched canvas.

But if he could break through the layer of ice that surrounded her, he might gain enough acceptance to permit him to call on her in Town. All he needed was an *entrée*. It would take all the charm he possessed to melt her. He held Miss Marshall's gaze and thought of the sweet taste of victory when he paid off Summersby's debts and exposed Redditch for the man he was.

There. That ought to make for a convincing smile. Successful, too, if the chorus of sighs from the surrounding young ladies was any indication.

"Finished!" Miss Abercrombie announced. The other girls flocked to admire her handiwork, but George stayed where he was. He'd seen enough young ladies' efforts at art, and in this case, he was far more interested in the subject.

Thus, he was barely prepared when Miss Abercrombie declared, "Mr. Upperton shall stand for my next portrait."

He held up his hands. "Ladies, I really don't think—"

"Oh please," they pleaded as one. Even Miss Marshall seemed to animate herself long enough to add her voice to the chorus.

"Well, if you insist. As long as you don't require me to stand like some statue, that is. The exercise will be far more enjoyable if I'm allowed conversation."

Miss Abercrombie jerked her head in assent. Thank God. If he had to stand there and think about how assessing her gaze was, he might well go mad. He took up his position where she indicated and tried to put her unnerving eyes out of his mind.

"Marshall, Marshall." He tapped his chin. "I seem to recall someone by that name a form or two below me at Eton. You wouldn't happen to have an older brother, by any chance?"

Miss Marshall peered at him frostily. "I regret that I do not."

He had to strain his ears to catch her murmured reply. "Pity that. A cousin, then?"

"No, sir." As she muttered the words, a trace of something—her eyes were too nondescript to call it a spark—passed through her glance. A flutter of a shadow. So the chit had something to hide, did she?

So did many members of the *ton,* but her family in particular was adept at hiding their foibles. Perhaps that's why she worked so hard at blending into the scenery. Under his scrutiny, she seemed to whither.

"Marshall, yes. It's coming back to me now. Henry, his name was. Always in some scrape or another. Almost as often as I was." He paused for the series of giggles that erupted from his audience. "Come to think of it, he favored you. Or you favor him."

She angled her head to one side, as if she was trying to make heads or tails of him. "I cannot possibly."

"Of course you do." Of course she didn't because Henry Marshall, her purported cousin, did not exist. "I see it now. His nose tilted the same as yours, and he was fair. With a bit ruddier complexion."

Her shoulders rose as she drew in a breath. Ghostly pale brows lowered. Two pinkish spots stained her cheeks—doubtless this was as ruddy as she ever got. Inside, she must be seething. "I'm afraid you are mistaken. I know of no Henry Marshall, not even among my acquaintances, much less any family connections."

The more she spoke, the more he became certain he'd

hit close to some mark. She was hiding something. Or perhaps not her, but a larger scandal within the family. But what? George sifted through his memory, but he'd never been one to attend to gossip, at least as long as he couldn't hear anything to his advantage. If the *ton* was abuzz over some lord losing big at the gaming table, he might lend an ear. If a man had earned a reputation for ruining young misses, he might pay enough attention to know who to warn away from his sisters.

But he'd never paid the Earl of Redditch the slightest heed before becoming aware of Summersby's difficulties. Well, here was his chance. He only needed to convince her to meet him under more favorable circumstances to see if he could draw her out.

That would require meeting with her. Alone.

PETER Weston would be all right, surely. Isabelle told herself as much as she left the vicarage. His mother was too indulgent. An overabundance of sweets would give any boy a bellyache.

A salt-laden breeze kicked up swirls of dust along the road through the village. She clapped a hand to her head to secure her bonnet as she made her way home. Coins jingled in her pocket, the very sound of security, or at least a full stomach tonight.

Two matrons, shopping baskets swinging from their elbows, emerged from the butcher shop. For form's sake, Isabelle nodded to them. They returned her acknowledgment with barely perceptible inclinations of their heads, as close to a cut as they could go without committing themselves to blatant rudeness.

She was far too accustomed to their reaction to let it bother her. When she first arrived here, heavy with child, she'd been appalled and hurt. Now she merely smiled a bit more broadly and suppressed a giggle when the two increased their pace. Heaven forbid she take their acknowledgment as an excuse to speak to them. How dare she possess the gall to comment on the weather?

She strode toward her cottage, suspecting without looking that the pair had their heads together. The whitewashed walls of her dwelling rose in a neat frame about the oaken front door. Not much, but she retained enough pride from her former life to keep the place as tidy as possible. A tangle of flowers trailed along either side of the path beneath the shuttered windows, their vivid colors bright in the sunshine.

As she came in the door, Biggles held out a folded square of paper. "I think this must be yers."

Isabelle blinked. "What's this?" A stupid question. Biggles could barely read.

"A note, it looks like. I found it there on the floor jus' waiting when I came in." She pointed to a space just over the threshold.

Isabelle lowered her brows. The only person she could think of with the audacity to slip notes under her door had no business doing so. As if her set-down earlier hadn't been enough. "We'll see about that."

She snatched the paper from Biggles and unfolded it.

Meet me in the garden at Shoreford House. Midnight. Come alone. I know something important about your son.

Isabelle scanned the elaborate scrawl twice in utter disbelief, but the words read just as terse and ominous the second time. She closed her fist about the note to stop her hand from shaking. Could Mr. Upperton have sent her the message? But that made no sense. Before yesterday, Mr. Upperton had known nothing of Jack's existence. What important information could he possibly possess?

Nor could it be anyone from the village. None of her neighbors would resort to cryptic notes. But that only left someone from her past. How could anyone have found her after all these years? And what could they know?

"What is it, dear?" Biggles laid a hand on her shoulder and squeezed. "Ye've gone all pasty."

"It's nothing. Just some foolishness."

Somehow she managed to hold her voice steady. She strode to the hearth and tossed the note into the flames, watching the paper twist and blacken to ash. She'd just told Biggles half a lie—because anything to do with Jack might be at once nothing and everything.

CHAPTER SIX

Gᴇᴏʀɢᴇ ᴘᴜʟʟᴇᴅ in a final drag on the cheroot and tossed the stub into the hedge. The chit wasn't coming. Naturally she wasn't, and why should he expect her just because he slipped her a note? Far too much of a risk for the upright Miss Marshall to meet a rake in the gardens without a chaperone. At any rate, he'd do better worming gossip out of one of the older ladies. One way or another, he'd charm the truth out of someone. Then, when he had the blunt to pay off Summersby's markers, he'd come armed—in more than one fashion.

He stomped toward the nearest French casement. It creaked as he pulled it open, the sound echoing through the empty ballroom. Of course. Deprived of the usual evening entertainments involving high stakes, the other guests had long sought their beds. The opportunity to invest his earlier winnings in a few more hands of vingt-et-un might be lost, but he could take advantage of the empty house in other ways.

To his left, the pianoforte loomed, a dark hulk of shadow in the night. That damned instrument that his sisters had turned into a torture device beckoned to him. Right. No one about this late. No one to mock him for undertaking such an unmanly activity as music. No one to laugh at him if he struck a false note—as surely he would. If he wanted this preoccupation to pass undetected, he couldn't practice daily as he ought.

He seated himself on the bench and the ivory keys stretched before him, a row of jagged teeth with spaces at regular intervals. He set his forefinger on middle C, drew in a breath and pressed. The note rang clearly through the darkness.

He positioned his left hand, and a tingle passed through him, half anticipation, half dread. Before his brain had a chance to engage, his fingers moved, rippling over the keys without direction. They knew what his conscious mind did not, but his ear told him every note was true.

Naught but a scale, simple enough, but the moment he closed his eyes, the music took over. His fingers found the path until a melody surrounded him, each note pure, each one correct, each one forbidden.

A miracle that his muscles retained the memory, the ability to execute the intricacies of an arpeggio. His fingers ought to trip clumsily over the keys like a toddler first learning to run. He practiced so seldom, they ought to have lost their stretch, yet he easily spanned over an octave. They recalled the necessity of lightness on the high notes to make them tinkle like silver bells. They remembered the emphasis in the lower register to accentuate the beat.

He didn't need to think this. He only needed to feel, to fill himself up with the music until the George Upperton that society knew—the rake, the gambler, the wit—ceased to exist. That man was a shell, a container, a bushel to hide this essential core of himself that not even his closest friends were ever allowed to observe, that even he denied.

At last, his fingers drummed out the coda, and the final notes drifted off into the darkened room. No sound broke the silence now, except for his own ragged breathing, as if he'd just run a mile. A drop of sweat trickled along his cheek and hit the ivory with a plop.

He inhaled, seeking to calm his racing pulse, and that was when he heard it—the steady rush of another person's breath, out of sync with the rise and fall of his chest. He looked back toward the casement. Open, but had he left it ajar? He no longer remembered.

Could Miss Marshall have decided to defy propriety and meet him?

"Who's there?" His question echoed, low and rough through the stillness.

"Pardon me. I . . ."

He raised his head toward the whisper, the voice somehow familiar to his ear when it shouldn't be. Isabelle stood in the far corner, her moon-kissed white-blond hair a mere glimmer in the deeper shadows. From across the room, he sensed her tension, her uncertainty. He remained on the bench, the massive bulk of the piano a shield between them. But whom was it protecting? Him as much as her, for he'd never intended to reveal so much of himself—not to her, not to anyone.

"What are you doing here?" He kept his question deliberately casual. No need to appear upset, even if she might as well have walked in on him naked. Any other woman, and he would have preferred things that way. Far more fun to be had. Far more pleasure. Much better than enduring the scrutiny of her silence.

"I . . ."

An assignation, but not with him. What else could it be? The thought struck him like a punch to the gut.

"Has Jack fallen ill?" There. He'd thrown her a line, an excuse, something she could grasp. And bolt.

"No, he's long in bed. I left him with Biggles."

"Biggles?"

"I share her house. He's safe enough."

He studied her face for a sign. In the low light, she appeared otherworldly, like a fairy, with her wisps of silvery curls backlit by moon glow. What he could see of her expression was guarded, as if she was afraid to admit the reason for her presence.

He rubbed his palms against his thighs, the fine wool of his trousers hot to his skin, and waited. Waited for her to declare herself. She couldn't stand forever on the threshold of her world and his.

She moved, a tentative step, presaged by the flutter of her gown. Her hand stretched out and lit upon the polished wood of the pianoforte. "I had no idea you played."

"I don't."

She opened her mouth and closed it again. "Of course you do. I've never heard such . . . such virtuosity."

"I don't play," he insisted, the words harsh, hard. Why was he doing this? Why distance her only because she'd chanced on a side of him he revealed to no one?

"No, you're right. 'Play' is too frivolous a term for what I just heard. That was not playing."

"It certainly wasn't work," he snapped. He shifted his weight, suddenly aware of the wood beneath his seat. Hard, unforgiving, unyielding. How much could she see of him in this low light? Too much. And she didn't need her eyes, not when she'd just experienced—

"Beauty, that's what it was. Ideal beauty."

He released his breath in a loud splutter, the sound just as discordant as any note his sisters produced. "Indeed. How manly of me to produce such heights of aesthetics. Why have you come here?"

She withdrew her hand. "I heard you playing, and I couldn't help myself."

"You heard me from your house in the village?"

"No." The whispered admission barely grazed his ear. "The garden."

"Did someone ask you to meet him?" He pushed himself to his feet. Despite the low light, he picked up on the rigidity of her shoulders. "What did you imagine would occur out there? Come," he added when she didn't reply.

"You've brought a child into the world. You cannot pretend ignorance of what passes between men and women."

She looked away, turned her head to the side and down, and he immediately regretted reminding her of her past scandal. "Forgive me. That was an unconscionable thing to say."

"Indeed." The word was frosty. "Most especially when you do not know the circumstances."

"Circumstances, yes. There are always circumstances." He waited. Would she go on without further prompt? Not that her past was any of his affair, but part of him was curious. She was obviously well bred. Her speech, her manners spoke to that. Her family was well-heeled enough to provide.

"I do not wish to say more," she said at last, as if he'd prodded her. "I've never heard anyone play so finely. Haydn, wasn't it?"

"Yes." Oh, she was educated, all right, as educated as any young lady of good family. Enough to recognize the work of a composer better known for his symphonies than his piano sonatas.

George probed his memory, searching for any recollection of a scandal involving a young lady. She'd have been making her debut, certainly, but six years ago he spent more time in gaming hells than ballrooms. Hardly surprising a young miss's unexplained absence from society had passed his notice.

But if they had been introduced, he'd have remembered this one, in particular, with her fine features and slender hands. As much as he made a habit of avoiding the marriage mart, the sight of Isabelle in a ball gown, gloves covering her long, white arms, her curls tamed beneath a fashionable headdress, might well make him reconsider the prospect.

Thank God he'd never laid eyes on her then. He'd

have made an utter ass of himself, when obviously, her heart had been engaged elsewhere.

"You must have learned from a master."

"I learned from the same tutor who instructed my sisters, and you may thank the heavens you've never been subjected to their performances."

"Oh, come." She smiled faintly, a mere shadow amid others. "They can't be that bad. Not when their brother displays such talent."

"I'd gladly let them have a measure of mine. They might each end up tolerable."

"Won't you play something else?"

The very request he'd been dreading. "No. I never meant to perform for anyone at all."

"Pity." She caught her lower lip between her teeth for a fleeting moment. "I liked you better when you were playing."

"Liked me better?"

"Not that I disliked you before, only . . . Oh, I'm making such a hash of things. How to explain this? When I was listening to you play just now, you seemed, well, less threatening."

"Threatening? My dear, you'll have me blushing soon if you don't leave off with the compliments. Do I threaten you now that I'm not playing?" He waited for her reply. How had he posed any sort of a menace to her at all? But he had. That first day down at the beach, she'd been on her guard. Fearful, really, beneath the veneer of anger. But what had she to fear from him?

The silence stretched out too long for her to deny it. "A little." She waved her hand. "Should anyone find us, my reputation shall be in tatters."

Again.

Neither one of them dared pronounce that truth, but it hung between them all the same. "A pity you have nothing to show for it then."

She held her hands clasped in front of her, the very picture of a demure and biddable miss. "Yes, a pity."

He cleared his throat. "Would you like something?"

"Not from you."

No, of course not. He hadn't requested the pleasure of her company. Someone else had. "And yet you stand there. Were you going to meet someone in the garden? Off with you, then."

She remained on the spot, her face turned away. Well. Whoever she planned to meet, she was clearly displeased with the prospect.

"Perhaps I ought to pity the poor fellow. Your eagerness is overwhelming."

"You know nothing. Nothing at all." She'd likely meant the words as an attack, but somehow they lacked force.

"Yet, you're here," he pressed. "With me."

Her hesitation tore at him. He was used to experienced women, women who knew what they wanted and weren't afraid to ask for it. Some were even bold enough to reach out and make the first move. Isabelle was different, experienced to a degree, and yet so completely innocent. He usually ran from virgins. Virgins expected a courtship. They expected flowers and escorts through the park and proposals. Isabelle, while no longer a virgin, retained that shyness, that hesitance that usually sent him scrambling in the opposite direction.

So why wasn't he running from her? Why was he skirting the pianoforte to stand before her? Why was he tipping her chin up and forcing her to look him in the eye?

Her lips parted at the contact, and he studied them, plump and open and soft, but not quite inviting. Some slight tension in her cheeks prevented her from relaxing completely.

"You've nothing to fear from me," he murmured.

"I've never once forced my attentions on a woman, and I don't mean to begin with you."

If anything, she tensed further. Her mouth closed and pressed itself into a line.

"What is it?"

Instead of replying, she picked up his hand and laid it flat, fingers splayed. She fitted her free hand over it, palm to palm, her soft skin a glimmer of white against his paw. His long fingers extended beyond the ends of hers. He could easily curl them into a fist and crush her hand if he chose.

He understood. She wanted the assurance of gentleness from him. He lifted her arm and pressed his lips to the back of her wrist. She sucked in a breath.

"I will not hurt you, and I will do nothing you do not wish me to do." He turned her hand over and brushed his lips over the tender skin at its base, inhaling as he did so, drinking in her freshness, her lightness, her otherworldliness. She smelled of lavender, the sharpness of sea air, and the earthiness of woman. He thought of taking his time, taming her slowly until he moved above her, sheathed in her softness and heat. Blood rushed to his groin.

He released her hand, placed it on his shoulder, and drew her close enough that the tips of her breasts brushed his chest. He stroked the length of her spine, his fingers tracing each bump of her vertebrae, feeling the tension ease from her as his hand traveled toward her waist.

Her breath released in a warm gust that wafted against his neck. He touched his lips to her temple, her cheek, at last grazing her mouth, gently, slowly, returning with greater insistence when she didn't freeze up on him. He raised his hand and pressed it between her shoulder blades, eased her closer. He teased her lips until he coaxed a response from her, a gentle pressure in return, unschooled, a far cry from his mistresses' practiced caresses.

And yet, with her, the patience to teach came so easily. Hell, someone ought to instruct her properly. The idiot who'd got her with child clearly hadn't bothered with the task.

Cradling the back of her head with his hand, he traced the seam of her lips with his tongue. When she stiffened for a moment, the reaction came as no surprise. So hesitant, his Isabelle, but then she'd landed herself in trouble before. No shock she advanced with caution now. He stroked her back again, and like a cat, she arched into his touch.

"Open for me, my dear," he whispered against her lips. "I swear I'll only kiss you."

Her hand slid to the back of his neck, and the tips of her fingers bit into the skin about his collar. Tempted and yet still hesitant.

"Trust me."

Oh, how she wanted to. Those gentle initial kisses had kindled a familiar fire within her belly—but down that path lurked disappointment and ruin. She could not give into passion with a man yet again, not even with George Upperton, whose gentleness and patience inspired trust.

When she'd placed her hand to his, she'd meant to show him how easily he might break her if he so chose. He'd taken the hint. He would not overpower her. But eventually he would demand more than she could give him.

And yet—his body was so firm against hers. He awakened in her an insidious longing, a curiosity to know him fully, and the feeling threatened to outweigh her memories and fears. Yes, she could kiss him, but no more.

As if he sensed her acquiescence, he bent his head once more and captured her lips. She parted them for him, let him explore with his tongue, raised her own to twine with his. Oh God, yes. She recalled this sensation of being swept along in a rising tide of passion, the pleasure, the pure heat, the awakening ache in her belly. At the age of eighteen she hadn't known what it was. Experience had taught her the depths of shame and humiliation, but while it was happening—at least in the beginning—how wonderful.

And with George it was even better, the fire hotter, the ache more bittersweet. He tasted and smelled of lingering smoke. The strands of his hair slipped like silk through her fingers. His chest pressed against her breasts, and her nipples tightened into buds.

With a groan, he tore his mouth from hers, his chest heaving raggedly. She opened her eyes to find him devouring her with his gaze. Gracious, such finely veiled fire. It was nearly naked. She caught her lower lip between her teeth, and his fingers curled tighter.

"Already you tempt me to break my promise and ask for more than a kiss." He dipped his head for another sip from her mouth.

"I would deny you," she said when he broke off. Her voice had faded to a low, husky note.

"What would it take?" He kissed her again. "How many more kisses until I've got you so drunk with passion you consent?"

"Too many." Too few, but she could never admit as much, lest she find herself on her back and increasing once more. "I already know the outcome. I prefer not to live through the shame a second time."

He pressed his lips to a spot just below her ear. How did he know? How did he know just where to touch and drive her mad with want? "There are precautions one might take."

"The surest is abstinence."

He dropped that soothing hand from her back and tugged at his hair. "I would protect you."

"Protect me?" The words stung like a slap in the face. She dropped her arms and wrapped them about her waist to ward off a sudden chill. "You wish me to become your mistress?"

"No, you misunderstand."

"Then pray, explain it, because the only other significance I can ascribe to your words is far worse."

He did not respond straightaway. His mouth worked, and his cheeks darkened, gray under the moonlight, but in the full sun they would be flushed a dull red. Mistress indeed, but as insulted as she was, part of her acknowledged that a role as a man's bit of muslin was all she was fit for now. She'd managed to ruin herself and could expect no better.

But she would not expose Jack to such an arrangement. He was an innocent child, and she would ensure he remained so as long as possible. There was pain enough when one's illusions were suddenly stripped away. She could spare her son that much.

"I meant no insult," Upperton replied at last.

She crossed her arms. "Indeed."

He exhaled, and she took a perverse satisfaction at his discomfiture. She'd pushed him into a corner, and she rather liked him there.

"Isabelle, you are a breathtakingly beautiful woman. Have you never considered you might improve your fortunes by taking on a protector?"

Oh, but he was beyond the pale. "My fortunes are perfectly acceptable as they are. A woman in my circumstances can hardly hope for better."

"No?" He stepped closer, near enough that she caught a hint of his scent with every intake of breath. "And when you lie abed at night, alone, and sleep doesn't come, and you long for another body beside you, a little warmth, a little companionship?" He tipped her chin up. "A little passion?"

She clamped her lips shut. He meant to seduce her, but she wasn't about to yield. Not after the sort of offer he'd just made. "I manage quite nicely, thank you. Now if you'll pardon me, the hour is late, and I need to be off home. I have responsibilities, you see, and I cannot simply wave them away or expect a servant to see to them for me."

He dropped his hand, and she allowed herself a smile at his stiffened posture. So he'd caught her insinuation. So much the better. Useless, idle members of society. What good had any of them ever been to her? Why would she wish to consort with any of them, most especially a man who wanted nothing more than a few hours' pleasure—his pleasure, not hers—and who would move on the moment he tired of her. She'd be fortunate not to find herself with a permanent reminder of his passage through her life.

"Good night, *my lord.*"

She didn't wait for his reply. Squaring her shoulders, she took herself through the casement and into the gardens. Her feet crunched briskly across the graveled path. Mistress indeed! Why any woman would commit herself to such a life—paid to live at a man's beck and call, to serve him in the most distasteful manner.

It's the best you can do.

She tried to push the thought aside, but it persisted. No man would look upon her as a suitable wife, and no respectable family would take her on as a governess or companion. She was fortunate to have found a comfortable dwelling. Otherwise, she would have succumbed to selling herself out of desperation long since.

She rounded the end of the house and strode down the footpath that led to the village. The moon cut from behind a cloud to cast the world in eerie shades of gray. A sharp breeze blew up from the sea, carrying with it the dull pounding of surf on the unseen beach at the cliff's base. Her cove lay nearby, bathed in that same otherworldly light.

That cove was no longer her and Jack's secret, not since the day Upperton had come upon them. He was no better than an intruder, and a rude one at that. What had she been thinking, entering the manor when she ought to have waited for whoever had left her that note?

Blasted curiosity, always leading her astray. And it had made her miss her meeting. Whatever *he* had wanted with her . . . He, yes. Curlicues aside, there was something masculine about the handwriting on that note. She'd trudged up the path to Shoreford house, her heart heavy. What could anyone know about Jack after all these years?

But she'd gone and let Upperton distract her. Although he'd kept his word and done no more than kiss her, bitter experience ought to have taught her to exercise more caution. She intended to, starting now. She'd go back to her cottage, mind her own business, raise her son, and never look in the direction of the likes of George Upperton again.

A crack from the hedge to her left brought her up short. Her heart slammed into her ribs, and her senses tingled to the alert. The night air, still but for the distant rush of waves on the shore, pressed in on her. Before her, the path stretched out, empty. Neither, she was certain, did anyone lurk at her back. Not Upperton, surely. Not even he was so insufferably arrogant that he'd have followed. Not the way they'd left things.

Drawing in a lungful of salt air, she willed her leaden feet forward. Awareness prickled at the back of her neck. How she wished she'd stayed home. Home was safe. Home was secure. It posed no danger to her reputation or to her person.

But a young woman wandering alone in the dark was a different matter altogether. She lengthened her stride until she wasn't quite running. No sense in allowing her fear to show. For all the lane appeared deserted, a sense of watchfulness grew until it weighed on her, sullen and oppressive as the air before a summer storm. Her breath came in ragged puffs.

Just ahead, a figure loomed out of the darkness—a large, imposing figure. It blocked the path.

She stopped, whirled. If she ran full out, she might make it within shouting distance of the manor before she was caught. A hand lashed out and clamped about her wrist, the fingers strong as five iron bands. The shocking force of that grip brought her face-to-face with a stranger.

"Did you really think you could throw me over tonight?" he growled. The menace in that voice sent a knee-weakening shiver through her. "Did you expect me to lie back and take it?"

She opened her mouth and screamed.

CHAPTER SEVEN

AFTER ISABELLE'S abrupt departure, George once again found himself in the garden. He pulled in fragrant smoke from a cheroot, but for once in his life, he found no comfort in the taste. It did nothing to erase the feeling of Isabelle's lips moving on his. He strode to the end of the garden. She would have left this way, marching down the path to the village in a temper.

Damn, damn, and damn.

Could he possibly have phrased his question any more awkwardly? George Upperton, known for his wit and clever tongue. Only tonight they had failed him. Tonight he'd managed to insult a poor woman who likely endured enough gossip. He'd all but ensured she'd never consider his attentions again.

Some wit. Some cleverness. He was an idiot, pure and simple.

He cast the stub of his cheroot to the ground and crushed it beneath his heel. Why should he care, at any rate? Dallying with her would bring him no closer to the Earl of Redditch, or to settling Summersby's debts. He had enough troubles without involving himself in another entanglement, especially one that came with the complications of a child.

Another child.

And he was getting nowhere, standing here, mulling

over Isabelle. He was most certainly not mooning. Should anyone suggest otherwise, he would call them out.

A woman's scream tore through the night's stillness, a high, terrified note. Isabelle. Oh God.

He took off down the lane at a dead run.

HE spotted them at the last possible moment, as he turned a corner past a high hedge. Two shadowy figures—one seeming to tower over the other—struggled in the middle of the lane.

George didn't stop to size up his opponent. He ran full-tilt into the beast, shouldering his way between Isabelle and her assailant. With a cry, she stumbled backward. George turned to grab the oaf by his lapels, but the man heaved himself, shoving his way out of George's grip. George ducked just in time to avoid a flying fist. Next thing he knew, the thuds of the attacker's footfalls faded into the night.

George shook himself and straightened his sleeves, grateful for the shadows that hid the heat rising on his cheeks. But those same shadows had obscured the other man's face.

Isabelle had shrunk back against the hedge, her arms wrapped about herself, staring down the lane in her assailant's wake. A quiet whimper escaped her lips, as if she'd tried in vain to hold it in.

"Did he hurt you?" George asked.

She glanced at him, eyes wide. "No. No. He's gone back toward the village."

"I imagine it makes sense for the likes of him to retreat there, where he can hide among the houses."

"No, you don't understand." Her voice rose on a swell of panic.

"If you'd rather not head straight home—"

"*No*. I need to get home. Now." She lunged down the path.

"Now see here. I can't let you run off unaccompanied with such as him lurking."

She ignored him. Her pace quickened to a jog.

Well. Invited or not, he couldn't let her go haring off when oafish thugs waylaid unsuspecting women. He strode after her. "What did he want with you?"

"That's none of your affair." Isabelle clipped each syllable. She didn't even favor him with a glance. "And no one asked you to come along."

He lengthened his stride to catch up with her. "As a gentleman, I cannot allow you to return home unaccompanied."

She glared at him over her shoulder. "You thought nothing of kissing me, and I won't even get into what you suggested to me afterward. Hardly the act of a gentleman." The words stung like so many tiny needles pricking his flesh, or more accurately, his conscience. "Now if you'll excuse me, I've spent far too much time away from Jack."

SHE had to get away from Upperton. No, she had to get away from *both* of them, and most urgent, she had to get home to Jack. *Something important,* the note had said. A wave of panic rose from her gut, rose and mounted as if a hurricane drove it to drown her. But, heaven help her, she could *not* let it show. Not when Mr. Upperton had already come running to her rescue. Lord save her, he was feeling protective, and if he came to the conclusion she needed protection against something more, she'd never be quit of him.

And she had to get home to make sure Jack was all right, make sure some ruffian never got his hands on her little boy. Jack was hers, dash it all, hers to safeguard since his birth. He was all the family she had left.

She fisted a hand in her skirt to mask her shaking fingers. That blasted Mr. Upperton was still following, and as long as he continued, she couldn't allow herself the luxury of a full run. She settled for lengthening her stride until her teeth clenched with every exaggerated step.

She ignored the man dogging her and squinted along the path ahead. Where had *he* got to? He'd left the note. He knew which among the village's low huddled dwellings was hers. Had he taken a path directly there? Was he even now rousting Jack from his bed?

Her throat closed on a sob that swelled until she ached. Oh, blast it all. She broke into a run. Behind her, Mr. Upperton let out a shout. She closed her ears to his protests until an iron grip about her wrist pulled her up short.

"Here now, what's the idea? You can't think to outrun me."

"Let me go." She fought to keep her words even and officious, as if she were instructing a servant. Once upon a time, her father had taught her to do that very thing—to speak to servants with a quiet authority that ensured obedience if not loyalty. Those lessons had been part of a life she'd rejected. They failed her now. Her voice wobbled on a high note of hysteria.

"What's the rush? You'll never convince me you're suddenly upset over Jack."

She yanked at her wrist. "My reasons are none of your affair." She let annoyance taint her reply. She was past caring what he thought of her. "Unhand me."

"I'm certain he's perfectly safe, dreaming away in his bed and has been all night. Didn't you say you'd left him with someone?"

Biggles, yes, for all an old woman could do against

such a hulk of a man. "You don't know that, and you will kindly refrain from detaining me any further."

He blew out a breath, and his grip slackened. Thank goodness. She tugged away and set off once more, her stride lengthening into a run. She didn't stop until she came to her darkened cottage at the edge of the village. Compared to the manor where she'd grown up, she'd always thought it a mean little place, but it was her lot now. She deserved no better.

The door stood closed, a firm oak barrier set in contrast to neat, whitewashed walls. All lay quiet, so quiet the chirp of crickets echoed through her brain, loud enough to mask the heightened rush of her breathing.

Her heart fluttered. Her hand slipped on the door handle, and her chest ached with the fear of what she might find. Cursed imagination, always running wild. It had helped lead her astray when she was naïve enough to believe in a young buck's assurances he would not go so far as to ruin her. And once he had, he would offer marriage. When would she learn?

"Isabelle?"

She had to get inside. Mr. Upperton was striding up the path. What sort of fool must he think her for fearing to enter her own house? She grasped the handle, turned it. The door swung open with a creak, flooding the main room with ghostly moonlight.

Her sense of unease increased. It filled her chest until drawing breath became an effort. Not a single item stood out of place, and yet, yet . . . Something was wrong. Someone had been here. Someone strange. It was almost as if he'd left a trace of lingering scent.

Right. The door to Jack's bedchamber lay directly opposite. She straightened her spine and rushed across the bare planked floor, heedless of Mr. Upperton's booted feet thumping in her wake. While she had not invited him in, a small part of her was grateful he had not stood on ceremony.

She yanked open the bedroom door. Empty. Oh God, the bed lay empty, the tangle of sheets clearly limned in the moonlight. The curtains swayed in a breeze drifting in through the open window.

Open window.

She pressed her fingers to her lips and rushed over, as if she might somehow catch her son scampering through the back garden.

"No!" The back garden lay just as empty as the bedroom. The breeze that toyed with the curtains stirred the grass, green blades washed to gray beneath the pale moon. "No, he's gone. I knew it."

Her eyes burned, but she had no time for tears. Not with Jack missing. She turned to Mr. Upperton and launched herself at him.

"I never should have come. I never should have left him." She balled her hands into fists and pounded on his chest. Anything to calm the shaking.

His hands gripped her shoulders, gentle but firm. "What's happened?"

"He's gone, you idiot. They've made off with Jack."

"Who has? Who would do such a thing?"

The nerve. This was none of his affair. His doing, perhaps in delaying her return, but never his affair. "We've no time to yammer about this. We might still find him."

Possible, yes. The culprit could not have gone far. He'd only had five minutes' head start. Given his size, why hadn't they heard him? Why hadn't Biggles?

"What of the person you said you left Jack with? Where is she?" Clearly Upperton was thinking along the same lines.

"She sleeps in the loft, but—"

"Call her."

"She can't have—"

"*Call* her."

She stiffened. Just like a high-born man to take such a high-handed tone.

"Is she even here?"

"Of course she is, and how dare you imply—Biggles!"

But Biggles was already making her way down the ladder. The thump of sturdy feet in the other room announced her descent. "Mum, what is all the racket?"

Isabelle brushed past Upperton into the main room. "Where is Jack?"

"Why, he ought ter be sleeping by rights, although how anybody can sleep with all these carryings on—"

"What have you heard?" Upperton's terse question cut the woman off.

She blinked and drew her tattered woolen shawl more closely over her night rail. "I don't hold with such." Her jowls quivered. "It ain't proper."

Upperton took a step closer. "What have you heard?" He enunciated each syllable precisely, as if he were declaiming before a schoolmaster.

Biggles drew herself up to her fullest height—she'd have topped five feet if she'd bothered to put on shoes. "All manner of clattering about. It's enough to rouse the dead. How a body can sleep—"

"Clattering," Isabelle broke in. "We haven't clattered."

"Ye have so." Biggles sniffed. "Stomping about, making all manner of noise."

"We haven't made that much noise," Isabelle protested.

"I beg to differ. Why—"

"It means they can't have gone far," Upperton said over Biggles's muttering. "Stay here. I'll have a look in the garden."

"No, he's my son." Isabelle started for the door. "My responsibility."

"Wot's this about the boy?" Biggles asked.

"He's not in his bed," Isabelle said, her voice unnaturally calm.

So many years having to hold a tight rein over her emotions where her son was concerned—so that strangers might not guess their true relationship—had made her an expert in detaching herself. She appeared cold and uncaring. Half the time, she feared the front was all too real, that she'd encased her emotions so deeply in ice, she might never thaw. But beneath that frozen veneer, her stomach knotted.

The color drained from Biggles's fleshy face. "Save us."

"If you heard so much noise, why didn't you investigate?" Upperton stepped closer to her, and she seemed to shrink before him.

Her shoulders collapsed, and she tucked her chin into her chest. "I thought it were mum coming home. I swear it."

He nodded. "Go put on some tea and when it's ready, pour a healthy shot of whatever spirits you've got into it. Miss Mears is going to need it."

Of all the nerve, giving the orders in her house. She crossed to him and yanked at his hand. "I am not. I'm coming with you."

A sandy brow arched, and he glanced at her fingers curled about his. "You'll stay right where you are. There's no telling who made off with Jack."

"He's my son. Mine." She spit the words. "And the longer we argue, the farther he gets."

"Why would someone make off with the boy? He's not some secret heir to a dukedom by any chance, is he?"

Why indeed? None of it made any sense. Some stranger had summoned her to the manor. How had anyone even discovered she was living here? And how had they learned which house was hers, unless—a cold finger of fear traced down her spine and raised the hairs at the nape of her neck. Unless they'd been watching for a while. Unless they'd planned for this chance to lure her away and leave Jack unguarded. Perhaps . . . perhaps Jack had already been abducted when the man stopped her in the road.

Upperton shifted his grip so that his fingers entwined with hers. "What is it? You look as if you've seen a ghost or worse."

"That man in the road tonight. I think . . . I think he's made off with him." Her reply emerged thready and shaking. "Only I don't know why. Please . . . please, let's just find him."

"Of course we will."

BUT an hour later they'd turned up nothing. A search of the garden had revealed not so much as a footprint in the soft earth at the edge of the house—and it was far too late to consider waking the neighbors. If anyone had heard anything untoward, they'd have come forward on their own.

"I don't understand it. A full-grown man just doesn't disappear like that." George tore a hand through his hair. "And making off with an active boy."

"We need to keep looking. Surely something will turn up." Isabelle's voice wobbled on the final words.

"And you've still no notion as to why?" If he'd asked the question once in the last hour, he'd asked it ten times.

"No, nothing." For the tenth time, she gave him the same answer. "Why anyone should care to make off with . . . with a natural child . . ." The rest of her sentence was lost in a choking sound.

He snapped his head toward her. The night breeze

stirred her hair, long since fallen out of its pins to trail in tendrils about her cheeks and neck. Moonlight shot through it, turning it to a nimbus that framed her face. She pulled her lower lip between her teeth.

"Isabelle." When she didn't protest the use of her given name, he took a greater chance. He strode to her and gripped her shoulder. "We're never going to find anything in the dark. The best we can do is wait until morning. The new day might well show something we've passed over in the night."

"And if it doesn't?" Her voice hardened. Somewhere she'd drawn forth the strength to protest.

He squeezed her shoulder. "We'll comb the village. It isn't that big."

"They could be long gone by then."

"They'll never make it unnoticed." He placed his free hand on her other shoulder but resisted the surge of desire to pull her into a full embrace. He might only wish to show her comfort, but she'd not take the gesture as such. "I have friends up at Shoreford. They'll help us."

"They'll not help me."

"What makes you say that?"

She tossed her head. "I might have been one of those people in that fancy manor once. They turned their backs on me. All of them—even my own family."

In spite of himself, he gathered her closer. Not quite a hug, but near enough that her scent of lavender tickled his nostrils. "I haven't turned my back on you. I'm willing to help."

"It's not the same. You're only here until you realize you won't get anything from me. Then you'll be gone like the rest of them."

He dropped his hands. "I ought to take a great deal of offense at that. In fact, I would, only we've more pressing matters to consider. So the offense is merely set aside until we've found Jack, and then I shall demand satisfaction."

She gasped. "How can you—"

"Oh, nothing as prosaic as pistols at dawn. I've been a party to that sort of thing, and once was enough. But I do intend to prove you wrong, and then you shall make me a proper apology. Until that time, I suggest you take what rest you can. I shall come back in the morning with reinforcements."

He turned to go, knowing he well deserved her outrage in light of his blunder earlier this evening. What had he been thinking, asking this lovely, proud woman to become his mistress? He should have known she'd never stoop to such a level, not for him, not for any man. She might have commanded a high price from any number of moneyed gentlemen of the *ton* had she chosen to take such a path. She might have done so long ago, and they'd have never met. Even as a kept woman, she'd have been far beyond his means—and she set herself above that. A man such as him didn't deserve her favors.

But he could make up for his blunder. He could restore her son to her and quietly walk out of her life to return to his own problems. Next to her clear desperation over her child, what were a few thousand pounds of debt?

She reached out and laid her fingertips on his arm. The touch burned through the superfine of his topcoat in four tiny ovals. "Wait."

In obedience to her command, he stilled. What more might she possibly want of him? "Please . . . I . . . I don't wish to remain alone. I'll never sleep, not until my boy is back home . . ."

She couldn't possibly be implying she wished for distraction in the form of his body. Not when she'd already refused him outright. He cleared his throat. "I don't know that it's the best idea for me to stay. What of your reputation?"

"What reputation I had was destroyed long ago, and you've already been here longer than is seemly. Please. I do not wish to face the long hours of the night alone."

CHAPTER EIGHT

SHE WAITED, fully expecting him to turn away. He'd every right to, the way she'd impugned his honor. His integrity. Not only that, she'd just betrayed weakness in expressing her need for comfort before him. Her stomach burned with self-loathing.

The moment stretched between them until the quiet rhythm of chirping crickets embedded itself in her ears. Her heart echoed the beat. No other sounds broke the night's stillness, not the turning of a carriage wheel, nor the thud of a booted foot or the even softer pat of an ill-shod child's tread. Jack.

She closed her eyes against the renewed pain in her heart. How many times over the past few years had she struggled against resenting an innocent child for his very existence? How often had she thought with longing on her one season and what she might have had if temptation hadn't changed her life's path? Jack hadn't asked to come into the world, and certainly not under such circumstances. She fought a daily battle to treat him fairly—to avoid assigning him blame for what her life had become.

But now, in the face of the uncertainty, confronted with the knowledge she might never see her boy again, she wanted to pull that sturdy body into her arms and bask in the scent of an inquisitive child—grass and earth and the salt of seawater.

Her throat swelled achingly tight, and she swallowed against a sob. Without warning, a pair of arms enfolded her. George. Why was he still here lending her comfort when she didn't deserve it?

Another sob wrestled its way past the obstruction in her throat, and she released it on a shuddering breath. The weight of his palm settled on the back of her head. His fingertips burrowed into her hair, exerting gentle but insistent pressure until she rested her cheek against his shoulder.

The sheer size of him surrounded her. Never had a man held her like this with no expectation of more coming from the embrace. He gave without demanding anything in return. Lord, where had this man been when she was a green little chit, completely unprepared for the lure of a determined rake? Would he have saved her? Or would he have lured her in, too?

At the idea, she stiffened.

"Come into the house, and we'll see if Biggles ever made us a pot of tea." She pulled out of the embrace and attempted a smile—a hostess's sort of smile, one that would have done her father proud, if she succeeded. She feared she'd managed no more than a grimace.

George—heavens, she was referring to him by his given name in her head—gave her an odd look, somewhere between a question and approval. "A cup of tea would be just the thing."

He hated tea, unless it was liberally laced with brandy, hated the stuff because it reminded him of social calls where his mother forced him to sit and make stilted conversation with retiring young misses fresh from the schoolroom. Come to think of it, he wasn't much for scones, either, and those fussy little slices of toasted bread bedecked with cucumber and watercress turned his stomach.

Thank God Isabelle's kitchen contained none of those transgressions—only a stone-cold teapot and a flustered Biggles.

"Ye didn't find hide nor hair of him?" Her hands twisted a tattered bit of linen—no doubt it had been a handkerchief in its misspent youth. "Oh my poor, poor Jack, spirited from his bed. And what can we do? They'll have all night to take him Lord knows where, and then we'll be in a pickle. And what could anyone have wanted with a mere little scrap like that?"

She sank to a bench by the fireplace. "What is the world coming to that strangers make off with children in the night?"

Isabelle let out a choked sound and pressed her knuckles to her mouth.

"That will do." George looked hard at the older woman. "No sense in working yourself into a dither. We need to think about this."

"And while we're thinking, that poor boy is getting farther and farther away," Biggles muttered.

"No, I don't believe that's the case."

Isabelle pulled her fist away from her mouth. "What makes you say so?"

"There wasn't a sign of a carriage in the road. No hoof prints if they went off on horseback. No sign at all. They have to be on foot, and if they are, how far can they get with a small boy who's used to sleeping at this time of night? No, whoever did this is still nearby. They probably won't move before sunrise."

Isabelle's eyes glittered as they hardened into a glare. "Then why aren't we out trying to find them before they discover a better hiding spot?"

"How do you propose we do that in the dark? We've searched this property and the nearby lanes as well as we may. Are you prepared to rouse your neighbors with a search?"

"No." She heaved a telling sigh. Given her situation, her neighbors might not be so inclined to help, at least, not in the middle of the night.

He laid a hand over hers. "As soon as it's light we'll try again, and then, if we've still found nothing, we'll bring in the others."

THE butler's glance landed on her, and his eyes narrowed. Isabelle drew her shawl more securely about her shoulders. She ought to have anticipated the reaction. Even in the country, the servants judged her. One look, and they knew, as if the words "scarlet woman" were embroidered across her forehead.

Granted, it didn't speak for her respectability that she turned up at the front door of the manor at sunrise, hair astraggle, still dressed in yesterday's garments, trailing after Mr. Upperton. Yes, as long as she was at the manor, she *must* think of him in polite terms. Distant terms. Nothing so intimate as a given name must pass through her mind, much less cross her tongue.

As it was, the women would put their heads together and whisper. No need to fuel their speculations by treating George—Mr. Upperton—as anything more than a helpful stranger.

"Is Revelstoke about?"

The butler snapped his attention to George and drew himself up until the top of his head nearly reached George's chin. What he lacked in size he more than made up for in imperiousness. He sniffed, actually sniffed at George. Her father would have given their own butler a sharp reprimand for such an offense to a guest.

"I shall have to inquire." Frost edged his reply. The man turned and left them standing on the doorstep.

"Can you imagine that?" George muttered. "The fellow suddenly thinks he's in Grosvenor Square and not in the wilds of Kent."

Isabelle cleared her throat. "Perhaps I ought to leave. This was a terrible idea. I don't know what—"

"Hush." He turned to face her and curled his fingers about her shoulder. Warmth seeped through the layers of fabric separating his flesh from hers. Thank goodness. Direct contact would be as hot as a brand. "You shouldn't be alone right now. You need company to distract you, and I can provide that while we look for Jack."

She shrugged, but his grip merely tightened. "I know when I'm not wanted."

"What makes you say such a thing?"

"Be honest. You're friends with the man's employer, are you not?"

"Yes, of course. Revelstoke and I have known each other since our school days."

"And has he ever left you cooling your heels outside before? He does know who you are."

George's brows lowered. "Certainly he knows who I am. He's been with the family for years. I might have walked right in just now, but for—"

"But for me, which explains why we haven't at least been shown into the foyer."

He dropped his hand and focused on some object over her shoulder—a tree or perhaps the gamesman's house they'd passed on the way up the sweeping drive.

"You can't come up with a good answer to that, can you?" she pressed. "Or you won't because you don't wish to insult me. They know. Even the servants take one look at me and they know. What are the ladies here going to make of me?"

"Revelstoke's wife isn't like that." Isabelle shook her head, but George continued, "Give her a chance, will you? Once she hears what has happened, she'll be all sympathy."

"Once she hears what has happened, she may well consider I only got what I deserved. Oh, she'll be too polite to say so, but she'll think it. They all will."

"You are insulting a dear friend of mine by even implying such a thing, and sight unseen, no less."

"Is she such a paragon she'd overlook a fallen woman with a bastard son?"

"Has it ever occurred to you to lie about your circumstances? Say you're a widow. Who would be the wiser?"

Heaven only knew she'd thought of such a ruse on her arrival in the village, and she'd tried to hide her relationship to Jack through appearances. Only her ingrained pride had kept her from lying outright.

Rather than admit to that, she diverted the subject. "Why are you doing this?"

He shook his head slightly. "Doing what?"

"Helping me? Last night was one thing, but this . . ."

"What a thing to ask," he practically spluttered. "What sort of gentleman would I be if I left a lady in distress?"

What sort indeed? The sort that expected something in return. She opened her mouth to retort, but the butler's reappearance stopped the words cold.

"Lord Benedict is out at the stables at this hour. I've sent the hall boy to fetch him. I daresay you might await him in his study. As for your companion—"

At the hesitation, Isabelle's cheeks burned.

"This is Mrs. Mears," George broke in. "She lives in the village."

"I believe most are aware of Miss Mears's situation."

A hollowing in George's cheek belied sudden tension in his jaw. "It's a disgrace to your profession to pay such heed to gossip. *Mrs.* Mears is here on a matter of utmost urgency. Now, you will let her pass, or I shall not be responsible for my actions."

The butler stepped aside, but his eyes glinted. Clearly, he did not approve, but he'd already trod too close to the line of insolence. "She might await you in the foyer."

"She will accompany me to Revelstoke's study. What I need to discuss with him concerns her. And I might recommend it does not concern you in the least." George stalked past the butler, his Hessians thumping loudly across the parquet.

The cavernous hall stretched toward the back of the manor, the ceiling soaring to twelve feet and yet, to Isabelle, the space felt confined and comfortless. The stone of the outer walls imprisoned the chill air from the Channel. Dankness crept into her bones.

What sort of people would tolerate life in such a dreary pile of stone high on a cliff, exposed to the ravages of the sea wind? A shiver passed down her spine. The man might well be a friend of George's, but once he realized who she was, he'd cast the sort of speculative eye any other man did, a leisurely perusal that began and ended with her breasts and made her all too conscious of her shame.

And his paragon of a wife would take note—they always did—and cast her own sort of speculative eye on Isabelle. A supposition, a judgment, and a warning. *You succumbed to temptation once; you'd best not tempt my husband to stray.* The shopkeepers' and artisans' wives in the village were bad enough. How much worse would a daughter of the *ton* treat her?

"Good God, where have you been all night?"

A broad-shouldered man clad in tight breeches and boots strode down the hall to meet them. Black hair flopped roguishly over his brow. Then he noticed her. His perusal swept over her from head to foot and back, coming to rest on her face. No doubt her countenance was haggard enough to draw his attention from her other attributes.

His eyes flitted from her to George and back again, while one dark eyebrow eased heavenward. "And who might this be?"

His tone was as cool as his glance, the speculative note nearly lost behind the casual façade. Nearly, but not quite. By all appearances, she'd just passed the night with this man's friend.

"This is Isabelle Mears. Mrs. Mears, Lord Benedict."

At the blatant lie, she nearly forgot to incline her head. She hadn't asked it of him. It was one thing to alter the truth for the butler; his friend was another matter. Indeed, the lie made her look just as bad as the truth, since it implied she'd just passed the night committing adultery.

"And haven't I seen you somewhere?" Revelstoke asked. "You look familiar."

"I live in the village, my lord. Perhaps ye've seen me selling my sachets and posies. Believe I've sold a few to yer lady wife." She did her best to imitate Biggles and the other locals, but she didn't know if she could carry off the sham for an extended period of time. Her cultured, *ton*ish accent was too deeply engrained.

Upperton narrowed his eyes at her, but she ignored him. If he could lie without warning, then she could dashed well carry herself off as a servant. In any case, servants stood a greater chance at passing unnoticed, and that was what she wished now in the presence of these titled people. To escape their scrutiny. To escape their judgment.

Upperton cleared his throat. "Mrs. Mears's son has gone missing. I thought to enlist your help as someone of influence in the community, and if not, at least you've another pair of eyes."

"I'll do you better than that. You can have my brother

and brother-in-law as well. And any other guest you might name." He turned to Isabelle. "Do not worry, madam. We'll find your boy safe and sound."

She curtsied. "I thank ye, my lord."

"Allow me to show you into the morning room. My wife and her sister will keep you company."

"Oh no, my lord. I wouldn't dream of imposing."

"I insist. A little company will help you pass the time."

She caught her lip between her teeth and inclined her head once more to hide the reaction. She could only let him see gratitude, not consternation. What had given her away and so quickly? If she'd really been a servant or villager, a woman reduced to selling what she could grow in her garden for a few pence, he would never have addressed her as madam and proposed she keep company with his wife. He ought to have sent her to the kitchen with others of her station.

But no, he insisted, and with one hand, he gestured to the corridor that led to the back of the house. She had no choice but to let him usher her into an airy room. Beams held up a high vaulted ceiling, and the morning sunlight fractured into a multitude of rays as it shone through two large diamond-paned windows. A fire crackled on the hearth. The air here was fresh with the scent of summer flowers—honeysuckle, lavender, and rose. Fresh-cut bouquets adorned several tables scattered about the room.

Near the windows, in twin armchairs, sat two women, close enough to Isabelle's age. One was blond-haired and blue-eyed with flawless skin, a true diamond of the first water, fit to grace any *ton* ballroom.

"Julia, my dear." Surprisingly, Lord Benedict addressed the second lady—no less lovely, but her darker hair and eyes made her looks pale in comparison to her sister. "This is Mrs. Mears from the village, and she has lost her young son."

"Oh dear." His wife rose from her seat with difficulty, hampered by her swollen belly. "How awful for you. We must do everything within our power to get him back."

"I'm about to organize a search party with the other men," Lord Benedict informed her. "Would you mind terribly if Mrs. Mears joined you and the other ladies?"

"Yes, you must join us." This from the as-yet-nameless sister.

Other ladies? But of course there were more of them. The pair in front of her seemed friendly enough, but Isabelle didn't actually remember them from her former life. Odd, that. At least one of them must have been out during her short-lived season. If neither one of them recognized her, she might stand a chance—at least until the others joined them.

"Do sit." Lady Benedict indicated a settee opposite her chair.

Isabelle perched on the very edge of the seat.

"You poor dear," said the blonde. "You must be worried sick. How did you come to lose your son?"

"I cannot say. I went into his chamber, just to look on him, and he was gone."

"Gracious!" She placed a hand over her heart. "Stolen straight from his bed."

Lady Benedict sat beside Isabelle and took her hand. My yes, the woman was a paragon. "And you didn't hear a thing?"

"No, my lady. I'm afraid not." Isabelle gritted her teeth and willed Lady Benedict to probe no further. She could hardly admit the real reason she'd heard nothing.

"Call me Julia."

"Yes, and you must call me Sophia," added the blonde. "We can hardly stand on ceremony under the circumstances."

Isabelle would not cry. She would not. She'd no reason at all to let herself get worked up over the sympathy these women showed her, when, once they learned the truth, their manner would change.

"And what shall we call you?" Julia asked.

"Isabelle." She folded her hands in her lap to stop their trembling and waited for the reaction. Not so common a name, hers, and they might have heard the gossip. Even if she didn't remember them, they may have heard of her and for all the wrong reasons.

Neither sister's concerned expression wavered in the slightest. Sophia took up an embroidery frame and stabbed a needle into it. Julia picked up a small bell, and its tinkle echoed through the room. "We shall have tea in no time, and perhaps the others will join us presently. They're not so used to country hours."

God willing, they'd sleep the day away so she wouldn't have to face any of them.

The teacart arrived, and Julia pressed a cup on her, along with fresh scones, jam, and clotted cream— luxuries she'd foregone for six years, along with proper tea from Ceylon. She couldn't possibly stomach the richness. Not when her mind kept turning to Jack. Raised on Biggles's good bread and solid country fare, the boy yearned for iced cakes from the baker's. Isabelle could never afford such. She broke off a corner of her scone and crumbled it between her fingers.

Julia stayed her stream of small talk and leaned forward. "How I go on. Your mind is on your son, of course."

"I'm only thinking how Jack would love a bit of scone. And chocolate. He's never had hot chocolate." She pushed her plate away. "I'm sorry. I'm sure they're lovely, but I fear I have no appetite."

"I should say not," Sophia said. "If I lost my Frederick, I'm sure I don't know what I'd do. Bad enough I've left him with his nurse. I've never left him alone for so long since he was born."

"How old is he?" Isabelle asked.

"Three this November, and such a clever boy." A prideful smile tugged at her lips for a brief moment. "Highgate's taught him his letters already and means him to write his name before his next birthday."

"Highgate?" Isabelle clamped her mouth shut before she could blurt out anything more.

"Why yes, he's my husband." Sophia's smile stretched her cheeks even wider. "Do you know him?"

Only by reputation, but doubtless the rumors were exaggerated. But if the talk of him killing his first wife and becoming a recluse as a result had been bandied about enough to reach her ears, what sort of gossip had circulated about her? What sort was still whispered behind lacy fans and gloved hands in scandalized undertones?

So brazen, that Isabelle. She never went to the continent, you know. She's disappeared into the country to raise her natural son. The father wouldn't even offer for her. No one will have her now, not even her own family. Such prospects she had. An heir to a dukedom going to offer any day, and she threw it all away.

All of it true. She had thrown it all away, but at the time, she couldn't imagine facing a future tied to that man. Tied to that life.

"We've never been introduced, my lady." Isabelle pretended to sip at her tea. Of course they wouldn't have been introduced. Not if she was moldering in the country.

Sophia—Lady Highgate—leaned over to lay a steady hand on her arm. "Now, none of that. You must consider yourself among friends here."

Isabelle had no chance to reply, for at that moment, several other ladies entered the morning room. House guests. Members of the *ton*. Isabelle studied her teacup, while Julia and Sophia greeted the new arrivals. Carefully, she cast glances at each one, but none of the faces seemed familiar.

Then came the inevitable introductions where she would learn for certain if any of them might recognize her. The younger girls all gave the appropriate murmurs of greeting. Henrietta and Catherine Upperton greeted her with solemn good cheer. Mrs. Upperton and Mrs. St. Claire exchanged glances behind their daughters' backs. Those two would bear watching. Clearly something about Isabelle triggered their maternal sense of potential trouble. They, no doubt, had heard of her real name, even if they'd never been introduced until now.

Soon enough, chatter and gossip replaced words of sympathy. At one time, such a gathering would have been a delight. She'd have happily exchanged *on-dits* with the others. When Catherine Upperton sighed over the Duke of Amherst's youngest son, Isabelle chewed on her tongue to stop herself from recounting the time she'd walked into his father's stables and caught him covered head to foot in horse manure. How the others would gasp in horror, but she couldn't admit the connection any more than she could admit she'd nearly accepted an offer from his eldest brother.

"And who are you connected with?" Mrs. St. Claire held her teacup halfway to her lips, eyeing Isabelle's decidedly unfashionable linsey garments. Nothing of pastel-tinted muslins for her. Only practical work clothes that hid the stains.

Isabelle made herself hold the woman's gaze. If the gossips would brand her as brazen, she must brazen this moment out. "No one of any consequence."

"She lives in the village, Mama," Julia said. "She's come to us for help."

Something flickered in the older woman's eyes. Nothing so decisive as recognition. No, it was more along the lines of doubt tinged with suspicion. She'd seen Isabelle somewhere before, and it certainly wasn't in some village in Kent. She just couldn't place where, exactly, or when.

Isabelle gathered all this in the time it took Mrs. St. Claire to sip daintily of her tea and set her cup back down. "And what sort of help do you need?"

She opened her mouth to reply, but the words jammed in her throat. She hardly wanted to call this woman's attention to her plight. Letting her know of Jack's existence was handing her another piece of a puzzle Isabelle had no desire for her to complete. She did not recall Mrs. St. Claire from the days before her downfall, but she knew the type well enough. Older women, unhappily married, who passed the hours listening to gossip, feeding themselves on the news of others' failings because it filled a void in their own lives, and perhaps, just perhaps, they kept an eye on their wayward husbands at the same time.

A new arrival in the morning room saved her from having to respond. A cheery good morning, the voice familiar. Her heart jumped inside her chest. It couldn't be. She turned and her heart plummeted. It was. In the doorway, still as a statue and staring directly at her, stood Emily Marshall.

Her cousin.

CHAPTER NINE

"You." The word issued from Emily's lips on a whisper of astonishment.

Isabelle's hands turned icy, and she set her teacup aside before she lost her grip on the porcelain.

"What are you doing here?" Emily advanced into the room. "What is the meaning of this?"

Isabelle hardly knew what to reply. The collective gaze of the other ladies settled on her shoulders as an unbearable weight. Her hostesses must be exchanging concerned glances. Mrs. St. Claire was no doubt hiding a smirk while she gleefully thought of repeating this juicy tidbit throughout the next Season.

Isabelle was obliged to surmise all of this, however. She couldn't take her eyes off her cousin. Emily had grown in the intervening years. Too young when the scandal broke to hear of its exact nature directly from her elders, she was still old enough to discover the gossip through her own means. By the age of thirteen, Emily had become adept at listening at doors when the adults spoke in hushed tones.

Emily stood tall in a morning gown of pale yellow muslin edged in the finest French lace. The height of fashion, of course. Nothing too good for the Marshalls, as long as you lived up to their standards.

"I demand an explanation."

The order, spoken as if to a servant, broke whatever

spell had held the room in thrall. Julia struggled to her feet. "Mrs. Mears is from the village. She—"

"Mrs. Mears, is it?" Emily kept her gaze trained on Isabelle. "Did you dupe some unfortunate soul into marrying you? Or have you lied to these good ladies?"

"Now see here," Julia insisted. "She's come to us for help. There's no call to accuse her of lying."

"That's quite all right, my lady." Isabelle's quiet statement cut through the tension. She kept her eyes downcast so as not to see the admonishment on Julia's face at the title. Under the circumstances, she preferred the distance created by formality. She no longer belonged to these circles. "I won't disturb your gathering any longer."

She leaned forward to stand, intent on stalking out with all the dignity she could muster. A hand on her shoulder stopped her progress. She turned her head to find Sophia had crossed to sit beside her on the settee.

"You aren't disturbing us in the least." The countess's normally breathy voice took on an edge of steel. "You're quite welcome to stay. If anyone feels offended by your presence, I daresay the problem lies with them."

Isabelle blinked and blinked again, but the sudden burning behind her eyes persisted. Her throat tightened until the only reply possible was a curt nod.

"It ought to be her problem." Emily sniffed, her expression so smug, so arrogant with her firm chin and taut lips. "No decent family would receive her. No decent family ought to."

Anger burned to the surface and dissipated the knot in Isabelle's throat. How dare she? If Emily had kept her mouth shut, they might have moved past this with no one the wiser. But Emily's self-righteous outrage had only served to call attention to the old scandal. Isabelle's shame reflected poorly on all the Marshalls, Emily included. Well, Cousin Emily had always been a spoiled brat.

"Do you mean to imply your hostesses are not of decent family? Perhaps you ought to leave, then, before they sully your pristine reputation and ruin your chances at making a suitable match."

A gasp came from one of the ladies as the echo of Isabelle's words faded. Too late, she realized, that in her anger she'd forgotten to maintain her accent. Her elocution had been just as clear and precise as she'd been taught by her governesses—perfectly in keeping with her cousin's.

Two red blotches formed on Emily's cheeks. "If I've not drawn the attention of someone suitable, it's because of the scandal you've brought on the family."

"Really?" Brows raised, Isabelle shot to her feet. "Papa hasn't ensured things were kept quiet?"

"He has his ways, as you well know. No one dares speak of you to his face, but behind his back . . ." Emily waved a dismissive hand. "Behind his back, he has no say."

"And in all that time, no one's found something else to talk about? Have you shot yourself in the foot by keeping old gossip alive? Because I can't imagine why else my doings would remain fresh in anyone's mind for so long. I haven't paraded myself through society lately. I've been living very quietly and out of everyone's eye for some time now. I might have continued if you hadn't dredged up the past."

She paused for breath and felt the burn of a roomful of rapt gazes at her back. Oh, she'd done it now. Tongues would be wagging for days, repeating the story of her disgrace with the addition that the intervening years had turned her into a shrew. There'd be no more hiding her antecedents, either. Not after Emily's outburst.

She caught Sophia's eye and experienced a pang deep in her belly. Sophia, a beautiful countess who had extended the hand of friendship, only to have it betrayed.

She stood next to Isabelle, pale and speechless, an emotion akin to pity in her blue eyes.

"Forgive me," Isabelle murmured. "I've intruded on your gathering far too long."

She straightened her spine, raised her chin, and marched toward the door. On her way from the manor, she met the gaze of no one else.

THE sun had begun its descent toward the horizon by the time George strode up Shoreford's broad front steps. He ought to have been exhausted after a sleepless night followed by a day of tedious searching. Who would ever imagine a small boy of little account could disappear so completely?

Only at the end of the afternoon had he come across anything closely resembling a solid clue. One of the stable boys at the inn may have heard someone moving about in the night. An investigation of the hayloft revealed an abandoned lace-trimmed handkerchief, but that may well have been left behind following a hasty assignation.

Still, it was more than he'd come across the rest of the day. Now all he wanted was to meet Revelstoke and the others to compare their findings. If he could bring any sort of hopeful news to Isabelle, all those fruitless hours would not have been a complete loss.

He strode straight to Revelstoke's study, fully expecting to find the others discussing the day over brandy. He pulled the door open to an empty room.

Damn and blast. Now what was he to do? He couldn't very well present Isabelle with the handkerchief, not when it smelled of roses. He pulled the scrap of linen from his topcoat pocket and sniffed.

No, he hadn't been mistaken. How odd. The handkerchief's erstwhile owner held the same taste in scent as his former mistress. He shoved the offending article back into his pocket. The last thing he needed was a reminder of those difficulties.

And if he spent this time helping Isabelle to locate her son, when, exactly, would he find a few hours to relieve some of the other gentlemen of their blunt?

They needed to find Jack and soon, before the gathering broke up and his creditors tracked him down. His creditors, who now included Roger Padgett. Lucy's brother. He pulled out the handkerchief and sniffed again. What were the odds?

Too long to wager on, but not long enough to ignore.

Damn it, where were the others? He might take care of both his problems over a few hands of vingt-et-un while learning of their findings. He might distract himself from this new quest, one Isabelle was right to question this morning. But, hang it all, he'd answered her truthfully. What sort of gentleman would he be if he ignored her plight? What kind of *human*? It was perfectly normal for him to feel this protective of a struggling young woman.

Wasn't it?

Upon closing the study door behind him, he wandered in the direction of the ballroom, in hopes of rousting someone up. But that space, too, was unoccupied. The lack of off notes jangling in the air ought to have alerted him to that fact. His sisters, no doubt, had joined the other ladies outside. The afternoon was warm and breezy, perfect for a walk in the gardens or sketching. No doubt Miss Abercrombie had found a worthy subject or two.

The pianoforte beckoned. No, he couldn't. Not with more important matters on his mind.

But his fingers ached to touch the keyboard again, and he thought of the peace it would bring him. Losing himself for a few moments was nearly as good as a glass of brandy. He'd sat at the instrument only last night, and Isabelle had discovered his secret, yet once more the need arose in him. Damned yearning for the feeling of the music flowing through him, around him, and in him, originating from somewhere deep inside, behind his heart, perhaps in the vicinity of his soul.

He stepped away, but could not take his eyes from the instrument. More demanding than any of his mistresses, it called to him. Mocked, even. *Yes, come to me. You know you want to. You cannot resist.*

God, yes, this feeling, this obsession, this joy, something he'd tried to bury years ago. But whenever he gave in—since he'd released the yearning last night—it clambered for freedom once more, to rejoice in the light of day.

The ballroom lay under the hush of the late afternoon humidity. Here, in the shelter of stone walls, no breeze chased the heaviness from the air. His boots thumped dully against the parquet as he crossed to the piano. The instrument dominated this end of the room, illuminated by a shaft of sunlight angling through a high, west-facing window.

He sat on the bench and rubbed a forefinger across the cool smoothness of a single key. One note, just one. Beneath his touch, the ivory warmed like a living thing. He applied pressure until the key descended and the note's purity tolled through the space. G, nine half tones above middle C. He knew without looking, based on pitch alone.

He closed his eyes and pressed another key and another. The second hand joined the first, and he gave himself over to the melody, the counterpoint, the low throb of the bass notes in contrast to the tinkling of the treble. The music transported him to another world where nothing but harmony existed, where time ceased, where he might lose himself . . .

"Gracious, I've never heard anything like it."

He started, his eyes opening abruptly, his fingers falling to strike a final discordant jangle. He winced and let his hands fall to his side. Henrietta stared, wide-eyed, from just beyond the empty music rack. Of course, he'd used no noted sheets. He'd been improvising, his fingers moving faster than thought. He ought to have stuck to Mozart.

His glance passed from face to face—a sea of them surrounded the piano, their expressions ranging from shock to intrigue to speculation. Miss Abercrombie's eyes narrowed, as if she were already revising his portrait.

"Mr. Upperton, I had no idea you played so beautifully." Prudence Wentworth batted her eyelashes at him.

He blinked twice. God, how could he have forgotten himself this way? Then he recalled he ought to incline his head in acknowledgment of the compliment.

"Oh please, don't stop. Play something else," another young lady twittered.

"Yes." A third clapped her hands. "If only the other gentlemen would return, we could have dancing."

This was it. They'd hound him now. Devilish compulsion that dogged him to give up his secret. He ought to take a sledgehammer to the goddamned piano and smash until nothing remained but slivers of wood, twisted wire, and shards of ivory.

He tamped down the urge and pushed himself upright. "I'd hardly be courteous if I continued when so many others might demonstrate their talents." He'd certainly never intended to put his on display. He gestured to the bench. "Please."

A chorus of feminine sighs went up. No one dared protest, not with their mamas and chaperones all watching for the smallest slip in decorum. Heat prickled at his nape. While he generally enjoyed feminine scrutiny, it was normally for his more manly accomplishments. The piano, as his father often berated him, was hardly a masculine bastion. Ironically, several of the younger misses were staring at him in open admiration, their cheeks pink with appropriately chaste excitement.

God save him.

He concentrated on his sister, who watched, her head turned away so that she regarded him from the corner of her eye. Was that hurt creasing her brow? Jealousy? He'd gladly give her this useless talent if he could.

At last, Miss Wentworth took a place at the keys and launched into a credible rendition of a Beethoven piano sonata. Her fingers fumbled now and then over the rhythm—clearly lacking the required feeling to create an emotional performance—but she struck far fewer false notes than Henrietta.

He plastered what he hoped was a mild expression on his face and backed up a step every so often, in hopes of slipping out the door unnoticed. He'd wasted enough time. He needed the men to return and soon, rather than pass the remainder of the afternoon with a roomful of hopefuls. And he hadn't seen Isabelle anywhere in the group.

"Don't you think you can sneak away like that, not when you had those girls completely enthralled."

George suppressed a groan. The last thing he needed was his mother badgering him into putting on another performance. Bad enough she put his sisters on regular display. And Mama would feel no compunction about the idea. Unlike his father, she would see no reason to criticize his musical ability as unmanly.

"I thought I'd be polite and let someone else have a turn."

Mama stepped directly into his path. Now that her position forced him to look her full in the face, he could see the tears shining in her eyes. "Never, *never* have I heard the like, and from my own son. How . . ." She pressed her fingers to her lips for a moment. "How have I never heard you play when your sisters are so accomplished?"

He would not laugh. He would not. Not when his mother was so convinced. Not when she was so *moved.* He tossed his shoulder in a half shrug.

"Papa preferred I pursue other studies." He pronounced the words carefully to keep the bitterness from his voice.

"Oh my dear, had I only known. I would have insisted."

She might well have, but nothing would have changed his father's opinions on what proper masculine pursuits entailed. Papa had been quite adamant in that regard. Gambling, drinking, whoring, dueling if necessary—all of those constituted a gentleman's daily regimen. Love of music—unless that love translated itself into a particular fondness for opera singers—was fit for women. Those men who indulged their talents were highly suspect—unnatural, even.

George had been nothing if not a dutiful son.

"No matter." It *did* matter, but that was no reason to dredge up the past. Not when his father had long since left this earth and could no longer answer for his shortcomings. Mama most likely didn't even know a quarter of Papa's vices. No point in upsetting her further by bringing them to light.

"You must give a performance."

God, no. The last thing he wanted was the entire *ton* staring at him. He was quite content with their view of him as a rogue and a rake. Tortured artistic souls had no place at the gaming hells and types of clubs he frequented. "Leave the performance to Henny and Catherine."

Her chin firmed, a sure sign she was about to dig in her heels.

"I've got a more urgent matter on my mind," he added

to forestall her. "Have the other gentlemen come back yet?"

"They have not. I don't understand. A house party, and all the young men have disappeared. The young ladies have been upset enough today as it is, without the added concerns of passing an entire afternoon with no opportunity to flirt."

She flapped her hands in front of her face, as if the very notion overheated her. Then she went still and looked him in the eye. "Come to think of it, you've been gone all day, as well. Please don't tell me you've been off convincing all the eligible young men in attendance to secret themselves away in avoidance of the fairer sex. It's quite unfair to your sisters."

"As a matter of fact, Mother, we've spent the day in search of a missing child."

Mama blinked several times before her eyes hardened. "Is this about that Mears woman from the village? Do you know who she really is? After Miss Marshall's outburst, we pieced together the entire sordid tale."

"Miss Marshall?" He fixed Mama with a hard stare. "What has Isabelle got to do with Miss Marshall?"

"Apparently"—Mama sniffed—"Miss Marshall is that woman's cousin."

"Cousin?" Such an inadequate reply, but his mind whirled with the implications. Mama knew nothing about his designs on the head of the Marshall family, and by God, he'd keep things that way.

"Yes, a cousin." She sighed. "And here I thought you might make an advantageous match. The influence you might have attained." The influence *she* might have attained as a result, but George refrained from pointing that out. "But Miss Marshall has already cut short her stay. You do remember, don't you?"

"No." He could hardly say any more. Not with his

pulse racing in his throat. It burned hot with a combination of anger and possibility.

"The family tried to cover it up, naturally. An earl's daughter throwing herself away like that. Imagine." Mama shook her head. "They claimed she'd gone off to stay with some feeble great aunt or other, but no one really believed that story."

This was exactly the sort of tale George paid no attention to, given that it involved a young miss. In keeping with his father's ideas on what constituted proper manhood, his interests gravitated to the older, the experienced, the widowed. If some young lady got herself into trouble and disappeared because of it, he gave no heed. Perhaps he ought to have.

"At any rate," Mama rattled on, "I cannot approve such a match now. Not knowing about the cousin."

"I'm surprised at you." Shocking how he could manage to sound so calm and controlled when inside outrage seethed through his veins. Fury threatened to erupt with every pulse of his heart. Good God, his own mother. "The woman's child is missing. I've always been under the impression you possessed a measure of compassion."

Her mouth worked for a moment or two. She cast a glance around the room as if to remind herself they were in danger of being overheard. They stood apart, and Miss Wentworth played on, but still this was no place for raised voices. "Don't be ridiculous. Of course, I possess a measure of compassion."

"When it suits you, you mean. Considering our position in society, you are the last person I'd suspect of being high in the instep. Congratulations, Mama. You surprised me today. Brava. I'd applaud you, but we mustn't cause a scene, now, must we?"

Hurt flitted through her expression. He ought to experience a certain level of guilt. He'd never turned his brand of biting sarcasm on his mother. He'd never had occasion to. Good-natured teasing was one thing, but he'd never crossed the line into mean-spiritedness until today. What was more, the emotions running through him pressed him onward. Go for the jugular. Twist the knife. Finish it. His own mother.

Christ.

But then her expression turned brittle. "You've taken the trollop to your bed, haven't you? And if you haven't, you're considering it. Consider well, because if she tries to entrap you . . ." Her voice rose, and she paused for breath. "You will not let that woman dupe you into marriage, do you understand me? I will not tolerate someone of her reputation in the family."

"If you'll excuse me." He didn't have time for any more of his mother's social climbing. He had to find Isabelle. Not only did he need to help recover her son, she might well lead him directly to Redditch.

CHAPTER TEN

GEORGE STALKED down the road to the village, muttering under his breath. Emily Marshall was no better than a cow, although that assessment might well be an insult to bovines. How dare she run her cousin off? Given her connections, though, he shouldn't be shocked. Isabelle's closer relatives had turned her out completely and left her to fend for herself.

Halfway to the village, he met Revelstoke in the lead of a group of grim-faced, dusty men. Damn it, that could only mean the others had come up with no leads, either.

George fingered the rose-scented scrap of linen in his pocket. "Have you discovered anything?"

"Not a thing." Revelstoke clapped him on the shoulder. "You?"

George shook his head. He saw no need to bring up the handkerchief. "I don't understand it. A child of six is small, but he doesn't simply disappear. Not without a great deal of noise."

"You going back for another look?"

"And to find Mrs. Mears," George said with a nod.

Revelstoke cast a glance at the others and lowered his voice. "Is there anything between you two I ought to know about?"

"That you ought to know?" George lowered his brows. "Not a thing."

"Seems to me you're rather involved. You've only just met her."

George glanced at the other men. Doubtless some of them would be interested in any hint Isabelle was open to receiving callers. Thank God Leach didn't appear to be present. "Yes, well. You'll agree she's rather easy on the eyes."

He could admit that much. He preferred to keep the latest gossip to himself for now. Revelstoke might well discover Isabelle's connection to the Marshalls soon enough, but George would rather not be present when that happened.

"Oh yes, quite." Revelstoke grinned. "And now you'll be off to comfort her."

George balled his hand into a fist. "Your wife and her sister had the same thought. And I hardly think it's time to make light."

Revelstoke, damn his eyes, simply broadened his grin. "Whatever you say." Then he sobered. "Tell her we'll try again tomorrow and for as long as it takes."

"We've lost a day as it is. We'll have to broaden the search."

"If we must, we must. But assure her we'll find the boy."

George set off once more. As much as he'd like to, he couldn't make her any promises. The child might be halfway to Yorkshire by now, God only knew why. How did a man appear from a hedgerow and snatch a boy away from his mother? Could Redditch be behind the child's disappearance somehow? This sort of scheme was exactly the sort of machination Redditch would dream up.

But why, and after six years?

A bastard was nobody's child. Jack's grandfather shouldn't want any claim. Unless Redditch had decided to punish Isabelle for her disgrace. But clearly Redditch had already turned her out of the family. Why wait another six years to chastise her further?

George might want answers, but he'd have to tread carefully in probing for them. Isabelle was already upset over the loss of her son. No doubt the scene the ladies had made this morning only added to that agitation. If Mama's reaction was any indication, Miss Marshall must have made quite a spectacle of herself. How humiliating for Isabelle. The last thing he wanted was to contribute to her distress by bringing up less savory aspects of her family. He preferred not to probe too deeply into the reasons why.

ONE last house. She would check one last house before giving in to despair. The vicarage rose before her, a larger and better kept dwelling than most of the others in the village. Manicured flower beds surrounded the path leading to the front steps. Isabelle let the knocker fall and awaited her fate.

Mrs. Weston responded on the third try. "Oh my goodness. Here it's the maid's half day, and I've done nothing but respond to inquiries." Even though the day was not hot, her wren-brown hair hung in sweaty straggles about her glowing face.

"Your pardon." Isabelle caught herself just before she dropped a curtsey, as if she were a servant. How ridiculous. "I'm looking for Jack. Have you seen him?"

"I'm sorry, no. As I told the gentlemen who asked earlier." Of course. The story had been the same at every other house in the village, delivered in varying levels of coldness and speculation. Mrs. Weston's version was fairly neutral and thus seemed nearly friendly.

A low groan sounded from somewhere in the house. Mrs. Weston glanced behind her, paling. "Please. My boy."

"Is he still poorly?"

"He's worse."

Isabelle tucked her lower lip between her teeth. Had she made an error with her remedy or was the boy's condition more serious than an upset stomach caused by an overindulgence of sweets? Nothing in the other woman's tone indicated an accusation, but that could soon change. At least if Mrs. Weston wanted more medicine, she might get it from Biggles.

"How much worse?"

"See for yourself." Mrs. Weston stepped aside and admitted Isabelle to the vicarage.

Stepping across the threshold was akin to entering another realm. Since her arrival in the village, Isabelle had never been admitted to another dwelling as if she was paying a social call. In the shops, she was tolerated so long as she was giving her custom or selling sachets, but not even the vicar's wife had ever offered her so much as a cup of tea.

The parlor was a rather shabby room furnished in fading brocades and limp velvets whose pile had long ago worn thin. A sour odor tinged the air. A pasty-faced boy lay on a settee, clutching his distended belly. His cheeks were loose and flabby, his pudgy hands dimpled at the knuckles, more like a child of six months than a boy of six years.

"It hurts, Mama."

Mrs. Weston brushed the boy's blond fringe out of his face. "I know, dear."

"Are you certain he doesn't need the doctor?" Isabelle asked.

At the word "doctor," Peter Weston let out a whimper. "Don't let him stick me."

Isabelle was at a loss for a reply. Clearly, the boy was beyond Biggles's remedies. "What have you eaten today?"

"Oh, hardly anything," said Mrs. Weston, "and normally he has such a vigorous appetite." An appetite for cakes and biscuits if Isabelle didn't miss her guess.

"A good cleaning out is what he needs," Biggles said every time Mrs. Weston asked for a stomach remedy for the child. "If she'd make him eat properly, he wouldn't be so poorly all the time. And she might let him run and play like a regular boy. He wouldn't be so soft."

But Isabelle couldn't point that out. "Have you tried feeding him stewed fruits?"

Peter pulled a face. "Nasty."

"Yes, well, it might help you feel better to try a little." Jack would have gobbled such as a treat, since she couldn't afford to buy him sweets. He also never suffered regular stomach ailments. "Shall I send Biggles with more of her remedy?" she asked Mrs. Weston.

"Oh, would you?"

Free of that stuffy house, Isabelle crossed the road and stumbled up the street toward her door. After a sleepless night and trying morning, so many hours enduring false murmurs of sympathy, shaken heads, obdurate doors that never opened had finished her.

Thank goodness for Biggles who could mix her a soothing concoction along with an infusion for Peter. She'd ask for something bracing added to her mixture. She'd need her strength, for she refused to rest until Jack was found.

Her boy, safe once more. She wouldn't let him out of her sight again.

"There you are."

At Upperton's pronouncement, she turned, jaw firmed. His expression betrayed nothing.

"I thought it best not to wait at the manor." She waved her hand. "Not after . . ."

"I know." He stepped toward her, arms outstretched as if to take her by the shoulders or pull her into an embrace. But then he dropped his hands to his sides. No, it was best he not make a show of affection or comfort in the middle of the street. "My mother told me of the scandal. It does not matter to me."

She brushed the statement aside. Naturally it wouldn't matter when he'd known from the outset. "Have you found anything? Any clue?"

He jerked his head to the side, lips pressed together. "No one's come up with anything. You?"

She released a breath, and her shoulders sagged under the weight of his statement. "Nothing. I don't understand it. Why—"

A line sketched itself between his brows, and he nodded in the direction of her house. "Not here."

"No, of course not." She stepped up the path, but stopped short of opening the door when she nearly tripped over a large wicker basket. An apologetic note pinned to the checked cloth covering the contents indicated the gift came from Julia Revelstoke and Sophia Highgate. "What on earth?"

"It looks like a peace offering."

"Yes, but why did they leave it out here and not with Biggles?"

She took the basket and let him into the kitchen, fully expecting Biggles to set upon them for news. But the room lay silent. No welcoming scent of freshly baked bread greeted her. No stew bubbling on the hearth. Even the fire had burned down to embers. Something leaden settled into her stomach.

"Biggles?"

No reply. The silence expanded toward the ceiling beams, where bunches of drying herbs perfumed the air. The absence of sound suppressed the delicate odor.

"Do you think she's taken it upon herself to search?" Upperton asked.

"No." Isabelle touched trembling fingers to her lips. "Not without telling us."

"She couldn't well tell us if we've been gone all day."

True enough, but the thought was no comfort. "No, she'd have stayed here. In case Jack came home on his own."

Upperton moved about the room, scanning. "Would she have left a message?"

"She can't read or write." Isabelle's voice wavered on the final vowel.

The situation looked ominous, but she had to make sure. Ignoring Upperton's grunt of protest, she gathered her skirts and scrambled up the ladder to the loft. The area under the slope of the roof lay shadowed in the late afternoon. A straw tick sat beneath the eaves, its coverlet neat and precise as always, but the nails in the wall where Biggles hung her spare wardrobe stuck out forlornly, denuded of their usual practical cotton and linsey garments.

Gone then.

The thought struck Isabelle like a fist to the gut. She rested her brow against her forearm and drew several breaths. First Jack and now Biggles. Lord only knew Biggles had looked after herself for far longer than Isabelle had been alive. She had to be all right. She had to.

"What is it?" Upperton's voice drifted from the base of the ladder.

"She's taken her things." Isabelle could manage no better than a whisper.

She inhaled once more, but the air refused to expand in her lungs. She still felt as if some invisible hand had wrapped itself about her throat to squeeze the life out of her. The rungs beneath her toes seemed to sway, and she tightened her grip on the ladder until her nails bit into the wood.

Her knees wobbled. She'd never make her way down to the floor. A single shuffling sound reached her ears. Upperton. His fingers curled about her ankle.

"Come on, now," he murmured.

Under any other circumstances, she'd tell him off for his cheek, only his action wasn't forward. He meant to guide her off the ladder. Somehow her toes managed to find the rungs below them, one after the next, until solid planks of wood supported her feet once more.

Too bad her knees refused to cooperate. She swayed, but Upperton caught her with one steady arm about her waist. She shouldn't lean. She should stand on her own, but in this moment, with both Biggles and Jack gone, she lacked the strength. She settled against his chest and let him hold her while her throat thickened.

Surely she was permitted to take comfort for a few moments at the end of a trying day. Surely that much came without a price. Surely Upperton would not exact payment in the form of favors. His arms tightened about her, and she let loose the sob that had been blocking her airway all this time.

She would take this moment because she needed it, but once it was over, once he relaxed his grip, she would slip away and see him off. She could not lead him to expect any more from her, even if she was ruined.

"We'll find the boy," he rumbled. "We will."

"We have to find Biggles now, too." She hated how small her voice sounded. Doubly so, for Mrs. Weston had requested more medicine.

At the thought, Isabelle pulled out of his arms and ran her forearm across her eyes. She strode to the shelves and rummaged among the jars that comprised Biggles's store of dried herbs. Comfrey, sage, rue. Where was the peppermint? Her hands shook, badly enough to send one of the containers crashing to the floor, where it shattered. A pungent scent of anise filled the air.

"Blast it all." She jammed the heel of her hand against her mouth, biting down on the fleshy pad to imprison another sob at the back of her throat.

"Here now." Upperton set his hands on her shoulders. "Sit."

"I can't. I have to do this. I promised."

"Do what?" He kept his voice low and steady and soothing.

"The vicar's son is ill, and Mrs. Weston needs an infusion." She twisted her hands together. "Biggles . . . Biggles normally makes this sort of thing, only . . ."

"Sit." He exerted a gentle pressure on her shoulders until he'd coaxed her into a place at the table. Numbly, she sank to the bench. Her fingers still trembled, and she folded them in her lap to hide the reaction. Upperton located a broom and began to sweep up the shards of glass and dried anise. Upperton, with a broom, like a servant.

"Oh, don't." She angled her knees, about to rise. "I can't just sit here. I have to—"

"Stay where you are." Steady as any downstairs maid, he stooped to gather the shards into the dustpan. "I'd make you tea, only I don't know where you keep it."

"I'm out of real tea." She kept her eyes trained on her hands, folded once more in her lap. "It's a luxury. Biggles makes all manner of substitutes. But—"

"What do you need for this medicine of yours?"

"Peppermint and, and . . ." Her mind went blank. Beyond an image of a jovial, gray-headed matron and a sprig of green, oblong leaves, nothing else would surface. Goodness, when was the last time Isabelle had ever felt so useless—besides when Jack had first come into the world and she had no idea how to care for him? And Biggles had helped her then, too. "I can't remember."

Upperton looked at her sharply. "Have you eaten anything today?"

She had to think about that. "I may have nibbled at something or other at the manor."

"Let's see what's in here, then." The basket. She'd forgotten.

He pulled back the checkered cloth and withdrew a pot of jam—peach, perhaps, or apricot. She hadn't savored the sweet tang of apricot jam on her tongue in forever. Another pot contained some sort of dark preserves, possibly blackberry. A golden loaf of bread and a crock of butter followed, along with a wedge of cheese wrapped in brown paper. Next came a gritty brown tablet, also wrapped.

"Chocolate." She forced the word past the lump that had risen to her throat. Heavens, that was for Jack. Julia had remembered her mentioning her boy never had such. Her generosity pierced Isabelle's heart. "How shall I ever thank them?"

"Now this might come in handy." Upperton produced a bottle of burgundy from the basket's bottom. With a knife, he uncorked the bottle and located two mismatched teacups. Fine burgundy in teacups. She wanted to melt into the floor. He was surely used to crystal goblets.

The rich red liquid swirled into the stoneware. Her father would be horrified.

"I'll take this over tea any day." He kept his tone light, as if her world hadn't just come crashing down about her ears since yesterday. Not that he was making light of the circumstances. Rather, he was trying to set her at ease, trying to stave off the paralyzing sense of panic that wanted to strangle her.

He set a cup before her. "Drink it down."

The wine's fumes burned her nostrils. This was good burgundy, heady and strong, not the watered down claret normally served to young ladies, or the swill she purchased from the inn on the rare occasions when she could afford it. She took a tentative sip. Rich flavor overwhelmed her tongue with dryness, and the wine burned a path to her stomach.

Gasping, she set the cup aside. "I'm out of the habit."

He grinned at her before taking a healthy swig. "Very nice. Don't stop now. The second swallow is easier."

At his prompt, she took another sip, feeling her courage burgeon alongside the growing warmth in her belly. "It will go to my head if I'm not careful."

"And after a sleepless night." He tore into the loaf of bread, and set a piece in front of her. "You'll need to keep up your strength."

As she reached for the butter, more to please Upperton than to appease a nonexistent appetite, her glance fell on another parcel. What else could Julia and Sophia possibly have sent her? She reached for it, and undid the paper wrapping. A selection of dried fruit spilled onto the table—apple, figs, currants, raisins, golden rounds of apricot.

"Dried apricot." The very thing. Bolstered by the wine, she bolted from her seat.

Fingers trembling, she wrapped up the package and strode out the door. The village streets lay quiet in the lengthening shadows as she made her way back to the vicarage. If Upperton followed, he held back. Thank heavens. She didn't wish to explain the association to Mrs. Weston.

Isabelle knocked, and the door opened presently.

"My goodness." Even though the light was fading, Mrs. Weston hadn't changed out of her day dress.

"Is Peter the same then?"

"I'm afraid so." Mrs. Weston's gaze lit on the parcel in Isabelle's hands. Her eyes gleamed with hope. "Have you brought me the infusion already?"

"Biggles . . ." She didn't wish to explain Biggles any more than she wanted to explain Upperton. "Biggles is in no condition at the moment."

"Oh dear. Is she ill, as well?"

"In a manner of speaking." Isabelle clipped the words, hoping her tone would forestall any further questions. "But I did bring you this." She thrust the packet at Mrs. Weston. "If you can coax Peter to eat some, he ought to be feeling better tomorrow sometime."

Mrs. Weston opened the paper. "I don't know. He can be so difficult when he gets this way."

"Tell him it's a new kind of sweet."

"But that . . ." Mrs. Weston advanced a step and lowered her voice. "That would be untruthful."

"Not entirely. Dried apricots are sweet. So is the apple."

The vicar's wife still hesitated.

"Take them. They'll do your boy more good than the infusions." Or any infusion Isabelle might concoct under the circumstances. *They'll do your boy more good than mine*, was what she wanted to say.

No, she must chase away those thoughts. It would help no one if she broke into a fresh spate of sobs on Mrs. Weston's doorstep. "I must go."

She turned, but not before she caught a sidelong glimpse of Mrs. Weston's narrowed eyes. Splendid. The vicar's wife had seen Upperton. Let the speculation and rumors begin. No doubt such would begin circulating by morning.

Isabelle straightened her back and marched toward the street. She had nothing to be ashamed of.

"I think she spotted me." Upperton pushed himself away from the gate to the vicarage and offered his elbow.

She stared at it, pointedly. "And how will acting as my suitor improve the situation?"

He cast a glance over his shoulder. "She's watching— still in the doorway."

"Of course she is." The busybody. "She'll watch until she sees me admit you to my house."

"Then shouldn't we make it worth her while to watch?"

If it hadn't been for the audience, Isabelle would have stopped cold in the street. He couldn't have just insinuated . . .

"Or would you rather we confound her by taking a stroll?"

A stroll. As if they were old friends. As if he were, indeed, courting her. How long she'd foregone such simple, ordinary pleasures. She'd be tempted if she hadn't passed a sleepless night and harrowing day—and if she weren't so worried. "I do not think that's the best idea."

"No? I think it is a capital suggestion. You need a distraction from today's events. However," he added before she could protest, "I might suggest other means of distraction."

An unexpected—and certainly inappropriate—rush of heat uncurled in her belly. But he couldn't possibly be hinting at anything untoward. Not under the present circumstances.

He wants you for his mistress. Isabelle pushed the irritating reminder aside. Now was no time to entertain such propositions, even when they hadn't been repeated.

"Distraction?" There. She'd managed one word in a neutral tone. Trying for more would be pushing matters.

"Nothing indecent, mind you," he said quickly. "Do you enjoy card games?"

Cards? Nothing but cards? She nearly laughed. "I have in the past."

"Excellent." He pushed her door open and steered her into the kitchen. "But I'm going to insist you eat something first. You need to keep up your strength."

"Yes, because now we'll need to find Biggles, as well as Jack." For the life of her, she couldn't have said how she kept her voice steady. She sank to the bench and contemplated the hunk of bread. It ought to have tempted her, but she suspected the firm crust would only turn to sawdust in her mouth.

He pushed the butter crock at her, along with the knife he'd used to open the wine. "You . . ." He paused, as if he didn't like what he was about to suggest. "You don't find it odd that Biggles disappeared at nearly the same time Jack did?"

She paused in the midst of buttering her bread. "What makes you ask something like that?"

His cheeks colored. "Your pardon. I've barely met the woman, you see."

"You don't understand." She couldn't keep the hard edge from her tone. "Biggles would never be involved in anything of the sort. She saved my life when I discovered I was expecting Jack. I owe her."

He cut a wedge of cheese and set it on her plate. "Saved your life?"

"When my family turned me out. I disgraced them, you see. I couldn't be allowed to remain and taint their good name." Her throat swelled shut and cut off her words. The memories of her desperation loomed large in her mind at the prospect of being alone once again.

"If they turned you loose with no resources, how did you find your way here?"

She swallowed. "That's just it. I didn't find my way. Biggles brought me here. She'd been turned out, too. Left with no references. She took pity on me and brought me with her."

More than that, Biggles had helped her smuggle her collection of ball gowns out of the house. An act of thievery, if they'd been caught. Thank the heavens they hadn't because the proceeds from the sale of those gowns had allowed them to feed and clothe themselves over the years.

"She possessed the means to buy a house when she worked in London as a servant?"

"This place belonged to her sister. She took us both in. But she's gone now. Biggles couldn't save her." Isabelle closed her eyes against the memory. That, too, had been a black time with Jack a new baby and deadly sickness running through the village. "If Biggles hadn't brought me here, I'd have had to sell myself long since."

She closed her mouth on the other half of that statement—that she might yet have to if she meant to survive.

Upperton could well draw that conclusion himself. Indeed he had, if the firmness about his jaw and the line between his brows were any indication. "You shouldn't remain alone."

"I've no choice." Her voice caught on the last word. Her son and a woman who'd looked after her like a mother—indeed, who'd shown her more love than her actual family—gone in the space of a day.

She stared at the untouched bread before her, as if the sight might stop the burning at the backs of her eyes.

CHAPTER ELEVEN

GEORGE POPPED the last of the cheese into his mouth and pushed his plate away. Isabelle had managed to choke down a bit of bread and butter. Now she tore apart the remains of the crust, her movements sharp and abrupt like a nervous wren. Her gaze darted to the window.

Outside, the sun had fully set, ending another languid late August evening. The bright blue sky was fast fading to a deep black.

"Hadn't you ought to return to your house party?" she asked quietly. Her tone belied a certain tension, an expectation that he'd depart. Indeed, propriety demanded it, but he knew she didn't want to remain alone.

"I won't leave you by yourself to brood." Unthinkable, the idea of allowing her to pass the long hours of the night with nothing to ponder but her solitude. "And I've promised you a distraction. I wish I might do more."

"You've done all you can," she whispered. "Involving your friends in the search. I could not ask for better."

"Revelstoke would have involved himself without my intervention. You had only to go to him." George rose and lit a branch of candles before reaching into his pocket. He still carried the pack of cards Leach had left behind at the inn. Casually, he pulled a few off the end of the pack and stuffed them in the middle. "Tell me. What do you like to play?"

"I haven't played cards in years. I'm sure I've forgotten how."

"What rot." He slapped the pack against the table to align the cards. "You don't forget how to play. What's your game?"

"Whist." With a forefinger, she traced the rim of her teacup. "But I don't know that we should."

He knew her son was ever on her mind, but with night coming on there was nothing left for them to do but wait for the long hours to pass before searching again. "It's better than dwelling."

She lifted her cup halfway to her lips before setting it down without drinking. The stoneware rattled in its saucer. "We can't play with only the two of us."

He leaned back, stretching his legs beneath the table. "If we used half the pack, we could."

"What?" She frowned. "Take out two suits? That would take the challenge away."

The challenge, yes. He smiled. Now he'd piqued her curiosity. Perhaps he could convince her to push her worries to the back of her mind for a little while.

Awareness of her on a very basic level crackled to life in the air between them. Not awareness of her as a woman so much as awareness of kindred thought. He agreed—he recognized that the more difficult a thing was to obtain, the more valuable in the end, whether a simple matter of a card game or something more complicated.

Like a difficult passage of music that took hours of practice until the notes became a part of his fingers. Until his fingers reproduced them without prompting from his brain.

Or like a woman.

He gave himself a mental shake. And where had that idea come from? He needed to consider its origin and banish it to the farthest ends of the realm, for that sort of thinking could only lead to trouble.

"And you claim you've forgotten how to play," he said. If she thought in those terms, she'd probably laid a wager or two in her lifetime.

"We'd need all four suits for a proper game."

He refilled his teacup with wine and took a sip. "We could deal four hands and only play two."

"Or we could choose our cards."

"How is that fair? If I play the gentleman and allow you to choose first, you'll take all the high cards for yourself."

"Not if we alternate." She held out her hand. "Give me the cards." She placed the pack between them. "I choose a card of the first two, then you choose, and so on until we each have a hand."

"You'll know what other cards aren't in play."

"So will you, and they won't be the same cards." She blinked and blinked again. "But if you really want, we can do it this way. I take the first card, and if I like it, I keep it and lay the next one aside without looking. If I dislike the first card, I can take the second, but then I must keep it, even if it's worse."

"That would work. How would you determine trumps?"

"Last card is trumps, just like real whist."

He grinned, caught up in the novelty of inventing a new game. "What shall we play for? Forfeits?"

"Forfeits?" Naturally her eyes narrowed. Experience had taught her to distrust. If he wanted answers to his questions, he would have to ease into the matter. "What sort of forfeits?"

"Nothing scandalous. Not unless you prefer higher stakes," he couldn't resist adding.

"I do not."

"I'd never ask for more than you're willing to pay. For every point, you must answer a question with the truth."

"And for every point I win?"

He allowed himself a rakish smile. If she believed him to be after kisses and such, she might be less suspicious of his true purpose. "You may name your price, and I shall be happy to pay whatever you demand."

She smiled in turn, and he wasn't sure he liked it. That impish gleam in her eye promised all manner of mischief.

One after the other, they drew cards. Her method of determining the hand proved devilishly clever. He might well build himself a long suit only to have another turn up as trump. Or he might hold a king with no way to tell if she had the ace or it lay in the pile of discards. He might attempt to count cards and remember the honors that had been played, but such strategies were hampered with half the pack an unknown quantity.

As play progressed, Isabelle showed herself quite adept. In a true game with the play deep and her as his partner, he might easily win enough to cover Summersby's markers plus a nice cushion for himself—enough to set Isabelle and Jack up in a nice area of London, enough to acquire her a servant or two. Enough that she might live the way she was meant to.

Isabelle slapped a trump on his last card. Blast it, she'd already closed her book, which meant . . .

"I win the point." She sounded all too pleased with herself.

"Imagine, once you remember how to play."

She rested her hand on her chin and contemplated him for a long moment, until he shifted his weight on the bench. "Well? Do your worst and have done."

"I want to hear you play the piano again."

Damn it, anything but that. His music might drive him, but it wasn't a talent he shared with anybody. And he couldn't refuse. He had said she could claim any-thing. "How shall I play with no instrument to hand?"

"You may repay me another time." On the other hand, that implied she might meet him again at Shore-ford. Given her reception earlier, she'd have to plan an-other midnight rendezvous.

With a grin, he passed her the cards. They composed new hands for another round. He watched her carefully as the game progressed. She'd begun to make elementary errors, leading a ten to his ace. By the final card, her fin-gers were shaky.

George took the last trick. "Two points. That means you answer two questions."

"Very well." Head bowed, she folded her hands be-fore her.

"Tell me . . ." He couldn't jump right in with Red-ditch. "Tell me about something that makes you smile."

"Oh." For a moment, she looked lost.

Perhaps that much was true. In the past two days, she'd lost her son, lost her support. And every day, she strug-gled. Struggled for acceptance as much as she struggled to live. Earlier, he'd seen the reaction of the other villag-ers the moment they realized who he was searching for. Their expressions had hardened, and they'd eyed him with speculation, the same as the butler this morning.

"Well. Jack . . ." Her voice caught on the name. "Jack's always one for stories. He usually wants me to invent something with dragons and such." She fingered her empty teacup. "The other week, I was too tired to come up with anything, so I thought he might like to hear about Jack and the beanstalk. Because of the name, you see."

"Wasn't he afraid of the ogre?"

"Not at all. He tromped about for days shouting, 'Fee, fie, foe, fum!' Do you know what he said?"

He propped his chin on the heel of his hand. "No. Tell me."

"He said an ogre worth his salt wouldn't say anything so namby-pamby." She nearly laughed at the memory, but somewhere her laughter snagged on a jagged edge to emerge as a choked sound.

George settled himself more firmly on the bench. Like the card game, he'd meant his question to distract her from her missing son.

"You still have another question," she said thickly.

He ought to ask about Redditch, but how? How did he bring up the topic and not appear cruel by reminding her of yet another loss? He couldn't do it, not after all she'd been through. "Perhaps I shall claim my second question later, when I've had a chance to play for you."

"Can't you think of anything else to ask me?"

"I'm holding out for something extra scandalous." There. Let her think he only meant to flirt.

"And you can't imagine that now?"

"Well, if you insist. Never let it be said I backed down in the face of scandal." He made a show of contemplating, tapping his fingers on his chin while giving her a wolfish grin.

Her cheeks turned a fetching shade of rose under his scrutiny. So much the better. The past few days hadn't done any favors for her pallor.

"Gracious." She touched her fingertips to the base of her throat. "What are you thinking?"

"Shall I answer you truthfully when it isn't your forfeit to claim?"

"Yes." That single syllable emerged on a throaty note, much more appropriate to the bedroom. But then she clapped a hand over her mouth. "Good heavens, what am I thinking?"

Her voice wobbled into an alarmingly higher register on the final syllable. Her face crumpled, and she screwed her eyes shut. Damn it to hell, he'd nearly succeeded in his distraction. He'd had himself believing he might coax reserved little Isabelle Mears into flirting with him yet.

"I shouldn't," she murmured into her palm. "What kind of person . . ."

She was melting before him. All her composure drained away before his eyes. Something like a fist squeezed his heart. He pushed the bench back, stood and circled the table to her side.

"Budge up, would you?" Deliberately, he kept his tone light, while he nudged with one shoulder.

Choking, she inched to the side, let him sit, let him wrap an arm about her. Her head settled on his shoulder, and one of her small hands crept up his free arm until she clung to him. Her breath tore from her in ragged spurts, and her body trembled against his chest.

She felt so small in his arms, small and vulnerable, this slip of a woman. Mentally, he cursed Redditch for turning her out into the world, for that night had led to this—a night she'd lost everything yet again. He tightened his hold on her, and sifted his fingers through her hair. If he could, he'd have saved her this pain.

She burrowed closer, buried her face in the side of his neck, and inhaled, steady now, as if she were taking his scent into herself. As if she might take him into herself. Her breasts pressed against his chest.

In spite of himself, his body reacted to her nearness, her softness. Good Christ, she was nearly in his lap. She might even feel him against her thighs—white, slender thighs that he wanted wrapped about his waist.

He swallowed a groan. The last thing she needed was to fend off his advances.

She raised her head, eyes wide and brown and luminous in the candlelight. No, those were unshed tears, not the reflection of desire. Her lips parted. Her teeth tugged at the plumpness of her lower lip, and his mind flooded with the memory of that sweet pliancy beneath his mouth.

Under his tongue.

She'd reacted to gentle persuasion, but now his mind focused on a single question: How would she react to a more carnal assault? For that was how he wanted to take her: rough, forceful, hard, and fast.

Only a scoundrel would act on the impulse. A scoundrel would take advantage of her innocent vulnerability—for she was still innocent, even though she'd borne a child. A scoundrel would think with his prick and strip that away from her.

She blinked, and her lips parted once more. The pink tip of her tongue darted out. Heated need shot to his groin, and he forced himself to loosen his grip.

She must have sensed his hesitance, for she moved closer. "Please."

Oh, damn. If she planned on begging him in that cracked little voice, he was well and truly buggered. "Isabelle—"

"Please, I need . . ."

He touched his fingers to her lips to stop her from completing that thought. "It's not a good idea. I should leave."

But he couldn't very well rise with her nearly in his lap, couldn't dump her onto the floor.

"I cannot bear to be alone." She formed the words around his fingertips, and his resolve slipped a bit further.

"There's a difference between keeping company and asking for trouble."

"Please." That word again. It burned through him.

And then she took away his choice along with his chance to protest. Seizing him by the lapels, she covered his lips with hers.

Her kiss, God, her kiss. As gentle as their first had been, this one was its complete and utter opposite. It was the antithesis of demure. It was every bit as rough and forceful and hard and fast as he craved. She tasted of desperation and need entwined. She shattered his will with all the finesse of a racehorse charging ahead on to the finish line.

Her palms flattened against his chest and slid upward to his shoulders. Her fingers tugged. Good God, she was unknotting his cravat. He had to slow her down before she pulled him over the cliff with her. She might well seek some release to her emotional turmoil, but he was certain she'd regret it if he took her to bed—by tomorrow morning if not the moment they finished and she drifted back to earth.

He tore his lips away, but she only settled her mouth against his cheek, while her fingers still fumbled with his neck cloth.

"Isabelle," he grated. By God, he was going to regret what he was about to do—or parts of him were. "Isabelle."

He pressed his hands over hers, halting her fingers. They were trembling, whether with desire or despair, he didn't know. "Slowly. I'm not going anywhere."

She blinked up at him, her eyes round and dark and huge in her pale face. It was the wine. It had to be. She'd barely eaten all day and the strong burgundy had gone to her head. Her breath ghosted across his lips. "Don't stop. I . . . I need . . . I don't even know how to say it. You'll think me scandalous."

"Hush." He gave her hands a warm squeeze. "I know what you need."

Lord help him, he needed the same, but for different reasons, reasons he was in a position to ignore. This one time, he could give without taking. "I swear to you, I won't do anything you'll regret later, but you'll have to trust me."

Her gaze focused on his mouth, and she leaned in. Before she could advance on him again, he met her halfway in a gentler caress. If he wanted her trust, he had to earn it, starting now. "Do you, Isabelle? Do you trust me?"

CHAPTER TWELVE

THE OVERPOWERING hunger for closeness to another person—to feel a heartbeat against hers—overwhelmed any protest her brain might mount. She craved this escape, however ephemeral. And if he could give her that much without forcing her to risk once again her virtue and reputation, then how could she refuse?

How could she *not* trust him? She'd already thrown herself at him in a reckless offer of her entire being. Her past might well have taught her caution, but in this moment when she'd lost everything, she could not tolerate any less than the comfort intimacy bestowed. His lips on hers. His tongue and hands seeking out her secrets. Skin against skin.

Above all, the oblivion of passion.

"Yes, I'll trust you when I should not." Her voice sounded foreign to her ears, something low and enticing and compelling.

Imagine such seduction dripping from her tongue, when she had once fallen prey to that very siren's song. But it was as if someone else controlled her actions now. Someone or something. Not reason, certainly. No, somewhere inside her, a need had awakened, a small spark that had ignited in dry timber to become a raging inferno. Reason and logic held no power against such forces.

Neither did her conscience.

She didn't want to think, only feel until the sensations overtook her and blocked out all else.

"Why should you not trust me?"

Because he was a rogue. Because his charm captivated her. Because, right now, she wished these things had never led her astray. "Perhaps . . ." She focused on the front of his topcoat. "Perhaps it is myself I should not trust."

He closed his eyes, and a groan erupted from deep in his chest. "Do not say such things." He raised a hand to her cheek. His fingers trembled against her skin. "You play utter havoc with my resolve to respect your wishes."

Wishes? She'd expressed no wishes.

His mouth covered hers, hard and demanding, before she had a chance to reply. His tongue invaded her mouth and forced her to hold back the questions that clambered into her throat. In another moment, she forgot them, as he hauled her up against his chest. He set her mind awhirl until she could only respond to the darkness of his kiss. She clutched at him, ran her hands across his broad shoulders and down his back, pulled him into her.

Yes, yes, and yes. She longed for him to be part of her, to fill her and erase the past and let her believe in a brighter future.

Brighter future? That was carrying matters a bit far.

With a groan, he pulled away, his breath coming in warm puffs across her cheeks. "Don't think." He ran a finger along her jaw, tracing a line to her throat and pressing on her racing pulse. "Feel. Trust. The last thing I want is to harm you."

But he would, when he left. He'd do both—leave and hurt her in the process. She buried her face in the crook of his neck, and his embrace tightened about her, a blanket of warmth and protection.

He pressed his lips to her forehead, a mere shadow of

a kiss, barely there. Again came the gentle pressure, a fluttering, over and over in a line down her face. The corner of her eye, the jut of her cheekbone, the lobe of her ear. She lowered her lids and settled into the tenderness, the simple affection behind the gesture.

So long she'd lived alone.

So long without such comfort from another adult. A child's enthusiastic hugs and grubby kisses weren't enough. Only an adult could envelop her so fully, could surround her with the sense of well-being. She let it infuse her.

She'd take what affection he was willing to give. Take it and return a measure of her own. Her body craved the security the way her lungs craved air.

Fingertips trembling, she stroked the side of his face, to press the gentle rasp of his beard against her skin, to revel in his nearness. Warm, wet heat skated along her neck as he branded her with his tongue.

Her fingers slipped into his hair. Like warm silk, the strands slid against her palms. He pressed closer, nuzzled and then moved on. Her collarbone, the notch at the base of her throat. The upper swells of her breasts.

Her nipples tightened in invitation, and she arched back in a wordless plea for more. She ached for him to fill his hands with her flesh, to bare her to his gaze, to suckle.

His deft fingers moved to the tiny buttons at her shoulders that held up her bodice. Then they tugged at the ties beneath. Her loosened stays fell aside easily along with the straps of her chemise. Cool air rushed over exposed skin, and her nipples puckered to buds, begging for his attention, his lips, his tongue, his teeth.

He pulled in a sharp breath. She opened her eyes to find him staring, eyes dark and hard as granite, but never cool. No, his gaze burned into her. Deep in her midsection, an answering spark burst into flame.

He raised his hands, and she inhaled, waiting for his touch, yearning for it. Needing it. But his fingers curled about her waist strong and steady on either side. Before she could question, he stood, raising her at the same time, crowding her, forcing her back. The firm edge of the table nudged at her bottom. He lifted and pushed until she sat, until her face hovered level with his, but his gaze was fixed on her throat.

Once more, he stepped closer. His slim hips angled between her knees and pushed them apart. His hands slipped to either side of her thighs, his arms a brace for his body and a cage to hold her in place.

Not that she intended to move from the spot. Not when the bulge at the front of his trousers pressed against her most intimate flesh, searing her through layers of fabric. Not when he dipped his head to draw a straining nipple into his mouth.

She cried out, a high note tinged with desperation. How did this man ignite such a fire in her? She didn't quite recall it being this way—all her reactions intensified. An aching knot of need tightened deep in her belly with every hot swipe of his tongue.

He edged forward and pushed her back against the unyielding wood. God, he'd laid her out on her own kitchen table. Next to the mismatched teacups, their hollows stained red. Beneath her, the scattered pack of cards and crumbs of their meal. Completely wanton. She no longer cared. All she wanted was more. More pleasure. More of him.

Until he filled her.

She tangled her fingers in his hair, pressed him closer. Arched her back, her head digging heedlessly into the oak's bite. For a moment, he pulled away, and the heat of his breath blazed across her swollen flesh, harsh and rapid. His eyes, darkened to black, branded her with the intensity of his gaze.

Still fully clothed, he loomed over her, hair in spiky disarray. Power lurked beneath that precisely tailored topcoat, beneath that rich waistcoat with its gleaming buttons, beneath the fine linen of his shirt. Power and rippling muscle. She'd felt it through the barrier of his garments. Her fingers itched to learn his texture, to experience the leap of his pulse beneath his skin, to trace their way down fire-gilded flesh and corded sinew, to learn, to know until the pair of them ceased to exist as man and woman alone.

Until they moved as one at passion's decree.

She reached for the band of silk that bound his neck, to finish loosening the first ties that separated them.

He grasped her wrist, pressing it over her head. "No, Isabelle." A grin stretched one side of his mouth, or perhaps it was more a grimace of pain. "I've sworn to leave you without fear of another child. But I'm only made of flesh and blood."

"I would know the flesh." Her voice was nearly unrecognizable. It floated over them both, low and sultry, as if she were indeed the temptress, the experienced one.

He closed his eyes, and a shudder passed through him. She felt the tremor at every point where their bodies touched—her wrist, her belly, the junction of her thighs, wedged apart and pressed against the solid length of his arousal. Something pulsed between them—her or him, she couldn't tell.

"Not tonight. I've given my word and, by God, I intend to keep it. How else am I to prove you might trust me?"

Lord, he was going on about trust when it was the last thing on her mind now. She ought to heed him, ought not to take another chance, but her body was making its own demands. She recalled the sensation from last time, only with him, it was somehow magnified. Insistent. Urgent. Implacable.

She might once again be disappointed in the actual joining, but she had to know, had to experience, just once with him. She tilted her hips. The hard length of his erection pressed into her just *there*, just at that sweet, sweet spot. Her breath released on a sigh.

"I won't deny you, love. I know just what you want." Leaning forward, he feathered a kiss across her lips. "I know just what you need."

She peered at him from beneath half-closed lids. Nothing about his voice had changed, but he couldn't have given in so quickly. Not after all his insistence on trust. "How?"

He laughed, a low, sensual rumble that originated deep in his chest and vibrated through her. "You poor, innocent creature. I might have known the ape who ruined you didn't go about the matter properly."

"I believe he managed well enough."

"For him, perhaps, but not for you. Don't think about him anymore. Let me show you how it ought to be."

Ought to be. Such promise in those words. *He* had made promises of pleasure, as well. Naturally he had—promises he hadn't kept. George was different somehow. She saw it in his eyes, the reverence, the determination. She felt it in the way his touch focused on her, worshiped her. It rang through the conviction in his voice when he spoke the vow.

How could she refuse? How could any woman, even laid out before him on a rough table like a banquet, a half-finished bottle of wine next to her head. Already he was devouring her with his eyes. She wanted to be consumed.

Yes. She swallowed to relieve her parched throat, but the word wouldn't come. Weakly, she nodded her assent.

Heat flared in his gaze and sent an answering spear of flame straight to her midsection. Intimate muscles clenched, and without thinking, she tightened her thighs about his flanks.

With a growl—there was no other word to describe the feral noise in his throat—he straightened. Seizing an ankle, he placed the sole of her foot on the edge of the table. His fingertips trailed fire up her calf. She sucked her lower lip into her mouth. Cool air teased the bare skin above her stockings as he raised her skirts.

He positioned her other foot, leaving her splayed, exposed, vulnerable, but as he looked his fill, an odd sense of power surged through her. He held her in thrall as she waited for him to fulfill the promise of his words, his gaze, his touch, but the expression of sheer worship on his face—the line of his mouth, the rigidity of his jaw, the pure intent in his eyes—revealed the truth.

This was all for her alone.

Not just any woman, no matter how skilled, but her, Isabelle, impoverished and ruined in the eyes of society, perhaps, but not in this man's. No, to him, she was precious, worthy, deserving.

A shudder passed through her, a reminder of the unforgiving plank on which she lay, and she lowered her lids to shut him out. A nameless emotion fluttered near the surface of his expression, a depth she wasn't yet ready to face, for it was dangerous. She couldn't afford to fall in love with a man who would, in the end, leave her and return to the society that had spurned her.

At the dull scrape of wood on wood, she opened her eyes. He had pulled up the bench. Even now he was taking a seat before her.

"What?"

"Hush." The order was no more than an outrush of hot breath against her inner thigh as he settled himself— directly before her . . . cunny.

The word echoed through her memory. She oughtn't know such a term. The way *he* had used it all those years ago, had been enough to indicate how very improper it was. More than that, it was ugly and dirty, just the way she had felt once he'd finished with her and left her to readjust her skirts as best she could, to wipe away his seed and her blood with her chemise, to find her way back to the ball, ashamed of what she'd just done, fearful the entire company would know her immediately for a trollop. How could she hope to hide it when she reeked of his essence?

No, no, she wouldn't think of that night. Not now. Not with George. Not when . . .

A mere rustle of fabric was all the warning she got before the hot swipe of his tongue pulsed against her most intimate self. Pleasure, sharp and white hot, coursed through her. She arched her back, and her head pressed into the tabletop. A low moan floated from the back of her throat.

Oh, God, what madness was this that he should dare to lick her most secret places? Surely this was wanton, forbidden, sinful. No proper lady would allow such ministrations, but she was hardly a proper lady anymore.

He grasped her hips, his fingers biting into her flesh, and pulled her closer. The next caress brushed, long and languorous, from her opening up to the top of her cleft, to that spot that ached and throbbed for his attention. He circled it lazily, and the pressure inside her increased. Her breath escaped on a hiss.

He paused a moment, pressed his lips to her inner thighs, and his whiskers rasped against her quivering flesh. She bit her lip and tensed in anticipation of the next stroke, a stroke that didn't come. Instead, a rush like a hot breeze bathed her nether region.

She inhaled, held the gulp of air, and waited. His hand slid from her waist, glided along her thigh, pressed against the back of it and up the inner edge to brush against her curls, so close, but too light.

She gurgled a protest and bucked her hips.

He rewarded her with the scrape of his teeth against her inner thigh. "If we're to do this properly, I shall require some guidance."

She tilted her head and raised herself on her elbows. Lord, the sight of him seated thus, between her legs, face flushed, eyes burning, shoulders hitching in shallow pants. How utterly decadent that he should place himself as if at a feast.

"Guidance? I've never done such a thing."

He grinned, a devilish quirk of his mouth. "I know. But you might tell me what you like." He arched a single brow. "Am I to surmise you're enjoying none of this?"

He dipped his head for another taste. That wicked, wicked tongue of his circled once more, just *there*. Oh, how could he know her body better than she did herself? She lay back and let herself feel. How did he know where to kiss and where to touch so that the pleasure drove her utterly mad with need?

"It's strange," she panted. "I never expected . . ."

"Not so strange. It's not so different from a kiss."

A kiss, certainly, but she'd never dreamed he'd set his lips to her private self. The thought sent heat rushing southward, heat and blood, a sense of vulnerability and devastation that also uplifted.

"It may be strange," he practically hummed the words against her flesh. The vibrations twisted into her, drove her higher. "But is it good?"

Good. Such a pale descriptor for what he aroused in her. This wasn't good; it was paradise—or it would be soon. With his tongue alone, he was driving her toward some unknown destination, driving her to a stark need to arrive. Soon, soon. "Don't stop."

He slid a finger inside. She cried out as her inner muscles clenched about him. He moved within her in time with the relentless circling of his tongue, sending streaks of fire through her limbs. The pleasure tore her breath from her lungs in ragged bursts.

"Touch yourself," he urged.

The words barely penetrated the haze of passion that enveloped her. "What?"

He reached for her hand, cupped her palm about her own breast. It swelled into her grasp, the nipple straining against her fingers.

"Yes, God, yes," he muttered before he pressed his lips to her once more, pulling in air at the same time, pulling *her* into his mouth. Her. Lord, yes, her. She'd known he might penetrate her, but it had never once entered her mind that he might take part of her into himself.

He thrust hard with his fingers. A second entered her now, stretching, stretching, while all the time his lips suckled the bud of flesh at the apex of her thighs. She bucked and twisted beneath him. Utter bliss mounted and mounted until at any moment she felt as if she might shatter. A tremor passed through her thighs, and the pleasure burned through the soles of her feet.

And then the world splintered. Her body pulsed and soared about his fingers. She gasped her release, on and on, until she thought she might faint from its power.

A bead of sweat trickled along George's temple. His fingers curled into her flanks, no doubt biting into the delicate flesh. She didn't even seem to notice. She was still trembling with the aftershocks of her crisis.

His arm muscles contracted with the urge to enfold her against his chest, to caress her until she came back to herself. At the same time, his groin tightened and throbbed with the steady pulsing reminder that he remained unfulfilled.

The urge to unbutton himself and drive into her tight little sheath warred with his will. No. He would not do it. He could bloody well wait for once. Later, he'd take matters into his own hands, fueled by the memory of what he'd just witnessed. For now, winning her trust was far more important than slaking his lust on her. If he took advantage of her now, she'd never forgive him.

Why do you care?

He tamped down the nagging voice in the back of his brain. He cared because she deserved better than a quick tumble on the table. He cared because she'd been duped once before to disastrous result. The last thing she needed was another child to raise. The last thing he needed was another by-blow.

He cared, by God, enough to leave her now, his body's demands be damned.

Above all, he cared because she was Isabelle, tough and brave beneath her air of vulnerability and delicate exterior. She'd survived society's censure and carved a life for herself where she could raise her boy in relative peace and security.

"George?"

With a rustle of cotton, she pushed herself onto her elbows. Her hair straggled about her flushed face, her eyes wide and blinking. Her bodice gaped to reveal lovely, rounded breasts, nipples straining, even now begging for his attention.

His throat went dry. Ignoring his raging erection, he tugged at the ties of her dress. The pink in her cheeks deepened, and she sat up, smoothing her skirts back into place, before fumbling with her bodice.

"I don't know what came over me." She kept her eyes downcast. Her fingers trembled and the laces fell from her grasp. "Oh, bother."

"Isabelle." He framed her face with his hands, tipped her chin up until she returned his gaze. "There is no shame in what passed between us."

"I feel like such a wanton." She cast her glance around the room. "Heavens, on my own kitchen table. If anyone had looked in . . ."

"They haven't."

"I . . ." She pressed her fingers to her lips as if she were testing to see if they were still there. Or perhaps they still tingled. "I can't make a habit of this."

"Make a habit of what? Taking your own pleasure?"

"It's selfish of me. I've given nothing back. And how can I think only of myself when Jack may need me?" Her voice wobbled dangerously toward desperation.

He gathered her close, savoring the slightness of her body against his, the press of her breasts against his chest, the soft flare of her hips. God, he could lift her so easily and she'd be at just the proper height. No, no. He must focus on her. "You needed the contact. You needed someone with you. You still do. And I'm not about to leave."

CHAPTER THIRTEEN

ISABELLE AWOKE to an odd, rhythmic rumble. Her body felt strangely heavy, as if she lay at the bottom of a very warm well and the weight of the water pinned her in place. She cleared the cobwebs of slumber from her mind and opened her eyes. The feeble light of dawn painted her chamber in muted grays. She couldn't even remember dropping off to sleep last night.

One moment she'd been in Upperton's arms, and— Upperton.

No, she could scarcely think of him by that name anymore. Not after all that had transpired between them last night. Not after she'd shattered under his deft fingers and skillful tongue. He'd played upon her body like a piano and drawn notes from her, impossibly pure and high and wild.

George snored softly beside her now—on top of the blankets. He'd cast one arm over his eyes, ready to ward off the morning sunlight. His chest rose and fell in a steady rhythm, in time with the low rumble emanating from his throat.

Goodness, how had she managed to pass the night with him and not notice? His shoulders occupied more than their fair share of the straw tick. Why had he stayed, when he might have slept in more luxurious accommodations at the manor?

I'm not about to leave. So he'd claimed, and he'd honored his word.

Stubble peppered his cheeks and chin. She extended a finger and traced a path through the rough texture. Last night, he hadn't allowed her to touch, but she wanted to now. If only she could return a small measure of the heaven he'd shown her.

His breathing hitched before settling into a steady rhythm once more. She folded an elbow under her cheek and studied him. She'd never had occasion to observe a man this close. She inhaled his slightly foreign scent, at once spicy and smoky. That musk must now impregnate her pillow. A pity he hadn't tucked himself beneath the covers. He might have permeated her entire bed, a reminder of his presence when he returned to his world.

For he would, eventually. He might rend her with pleasure again and again, but he would not stay where he did not belong. She must remember that. Remember and not allow herself to become attached.

She crept from beneath the covers, and her chemise fell about her calves. Her chemise and nothing more. Not even her stays remained to hamper her breathing, which meant he must have helped her undress—slipped her garments from her, snuggled her into bed, and lain beside her all night, fully clothed like a perfect gentleman.

Although they'd been far more intimate, she ought to be mortified that exhaustion had prodded her to set aside propriety and let him play the lady's maid. Instead, a blossom of warmth took root in her chest at his kindness. She'd been so leery of his intentions, but beneath the rakish façade lay a perfectly decent man. Honorable. Trustworthy. He'd demanded her trust and proven himself.

A pounding on the door sent her heart slamming into her ribs.

George raised his head, blinking sleepily. His gaze

landed on her and raked downward. A lazy grin, full of promise, spread across his face. "Good morning."

Too late, she remembered her lack of proper garments, and her cheeks heated.

"Don't lose track of that thought." He tucked his arm beneath his head and contemplated her. "That shade of pink is nothing less than adorable on you, and whatever you're recalling to make you blush so—I want to hear all about it."

"Stop," she admonished. "There's someone at the door."

The pounding renewed, louder this time. At the sound, her heart flipped, and the pulse in her neck throbbed.

"So there is. Best you cover up and answer before they burst in and draw their own conclusions."

She owned nothing resembling a dressing gown. Normally, she'd be clothed by the time anyone knocked, but normally, no one knocked this early. The quality of light in the room was sufficient to indicate the time—not even an hour since sunrise. Could her boy have been found? *Please, oh please, and let him be all right.*

She wrapped herself in a shawl and pushed her wayward curls out of her eyes before rushing across the kitchen and yanking open the front door.

"My lord," she gasped.

Lord Benedict stood on her stoop, slapping a pair of leather gloves against his palm. Behind him, a large horse nosed at her flowers, reins secured about the low fence that separated her front garden from the road. Alone, unfortunately.

"You'll forgive the early intrusion." Lord Benedict swept into a bow, as if she were standing in a drawing room rather than barefoot in the doorway to a poor cottage. "I'm looking for Upperton, and I hoped you might be of some assistance."

"Oh." Her cheeks burned in the early morning breeze,

and she stared down at her toes. Oh, yes, she knew just how guilty she appeared, but she could hardly act otherwise. She *was* guilty, and, worse, she'd answered her door looking like she'd come fresh from a tumble.

"I wouldn't dream of disturbing you under any other circumstances," he went on, "but the matter concerns your son, as well."

A hundred questions jammed her throat, each jostling for attention. She wanted to shout them. She wanted to grab the man by the lapels of his riding coat, drag him inside and demand answers. Only she already knew the reply to the most important question of all. Jack was still missing; otherwise Lord Benedict would have brought her boy straight home.

Driving her fingernails into her palm, she reached for the well of dignity that had been engrained in her from childhood. "Please come in."

She stepped aside to let him pass, unable to look any higher than the middle of his chest, for fear she'd read judgment in his gaze. She ought to be long used to it, but from him, such censure would be doubly difficult to stomach, given his kindness to her yesterday. And that was to say nothing of his wife. Best to get the niceties out of the way.

"I owe you a debt of gratitude." She addressed the brass buttons on his riding coat.

"It's nothing. Anybody would be willing to pitch in and search for a lost child."

Anybody indeed. The villagers—her neighbors— hadn't lifted so much as a finger.

"I didn't mean about Jack, although I'm grateful there, too. Your wife sent along a basket yesterday." Her glance drifted to the kitchen table where the remains of their picnic still lay scattered. Cards, breadcrumbs, and teacups with the dregs of fine burgundy still staining the bottom, all abandoned for other pursuits. The reminder of what else had befallen on that table drove a spear of heat through her belly.

Dear Lord, and what did any of that matter? If she'd needed comfort last night, it was no one's affair but her own. Why couldn't he skip to the real reason for his presence and tell her what he knew of Jack?

"According to Julia, sending along a few trifles was the least she might do."

"To me, they were hardly trifles." Drat. That had come out colder than necessary. Lord Benedict couldn't know. He'd probably never wanted for anything in his life.

"What brings you here so damned early?" Thank God for George. Thank God, even if he had drifted in from the bedroom, his clothing rumpled, his hair mussed.

"It's your own fault. I'd have talked to you last night over port, only you never turned up." Revelstoke proclaimed in the same kind of tone he'd use to remark on the weather. *Oh, yes, it's raining again. Common enough occurrence in the south of England.* Rain, wind, Upperton not spending the night in his own bed. Nothing out of the ordinary.

Isabelle didn't think her cheeks could burn any hotter. And why, *why* couldn't they come to the point now that courtesy's demands had been met?

"I was needed elsewhere," George said in the same sort of tone.

"Oh, for heaven's sake, what of my son?" Isabelle clapped a hand over her mouth a moment too late.

"That's what I've come to discuss. I'd no intention of disturbing you." Revelstoke nodded at Isabelle, but his expression gave nothing away. "But this concerns you at any rate. More than it does Upperton, in fact."

"What is it?" Isabelle twisted the frayed ends of her shawl in her hands. The once rough wool had long since worn to softness.

"I see no choice in the matter but to broaden the search. We turned up nothing yesterday, and the village isn't that big."

George bolted toward the door. "You'll lend me a horse, won't you? Only not Buttercup. Surely you've got one with a sweeter disposition."

"I've already sent riders out."

"Oh, no." Isabelle pressed her fingers to her throat. "They oughtn't look only for Jack now. They must find Biggles, as well."

Lord Benedict's brows disappeared beneath his fringe. "Biggles?"

"Her servant," George clarified.

"She's not my servant," Isabelle insisted. "I told you." She turned to Revelstoke, digging her fingers once more into the wool of her shawl and twisting. At least the movement would mask their trembling. "Her name is Lizzie Biggles, and I suppose she looks like a servant or perhaps some farmer's grandmother. She's let me live with her, but she's disappeared now, too."

Revelstoke pulled his gloves through a clenched hand. "At the same time? And you don't find that suspicious?"

Isabelle suppressed the urge to scream. "No, not at all. I've lived with her since before Jack was born. If she meant him any harm, don't you think I'd have noticed by now?"

Lord Benedict glanced past her at George, who offered no comment. "You don't think we might find her with your son?"

"I don't see how or why. She only went missing yesterday, and if she knew where Jack was, she'd never have kept me from him." She had her own suspicions about what might have motivated Biggles to leave. Guilt, since Jack had been taken from under her nose. Under all their noses. "I can't blame her. I *can't*. Not when I wasn't even here."

There. She'd voiced her failure aloud, and the world hadn't come to an end. No, it kept on turning, the better to torture her with the knowledge.

"Do you think she might have set off on her own investigation?" Revelstoke asked. "Any idea where she might have gone?"

Isabelle sifted through her mind. "She has a friend she visits on occasion, in Sandgate, but why she'd go there to look for Jack . . ."

"We'll go then." George placed a hand on her shoulder. "You and I."

Isabelle met his gaze. She wanted to search for her son. Biggles, at least, could look after herself. But the riders were already gone.

"I think you should," Revelstoke said. "It will give you something to do while we wait on news."

GEORGE would have taken a carriage to Sandgate. Despite a sky full of scudding gray clouds, Isabelle insisted they walk.

"Biggles always goes on foot and makes a day of it," she pointed out. "Besides, with the condition of the roads, walking will get us there just as quickly. The footpaths are more direct."

Horseback might have been faster, but he swallowed that argument. He was no horseman, even if Revelstoke might spare them two nags. Walking meant they'd spend less time sitting and waiting for news. If he understood anything, it was a need to act, to feel as if he was contributing to the effort of finding Jack.

By the time they reached the outskirts of the town, his feet were protesting the prolonged constitutional. The journey on Buttercup would have been more pleasant—and they still had to make their way back.

The weather had turned against them. A sharp wind

whipped the waters of the Channel to whitecaps, while overhead, the sky had taken on a uniform shade of lead. In the distance, gray sheets of rain pelted the sullen waves.

"I'd wager my last shilling we won't make it home dry," he muttered.

Isabelle hunched her shoulders beneath her shawl. "If anyone's traveling back toward Shoreford, perhaps they'll take pity on us and give us a ride."

George eyed the road that snaked its way along the steep face of the bluff down to the pebble-strewn beach. Her hope held little foundation if they must rely on current traffic. But for the groups of houses, separated by green terraces clinging to the hillside above the Channel, the place looked utterly deserted. A sad sight for the month of August when people ought to be on holiday. If ever a parade of the fashionable graced this town's promenade, no colorfully clad gentlemen or ladies strolled along the shoreline today.

"Seems as if most people had enough sense to stay home."

She caught her lower lip between her teeth. "And the riders out looking for news of Jack? They won't get far, either, and if there were any clues to be found . . ."

She didn't need to finish that statement. A solid drenching would wash any sign away. Not to mention she must be thinking of her son, praying that, wherever he was, he'd found shelter.

Still, George had to say something to brace her spirits. He hated how dull her complexion had become in the last two days. Her skin was porcelain pale to begin with, but the upheavals of late had wilted the roses in her cheeks. In contrast, violet circles darkened the delicate flesh beneath her eyes. The inner fire she'd shown him that first day—her pluck—had faded along with everything else.

He drew his palm along the line of her upper arm.

Such an insubstantial gesture, when what she really needed was to regain hope. If only he could restore it for her. "While we're here, why don't we ask if anyone's had word of Jack?"

Her brow furrowed. "Why would he be here?"

She gestured to the sleepy collection of dwellings and shops huddled about a church and a public house. The town was every bit as peaceful as the village below Shoreford, nearly nondescript in its pastoral and provincial nature. Hardly a den of kidnappers. No, the only possible crime Sandgate's citizens might possibly undertake was smuggling, and the war with France had been over for five years.

"Why would anyone steal a boy from his bed?" he countered. "They can't think to ask for ransom."

"I don't know. There's no reason behind it, and I've no money to pay ransom."

"But your father has." He said it casually, as if he were pointing out a feature of the landscape. Yes, on a clear day, you can see all the way to France, and Richard Marshall, the Earl of Redditch has more blunt than he knows what to do with. And it's not enough for him.

"My father." She seemed to seize up on the words, but she didn't question how he knew the man's identity. She'd doubtless surmised he'd learned it from her cousin. "I no longer exist as far as he's concerned. It makes no sense to hold Jack hostage in hopes of gaining anything from my father."

"And what of Jack's father?" Another stab in the dark, but in the absence of solid clues, they had to begin somewhere.

"That makes no sense, either." She lengthened her stride, tromping up the road as if she might escape the subject. "I haven't seen him since . . . since that night. Why should he turn up after all this time?"

"Did he know he has a son?"

"He didn't learn of it from me. Someone else could have told him about Jack. Gossip, mind you." She honed her words to a sharp edge, each syllable like a little blade that cut just as deep as a society dragon's vicious tongue.

And the scoundrel had abandoned her to that. He'd left her to bear the entire burden of shame, when he could have saved her.

"Perhaps you ought to tell me more about him," George ventured. A perverse sense of protection drove him to ask. What if he knew the man in question? Hell, he might even like him. Jack's father could be one of his cronies, an old school chum, someone who had grown up to haunt gaming hells, clubs and card rooms.

Someone just like him.

An image of his former mistress rose in his mind. Lucy threw back her strawberry-blond mane and laughed, deep and full throated, while running a hand over a belly swollen with his get. Goddamn it.

Goddamn him.

"I can tell you very little. You see"—she paused to swallow—"by the time I was able to discover his direction, he was gone."

Naturally, the scoundrel wanted to make himself difficult to find. All the better to avoid his responsibilities. Responsibilities such as George now had toward Lucy. Although he'd had very little to eat today, his stomach grew heavy. That damned lead weight reappeared every time he thought of his impending fatherhood. And, like a child snug within its mother's womb, that weight grew over time. Guilt added layers the way an oyster produced a pearl from a grain of sand.

"If you don't mind," Isabelle said, "I'd really rather not discuss Jack's father."

If she preferred to drop the subject, George couldn't very well object. His probing of her past shame was no doubt proving painful. And perhaps it was for the best if he didn't learn the father of her child was one of his cohorts. George would be tempted to throttle the bastard next time they ran into each other.

As they wound their way up the hill, the wind took on a finer edge that robbed their breath. A stinging raindrop or two landed across his cheeks. "How much farther?"

Isabelle nodded toward a row of houses. "The one in the middle."

He seized her hand. "Let's step lively, then. I don't fancy a drenching."

All the walking had parched his throat, enough that he'd make do with water at a pinch. If Biggles's friend didn't offer refreshment, he'd convince Isabelle to stop at the public house.

They approached a front garden overgrown with leggy, neglected bushes. The door may once have been red, but the paint had long since faded to a muddy orange. Hardly auspicious or welcoming. A glance at Isabelle showed her squaring her shoulders and raising her chin, as if she were mentally girding herself for battle.

"Do you know this friend of Biggles's?"

"I've never met Mrs. Cox, no, but I'm sure Biggles has said a thing or two about me. She'll work out who I am."

George knocked, and they waited beneath the eaves while a few more raindrops hit the ground with ominous plops. A minute or more passed before the door creaked open.

"Yes?" Mrs. Cox might have been Biggles's relative, as the two women were built along the same lines—broad-bosomed, round, and jowly. Strands of graying hair straggled from beneath Mrs. Cox's mobcap.

George gave the woman his most winning smile. It had charmed ladies in ballrooms and card rooms all across London, but apparently its power did not extend to the Dover coastline.

Mrs. Cox swung a glare from George to Isabelle and back. "If ye've come for a love potion, I'm fresh out."

The devil? George cast an alarmed glance at Isabelle, who kept her gaze firmly fixed on the threshold. Right. No help from that quarter. "Love potion? No, we—"

"Don't try to deny it." She jerked her head into a nod that set the ruffles on her cap shaking. "That's the only reason nobs like ye come round. Come all the way out from Town, they do, all smiles. Think no one will catch on they're having troubles if ye know what I mean."

"Now see here." He would have advanced on her, but she stood guard over her doorstep like Cerberus at the gates of the underworld. "I am not having troubles of a personal nature."

She crossed her arms beneath her considerable bosom. "That's what they all say."

"And if I were, I would not discuss it on your doorstep."

"I haven't got reason to let ye in. As I said, I'm out." The door lurched ominously toward the jamb.

"We're looking for Lizzie Biggles," Isabelle put in before the mud-colored plank of wood could clip George's nose. "Have you seen her?"

Mrs. Cox turned her gimlet gaze on Isabelle. "I don't know no Lizzie Biggles."

Damn. Had Isabelle led them to the wrong house?

"But that's impossible." Isabelle stretched out a hand, but the older woman remained unmoved. "She comes once a month to visit you. She was here not more than a few days ago."

"Who's been telling ye such nonsense about me? I make all my own concoctions. Highly secret recipes. I certainly don't need any help. Anyone who says otherwise is a liar."

"Who said anything about help?" Isabelle let out a huff. "I'm looking for Biggles because she's gone missing. I thought she might have come here."

"Missing?" Mrs. Cox seemed to deflate. "But if she's gone missing, how am I to—" She shook herself. "Never mind that now. I haven't seen her."

"Have you seen Jack?" George asked. Might as well try to salvage something out of all this bother.

"Young man, most of my customers tell me their name is Jack, when it's not John Smith. Which would ye be?"

"Neither. I'm George."

"Well, there are plenty of them, too. They think they can hide behind the king's name."

"Jack's more important here. He's a little blighter. Blond and lively, about so high." George held his hand at waist level. "Takes after his mother."

"Ah." Mrs. Cox nodded. "You'd be Isabelle, then."

He sensed Isabelle's stiffness. She drew herself up as if donning armor. Six years of society's judgment had no doubt taught her the reaction. "I am."

Only two words, but she'd said so much more. *Is there some sort of problem?* echoed in their passing.

"Yes, Lizzie's told me about ye." No judgment lay behind the reply, but no sympathy bolstered it, either. "And yer boy. Ye say he's missing?"

"He is."

"I'm sorry to hear it, dear, but I can't help ye find him." At long last Mrs. Cox's tone softened. "Not even Lizzie knows how to mix a potion for that."

George shifted his weight until he was leaning against the jamb. "I don't suppose you'd have an idea where Biggles might go if she hasn't come here."

"I'm certain I don't, and more's the pity."

Once again, Isabelle stretched out a hand, and this

time laid it on the older woman's forearm. "If you see her, will you tell her we were asking after her?"

"I'll do ye one better." Mrs. Cox drew her shawl more tightly about her shoulders. "I'll tell her to be sensible and go home. I haven't got any place to put her up and from what she tells me, she's comfortable enough."

"Yes, tell her that. Tell her she's needed at home."

Mrs. Cox nodded. "I'll do that."

George turned and cast a glance at the sky. The pall of clouds had not yet opened up. Rather, it spit out a drop or three now and then as a simple reminder. Or a warning. "We won't keep you then."

"Wait." Isabelle laid a restraining hand on his shoulder. "You've said you're out of love potions, but would you have anything for an upset stomach?"

Mrs. Cox's expression hardened into the glare she'd worn to answer the door. "Whatever for? The pair of ye look quite healthy."

"Not for me. It's for a neighbor boy. His mother allows him to indulge in all manner of sweets, and it affects his digestion."

"Now there's something I can manage." She disappeared into her dwelling while the clouds fired off a few more warning shots.

"I hope she hurries," George muttered.

Isabelle hunched closer, her body slight and warm against his flank. "We'll never make it home. Not if we want to arrive dry."

"Here we are." Mrs. Cox appeared and handed Isabelle a square of linen knotted into a pouch. "Infuse this into a tea, and the boy will be all set. But I suppose ye already know that."

George reached into his top coat for a few coins. "How much do we owe you?"

She stepped back, eyes narrowed, and looked him up and down. He'd seen similar expressions on society mamas, assessing his worth, deciding if his income made him worthy of courting their daughters. "Half a crown."

"Half a crown?" Isabelle protested. "That's fully three times its worth."

"Never mind." George counted out the amount. "Let the lady make some profit. She won't be selling any more love potions for a while. Not with Biggles gone."

Mrs. Cox bit down on a shilling before tossing it into the air and catching it again. "Thank ye kindly, sir."

Isabelle glared at the door after it slammed shut. "I'll be having a word with Biggles about her. Half a crown. You must realize I cannot repay you."

"No matter." George eyed the sky. The deluge held off for now, but before long, the clouds would let loose. "In fact, I'm about to spend a bit more. I could stand with something bracing. Let's see if we can't get a meal and a drink while the storm passes."

CHAPTER FOURTEEN

They nearly made it home between squalls. The first one lashed in great gusts of wind and rain against the grimy windows of the Sandgate public house while they warmed themselves with a hearty stew and mugs of ale. After an hour, the storm exhausted its fury and made for parts farther east, but halfway to Shoreford, the clouds lowered once more, and the threat of a dousing increased with every hurried step.

Beside George, Isabelle's breath came in labored puffs as they jogged up the road. "I must rest."

He cast a wary glance at the sky. Just ahead, a low wall lined the wayside to mark the boundary of Shoreford. The leafy boughs of thick-stemmed oaks overhung the road, perhaps shelter enough if the weather contained itself to a light drizzle. He took her arm and guided her to the crumbling sandstone. With a relieved sigh, she settled herself on the ledge. Arms about her knees, she rested her head on them, her face turned away. A sudden breeze stirred, and wisps of blond hair escaped their pins.

George caught himself, his hand extended in the air. The long line of her neck beckoned. His fingers itched to touch the smooth, white skin, to brush away the wayward curls and clear a path for his lips.

"What are you thinking?" he asked, as much to distract himself as to hear the reply. His voice was shockingly hoarse—and over her neck, hang it all. When was the last time a woman's nape had driven him to such a state his breeches no longer fit properly?

She turned her face toward him. Her cheeks were flushed pink. He might have mistaken their color for a sign of arousal, but for her eyes. They glimmered in the low light with unshed tears.

"Jack, of course." Her tone mirrored her expression—bleak, defeated, desperate.

Blast it, why should she pull at his heartstrings like this? He'd give everything he had to coax a smile, to hear her laugh again. All he needed was to restore her son to her.

Her son. The little blighter who managed to worm his way into the affections of even a man like George. A man for whom children were nothing but a necessary evil because he needed an heir. Eventually.

Or so his father had taught him through word and deed.

He gave in to his urge to touch her. The tips of his fingers brushed an earlobe as he fitted his palm about the curve of her neck. The vertebrae beneath his palm went rigid, and he waited for her protest. He maintained a steady pressure—not the flutter of a caress, but a solid grip.

"We'll find him."

After a moment, the tension beneath his fingers eased, and she leaned into him, shoulder to shoulder, her head resting against the side of his neck. Her breath feathered warmth against his skin.

Had he ever done this? Had he ever sat with a woman in silence and given no more than simple comfort? Before last night, he couldn't recall a single instance, any more than he could recall being satisfied with nothing beyond her presence, the soft weight of her head on his shoulder, the tickle of her hair against his cheek, the clean scent of lavender filling his nostrils.

This had nothing to do with arousal and everything to do with companionship. Never in his life, since he discovered the delights of the female body, had he suspected anything like this moment could exist. He could spend a great deal of time, seated thus, basking in her presence, while Redditch and Summersby, his creditors, and Lucy all faded into the background.

He would, of course, have to find a solution eventually, but for now he'd concentrate on Isabelle. He could restore her happiness simply and concretely in finding Biggles and her son—in restoring her family to her, such as it was. His own troubles could wait.

Thunder rumbled, a low menace in the distance. To the west, the sky filled with a pall of darker cloud. A flash of lightning stabbed through the mass, and the breeze turned sharp and cold, laden with a renewed scent of rain.

George pushed himself to his feet and extended a hand. "It looks as if our reprieve is over."

Isabelle clambered upright, her fingers curled tightly about his. She cast a worried glance toward the sky. "I'll never make it to the village before the storm."

"We may have time to make the manor." He took a step, but she remained planted where she stood. Her grip on his hand tightened.

"Come," he urged.

"No, not the manor. I won't go back there again."

Another flash of light blinded him for a moment. The crack of thunder followed shortly. "Not even if it's a choice between shelter or a dousing?"

"I'll take the dousing." Her words were clipped and grim.

Certainly some of the ladies would have fits if he brought her back to the main house. Not Julia and Sophia, but his mother was another story. Part of him wanted to take Isabelle to the manor and set her in the best parlor for that very reason. His mother had no right deciding which ladies were fit for his attention. He was nearly thirty, damn it.

But he couldn't put Isabelle through that again, not when she was already upset over her son. What's more, he recalled her behavior in Sandgate—the way she steeled herself as they entered the public house, as if someone might recognize her and accuse her of all manner of sins. "There's a cottage on the estate. We'll come to that before we come to the main house. It ought to be unoccupied."

UNOCCUPIED sounded perfect, except it meant she'd be alone with him again. She breathed in storm-laden air. Alone, she could manage. He'd proven himself trustworthy last night, and if he turned his seductive talents on her, she could resist a determined assault. She had only to keep the consequences in mind.

A flash through the sky made her jump. The answering roar sent a tremor of fear through her. She clenched her fists against it. She'd never liked storms. It was as plain as the lash of the wind against her face that she'd never reach home ahead of this one.

George reached for her hand and helped her scale the wall. He strode off through the trees across an open field. Already breathless from the jog from Sandgate, she stumbled in his wake, unable to make her legs match his gait. Another crack of thunder spurred her on.

Ahead, a second stand of trees lined the long drive to the manor, but nestled among them stood a cottage, its whitewashed walls a glimmer in the oppressive air. She

focused on that goal. Only a little farther now. But halfway across the open ground, the skies released a torrent
of ice-cold rain.

She arrived at the door of the small cottage, her clothes
plastered to her skin. Window boxes filled with gerani-
ums did little to brighten the gloom beneath cloud and
tree. George pressed his shoulder into the solid wood
plank door and shoved it aside. She tripped after him and
caught her breath. The place was dusty from disuse, but
its layout—spacious room, stone fireplace dominating
one end, beamed ceiling, rough-carved benches and tres-
tle table—reminded her of home. The place lacked only
Biggles filling it with the aroma of her cooking and the
fresh scent of herbs drying in bunches from the rafters.

George fought the wind to shut out the storm. Thunder rumbled outside while rain drummed on the roof.

"Rather a moment too late," he said. "Although we'd
have been even more bedraggled if we'd made for the
main house."

She glanced at him, eyebrows raised. "I'm not convinced that's possible."

Smiling sheepishly, he tugged at his coat sleeves. The
high-quality fabric might absorb more rainwater than
her simple cotton and linen garments, but the stink of
wet wool wrinkled her nose. Droplets clung to his hair,
and slid down his cheeks and neck to disappear beneath
his sodden cravat.

Isabelle knelt before the fireplace. Of course, no one
had thought to lay a fire. The place was uninhabited.
"The first time was more than sufficient."

"More than sufficient? What does that mean?"

She found kindling in the wood box, and enough fuel
for a few hours. They might, at least, wait out the storm
in relative comfort. "We both got rather wet the day
you pulled Jack from the Channel, wouldn't you say?"

"Ah, yes." His voice came from directly behind her.

She shivered for reasons having nothing to do with rain or storms. How on earth did such a large man move so quietly? The thought of him hovering close enough to reach out and touch without warning made the fine hairs on her nape stand on end. "Do you need any help there?"

She looked over her shoulder, straight into his gray eyes. He crouched behind her, near enough that the heat of his body radiated into her, warmed her skin beneath her dripping clothes. "What do you know of laying a fire?"

"Plenty. I had to learn at school, didn't I?"

She pressed her lips together and nodded. "I had to learn of necessity. I'll manage."

He reached around her and took her hand in his. The pad of his thumb brushed across the back of her hand. Then he turned it over and traced the lines of her palm. She had to will herself not to move, not to lean into the touch or close her fingers about his.

Her hand trembled, skin mottled with the chill, but at the same time, heat raced to her cheeks. He was tracing calluses, not the smooth palms of a woman who spent her days stitching or painting and her nights attending parties. That was the sort of hand he was used to, the hand he expected, soft and yielding. Since her arrival in Kent, her hands had known nothing but work.

She pulled away from his grip. She didn't want the scrutiny of a man whose hands were still as soft as hers once were. Not when he might somehow see through her and realize she wished her hands were untouched.

"Isabelle."

She dropped the sticks she'd just pulled from the wood box. They clattered onto the hearth. "Let it be," she murmured to stave off the questions she could feel hovering in the air between them, as heavy as the storm clouds outside and just as menacing.

"You're a lady. You still speak like one."

Just as she feared, he had read her mind. She stared at the beginning of her fire. If she concentrated hard enough on placing the kindling just so, she might ignore the memories of her former life. She might ignore the flood of feeling that rose in her gut along with the images of balls and social calls and gowns and teas. She gritted her teeth and clutched the wood until her fingernails lodged in the bark. "If I don't get a fire going, we'll freeze."

Something soft hit the floor with a sodden thump. She glanced sideways. His topcoat lay in a puddle of water. The flint tumbled from her boneless fingers and struck a spark on the fieldstone hearth.

"What are you doing?" She would not look. Could not. Already the image of him, his breeches plastered to his thighs after his dip in the sea was etched into her brain. She did not need to accompany it with the sight of him in a wet shirt. The linen would be transparent. He might as well be bare-chested. Oh, God.

"Once I get the fire going, we'll be fine." Even her voice shook now. It was only because she was soaked and miserable. In no possible way was her trembling due to him or the fact he was disrobing.

Something else thumped to the floor. That had to be a boot. Her heart skittered in her throat. If he was removing his Hessians, his breeches wouldn't last much longer.

"Your clothes will dry more quickly if you're not wearing them."

She scrambled for the flint, tried to strike it, but once again, it slipped from her fingers. What on earth was the matter with her? *You're alone with a man again, and this time, he's disrobing behind you.*

Not just any man, one she found far too attractive.

One she wanted to see unclothed. One she wanted to touch and taste. One she could not have.

The risk isn't so great, a traitorous thought prodded. *You can't be so unlucky a second time.*

Her courses were nearly upon her. She'd learn the truth soon enough if she took the chance. But she wasn't taking the other hazards into consideration. If she lay with him—if she gave him her body—could she do so and preserve her heart?

She didn't think so. Not this time. Everything he'd done for her—from saving Jack that first day, to doing all he could to find her boy now, to remaining by her side so she wouldn't face the night alone—had already carved out a place in her memory. He would leave Kent and return to Town, but she would always carry a piece of this man in her mind, entwined with the clear notes of his fingers striking the piano keys, enmeshed with the pleasure he'd already wrung from her, comfort mingled with ecstasy.

"I will not undress in your presence." No matter that he'd already seen a great deal. No matter he'd already kissed her in the most intimate, shocking manner possible.

"Pity, that."

She whipped her head about to glare at him for his cheek. A colossal mistake. He stood, his shirt dangling from one hand. Drops of rain dripped from a sleeve, but her gaze barely halted there. It followed the contour of a corded forearm, across the bulge of his biceps to his shoulder. The back of her throat dried, and the simple act of breathing became a chore. His chest was broad and muscled, as if a sculptor had chiseled each perfect ridge. The hair scattered across that expanse of skin tapered into a line that arrowed down to his navel and disappeared beneath the waistband of his breeches. The fine wool still encased his thighs, the fabric so tight she could well imagine what lay beneath, and it was just as fine-hewn as the rest of him.

She opened her mouth to protest but managed no more than a squeak, more frightened mouse than admonition. And she was frightened—of her body's demands. For her fingers itched to trace the solid planes of his chest, to feel the leap of muscle beneath her touch, to chart the places on his body that would elicit a groan or a tremor of pleasure.

His low chuckle pulled her back to reality. "Perhaps I should light the fire."

He knelt beside her, damp tendrils of hair flopping into his eyes. He could not possibly be cold. Heat radiated from his body and settled over her, not enough to halt her trembling, but enough to change its character. She wrapped her arms about herself to mask the reaction. Water from her gown moistened her hands.

He struck the flint and ignited the tinder. Crouching closer, he blew encouragement at the base of the flame. Firelight soon gilded the planes of his chest and the muscled delineation of his arms and shoulders.

And heavens, the magnificently firm backside encased in nothing but breeches. The way the wool fabric molded to taut curves was positively indecent. The small amount of moisture lingering at the back of her throat evaporated. Good gracious, if she had an extra shilling to her name, surely she could bounce it off that steely flesh.

He sat back on his heels, hands flat against his thighs, and eyed her sidelong.

She looked away, straight into the dancing flames, and hunched over, hoping the small blaze might ease her shivering.

"I believe there's a bedchamber of sorts." George nodded over his shoulder at a door in the opposite wall.

"We might find blankets to wrap about ourselves while we wait."

"That sounds like a perfect solution to our predicament." Perfect indeed.

While he plodded to the other room, she scrambled to her feet and began working at the fastenings of her dress. Heaven forbid he decide to play lady's maid with her, now that she was awake to remember it. To experience his touch once more. Out of necessity, she had learned to manage even the intricacy of stays without help, but now when she was in a hurry before George came back, the knots of her laces quite defeated her efforts. Water had caused the cord to swell, and her shaky fingers only added to her difficulty.

"Do you need help?" His voice rumbled just beneath her ear. How did he manage to move so soundlessly?

"I'll be just fine."

"Of course you will."

His warm fingers pushed hers aside. She held herself rigid while he tugged at her laces. God help her if he touched her, but he couldn't possibly undo her stays without his knuckles brushing her back. At the glancing contact, her knees threatened to give way, and she remembered the previous night when he'd caressed her with purpose. She wanted nothing more than to melt against him, to rest her back against the breadth of his chest and allow him to support her for an hour or two.

His breath feathered along her neck, rhythmic little wafts of warm air that increased in tempo as he worked. Something deep inside clenched at the realization. He was reacting. He wanted just as badly. Perhaps needed . . . Any moment now, he might give in to the temptation and press his lips to the pulse that fluttered just beneath her ear.

Oh, please.

Her stays loosened and fell to the floor in a sodden heap. She stood, clad only in her chemise, and waited. The back of her neck burned at the thought of what he must be staring at. The thin cotton of her undergarments must be all but transparent.

She breathed. In. Out. If she concentrated on something so basic, she might keep control. Might not turn and run her hands over his flesh like some brazen trollop.

A scratchy weight settled over her shoulders. The blanket. She drew in a long lungful of air. Relief and frustration mingled as she let it out again. When she opened her eyes, he'd moved to stand before her, a dark swath of wool shrouding his bare chest. He watched her from beneath half-lidded eyes as if waiting—waiting for her to set the pace.

A current streaked through her at the thought, as if a stroke of lightning had taken up residence inside her. He was handing her the power to decide. If she wanted him, she need only make a move, and he would restrain his passion no longer. And if not, if she hesitated, then . . .

He tore his gaze away and moved to the bench. "I'm sorry this trip has been a loss."

"It's hardly your fault." She pulled the blanket more tightly about her shoulders, shocked she could even reply in a coherent fashion.

He settled his weight on the plank of wood, leaving space beside him. Space for her, if she so chose. "Over and above hoping we'd get some word on Jack and Biggles, I thought we could make some sort of outing of this."

She met his gaze. Heavens, he was serious. "An outing?"

"Well, yes. I suppose it's a novel concept, but such

things are all the rage in Town. Getting away, doing something different, like strolling along the beach."

Strolling along the beach—just as she and Jack had done the day she'd met George.

"A pity the weather decided not to cooperate," he went on, "but we still might make the best of it."

As if he were courting her. A ridiculous notion. He was merely attempting comfort. No respectable man would court her. Despite the fire, a chill passed through her, and she drew the blanket more securely about herself.

Eyeing her, George patted the empty space next to him. "Why don't you sit? You've been walking half the day."

Unlike his words to her earlier, he kept his tone and expression deliberately neutral, all hint of seduction vanished. He'd read into her actions, then. Even if they were alone and likely to remain stranded here long past nightfall, she would not step heedlessly into his arms, no matter what her body demanded. Not again. Not when she knew the pleasure he was capable of granting her.

She dropped to the seat next to him, and he made no move to touch, no move to embrace her. Awareness of the action—of what he *could* try—arose from the very absence of the attempt. A silence fell between them, during which her mind filled with a single thought: *He's so good to me.* He was. All his actions, from rescuing Jack to last night to paying for Peter's stomach remedy and her meal at the public house, were selfless. She found herself shuffling her feet, the worn soles of her shoes a mere whisper against the wooden planks.

"I don't suppose anyone's spirited away a pack of cards or some such," she said, to fill the space between them. She needed to fill the silence with words, to fill the emptiness with pointless amusements, anything to hold back the reminder of their circumstances.

"I doubt it. This place doesn't see much use." His voice

cracked on the final syllable, and he broke into a fit of coughing.

She angled herself toward him to find his face red, as he hacked into his fist, an odd, false cough, one she suspected might have been a laugh under different guise. "What is it?"

He cleared his throat. "Naught but a memory."

"Of this place?" She glanced at the layer of dust on the mantel. "If you've a memory to make you react like that, you must have been here to some nefarious purpose."

"Oh, I was. Not the most nefarious, mind you, but bad enough."

When he didn't clarify, she prompted, "Are you going to leave it at that? If you've a story to tell, out with it. We may as well fill the time."

"I couldn't possibly." He leaned into her until she felt the ghost of his breath warm on her neck. "It's far too scandalous."

A wicked gleam sparked in his eye—or perhaps it was a reflection of the firelight. Either way, that flash dared her to prod. "I expect no less of you. What did you do? Lead some poor girl astray?"

He drew himself up slightly, surprised, no doubt, that she'd hint at her own situation. And why had she? If he was a seducer of innocents, she was better off remaining ignorant. But part of her already insisted he'd done no such thing. He could have seduced her last night, if he'd chosen, when he had her open and willing on the table. Yet he'd denied himself the ultimate pleasure.

"That wasn't me," he said. "That was Revelstoke."

"What?" She couldn't fathom the notion. The man she'd met appeared so upright and staid.

"Of course, the poor girl in question is now his wife, so it worked out in the end."

"And what did you have to do with that?"

"He dispatched me to bring a special license."

"Your scandal is becoming more respectable by the moment. I'm beginning to think you nearly entered the church." She couldn't resist the gibe just to see his reaction.

"Oh, now they definitely wouldn't have me." Not with a grin that promised all manner of sin, no.

An answering smile stretched her lips. And yet she wanted to dispute his statement. He might fancy himself sinful and unrepentant, but beneath that front lay an inherently good man. She opened her mouth to tell him so, but a blinding light bathed the cottage in white for an instant. The clap of thunder that followed shook the roof. Her heart jumped a mile or more, and the stab of fear cut the bottom out of her stomach.

George reached for her and pulled her against his chest. "All right there?"

She swallowed her racing heart back into its usual spot. "I will be."

He settled his arms about her, his fingers tangled in the wisps of her hair. "It'll be over soon."

She inched back. "Will it?"

"The storm, yes."

"But we're still no closer to finding Jack. The riders won't have got far. Any clue will be washed away in this deluge."

He swept his hands to either side of her face, fingers splayed across her cheeks, and forced her to meet his gaze. Sincerity and intensity entwined in the gray depths of his eyes. "We will find him."

"You cannot promise me that."

He leaned closer until his breath wafted across her lips. "It's not a promise. It's a vow."

A vow. George caught himself before he shook his head. What the hell had he just done? Sworn to an impossibility, perhaps. Not only that, he'd laid his own plans aside to focus on Isabelle's difficulties.

He ought to know better, but something about her moved him. Something about her aroused a need in him to protect, and at the moment, she needed protection from her own thoughts and fears. She needed her son back.

She stared at him, unblinking, eyes huge and round beneath the shadow of her brow. When he put his arms about her, his only intention had been comfort and support. Seduction was out of the question. She'd sent him a clear message on that score, and damn it all, he'd respect her wishes.

Still, he couldn't prevent his fingers from testing the softness of her cheeks, a gentle caress of affection, not arousal.

Her lips parted, and she emitted the tiniest gasp. Good God, she was skittish. Skittish yet vulnerable to his attentions. Try as she might, she couldn't completely hide her reaction. Images of her response to him the previous night filled his mind. Like a dream, they unwound before him, and he experienced once more her cries, her movement against him, her body's salt taste, the way she'd opened to him. Trusted.

What he wouldn't give to witness that again. Here. Now.

"Isabelle." He touched her again, more boldly this time, the pad of his finger tracing her cheek to skate across her lower lip. "If I kissed you now, would you allow it?" Another pass with his fingertip. The flesh beneath it was warm and moist and invitingly pink. "Would you allow it or would you slap me?"

She did not shrink away. Thank God. "I shouldn't allow it, but I'd be discourteous to return all your kindness with a slap."

He inclined his head until his brow rested against hers. "You should allow it."

"I should?" She wanted to, certainly. Her unwavering gaze, the husky note to her voice, her utter focus on him all indicated he held her in thrall.

He inched closer until his lips were a hairsbreadth from hers. "I believe it's customary to seal a vow with a kiss."

CHAPTER FIFTEEN

THE WAY he'd been looking at her, she was expecting an assault to rival what she'd lived last evening. But he kept this kiss light and easy, a simple give and take of his mouth against hers. A dance, but not a waltz. No, this kiss was more akin to a reel, meeting and pushing away, together and back again. Not demanding, yet arousing.

Arousing because she now knew what he was capable of.

But then he eased away to tuck her into an embrace. One palm fitted to the back of her head, he pressed her into the crook of his shoulder. Her cheek stuck to his dampened skin.

She breathed in his rich scent and listened to the steady rhythm of the rain drumming on the roof. The fire crackling on the hearth scattered the shadows of the deepening evening and lent warmth. But the true heat in this room emanated from him. It penetrated the thin layer of her chemise and set her nerves aflame.

Her breasts felt heavy pressed against him, heavy and full and sensitive almost as they had when she was expecting. He drew in air, and his hand skimmed along her neck, tracing a deliberate caress to her waist. She quivered.

He shifted slightly, and she raised her head to find him contemplating her. His eyes caught the fire's glow and reflected it with hunger. The air about them thickened, and her lips parted. He'd lent her comfort, but the atmosphere between them had become charged with a different energy.

One that quickened her pulse and made her breath come in shallow spurts. One that demanded she set her tongue to the notch at the base of his throat and taste the salt of his skin. One that urged her hands to explore the broad planes of muscles that banded his chest, to feel them ripple beneath her fingertips, to search out the places on his body that would elicit a groan, a hiss, a shudder . . .

"Isabelle," he whispered, "if you don't stop looking at me like that, I shall not be responsible for my actions."

"How am I looking at you?" Her question ought to have been a challenge, but instead, it emerged from her lips in a seductive purr.

He leaned his forehead against hers. His lips hovered less than an inch from her mouth. She could nearly taste his breath. "Like you're ready to devour me on the spot."

Dear Lord, was she so transparent? "Oh."

"Believe me, my dear, I should like nothing more."

He closed the gap between them all too briefly, his lips a fleeting brush against hers. She tried to follow, tried to prolong the contact, but he eluded her.

A flash of lightning bathed the cottage in brilliance for an instant, followed by a low growl of thunder.

"It seems we shall be stranded for quite a while." Still that yearning note in her voice. Why couldn't she be sensible around him? Why must she continue to play with fire whenever he was near? Not simply fall the way she had the first time, but leap into the flame. Already her foot teetered on the brink of a precipice.

"Yes, it does."

She leaned toward him, caught his lips with hers, but

once again, he pulled back before a true kiss could take hold.

"Before we take this too far," he added, "I need something from you."

"What?"

"Your assent." He kissed her temple. "Your trust." Another brush of his lips against her brow. "I ask a great deal, you see, but never more than you're prepared to give."

She lowered her lids against the intensity in his gaze. He wanted her, of that there was no doubt. Seduction laced his tones, but it was enmeshed with something else—caution, perhaps. A readiness to stop, should she call a halt. And he was letting her know now, before desire sunk its claws in too far, before lust clouded their judgment and urged them on.

Ironically, the knowledge made her decision all the more difficult. He was placing the power in her hands, allowing her the lead. It was a singular moment in a life that had always been guided by the dictates of others— her family, society, circumstance.

When she'd trysted with Jack's father, she didn't know what she was letting herself in for until it was too late. He'd pushed her to the point of lust-fogged judgment all too easily, and then her body had taken over and responded to his and kept on responding until her virginity and her reputation lay in the tatters of her ball gown.

But this was different. *George* was different. He'd been nothing but a support to her through these last worry-filled days, always there, always solid, always doing his utmost to find her son. And now he'd given this gift, beyond price, to her who had once possessed every possible luxury.

She knew the value now, having lost it all. And she also

knew this: She'd willingly trade all of these if it meant getting her son back. She owed George.

But she shouldn't do this because she owed him. She should do this because she wanted. Because she cared, and how could she not? Cared because he'd given, yes, but more than that. His charm, his wit, his nonchalance, his willingness to tell the rest of society to bugger themselves. How she wished she possessed such courage.

And that was just on the surface. He possessed a depth, one he kept well hidden, but she'd witnessed it that evening in the ballroom when he'd sat at the pianoforte and let the music flow through his fingers. He'd let her in that night and shared with her a secret piece of himself he shared with no one. Not even his longtime friends.

He caught her chin in the palm of his hand, his long fingers splaying about her jaw. Her heartbeat raced onward. She'd waited too long to reply.

He would withdraw now. He'd leave her untouched, and when the rain let up, they'd each return to their separate worlds—she to her empty home in the village and he to the crowded manor where he felt utterly alone.

Where had that thought come from? It had popped into her mind, but her gut reacted to it, and she knew it for the truth. This charming wit of a man who easily surrounded himself with family, friends, acquaintances, who eased through life with a smile and a snappy rejoinder, was essentially alone in the world, because none of that was him. None of the façade he presented to the *ton* was real. It was armor, a shield to protect his essential self from ridicule.

"Wait," she whispered.

"I am waiting, waiting for your reply."

She swallowed. "Yes. The answer is yes."

That one word sent a jolt through him. She felt its tremor beneath her thighs. "Yes what?"

Still wary. Still ready to withdraw before they got carried away. She *wanted* to be carried away—with him. Only with him.

"Yes, you have my assent." She leaned close and pressed her lips to his. "You have my trust." Another kiss, this one longer, more lingering. "You have me. For as long as you want me."

With a groan, he tightened his embrace and drew her into a devouring kiss that stole her breath. His tongue swept between her parted lips, and she gladly responded. Too long. Too long her feelings had been deadened. What joy to discover them once again, and so much more intense than she recalled. Each thrust of his tongue, each brush of his fingers against her throat, her temples, her nape elicited a pulse of pleasure that rivaled what she'd experienced last night.

A growl emerged from deep in his throat, and the sound released an answering throb in her belly. Not close enough. Not even with the negligible barrier of her thin cotton chemise between them. She wanted his skin against hers.

All of it.

She wanted to wrap her arms and legs about him and pull him into herself. She wanted to be filled with him, to merge so completely that both of them ceased to exist as separate entities.

His insistent tugs at her hips sent her scrambling, and somehow she landed in his lap without their lips breaking contact. Her fingers plunged into his hair, and beneath her bottom, the hard length of his arousal pulsed insistently through his breeches.

Her core throbbed in response, aching for him. She pressed her thighs together in a vain effort to ease the delicious discomfort, and he groaned into her mouth.

He tore his lips from hers, leaving them swollen and tingling, while his breath puffed warm and shallow against her cheeks.

"If you don't sit still," he rasped, "I shall go quite mad."

She grinned. She couldn't help it. The sheer need driving those words unleashed a torrent of utter wickedness. Slowly, deliberately, she canted her hips. "Perhaps I want to drive you mad."

His breath released on a hiss, and his eyes seemed to roll back for a moment. Then he seized her by the hips and turned her until she faced him. Somehow, he wedged her knees on either side of his flanks so that the delicious, hard length of him pressed just where she wanted it. "Then let's do it up right, shall we?"

He shifted his hips beneath her, a thrust that sent a spark of pure pleasure arrowing from the apex of her thighs to her womb. Heat radiated through her limbs. She dug her fingernails into his bare shoulders, closed her eyes and arched her back.

"God, so beautiful," he muttered, the sound a low rasp in his throat. "Just as you were last night." He set his lips at the base of her neck and gathered her close. Through the thin layer of her cotton chemise, her nipples peaked against his chest. Warmth and power welled from him to her.

Beneath her fingertips, the muscles of his shoulders bunched. His lips slid along the column of her neck, his tongue tracing a path to the spot where her pulse raced. He nibbled, and she jerked against him. The movement elicited a groan, while sending another jolt to her midsection. Her inner muscles clenched on nothing, and her ache for him expanded.

Lord above, it would take so little to complete their joining. Nothing but a couple of flicks to release the fall of his breeches, to release *him*. A slight adjustment, and she could sink onto him, letting her weight multiply the sensation of being utterly filled with him.

And she was ready. Heavens, she was ready.

She slid herself along his length and felt the moisture seeping from her. She repeated the motion, gasping as the knot of desire tightened in her midsection. She thought of that wonderful rush of ecstasy he'd shown her with his tongue and his fingers buried deep. It lurked within once more, elusive, but each movement brought her closer.

"Please."

She buried her face against his chest, breathing in his scent, panting. A thin sheen of sweat coated his skin, stuck her to him. She closed her eyes and let herself feel. Experience. Surround herself with him. With George.

This was nothing like some hasty encounter in a darkened drawing room, each movement furtive, each sound from without like an alarm that they might be caught at any moment. Here, the world receded until only the pair of them existed, only, soon, they as a pair, as separate man and woman would cease to exist altogether.

"Please, please."

His hand slipped along her thigh. She drew in a harsh breath in anticipation of his touch just *there*. Yes, there. Oh, yes. Oh, God, yes. His fingers parted her flesh, explored among her folds until his thumb grazed the spot.

She turned her face into his shoulder, pressed her lips against his heated skin, tasted him. He moved with her, his thumb on that bud of flesh, his erection beneath, thrusting in a mimicry of their ultimate joining. The pleasure rushed in on her, a great wave that rose, crested, and crashed until it engulfed her. Its salt filled her mouth. It tore the air from her lungs and left her gasping on a wordless scream of joy so powerful, so all-encompassing she could die of it.

Part of her, in fact, just might have.

He'd taken her fear into himself, taken her need, and now he'd taken another, far more essential part of her. Joy, pleasure, and pain combined, and she gave it. She gladly gave it for him to possess as long as he would.

And they were, as yet, clothed after a fashion. She opened her eyes. Her mouth was plastered against his shoulder, agape, her tongue tasting his skin—and something coppery. Blood.

She jerked her head upright. "Heavens. I've bitten you."

His laughter vibrated through his chest. "That you did, but I believe you might still make it up to me."

He took her hand and pressed her palm to the spot. Beneath her fingertips, his heart beat, rapid and powerful.

"Better already," he whispered. "Just keep touching me."

The note of harshness in his voice, the insistent thrust of his erection between her legs reminded her they weren't finished yet. Not tonight. Tonight he wouldn't be content with her pleasure alone. He was about to demand his due.

A tremor of renewed desire thrummed through her. Oh, yes, his pleasure would be hers, as well, the ecstasy shared and redoubled. She watched from beneath half-lidded eyes as her fingers traced along the plane of his chest, swirled a pattern through the crisp hair scattered across it.

His breath hitched. She glanced up to find his eyes closed. His fingers curled into her waist, holding her steady in his lap while she explored. Her nail grazed the raised disc of his nipple, and his grip on her tightened. She circled the tiny peak, marveling at its soft texture.

A tremor passed through him—it passed through her

as well, shuddered through her core, where they were pressed so intimately together. She thought of his tongue on her nipple when he'd kissed her breasts last night, when he'd drawn her into his mouth and suckled. Such exquisite pleasure. She tapped the tiny knot beneath her fingertip. What if . . .

Before her mind could complete the question, she dipped her head and licked. His entire body jerked beneath her, and a groan burst from his lips. She kissed the spot again, allowing her tongue to circle and savor the taste of him, the musky scent of his arousal. His fingers threaded through her hair, holding her in place, while she grazed the sensitive flesh with her teeth. His breath rushed between his lips in shallow pants, as if he'd run five miles.

Emboldened by his reaction, she let her hands explore further, down the ridges of his abdomen, tracing the line of hair that extended from his chest to his navel, and lower.

Lower, it disappeared beneath the waistband of his breeches. Two flicks—that's all it would take to release him from the confines. She wriggled on his lap, bringing forth another groan as her sensitive flesh tortured the length of his arousal. Her hand slipped to the left button, but unfastening it required too much concentration the way her fingers trembled with anticipation.

He grunted and stiffened. He straightened his spine— somehow he'd slumped, his back against the edge of the table. How they'd managed not to crumple into a heap was anyone's guess.

His hand encircled her wrist. "Hold on a moment," he rasped. "I believe we'll be more comfortable in the bedroom. You deserve better than a tumble on a wooden bench."

She focused on the fingers curled just above her hand. "It isn't as if it's my first time."

He slid his free hand from the back of her neck to her jawline. His thumb traced the curve of her cheek. "It isn't a question of first time or tenth or hundredth time. It's a matter of what you deserve."

"What I deserve?" she echoed. She had all she deserved in a tiny cottage in a godforsaken village in Kent. After she disgraced her family, they hadn't even deigned to give her that much. She couldn't deserve any more—or a hard bench or a rough wooden table or, at most, a straw-filled mattress covered in musty sheets.

"What you deserve is the finest linen, feather mattress, a canopy, velvet hangings." He arched a brow. "Cherubs, perhaps?"

"Oh, no, not cherubs." She tamped down the urge to giggle over his sudden, fanciful turn.

"Just as well. I doubt we'll find any in there." He nodded toward the door on the opposite wall. "However, there is a bed of sorts." He clasped her about the waist and set her on her feet. "We might make use of what we have."

She wobbled for a moment, her knees shaky. His mood had changed so quickly, from dark and intense, to playful in the space of a sentence. She studied his expression as he pushed himself upright. The hunger still flickered in the depths of his eyes, but he'd exerted an effort to quell it. To rein it in.

Then it struck her. He was steeling himself to stop, even now. Even after she'd fallen apart in his arms without promise of repayment. He would let her go once again—in case she was still fearful of the consequences of this evening, he would allow her to withdraw while there were none. Before she placed herself in danger of conceiving again.

Once more, he was giving her a choice. Giving her power, and the power, in turn, lent her courage. Emboldened, she flattened her palm against the ridges of his belly, her fingers spread across its breadth. She pressed her hand into his skin, as if she might brand him with the imprint, and stood on her tiptoes to kiss the underside of his jaw. She touched the tip of her tongue to the roughness of his beard sprouting just beneath the surface, while, with her hand, she pushed downward.

Her fingers delved beneath his waistband. The slightest of sounds burst from his lips, a near nonexistent groan. He swayed toward her, actually swayed, as if he, too, was struggling to keep his balance.

Such a strong, solid figure of a man, and yet she'd weakened his knees with a bare touch. Then the floor tilted beneath her feet, but his arms encircled her, supported her, lifted her against his firm body, cradled her close as he strode across the planked flooring.

He kicked at the bedroom door, and it burst open, banging against the inner wall. She barely caught a glimpse of a white coverlet before she landed in its midst. The bed ropes groaned as he dropped beside her, his grin boyish and full of sinful promise.

An incongruous giggle bubbled to the surface, and she gave it voice. The sound echoed through the spare chamber, high and girlish and joyous. A sensation of lightness buoyed her until she felt as if she might float on the currents of air, drifting among the heights.

He stretched out beside her, the length of his body warming her in the cool air of the unheated room. He reached for her, but his touch landed first on her temple, brushing back the stray curls of her damp hair from her forehead. From there, it swept along her face, feather-light, almost worshipful, to graze her brows, her cheekbones, her lips, her chin.

Such tenderness, so wholly unexpected.

Based on her experience, she'd braced herself for an assault, sensual to be certain, but an assault all the same. Somehow this, too, this reverent caress, fit his change of mood. Not that he would hold back for much longer, not that he still doubted her intention to continue, certainly not that he was suddenly experiencing a bout of shyness.

Perhaps he, too, felt the lightness, the joy, the soaring nameless emotion that welled, bittersweet, in her heart. For sweet it was, unbearably so, but bitter, as well, for her time with him was finite. Once the house party ended, he would return to the social whirl of London. Oh, he might spend the autumn wandering from one country estate to the next, but he'd eventually return to Town, while she went back to her cottage.

If she was fortunate, she might see him once a year for a week or so, before he moved on. Or perhaps that would be her misfortune, to have him come back from time to time as a reminder of what she might never have. This tenderness on a regular basis. A pair of strong arms willing to wrap themselves about her and lend her comfort.

She oughtn't venture down this path that led only to heartbreak, but she wouldn't for anything leave this bed. Not when he touched her so reverently. Not when he pulled her flush with his body and rolled her beneath him. Not when he captured her lips in a kiss that soon turned carnal.

His mouth moving on hers, his weight bearing her into the mattress, his hands trailing fire along her ribs, down her flanks, reaching for her thighs and the hem of her chemise, all of it scattered rational thought and drowned her in a sea of pure sensation.

His musk surrounded her, blocked everything but the pressure of his lips over hers, the short bursts of their breathing, the cool air that rushed between them as he pulled the last scrap of cotton from her body.

The barest flicker of the small fire penetrated from across the main room, casting the bedchamber in hues of gray, enough to make out the expression on his face once her eyes adjusted. And how much could he see of her naked form? She blushed, its heat radiating from her chest to creep up her face and lose itself in her hairline. She'd never been so completely exposed before any man, never so vulnerable.

Never so alive.

He breathed in sharply, a rough, harsh sound in the blackness. He bent, touched the tip of his tongue to her breast, drew the aching peak into his mouth. She arched off the bed, directly into his touch—into him. She grasped at his bare shoulders for purchase, and he became her sole anchor in a world spinning off its axis.

His knee slid along hers, the wool of his breeches rough against her sensitive skin, providing a counterpoint to the sheer pleasure of his hands. Fine, soft hands that had never known a day's work, that had never known more abuse than the abrasion of a pair of reins, cushioned by leather gloves.

So unlike her hands now. She slipped her palms along his back, enjoying the jump of muscle beneath the smooth skin. Her callused fingers caught on his flesh as she explored. She pressed to his waist and lower, digging her fingers beneath his breeches, kneading the rise of his taut buttocks.

With a grunt, he reared to his knees. His fingers made quick work of the remaining buttons, and he kicked free of his breeches—the last barrier between them.

She pulled him back to her, her lips seeking his. His erection probed at her belly, the tip leaking moisture. His knees settled between hers. She parted her thighs for him, tilted her hips, and braced herself for the remembered discomfort of a man's body invading hers.

She pressed her palms down his spine to his rump, tried to push him into her, even as she gritted her teeth.

He tore his lips away from hers. "No, not yet."

She released her breath. "What?"

"Not yet. Relax."

Relax? How was she supposed to relax with him poised on the brink of plunging into her? Of hurting her for a brief moment or two? But she was ready to bear the discomfort to appease the demands of her body. She ached too much, ached for him as she'd never ached for Jack's father. As she'd never ache for another man, ever.

"Relax," he insisted. "You're thinking too much. Feel."

He bent toward her and caught her lips with his. A gentle kiss, easy and tender, but underneath he shook with the effort of restraining himself. Muscles quivered beneath her fingertips, brimming with a wild energy he held in check. Like the pleasure he'd drawn from her on two occasions now.

At the thought of that rush of joy, her inner muscles clenched, longing to hold him. Fire raged through her at the idea of experiencing it again, only this time, she'd take him with her. Who was she to deny him after all he'd given her?

She returned his kisses, but at the same time slipped her palm across his back, over his hip. Her fingers brushed through coarse hair before meeting with hardened flesh. He sucked in a breath as she fit her hand about him. His flesh pulsed against her palm, the skin smooth and soft over the underlying rigidity. So solid, so hard.

Heavens, it must pain him.

She ran her hand along the length, and he groaned, his head sagging against her shoulder, the soft tips of his hair caressing her skin. A shudder passed through him, and he ground his hips against her palm, his breath shallow and harsh.

"Stop," he panted. "Stop before you unman me."

She couldn't imagine such a thing. How could he ever be less than a whole, vibrant man? Her man. Hers.

"Then come to me." The words burst from her throat—from her heart—with an animal ferocity. Her need for him far outweighed any vestige of fear, any apprehension. This was their moment, possibly the only one they'd ever have, but she meant to take it, meant to live again for a brief time with all the enthusiasm, all the recklessness that had led to her downfall.

It didn't matter. She'd done six years' worth of penance. It was time to take back a little of the joy she'd lost.

"Easy. I don't wish to hurt—"

"You can't hurt me any more than I've already been hurt." She curled her fingers about his length and raised her hips.

The tip of his erection met her entrance, and she gritted her teeth as he began to penetrate, slowly—too slowly. Her body stretched to accommodate him, not painful, not even uncomfortable. No, the fullness inside her felt right. It felt incredible. She clutched at his shoulders and wrapped her thighs about his flanks.

Ah, perfect.

He slid home—slid easily, as if she'd been made to receive this one man. She stretched beneath him, craned her neck, and pressed her lips to his throat.

He trembled, and she felt it within, without, beneath her fingers and inside her body where he filled her.

"Please." Her harsh whisper echoed in her ears. She knew what came next. If he didn't move soon, she'd go mad. "Please. You don't need to give me time to get used to this." Lord knew Jack's father hadn't.

Her heart swelled in her chest at the idea of George giving her what she'd missed the first time—consideration. Even now he put her needs ahead of his.

Another tremor passed through him, igniting flames along each of her nerve endings.

"Can you stand it if I pound you through the mattress?" He pitched his voice low, but each word dripped with tension. "God only knows I want to, and if you beg me one more time—"

"Please."

He let out a groan, and, at last, withdrew almost completely. He filled her again with a powerful thrust that left her gasping, not in pain but in the sheer ecstasy of such complete possession. He surged into her again and again, and each stroke drove her higher. She cried out and arched her back, letting him sweep her along with his passion.

Somehow her body managed to keep pace with his. She pressed her hips into his, her nails digging into his shoulders as her teeth had marked him earlier. He hissed his pleasure, his features twisted and animal.

A part of her wondered at herself for not finding him ugly in such a moment, but there was a wild beauty to him now. This view of him—so intimate, so close to his essential self—could be nothing less. And his expression must be mirrored on her face.

He pushed himself up onto his elbows, reared up against the ceiling, filled her vision, and with the movement, the angle of penetration changed. Her eyes widened. With every thrust, he struck at a new spot within her, achingly sweet.

Yes.

Her breath tore from her lungs now. She moaned and whimpered and pleaded while the tempo increased.

Yes.

Harder and harder, and with every surge of his body, he pushed her toward the brink.

Oh, yes.

Somehow it was higher than before. She reached, but

it moved further off. When she fell, she would fall long and hard.

God, please, soon.

Then, without warning, she was soaring, keening like a bird as she convulsed. He filled her to bursting, but her body rippled about him. Somewhere far away, she heard his answering shout, and he pulled out and away from her.

CHAPTER SIXTEEN

GEORGE SWALLOWED great gulps of air while his heart ceased its pounding and his body floated back to earth. Gradually, he became aware of the soft curves cushioning his torso.

Isabelle.

He pushed himself onto his elbows and contemplated her flushed cheeks. Her golden hair, tangled in a halo of curls about her head. Her lower lip arced in a half smile. So swollen, that lip, nearly pouty from his kisses. Its plumpness tempted him to take it between his teeth, to tease her into wakefulness, to start again.

Her breasts rose and fell against his chest, and her breath puffed out in a sigh, the very sound of contentment. A note of deep satisfaction such as he'd rarely heard from his lovers.

The warmth of pride filled his belly, and his cheeks stretched in a broad grin. Good thing she was still floating somewhere between this world and the next. No doubt she'd chide him for looking smug the moment those velvet brown eyes opened.

Hell, he felt smug. He damned well deserved it, too.

He rolled to his side before he could crush her under his weight. She was tiny beneath him, delicate and small-boned. How she'd managed to endure that onslaught . . .

But she had. She'd endured and gloried in it. Good Lord, her enthusiastic response had driven him mad, and when she climaxed around him, when her body gripped his in ecstasy and rippled along his length . . .

God, that had been a near thing. He'd been a hairs-breadth away from spending inside her.

With one hand, she groped for him, her fingers fluttering against his wrist as if she didn't quite possess the energy for a firm grip. He knew what came next. This was where his mistresses wanted to purr and preen and bask. It was where he wanted to drift away, but for some odd reason, the last thing he wanted to do now was sleep. In fact, every last nerve ending in his body fairly screamed at him to run.

He'd never in his life fled from a woman, but something had happened just now with this one, something he'd never before experienced. Tenderness of an unfathomable depth filled him. More than that, it overwhelmed and drew him under the way the waters of the Channel had tried to engulf Jack. He felt the bottom roll beneath his feet, the current sucking him under. He could fight or drown, but already the shore was nothing more than a pinprick on the horizon.

Her fingers encountered his forearm and curled about bare flesh. "Wonderful," she muttered, half-asleep.

It was possibly the most coherent thing she could utter under the influence of drowsy afterglow, but that single word encompassed so much more. She hadn't known how good relations between a man and woman could be. That much was easy enough to surmise. Hell, *he* hadn't known it could be that way—so intimate and intense and raw and deep—and he'd enjoyed the skills of more than one talented courtesan. But the relative skill wasn't so important as the response.

For all his experience, he'd never known one like Isabelle's.

Only the worst sort of scoundrel would run now and leave her utterly alone, most especially after the vow he'd made, the vow that had led to this. So he settled beside her, fitted her slight form against him, and pulled her into his arms. She rested her head on his shoulder, and her wayward curls tickled his nose. With his fingers, he combed them back from her face.

Lucy employed a maid who used hot tongs to shape her strawberry-blond locks into ringlets. Isabelle's curls formed on their own, wild, riotous, untamed. Like the woman herself, her hair had a mind of its own; it refused the kind of regimented order more fashionable coiffures required.

"How is it, after so many years, I've finally fallen on good fortune?" Isabelle murmured sleepily against the side of his neck.

"How indeed?" It was all the reply he could muster. What in blazes was the matter with him? At the least, he might invent a snappy rejoinder about his uniqueness among men, something to make her laugh and smack at him and deliver an appropriate set-down. He was long used to the sort of verbal sparring that occurred between bed-mates.

Not even lovers, but those who looked no farther than physical pleasure. With Isabelle, he was out of his depth.

"You don't regret what we've done, do you?" Less drowsiness fogged her words this time.

Oh, God, here it came—the reason he preferred mistresses and courtesans. Ladies who held no expectation beyond the pleasure they could give and receive. Ladies who wouldn't force him to examine his feelings. Not that he had any.

At least not where ladies whose name wasn't Isabelle were concerned. The devil take it all, he was a goner.

"What makes you say such a thing?" he asked carefully.

"You seem unable to relax." Her tone betrayed nothing.

He tilted his head to catch a glimpse of her expression, fully expecting to find her deep brown eyes turned on him. Analyzing. Perceptive. Piercing any barrier he might choose to erect. But her lids remained firmly closed, not as one asleep, but as if she made a concerted effort to shut out the world. "Why are you holding your eyes closed?"

"Because I don't want to lose this moment."

Her reply made him regret the question. Rather than divert the topic, he'd managed to bring it into even sharper focus, like a maid entering his chamber at noon to throw back the draperies onto a bright, sunlit day, one he did not wish to face. A flood of light after a night's carousing that invariably caused his head to pound and illuminated the stubble on his cheeks and the shadows beneath his eyes. It only served to emphasize his flaws.

"You don't have to lose it. You can hold it in your memory forever." There. That sounded sufficiently sentimental.

"Yes, and by next week, a memory is all I'll have." Another woman might have made that reply sound wistful. Isabelle stated a fact, but the fact was tinged with an edge that implied she was trying to convince herself.

"Isabelle—"

"Don't. Don't make empty promises to try to convince me otherwise."

He brushed a kiss to her hairline. "Sleep."

He tried to do the same, but his mind refused to let him drop off. Damn it, he wanted to make those promises. What was more, he wanted the words to have substance. He wanted to make them as much a vow as the oath he'd sworn earlier.

And that realization scared the hell out of him.

* * *

Isabelle awoke trembling. Shadows filled the bedroom, and rain drummed steadily on the roof. Beside her, the mattress lay cold. "George?"

Silence answered her question. She shook off the last vestiges of sleep and pushed herself upright, the soreness between her thighs a reminder of what had transpired in this room. Explicit images rushed through her mind—his hands, his lips, his tongue, his body had all combined to wring every last ounce of pleasure from her.

A shiver crept down her spine, and she groped for her chemise. The thin cotton was an insufficient barrier against the cold.

And why had George gone off when they might have blended the heat of their bodies to ward off the chill and night dampness? She padded to the other room. Empty. The fire had burned down to embers, but she didn't think she'd been asleep more than an hour.

Blast the man. The least he could have done was waited until morning. He might have allowed her a few illusions, long enough to last the night, before he stripped her of the fantasy. And what fantasy was that? That she might find a man willing to care for her, to share the burden of raising her son, to lighten her load just a little? Someone willing to bring her a little joy, a little laughter, and, yes, a little love?

Hadn't she learned the first time she couldn't depend on a man? He'd take what pleasure he wanted and abandon her. Clearly George Upperton was no better than Jack's father, even if he did come wrapped in a more attractive package. Charm and wit would ever be her undoing.

She strode to the fire and plucked her still damp gown from the hearth. George's clothes, of course, were already gone. She fumbled with the laces of her stays and shook out her skirts before easing the damp fabric over her skin. She pulled where it clung until it draped uncomfortably from her shoulders. It would have to do. She'd be more miserable by the time she returned to her cottage. Let every last raindrop that soaked her be a reminder, a layer in her armor she would use to shield herself. Men were not to be trusted.

Squaring her shoulders, she strode to the door, yanked it open—and collided with a solid wall of a man. She swallowed a cry and stepped back. The figure turned, and relief flooded her, but rather than warming her, the back of her neck heated, while her fists turned icy. "What are you doing out here in the rain? You'll catch your death of cold."

Darkness shaded George's expression. Just as well. If he was about to give her the cut, she preferred it swift and silent like the blade of a guillotine.

"I thought I'd return before you woke up." He ran his fingers down her arm, the barest of touches, but the gesture reassured. "I did not mean for you to wake alone."

"Then why didn't you come in?"

"I was trying to work out a solution." He glanced away, and she almost pictured him as a boy, hands clasped behind his back, dragging a toe through the dirt. The very way Jack sometimes acted when he'd done something laudable.

"Solution?" she prompted.

"Yes, well, I was hoping for a stroke of genius, or at least a stroke of lightning, but the storm seems to have passed. I was caught up in the absurd notion I might work out what's happened to your boy. I didn't want to come in without an answer."

"Oh." Her heart doubled its pace. And she'd doubted him after that heartfelt vow. "Oh." She stepped closer, out of the shelter of the doorway. Drops of rain struck her face and damp garments, but she hardly cared now.

"If you had something to work out, you must have some news."

"None, unfortunately. That's why my notion was absurd. I wanted to catch Revelstoke before he took himself off to bed and see if he'd heard anything from his riders."

"And?"

"It's as we feared. If there were signs to find, the rain has washed away all traces."

"Surely they'd have made inquiries at inns and such." George had already said straight out there was no word, but she couldn't hold back her plea. "As we did."

"I'm afraid the weather curtailed that bit of it, too. No one was able to get very far." Again that fleeting touch, as if he still thought her fragile. Or perhaps not her, but whatever lay between them now. "It'll likely be another day before we get a chance at any more news. I'm sorry."

"It's hardly your fault."

"Yet I am sorry for your sake."

She reached out and squeezed his arm, hoping this small token communicated what her tongue could not. He caught her hand, tangled their fingers and pressed back. Somehow the gesture felt as intimate as when their bodies had joined.

"Thank you, for everything. I don't—" Something filled her throat, blocking the rest of the sentence. Goodness, and it all sounded so final. "I don't know how I'd have got through these two days without you."

Had it only been two days? Those two days encompassed two lifetimes—Biggles's and Jack's.

"However long it takes, I'll see you through to the end." He still clasped her hand, and through that connection she felt the sincerity behind his words.

She drew in a lungful of night air, heavy with rain and the scent of the nearby sea. Life was going to be unbearable once he left. How had she allowed herself such an attachment in so short a time? Yet she couldn't deny it, even if she knew better.

"I'd kiss you, but I'm soaked again," he said through a smile.

"Then come in out of the weather." She followed his lead and lightened her tone, although the weight still burdened on her shoulders like an overlarge cloak. "You still owe me a forfeit."

His grin broadened in response, decadent, promising, sinful. He'd already fulfilled that promise once, yet her insides still melted. At last, she understood the attraction a man held for a woman. It wasn't simply the creation of a child within her. It was the pleasure in the act—at least with the right man.

"Did you have anything specific in mind? I'm yours to command."

Oh, how she wanted to take him up on that offer. Temptation nudged at her. She could ask for kisses. She could ask him to take her back to bed. She could ask him to show her something new. And yet . . . "You know what your forfeit is. I let you off last night. I'm calling for it now. You're going to play for me."

"But that would mean returning to the manor."

"I know. I'll take my chances." Besides, as late as it was, the other houseguests ought to all be in bed.

His fingers curled about her hand. "Then shall we make a run for it?"

She ducked after him into the drizzle. The rain soaked into her already damp gown and chemise, but she didn't care. George's mere presence and the lingering afterglow of his lovemaking warmed her through. They ran across the lawn toward the main house. Darkened windows overlooked the broad expanse of grass like so many blank eyes. Heedless of the growing dampness, he skirted the side of the manor.

At an out-of-the way door, he paused. "We can go in the back way. My room isn't too far from the servants' staircase."

She crossed her arms and leaned against a rough stone wall. "You have a pianoforte in your room, do you?"

"Er, no, but I have a change of clothes and a rather comfortable bed."

"Your forfeit didn't involve a bed."

He placed his palms on either side of her head and leaned enough that the warmth from his body blanketed her. "It could if you changed the terms."

"I'm not changing the terms." She ducked from beneath his embrace. "Yet. You'll have to convince me otherwise."

CHAPTER SEVENTEEN

CLAD IN dry clothes and raising a branch of candles, George slipped into the ballroom. "It's safe to come in."

The house lay in darkness, candles extinguished, fires banked. Even the servants had taken to their beds, and George had moved silently through the corridors to avoid rousing the hall boy.

Isabelle padded into the space behind him. In this room, like in George's bedchamber, the hearth glowed with the faint orange of dying embers. Crouching before the grate, he stirred the ashes until he coaxed a feeble revival from the remains of a blaze.

He glanced up to find Isabelle standing over him. "I might still lend you something."

"I won't parade about the house clad in a man's garments, even if everyone else is asleep. I'll dry out, eventually." She gestured toward the piano, lurking at the back of the space. "Your forfeit."

"Indeed. You stay here and let yourself dry, while I—"

He rolled back on his heels, pushed himself to his feet, and ventured deeper into the room. What looked like a sheaf of paper had been abandoned over on the piano bench. Someone's music? He picked it up. No, not music—the pages contained sketches. No doubt it belonged to Miss Abercrombie, she of the all-seeing gaze.

Idly, he leafed through the pages. Miss Marshall

stood, cold and composed on the first one. Miss Abercrombie had somehow managed to capture her subject's icy, superior stare in just a few deft strokes of charcoal.

On the next page, Leach grinned raffishly, the size of his teeth exaggerated. In his hand, he held a pack of cards, but an ace peeked from his sleeve. "She got that one wrong," George muttered to himself. "If he cheated, he'd win a lot more often."

The paper rattled as he turned the next leaf. Miss Abercrombie had captured Julia and Revelstoke in an unguarded moment. Their charcoal effigies stared into each other's eyes, holding one of their private, wordless conversations. The artist had all but portrayed the dialogue on the page.

At one time—not even a week ago—George would have asked one of his friends to put him out of his misery before he looked at a woman like that, all besotted and soft. Now all he could think of was Isabelle. Had she ever looked at a man with such a love-struck expression? Had she simpered over Jack's father?

The thought turned his stomach. And if she looked at George that way, what would he do? In the past, he'd have run fast in the opposite direction the moment a woman gazed on him with dewy eyes, but if Isabelle wanted to turn such an expression on him . . .

His heart sped up, but with an effort, he shook the image from his mind. He'd consider that possibility another time, ideally once he was out of her presence. When the chance of such a thing occurring in reality was remote.

In his haste, he practically tore the sketch of Julia and Revelstoke, but as soon as he'd turned the page, he wished he hadn't. Staring back at him was his own portrait.

"Whoever drew this is quite talented."

In spite of himself, he jumped. Isabelle had managed to creep up behind him.

"Talented, yes." Unnervingly so.

"Is that the way you dress when you're in Town?"

As with the other portraits, Miss Abercrombie had exaggerated a few key details. On him, it was the clothes. Somehow she'd managed to put a gleam on his boots that might have outshone the sun. His collar points rode impossibly high, until they nearly engulfed his face. His cravat was knotted into something absurdly complicated, and his hair . . .

Absently, he raised a hand to test. Just as he thought. Nobody wore his hair piled in such a ridiculous manner, not even Beau Brummell before his disgrace. Certainly not George Upperton. Was this how the world saw him then? Nothing but a useless dandy whiling away the summer and autumn months until the fashionable returned to Town and he could go back to sleeping off the days and haunting the gaming hells at night.

But that was exactly the sort of man his father wanted him to be. Shallow. Dissolute, if not quite debauched. With such lessons, George had proven himself an apt pupil.

He cleared his throat. "Not to this degree. I can't think of anyone who would."

"I can." Before he could ask her for examples, she pointed. "Did the artist know you play?"

Miss Abercrombie's penetrating gaze had seen through him. She'd sketched him standing, just as he'd posed for her outdoors, but she clearly hadn't filled in the background until later, until he'd inadvertently revealed his secret. She'd added the bulk of the piano looming behind him, and through his awkward stance, she'd managed to make it appear as if his portrait self were trying to hide the instrument from the viewer.

"Brava, Miss Abercrombie."

"You're stalling, you know," Isabelle prompted. "If I had anything to wager, I'd wager you don't wish to fulfill your forfeit."

HIS fingers stilled, and the final, pure note faded into the night. Such skilled fingers, whether they rippled across a keyboard or her body. She pulled her lower lip between her teeth at the thought.

As Isabelle Marshall, she had known dandies, such as the sketch of George portrayed. Men who spent hours deciding which topcoat went with which pantaloons, men who drove their valets to distraction until their cravats were tied just so. Self-aggrandizing braggarts. Men whose best friend was a well-polished cheval glass. Men who were just as shallow and flat as that best friend.

Something about Upperton struck her as different. With him, the emphasis on appearance was mere façade. He hid his true self behind that front, a far deeper person with far deeper concerns and, perhaps, pain.

His eyes blinked open, as if he were awakening from an hour-long trance. "Do you play?"

The question caught her off guard. "Not like you."

"You must have learned. Isn't the ability to pound a few notes out of pianoforte part of a proper young *lady's* upbringing?" A tinge of cynicism accompanied an undue emphasis on the word lady. It set her on edge. "That's how it was in my household."

"I was much better at stitchery."

He rose from the bench. "Come. Sit."

"But I've nowhere near your talent." Not to mention, she hadn't touched a keyboard in years. She curled her fingers into a fist.

"I've performed for you. I wish you to perform for me." His tone brooked no argument. At the same time, a stream of liquid warmth washed through her midsection. Part of her wanted him to perform as he had in the cottage. As he had in her kitchen.

Again, yes, again.

Perhaps if she acquiesced, this strange mood of his might turn into something more pleasurable. She took a seat in front of the keys, pausing to smooth her skirts beneath her, and set her hands the way she'd been taught—right thumb on middle C, the smallest finger of her left hand an octave below.

"It's been ages. Honestly, I'm not sure what I remember." The last time she'd sat at a piano and played for anyone had been before her debut. Just another innocent girl in white displaying her accomplishment to the *ton*. Making her family proud. "What shall I play?"

He shifted until he stood directly behind her. She fancied his breath stirred the hairs at the top of her head. "*Eine Kleine Nachtmusik.*"

"That's a serenade for strings."

"There's a piano arrangement."

"But Mozart." She dropped her hands to her lap. "Have pity."

"My sister Henrietta butchers it with shocking regularity." A surprising measure of bitterness infused his tone. "You can hardly do worse."

She nearly turned her head to look at him, but recalled just in time their relative positions. It wouldn't do to set her face in an embarrassing spot.

He leaned into her, his chest to her back, his cheek against hers. The scent of cheroot and brandy and male teased her nostrils. He placed his left hand on the keys and led her right forefinger to high G. "At least play the melody."

She depressed the keys, haltingly ascending and descending the first few measures, ever aware of George at her back, one arm nearly embracing her as his accompaniment quickly turned into counterpoint. She fumbled over a few more notes before stopping altogether. His left hand drummed out a merciless allegro rhythm. Even when she'd been in practice, she'd never have kept up.

He went on, humming the melody under his breath, until that too drifted into something unfamiliar. He kept the proper chords but changed the sequence. Improvising, the way the original composer was reputed to have done. So lost in the refrain, he hadn't even noticed she'd folded her hands in her lap.

"If you wanted Mozart," she observed, "you might have chosen one of his operas. I might at least attempt singing."

His fingers came to a rest for a moment. His right arm snaked around her, encasing her fully, trapping her against the instrument. Then he pounded several heavy chords. It wasn't until he reached a series of tinkling notes that sounded like mocking laughter that she recognized the opening strains to *The Magic Flute*. The opera, of course, had been scored for a full orchestra, but he managed to capture its spirit with a single instrument.

"I hope you don't expect me to be the Queen of the Night."

His laughter reverberated from his chest as his fingers reached for the high notes of the famous aria. "You don't like a challenge?"

"I've got enough of one in you."

His fingers came to an abrupt halt. "What's that supposed to mean? You saw my portrait. I'm a simple enough man. I like my drink strong, my wagers daring, and my women—" His hands moved from the keyboard to cup her breasts. He leaned his cheek against hers and nuzzled. "I like my women willing."

She pulled in a breath as her nipples tightened. "You're not as simple as that, not when you hide this part of yourself from the world. You ought to be in London performing for the king."

"I ought to be performing for you."

"You have been. It's been a revelation."

"I'm not finished yet." He squeezed gently and touched his tongue to her earlobe. "This was merely the warm-up."

"There you go, hiding once more."

"What I'm attempting"—he nibbled the side of her neck—"is moving along to more interesting pursuits now that I've fulfilled the terms of my forfeit."

Oh, but he was persuasive. Persuasive, seductive, a true sensualist. Another downfall loomed in her imminent future, and she would gladly plummet. But not just yet. She tilted her head and ducked away. "You are trying to distract me from the subject."

"The subject wasn't the divine way you taste right about here?" He dipped his head for a kiss, but she avoided him once more.

"The subject was Mozart. You know, the composer. The prodigy."

He pulled away, and the space between them filled with a different sort of tension. "I am no prodigy."

He pronounced each syllable with exacting precision. Let there be no doubt in her mind—or his. Was he trying to convince himself?

"There isn't a whit of shame in it."

"Tell that to my father."

His feet fell with dull thuds as he stalked away. Neither the candlelight nor the glow from the hearth was strong enough to chase the shadows from the far end of the room. But she could picture him, drawn up to his full height, shoulders squared, a frown etched across his face.

"Music," he spat. "It's a woman's pursuit. It's frivolous. It's unmanly."

She rose and followed him. "No."

"It's shameful."

"No."

"It was to my father." He tugged a hand through his hair, leaving it in spiky disarray. "Do you have any idea what it is to have this . . . this *thing* inside you? God, sometimes it feels like it's alive. It gets hungry, and it wants out. But it's a part of you, part of yourself. You'll never be free of it, but you have to deny it. You have to hide who you are, because it isn't acceptable. Do you know what that's like?"

He kept his back to her, and she wished she could see his expression, although she could well imagine. His anguished tone revealed soul-deep pain. A part of her wanted to pull him into her arms, to cradle his head against her shoulder, and run soothing fingers through his hair.

But another part of her mind recalled the past few years lived in disgrace. *You have to hide who you are.* Indeed. That part bade her cross her arms and set her foot tapping. "Yes, I believe I do."

GEORGE pressed his mouth closed. Hell, he'd never meant to reveal so much of himself, not his talent and not the pain of having to hide it. He'd never expected anyone to understand.

But Isabelle not only understood, what she had endured in the past few years trumped anything his father had put him through. Trumped, took all the tricks, and cleaned out his pockets at the turn of a single card.

A Jack, no less.

"God, I'm an ass."

"At times." Isabelle padded closer. "But your heart is in the right place. I can't think of too many men of your standing who would have taken up my cause with no expectations."

George cleared his throat. "Let's not talk about expectations, shall we? I'm afraid many of my recent actions might not appear so worthy when examined closely."

"Do you mean just now or earlier?" She'd come to stand before him, but he couldn't make out her expression in the darkness. Her tone betrayed nothing. If only she'd touch him—no more than her fingertips on his forearm and then he'd know he stood on firm ground with her.

"Last night. Earlier. Just now. All of it."

She went still long enough for a bead of sweat to trickle at his temple. The only sounds were her breath and a rustle of fabric, but at least she wasn't stalking away—or raising her hand for a slap. "You didn't seduce me last night. You comforted me."

"And just now?"

"I ought to expect you to try again where you've succeeded once. Isn't that what men do?"

Men, yes. The sort of man his father had raised him to be.

"But you haven't succeeded this time," she went on, "have you? I haven't let you. Yet."

Such promise in that one word. He reached for her, but his fingers only caught the edge of her skirt before she slipped away. "You're not making it easy."

"That's because you're going about this the wrong way." Still that hint of promise—it accented her words like a grace note.

"What other way is there?"

"Patience. Let me come to you."

"I've never been long on patience."

"And don't use seduction as a means of avoiding things you'd rather not talk about," she went on as if he hadn't spoken. "Perhaps tonight, I ought to return the favor and comfort you."

What in blazes was she talking about? Last night, she'd been frantic over Biggles and her son. He couldn't even lay claim to emotions like anger or hurt. Well, not *so* angry, not *so* hurt. He had no right to those feelings. She'd shown him as much with a simple, five-word sentence.

"So, Mr. Upperton—"

"After last night, hadn't you better call me George?"

"Mr. Upperton"—this time he heard the smile in her voice—"why don't you tell me about it?"

He shook his head, pointlessly, because she probably couldn't see it. "Tell you about what?"

"What's this thing inside you that your father so disapproved of?"

"I've shown you that. It's the music. People don't generally know—or they haven't. They will now."

"Who do you suppose I'll tell?"

"Not you. I slipped yesterday. I came in here in broad daylight to play and got lost. It does that to me. It makes me forget where I am. The next thing I knew, I had a passel of admirers."

"So far, you aren't making much of a case for needing comfort." Was that pattering rhythm her foot tapping?

"But all those young ladies know now. My *mother* knows, and if you don't think she'll nag me to perform in public, think again."

"You're not strengthening your case by any means." The woman could have been a barrister.

"What about the gentlemen at my club? What will they say?"

"I daresay you'll live it down." He could picture her crossed arms, her expression of mock severity, a smile pulling at the corners of her mouth. A comely barrister indeed.

"As I said, I'm an ass."

"Why does it *really* bother you?"

The question was far too incisive. He shouldn't answer her, not honestly, but part of him wanted to. She'd heard him play, which was more than his oldest friend could say. Of anybody, she'd heard him first. What harm to tell her part of the story? He could offer her that much, as long as he didn't reveal too much.

"I was never meant to have lessons. The music master was brought in for my sisters."

"But you wanted to learn."

"More than anything." He'd never be able to adequately express that need. "I listened to their attempts, and I knew I could do better."

A memory of himself as a boy flashed through his mind. How many afternoons had he spent lurking at the door while his sisters fumbled through their scales, his fingers itching to show them how it was done?

"Their teacher would demonstrate a new piece," he went on. "I only had to hear it once. I'd sneak out of my bed at night and play until I learned it."

"You must not have slept much."

"It took less time than you might think." He laughed, an oddly hollow sound. "Mama always claimed my sisters were prodigies, only they seized up with nerves in front of an audience. I wonder now if she heard me at night and thought it was Henny."

"Why did you hide?"

"I begged my father for lessons at first. He let me know in no uncertain terms that such pursuits were for girls and no son of his would undertake anything so unmanly as music." He stopped there. He need say no more.

"And then?"

Damn her and her perception. "My father came home from his club one night and caught me at it."

He still recalled the piece. Bach. Toccata and fugue in D minor. Learning it by ear had proven his greatest challenge yet. He'd practiced and practiced the complicated intertwining themes, slowly at first, until his fingers adjusted to the movement, and then faster to bring it to its proper tempo. He'd been close to playing it through flawlessly.

Of course, he'd become lost again. The music had taken him in like an enchantress's spell until he'd lost all notion of time. And then his father came staggering in the door, deep in his cups.

No son of mine will grow up a sodomite.

He wouldn't repeat such words to her. At the time, he'd only had a vague notion of what they meant. As Jack had repeated, *bugger.*

He nearly said it aloud. The glance of her fingers across his forearm stayed the vulgarity. Her touch fluttered to his shoulder, not yet an embrace, but threatening to become one. "What did he do when he caught you?"

"What he did best—a load of bluster." Easy enough to shrug off, but for what happened the next day. "Only he wasn't foxed enough to forget. The next morning, he swore he'd make a man out of me yet. He took me to his boxing club."

George scrubbed a hand across his face. "I rather suspect he hoped I'd break my knuckles."

Isabelle leaned closer—enough that he caught a hint of her lavender fragrance, enough for her warmth to seep beneath his skin. "But you didn't."

"No." He'd learned to dodge. He'd learned to wear an opponent down through endurance, learned to distract through chatter. Anything to preserve his hands. And when he had to strike a blow, he'd learned to make it devastating. "But I wouldn't take the chance of him succeeding eventually. He made me into what you see. A simple man who plays too deep, drinks too much, and enjoys too many ladies outside the bonds of marriage."

How empty that sounded. And now he knew first-hand the consequences of such a life, but he couldn't tell her that.

"You are more than that," she declared. "More man than all that. I know you to be."

She gave him no chance to reply. She sealed any protest with her lips.

CHAPTER EIGHTEEN

HER LIPS on his were tentative at first. Unsure, despite all that had passed between them. George would not demand more than she was willing to give freely. Let her discover her own brand of power, her own means of persuasion. Let her make the demands once she was ready. Once she knew her own need.

She sipped, rather than drank of him, although a full-throated draught would come as her insecurities fell away. He curled his hands about her waist, held her easily. Her fingers traced featherlight paths that somehow burned along his shoulders, his nape, his neck, his throat, seeking the skin beneath his collar.

Soon. God, let it be soon. Her innocent kisses tortured with their sweetness.

He tightened his grip and lifted her against him. Her small breasts flattened against his chest. Lord but he wanted them in his hands, he wanted to taste them, wanted the taut peaks of her nipples beneath his tongue.

Yet again, he pressed with his hands, this time holding her rigidly, not allowing her to melt. Not yet. Not yet, but soon.

She pulled away and opened her eyes. Her breath rushed between parted lips to fan across his cheek.

"Not here," he rasped. "The servants will be up to light the fires, and if we dally too long, they'll catch us. Come to my room."

She blinked, hesitant in spite of everything they'd done. His room, yes. It was a step into his territory to couple on the linens where he'd slept, perhaps to drift off together and awaken in each other's arms. Lord, she ought to hesitate.

And why in hell was he allowing it? He never brought his women back to his personal domain. But she was nothing like his other women, or indeed any woman. He could make the exception this once.

His body demanded it.

"It'll be more comfortable in bed." He bent and feathered a kiss beneath her ear. Her pulse fluttered just beneath the surface. "More pleasant." He touched his tongue to the spot. At her gasp, he smiled into her neck. "We can take our time."

He let her feel his teeth—just a nip. She clutched at his shoulders and sagged against him, her slender body fitting against his as if she was made for him.

Damn, if that wasn't a sobering thought, one that ought to scare the devil out of him, ought to send him running. But part of him wanted to stay and contemplate the notion. Like a powerful storm at sea, the idea combined both fear and wonder, enough to compel him to watch and yet raise the hairs at the back of his neck.

"Someone might still come upon us."

He let himself grin. "That's part of the fun, but if the thought bothers you, you'll have to promise to be very, very quiet."

He planned to enjoy coaxing as many cries of pleasure from her as he could.

He released her from his embrace and took her hand. "We'll steal up the servants' stairs."

By God, her fingers tightened about his, and she followed. The trust she placed in him. Granted, he'd asked it of her, but her words from just before their kiss rose to his mind.

More man than all that.

He wasn't so certain, when he was falling back into the rake's role to lead her astray.

And if you promised her more, you wouldn't be leading her astray.

Now that thought was truly frightening. Besides, he could not act on it. What might he offer her? A better home, a better position in society, perhaps, but polite society would never accept her.

And then there was the matter of his heart. He might offer her that, but what did he know of sentiment? His father's laughter echoed through his mind. Romantic attachment, yet another domain of females, along with silk and lace, along with watercolor, along with poetry and novels. Along with music.

The best he could do was restore her son to her—and he'd already made that vow.

ISABELLE'S heart pattered a frantic beat against her ribs. The outside world looked on her as a fallen woman, but for the first time, she was acting the part. Bold and brazen as she pleased, she'd thrown herself into George's arms, and now she let him lead her toward the temptation of his body.

Gladly.

He'd given her pleasure, and now she'd give back. She wanted to share herself with him and erase the ghost of the sad little boy she'd seen flit through the room as George recounted his childhood frustrations. She knew all too well what it meant to be forced into a mold of familial expectations—the rules that required her to present a façade of perfection. How they'd rankled. How they, in the end, had pushed her to rebel.

The servants' stairs ran through the back of the house, spare and rickety. Each creak of a loose board echoed in the night. When they emerged into the upper corridor, she half expected to find the other houseguests waiting to pounce.

"Do you think this is a good idea?" she whispered as loudly as she dared.

"I think it's an excellent idea." George pitched his voice low, and its warmth washed over her in a sensual wave. "See? We're already at my door."

He turned a handle and swung aside a panel to reveal his cavernous bedchamber. The light from his branch of candles chased the shadows to the corners. An arched casement broke the line of the far wall. A wide canopied bed dominated the left side, its hangings a steely blue that matched the stripes of the wallpaper.

"Nearly as big as my cottage," she murmured. She'd paid it little heed earlier, when he replaced his wet clothes for dry. "All this stone. It must be impossible to heat in winter."

He set a hand against her nape. "I can think of a few ways to keep warm." His fingers curled around her neck, pulling her closer. "What do you think? Two bodies beneath a coverlet ought to manage nicely."

He swept her into a full embrace, and his lips descended. He pressed feverish kisses to her mouth, cheeks, and forehead. Not enough. She hadn't followed him here for a few simple pecks like children hiding in a hedgerow.

With a moan, she grasped his shirt front and pulled him to her. Her lips met his in an urgent kiss. She held nothing back. He'd awakened these feelings in her, this craving, this sensuality, and for once, she was going to obey their demands. She might never again have such a chance. Her fingers entangled in his hair, her breasts crushed to his chest, and her hips cradled a fast growing hardness.

Oh, yes, she wanted that in her hands, between her thighs, slipping into her body and driving her to madness. With breasts and hips and thighs, she pressed closer.

He tore his lips from hers, his breath ragged. "Slow down, love. We've hours yet before dawn."

"I don't believe I want slow. Not just now. Perhaps later."

He bent until his forehead rested against hers. "Do you mean to test my limits?"

The smile that stretched her cheeks felt very wicked indeed. "That sounds like it might be quite diverting."

"Diverting." He gave a short laugh. "I'll show you diverting. Come here."

He hauled her up against the breadth of his chest, and his lips grazed a spot just beneath her ear. The tip of his tongue darted out to trail warm dampness over her skin. The flats of his palms smoothed along her spine from her shoulder blades to the dip of her waist and lower.

She gave herself over, let herself feel. How different this experience was from furtive groping in an abandoned corridor. How much richer, how much deeper, how much less fraught with fear. How much more alive.

George had demanded her trust days ago, and she'd given it to him. He'd reached out to her—an essential stranger—and helped. He'd shown her caring when no one else would. He'd refused to let her remain an outcast. And when she was with him, she no longer felt like one.

He awakened in her a sense of belonging that she'd never experienced, ever. Even before her family had repudiated her, they held their members at a distance. The Marshalls existed for gain—power, money, it didn't matter. What they wanted, they took, and no one dared protest. The reckless fool who possessed the audacity to break free of the rigid mold of their expectations was no longer acceptable.

And if she'd ever stopped to consider the situation, she might have realized sooner that she'd never been one of them. Not really. As she was now discovering, she craved closeness to another. She *needed* it.

Too many clothes separated her from George, too many layers of cotton and linen and wool. She slipped her hands between their bodies and fingered the horn buttons that fastened his waistcoat. Holding his gaze, smiling, she made fast work of each fastening and parted the fine fabric. Only a swath of linen separated her from his chest. She yanked the cloth free of his trousers, untied his cravat and loosened the closures at his neck. Gathering the crisp linen by the fistful, she pulled the shirt away from his body and tossed it aside.

Who could have imagined such pleasure in the simple act of undressing a man? She loved the expanse of flesh, gilded in the flickering candlelight, thus revealed to her. She reveled in it. She wanted to savor every inch.

The notch at the base of his throat beckoned. She leaned in and drew her tongue through the hollow. His hands found her waist and squeezed as she continued her exploration. She lapped at his skin, kissed, nipped, noting every nuance of his harshening breath, listening for groans, pushing him back toward the bed, one step and one touch at a time.

He collapsed onto the mattress and lay back, his arms bent behind his head, relaxed now. Surveying. He owned that blasted bed the way his body draped across it. His erection strained against the falls of his trousers. A few buttons more, and she could have its velvet hardness free in her hands.

Her mind filled with lust-driven images. He'd kissed her in the most intimate places. Did she dare do the same to him? A wicked urge to attempt an act of wantonness warred with uncertainty. And what sort of woman would he think her if she dared taste him?

"Wait." He caught her glance, held it, his eyes intense and compelling. "I want to watch you undress."

Her heart jumped in her chest and pattered against her ribs, but all the same, she raised her fingers to the fastenings of her bodice. Her gown was of the old round style—shoulder buttons to hold up the yoke, and beneath that, ties across her breasts with a free-falling skirt to the floor. She could be out of it in a trice, out of it and on the bed with him.

"Take your time," he added.

The heat in his gaze told her he wanted to savor, and the thought made her fingers fumble on the first button. She caught her lower lip between her teeth.

"Oh, yes. I like that expression on you. It's the perfect mix of innocence and assurance."

"I don't feel very sure." She didn't now. She felt as if she was on display. She'd only ever removed her clothes under the perfunctory glance of her maid or modiste. Certainly not anyone inclined to look his fill. Not someone whose scrutiny fell on her skin as a physical touch, as if he caressed her with reverent fingertips. He'd seen her already, but this disrobing before him was different in its deliberateness.

Her nipples peaked against her chemise as the worn cotton of her dress pooled about her ankles. Yet he stared at her as if she wore the finest silks and ribbons.

"Your stays now." His hand drifted to the waistband of his trousers. Idly, he fingered the button at the fall.

Throat dry, unable to look away from his lap, she reached behind her back and tugged at the knot in her lacing. The stance pushed her breasts upward.

"There is nothing lovelier," he drawled, as his fingers worked the fastenings of his trousers, "than a woman readying herself for my bed."

Such cheek, and he wasn't finished. She watched in

fascination as he released his erection and took it in hand. He stroked from base to tip and back.

Never before had she been so aware of her skin—the way it enveloped her body, the way it tingled, the way it warmed. Every sweep of his hand along his length set off an answering throb deep, deep in her midsection, a beat that at once made her melt and made her thrum with rising tension. Liquid heat poured through her, and she pressed her thighs together lest it escape.

She couldn't tear her gaze from the sight. Her fingers itched to replace his. Her tongue darted from between her teeth to wet her lips. His eyes narrowed over a gaze, intense in its focus. On her. Yes, he'd said a woman, as if to indicate any woman, but he meant her. Isabelle.

Fingers shaking, she pulled at the spiral lacing at the top of her spine. She couldn't drop her stays fast enough.

"Now come here."

She locked eyes with him and approached, step by measured step, sensing he wished to draw out the anticipation until it strung taut enough to snap. She reached the side of the bed, and he leaned forward to skim his hands along her ribs, up, slowly up, until he cupped her breasts. He pulled her to him, his lips closing about a hardened nipple, his tongue moistening the fleshy bud through her chemise.

Closing her eyes, she arched her back and moaned, the sound low and throaty.

"Are you ready for me so soon?" He did not give her a chance to reply in words, but suckled harder until her breath rushed through her teeth.

His hands stole beneath her chemise, whispered up her thighs. She shivered in anticipation of his fingers on her, in her, pressing and probing until they coaxed from her that vivid rush of ecstasy.

He dipped into her and groaned. "Good God, you're responsive."

"To you." She shouldn't admit so much, but the words slipped out.

"Raise your arms."

She obeyed, and he whipped her remaining garment from her body.

"Now come here and respond."

The command in his tone sent a pleasurable shiver straight to her core. She climbed onto the mattress next to him, and he pulled her down into a frenzied kiss. The contact of his bare flesh against hers sent heat tingling through every nerve ending. Sloughing his trousers, he rolled on top of her.

Now. Yes. Now.

He seized her thigh by the fleshy outer edge near her hip, hard enough that she felt the bite of his fingers. To-morrow, she might well find bruises. The passion driving that grip made her melt.

She needed, oh, she needed. Never had she experienced such depth to her desire. Never had she known such fierceness could exist within her, as if the wildness in him reared up and drew forth an answering force in her.

She reached for him with her arms and legs combined, wrapping herself around his flanks, his hindquarters, his back. Anything to bring him closer. Anything to merge them into one.

He drove into her in a single, smooth stroke, and she clung. She would not let him abandon her. Not this time. Again and again, he filled her, in a frenzied rhythm as if neither of them had been sated but a few hours before.

"Oh, God." She pushed her hips against him, meeting his every thrust. "Oh, God, yes."

She spiraled higher with the building pressure, the building pleasure. Somewhere paradise lurked. Somewhere close. Sometime soon. All she had to do was reach out and grab it.

George seized her hips, slid his hands beneath her, lifted her to him. His breath tore from his lungs in harsh spurts, his expression focused, intense. His gaze riveted on her, a silent plea, or perhaps a command.

She inhaled his scent, combined with the heady musk of their joining, and her breasts pressed into his chest. Her nails dug into the muscles at the tops of his arms.

Closer, yes, closer. She could never be close enough, not to him, not to the ecstasy mounting within.

"Yes, please. Soon."

He dropped his head to the crook of her neck, nuzzled with his lips in a gentle counterpoint to his deep pounding thrusts. She wrapped her arms around him, clasped him near, and let the storm take them both.

HEART still hammering in his ears, George braced himself on his elbows. Beneath him, Isabelle still hummed, lost in her pleasure. He couldn't remember a more satisfying bout of bed sport, couldn't recall ever delighting in a partner's satisfaction the way he'd delighted in hers. How her hot little passage had gripped him. How she'd pulsed about him when she'd reached her peak. Wave after wave rippling along his length until he could hold off his climax no longer.

Climax? Bugger and bollocks! A sudden stab of horror turned his insides to ice, and he rolled off her. His prick, limp now, slid free of her body. Good God, he'd finished inside her.

He'd never meant to lose control like that. He'd intended to pull out, *should* have pulled out the moment he'd felt the burn at the base of his spine, the instant his bollocks tightened. He was not some green schoolboy, and she would have taken no precautions if she'd known any.

They hadn't planned any of this. In spite of the damnable attraction between them, he would not have predicted this night would end in the most phenomenal swiving of his life. The least he could have done was spend into the sheets like a respectable gentleman.

Isabelle let out a whimper and curled into a ball on her side as if she missed his warmth. His heart thumped in his chest, slowly now, each beat loud in his ears, each beat contributing to the knot of terror in his gut.

She didn't deserve this. Not when her trust was so hard-won. And what did she get in return, but the risk of finding herself, once again, with a swollen belly and no husband to show for it, no protector, no provider?

He'd intended to help her find her son, to comfort her when the search proved fruitless, and instead he'd betrayed her.

He watched the steady rise and fall of her chest as she dozed on, oblivious. Long eyelashes fanned across rosy cheeks. Her slender body belied its true strength. Twice now, she'd borne his weight without complaint. She'd downright reveled in the pounding he'd given her. Reveled and begged for more.

He tried to picture her heavy with child—his child—imagine her holding a tiny babe in her arms, and he felt . . . He wasn't sure what it was, but he could name several things it wasn't. It wasn't revulsion; it wasn't annoyance; it wasn't disgust. It wasn't impatience that here was another drain on his overburdened finances. It wasn't a desire to empty his liquor cabinet. In short, it was the opposite of everything he'd felt when Lucy had announced his impending fatherhood.

Oh, God. Lucy. What was he going to do about her? And, more importantly, what was he going to do with Isabelle? His head whirled with solutions where she was concerned. Socially acceptable solutions—duty, even. The acquisition of a special license. His conscious thought admitted them all without hesitation, accepted them as the right thing to do.

God help him.

CHAPTER NINETEEN

Jack!

With a shiver, Isabelle blinked awake to an unfamiliar chamber. Slowly, she breathed in. She'd been running in her dream, chasing her son who eluded her at every turn. He still eluded her in reality.

The glimmer of dawn filtered through a window in the far wall, casting the space in monochromatic grays. The mattress she lay on was far too comfortable, the sheets that wrapped her too luxurious. As she shook away the cobwebs of sleep, memories of the previous night came flooding back. George kissing her fiercely, filling her again and again, wild and impassioned.

She rolled over and found him lying beside her, his hands tucked beneath his head, staring at the canopy. She had little enough experience with waking up beside a man, but she wasn't completely green. Something wasn't right here. Shouldn't he have cradled her through the night, matching his breathing to hers, sharing a pillow? Shouldn't he have woken her with a gentle kiss, or perhaps a bold caress someplace scandalous? She'd have preferred either to discovering him lying unmoving and silent, like a stone—if stones could generate tension.

She reached for his arm, but her hand lost its courage halfway across the sheet. "Did you not sleep at all?"

"No." A single, frosty word, after all they'd shared.

"Oh." She pressed her fingers to the base of her throat.

"I see." She tried to keep her tone flat, but she suspected he caught the waver at the end.

"I wonder if you do."

That did it. If she was cold before, she wasn't now. Impossible to feel the chill with rage erupting inside her. Of all the insufferable, arrogant rakes, she'd fallen in with the worst. And she knew arrogant and insufferable. She'd grown up surrounded by those traits. She'd adopted them herself. She'd been expected to marry someone of like temperament and pass that superiority down to her children so they could perpetuate the myth that they were so much better than everyone else, merely because they'd been fortunate enough to be born into the right family.

Well, it wasn't a good fortune, not when those traits became weapons when one failed to measure up. As she had.

"Oh, yes." The dead calm of her words betrayed nothing. Her fingernails bit into her palms to calm their shaking. "Oh, yes, I see. You've taken what you want of me and now you'll toss me aside."

He snapped his head toward her. "What's that supposed to mean?" He rolled to face her. The breadth of his shoulders blocked her view of the rest of the chamber. "For one thing, I never intended to cast you aside." He bit off each syllable.

She suppressed an urge to shrink toward the wall. She must not back away or cower. Not now. She'd never liked the simpering *ton* girls who fainted at the mere suggestion they'd displeased someone. She would not do it, would not play that game.

"You've an odd way of showing it. What on earth was I supposed to think?"

"You'll think whatever you like, of course. I thought we'd moved past this matter of you mistrusting me." He gave a harsh laugh. "Isn't that rich? Turns out you were right, in any case. I can't be trusted when it comes to you."

She pulled a long draught of air in through her nose while she tried to make sense of his ravings. Somehow while she'd dozed away the effects of his lovemaking, he'd managed to go mad. The only experience she'd had with madmen was her Uncle Erasmus, but he usually reacted well to a calm voice and a stiff shot of spirits.

She laid a hand on George's arm. "Why can't we talk about this?"

He shook his head. "I don't want to. Not here, where there's nothing to drink." He rubbed his forearm across his brow. "God, I need a brandy."

Wonderful. Now he'd all but accused her of driving him to drink. If they had a bottle of brandy, she'd be tempted to break it over his head. "It's nearly daybreak. You can't drink brandy for breakfast."

His shoulders drooped, and she took that for relenting, but then he rolled to his back, one arm cast over his eyes.

Isabelle bit her lip. What on earth was she to make of his behavior? She was still trying to work out what to say when he scrubbed a hand down his chin and caught her eye. Held it. "You realize I must make you an offer of marriage."

She gaped for the space of several blinks. "You hardly have to go to such lengths," she said weakly. "I'm not some young miss you've just ruined."

"No, but you are of good family."

"Not anymore."

He held up a hand, and she bit back the rest of her protest. "You may live under diminished circumstances, but it has not always been that way. Your breeding shows, whether or not you realize it. The way you lift a teacup. The way you sit in a chair so properly, back straight. The way you lean forward and attend whoever's talking, even if they're boring you with the details of their fourth-cousin-twice-removed's fascination with hieroglyphics. My own mother doesn't carry herself so well."

Heat crept up the back of her neck, and she grasped handfuls of the sheets. "No matter my origins, sir, I could hardly expect an offer of marriage from you. What's transpired between us does not signify."

"And if you find yourself with child again?" His eyes never left hers.

She rubbed her palms against her thighs. "That is the risk we took."

Or she'd taken. She'd gone to his bed, wholly prepared to face the consequences, even if it did result in another child. Oh, God, not just any child but *his* child. She closed her eyes against the image of a bright-eyed boy with an impish grin. George's son would get into twice as much trouble as Jack.

"I didn't mean to take such a chance. Not with you. I . . . I lost control. I did not intend to . . ." He shifted on the sheets and cleared his throat. "At any rate, I ought to do right by you."

She pulled in a breath. She ought to be flattered at his offer. It was far more than she'd ever gotten from Jack's father.

But something was missing. He'd said all the right words, but they lacked the force of conviction. His offer was made out of duty and perhaps a desire to compensate for her current circumstances. Whether or not he'd had anything to do with them. And that wasn't enough—certainly not for Isabelle Marshall.

Diminished as she was, it wasn't enough for Isabelle Mears, either. She'd managed just fine on her own. She would continue to do so.

Without George Upperton.

"You do not have to do this. I am far beneath you. What would your family say?"

He bolted off the bed, still naked and oh, so distracting. "To hell with my family. They have no say in this matter."

She shook her head, even as she wrapped the sheets about her and sat. "Forgive me, but it is quite naïve of you to think so."

He threw back his head and let out a shout of laughter. "Naïve? Oh, isn't that rich? I don't think anyone's referred to me as naïve since my first year at Eton. Come to think of it, they didn't even call me naïve then."

"You may think yourself quite worldly in most areas, but this is one where I believe I have a little more experience."

He crossed to her and seized her by the shoulders. "Do you really think so? Perhaps we should do a comparison. What your family expected of you and what mine expects of me. And we'll see which of us outdoes the other."

Men always had to turn the most inane topic into a competition. Well, she wouldn't have it. If she refused to play his game, perhaps he would stop this madness.

"Come now. Let's have a go." His fingers bit into her upper arms. "Let's start with you. I can guess easily enough. They wanted you to make a brilliant match that would enhance their social connections."

Only an heir to a dukedom. The memory of the Duke of Amherst's oldest son sent a shudder through her. If she'd gone through with her expected role and married him, she'd have doomed herself to an endless succession of parties, calls, routs, all of it expected. All of it predictable. Comfortable, luxurious, socially acceptable, but ultimately sterile.

Her lips stretched, but she feared the expression was only a poor semblance of a smile. "It hardly takes any kind of thought to work that out. The same can be said for any daughter of the *ton*. At any rate, I believe you'll agree I failed spectacularly."

"Would you consider telling me how that came about?"

Once again, the strangeness of his mood struck her. He flitted from one topic to the next and dashed if she could follow his thinking. "Do you really want the sordid details? And after you've made me an offer, no less?"

He started, as if someone had just pierced him through. "Not the sordid details, no. I only wonder how such a thing came about when clearly . . ." He grabbed a fistful of forelock and pulled on it. "It's just . . . In the eyes of society, you're of the highest breeding."

"That's what my family liked to think."

"But . . . but you don't believe that to be true."

"I know that not to be true. I *lived* it. Perhaps I didn't wish to live that way the rest of my life." She rolled to her back and contemplated the canopy. Heavy blue velvet, draped just so, comprised the hangings. "I hardly know anymore, but perhaps that was why I let myself be taken in. He was quite persuasive, you know, and not in the way you're thinking. He had a way of expressing himself. I think he fancied he could talk himself into and out of any situation. That's how he managed an introduction in the first place when my family would never have countenanced me consorting with him. That's how . . ."

"That's how he talked himself under your skirts."

"He did." She let the admission float in the air, stark in its simplicity. "And now I've let that happen again."

He grasped her shoulder, forcing her to turn and look him in the eye. "How can you say such a thing when I've just made you an offer?"

"It was hardly a serious offer." She waved a hand to shoo the idea away and at the same time convince him to release her—and cover himself.

The gesture didn't work. If anything, his grip tightened. "I was in complete earnest."

"All right." She sighed. "Let's suppose for a moment you were. My family would hardly consider it a brilliant match. I regret to inform you they would consider you beneath me. Or they would have. Then."

"I know that much," he muttered. "A mere mister wasn't good enough?"

"My family? They'd have settled for no less than a title, preferably a duke or a marquess. I'm afraid I ended up a great disappointment to them."

He looked away for a long moment. "Disappointment," he said under his breath. "Yes, let's talk about disappointment."

"If you bring me before your family, I'm sure you'll do the job quite nicely." She backed out of his grasp, as a new thought occurred to her. A disturbing, even disillusioning thought. "And that's what your offer is about, isn't it? Your family has put pressure on you to marry."

"My mother had been threatening me with young chits and introductions enough to drive me mad, yes, but . . ." He shook his head as if to clear it. "That isn't why I made you an offer."

"Well, it certainly wasn't because you ruined me." Her voice wobbled on the final word. Blast it, she'd been doing so well keeping control of her emotions. Why must she slip now when she needed to set him down? "Haven't I had enough men use me already?"

"Use you?" His arm slashed in a gesture toward the mattress. "Is that what you think happened between us? I don't recall having to coerce you in the slightest."

A soft knock at the door saved Isabelle from having to reply. A good thing, too, for her throat had suddenly constricted past the point where words would emerge. Once again, she was about to be caught.

* * *

"Whoever it is, I'll get rid of him," George muttered. "We're not through discussing this matter." Of all the damnable sense of timing.

He waited until Isabelle had recovered her clothes and retreated into a far corner, before reaching into the wardrobe for his banyan. He crossed to the door and cracked it open.

His sister stood in the corridor, already dressed for the day. "There you are. Nobody's seen you since yesterday."

Only Revelstoke when he'd gone to gather information, but he wasn't about to tell Henrietta that. "If Mama's sent you to remind me of my social duty, it's really not a good time."

Henrietta stepped forward, as if expecting him to invite her in.

Remembering Mrs. Cox yesterday, he planted his feet firmly on the threshold. "I'll come down to breakfast if my presence is required."

"That isn't the problem." Her eyes, suspiciously red-rimmed, narrowed. "Do you have somebody in there?"

"That is none of your affair. And you oughtn't know of such things."

She turned her gaze skyward. Come to think of it, her nose was rather puffy as well. "I am five and twenty, and I've listened to enough gossip. Really, George. You'd better not have lured one of the younger ladies in there."

"And give Mama a chance to thrust me in front of a parson? The very idea." He nearly caught himself wincing at the idea of Isabelle overhearing this conversation, given what they'd been arguing about. "Now who's been putting such ideas into your head? If it's that Leach character, I'll be talking to Revelstoke about acting as my second."

Her face went oddly blank. "No one's seen Leach in

two days. I thought perhaps you knew something. If he's been helping in the effort to find that boy, for example, I might feel a bit better."

He reached out hesitantly and patted her shoulder. "There, there. The man's clearly an idiot. You can do far better. Unless—" He broke off as a new thought clicked into place. "Good God, did you say he's been missing for two days?"

"Yes, and what of it? You've been nowhere to be found for about the same time."

Two days. The timing was too damned convenient. Jack, Biggles, and now Leach. "That's not true. You've found me. Leach is still conspicuously absent."

She let out a puff of air too anemic to be termed a sigh.

"Chin up. I thought you'd decided not to marry."

"I have. This only decides the matter. Still, a girl likes to know a man might find her fanciable."

"Worry about that when you've found someone worthy of you." Leach in no way fit that particular bill. Not if George's growing suspicions amounted to anything. Although what a grinning idiot like Leach might have to do with a young boy's disappearance was anybody's guess.

Henrietta squared her shoulders. "Make sure you turn up at breakfast. If you've got someone spirited away in there, you don't want Mama coming up here next."

George drummed his fingers against the side of the door until the pink flounce of Henrietta's day dress disappeared round the corner. He forced himself to turn the latch carefully before he faced Isabelle. She still stood in the far corner, dressed now and half hidden by the bed's hangings. "How much of that did you overhear?"

"I don't make a habit of eavesdropping." So stiff and polite she was. He could almost imagine the young lady she'd been before her downfall, clad in a white ball gown like any other chit who had just made her bow, but more regal.

"I should have asked you this days ago. I'm an idiot for not thinking of it sooner." He strode about the end of the bed to stand before her.

"What?" She eyed him warily, as if she already knew she wouldn't like the answer to her question.

"Who were you meeting that night in the garden?"

The color drained from her already pale cheeks. "I . . . I don't even know. I received a note, but it was unsigned, and I did not recognize the handwriting."

George rubbed his stubbled chin. "What are the odds?" he muttered to himself.

"The odds of what?"

"According to my sister, there's been another disappearance. You wouldn't happen to know a chap by the name of Reginald Leach, would you?"

Isabelle shook her head. "No, definitely not."

"Jack gone, Biggles missing"—he counted the names out on his fingers—"and now Leach. And a man accosted you in the road that night."

Only the ape George had confronted was a lot bigger than Leach. Poorly dressed, as well. In fact, the man's size and dress reminded him of someone—the man who had pounded him in Lucy's bedroom. Her brother—supposedly. Which made no sense. What did the one have to do with the other?

On the other hand, Isabelle did receive a note, and George still had Leach's marker. It was worth a try.

He crossed to her and placed his hands on her shoulders. "You wouldn't still happen to have that message, would you?"

"No, I burned it."

"All right." He ran his hands down her arms in what he hoped was a soothing manner. Pity it was doing nothing for him. "All right. We'll just have to hope another clue will turn up."

Footsteps echoed in the corridor, gradually getting louder and then fading. The household was wakening. At any moment, a maid might beg entrance to see to his fire. He had to get Isabelle out of here before then. It wouldn't do to expose her to another bout of female shrieking over scandal and ruin and lack of morals.

"For now," he added, "I think I'd best see you home."

GEORGE might be turning over some sort of plan in his mind, but maybe he was also grateful for the distraction that had forestalled their earlier argument. He was hiding something. Isabelle knew as much without a doubt, the same way she could always tell when Jack had been up to no good. Her son had a particular smile, too broad and innocent to be truthful. *Heavens, Jack.* And when would she have news of her boy? *Please let it be today.*

George, apparently, possessed the same expression. Perhaps all males did.

Dressed now, they walked down the main thoroughfare of the village, George chattering about inconsequentialities and beaming like an idiot. Did he expect her to fall for it?

No doubt he did. She'd fallen for the rest, after all, and let him have her body. Images from the previous night flashed through her mind. Hot, fleshy images accompanied by a melting sensation at her core.

Oh, yes, she'd fall again, given any sort of provocation. He'd awakened something inside her, something insidious and demanding like his talent, only this was a hunger for more of him. If she closed her eyes, she could see the angles and planes of his chest. Her fingers recalled the texture of those muscles. Her tongue recalled the taste of his skin. A hunger, yes, but one that required all of her senses to fulfill.

All her senses, all her body, all herself. More the fool, she, if she gave in to it. But she would. This compulsion was beyond her resistance.

The note lay just past the threshold when she opened the door. An innocent little folded square of paper, all pristine whiteness, the same sort of stationery as the first. Her pulse throbbed in her neck. This must be news. It had to be.

Pressing a hand to her throat, she snatched it up.

If you want to see your son again, you'll bring one thousand pounds to the crossroads where the drive from Shoreford house meets the main highway to London. Tomorrow night. Come alone.

She blinked, but the terse note read the same on the second try. Her legs suddenly refused to support her weight, and she swayed. A pair of strong, long-fingered hands at her waist steadied her.

George. She'd nearly forgotten his presence. "Here. What is that?"

Wordlessly, she handed him the scrap.

"A thousand?" He balled his hand about the paper. "Good God."

"I haven't got a thousand," she replied mechanically. Breathing was difficult when someone had just stuck his fist in your gut. Or perhaps a pole-axe was nearer the mark. "Not tonight. Not even next year."

"I have."

"George, no." She turned. "I cannot take your money. Not after last night. It would make me feel as if you paid me for my favors."

Pay for her favors, and yet she'd do anything for her son. Could she stoop to selling herself for the money? What was her pride and dignity next to her boy?

He seized her, his long fingers like shackles curled

about her upper arms. She felt as if he could crush her small bones, should the notion take him. "Whatever passed between you and me, Jack's kidnapping had nothing to do with it. What I—Christ."

The expression on his face stunned her. Never in all her girlish dreams of a future suitor had she imagined such intensity, such gravitas mixed with pure emotion. The heat in his eyes liquefied their steely gray. It pinned her to the spot, while an answering fire ignited within.

"Let me do this." Even his words were weighted with whatever had moved him. Lord above, with that voice, the man might entice an angel to sin.

"I need to know why." How she'd managed such a steady tone, she'd never know. Inside, she was all aquiver.

He reached into his topcoat and withdrew a purse. Its knit sides bulged. He tossed it onto her table, where it met the wood-planked top with a heavy clunk. "I have the blunt. You do not."

Good Lord, the man carried vast sums in his pockets and cast them away like pence. She placed a hand over her racing heart. "You just happened to be carrying a thousand pounds on your person?"

A taut smile stretched his lips. "I doubt there's even five hundred there, but it's a start. And no, I don't make a habit of carrying so much coin on me." He waved a hand, the gesture only apparently nonchalant. An odd tension settled over his face, pulling his cheeks rigid. "I won at cards."

"You must know I cannot repay you."

GOOD God, he was on edge. Only moments ago, he'd nearly spouted his feelings like some hysterical female. Ridiculous. He might well care, might well be prepared to protect her at all costs, might well want to spend every waking minute with her.

Hell, he'd *meant* that proposal, not because he'd spilled inside her, but because of these damnable feelings. And she'd refused to take him seriously.

At any rate, a man didn't just admit to such things. He expressed them through gifts and through sacrifices and through pleasure rendered. He offered bloody marriage. If worse came to worst, he expressed them through music, but to put them into words?

"I do not require repayment. Your happiness is repayment enough."

Her chin puckered, and she choked on a sob, falling against his chest, shoulders heaving. He slid his hands to her back, his palms mapping her shoulder blades before slipping upward to tangle in her hair.

What a rotten liar he was. He'd even lied to himself. Feelings be damned. Whatever was welling in him could not be described in such flimsy terms as feelings. In a matter of days, she'd worked her way into his heart with her unique blend of pluck and vulnerability. Raised to be the consummate lady, quiet and dignified, she didn't wilt beneath the weight of her reduced fortunes.

He looked over the spare room—stone hearth, rustic table and benches, herbs hanging from the ceiling, open cupboard full of vials. This was all she had, and it wasn't even hers. He could offer her better, offer to take her away from all this and give her some semblance of the life she'd once known.

He had, damn it, and she'd all but turned him down.

Such a tiny thing she was, burrowed against him, and yet she managed to take up his entire heart. She stirred, but instead of nestling closer, she raised her head. Reflexively, his arms tightened, but she resisted, her body going from boneless to just stiff enough to warn him.

She was thankful, but she had not completely surrendered. A well of unshed tears glittered in each eye, but rather than soften, the liquid had the opposite effect. No frightened doe, his Isabelle.

"I hate it." She pushed away from him, her kissable mouth firming into a line.

"What do you hate?"

"That I am in a position to take and never give." She turned slightly, showing him her shoulder and the soft curve of her breast. She wrapped her arms about her waist, hugging herself, replacing his comfort with her own. Proud as any princess, she tipped her nose toward the ceiling.

Yes, he could imagine her in a sumptuous ball gown, standing in the light of a hundred candles, fending off suitors. He'd never have stood a chance.

"I keep no tally, and I ask for nothing in return."

"That isn't the point. Even if you ask nothing, I feel the debt, and it rankles."

"What if . . ." He fumbled in the pocket of his waistcoat. Thank God. He still had Leach's marker—a long shot, but better than nothing. "What if we can work out where Jack is and you won't have to pay any ransom?"

Her eyes went round. "How are you going to manage that," she said faintly, "when there's been no sign?"

"On the off chance . . ." He unfolded the scrap of paper. "Leach gave me this the other day, and since he's gone . . ."

George lined up the messages and compared the handwriting. Both contained the word *thousand,* and the particular flourish on the upstroke of the D, the sweeping curlicue on the cross of the T, the enlarged loop on the H . . . Leach had definitely sent the notes, but he couldn't have been the man who accosted Isabelle in the road. "Well, I'll be damned."

Isabelle craned her neck. "What is it?"

"The writing's the same, and yet." He caught her gaze. "You told me you didn't know Leach."

"I don't. Do you think I'd forget a name like that?"

No, of course she wouldn't. No one would. "But none of this makes any sense. Why would Leach make off with a random boy from the village? Why would he think such a child might be good to net him a thousand pounds? He'd have to know who you are. It's almost as if he's the boy's father."

Isabelle stiffened. "Jack's father disappeared from society about the same time I did."

"So you're saying the man's name cannot be Reginald Leach."

"Not unless he invented a new one." She looked away. "Jack's father went by the name of Roger Padgett."

CHAPTER TWENTY

PADGETT. GODDAMN him. The man was ever damned to shadow George, it seemed. But who was the real Padgett? George tried to imagine the ape who had beaten him as a seducer of young girls and couldn't quite manage the feat. The flashy dresser he'd met at Revelstoke's party, the one who'd charmed Henrietta, stood a far greater chance.

Devil take him, he better not have touched Henny.

"Judging by your expression, you know the man." Isabelle's cheeks had gone pink, and she didn't quite meet his gaze. Yes, she ought to be ashamed. She could have done so much better. "But I don't understand how."

Not that he could tell her. *He's my mistress's brother*— or so George surmised from the name. Yes, that would go over well. No. God, no.

A sudden chill turned his hands clammy, and another piece of the puzzle clicked into place. No wonder they'd never found Jack in the village. Padgett and his sister wouldn't keep him there, not when they could take him back to London to that overpriced townhouse in Bedford Street that Lucy had insisted he rent.

"Are you feeling all right? You've gone pale."

"I'm fine." He shook his head to clear the haze of his whirling thoughts. He could fix this. He could restore Isabelle's son to her—as long as he kept her from accompanying him. But how to leave her here alone with no inkling of what he was about? Damnation, what a mess.

"I want to know how you came to be acquainted with Padgett. He can't run in the same circles you do."

"When you knew him, did he have a penchant for gambling?" When he wasn't ruining innocent girls, that was.

"He played cards, same as any gentleman."

"Yes, well, he might make a living at it now. He's managed to accumulate a few of my vowels." Vowels, yes, such as Barnaby Hoskins's marker. And if Leach were actually Padgett, the bastard was right there when George received the message. He'd probably gloated to himself at the same time he was charming Henrietta.

George ran a hand through his hair. Hang it all, he was going to have to admit his suspicions as to Jack's whereabouts. As long as he was careful, though, he might still save the situation. He'd have to be damned careful. He was about to make her very angry.

"Given this development"—he measured his words slowly, the better to put off the ultimate admission—"I think I can arrange for Jack's return without paying the ransom."

She stiffened, visibly, like a small tremor racking her body. Slowly, she released her grip on herself, and her arms drifted downward. "You know where Jack is."

He cleared his throat. If only he could draw the moment out forever. If only he could turn back time and hold her once more. For as soon as he responded, she would turn her considerable determination on him. She might well never forgive him.

It was no use. The longer he delayed, the worse her reaction. He nodded. "I have a good idea, yes."

* * *

In his exuberance, Jack had once run headlong into her belly. The force of his head colliding with her gut had forced all the air from her lungs. That burning gasp for air was nothing to how she felt now. She struggled to draw one painful breath.

"What? How?" She was incapable of anything more coherent, despite the jumble of questions that filled her throat.

"Because I know who Roger Padgett is," he said slowly, as if reluctant to make such an admission.

"So you've just said. Something about gambling debts."

"No, I know more than that. I've met the man."

"When? When would you have met him?"

A dull flush reddened his cheeks. "Yes, well, that's actually a good question."

And what on earth was that supposed to mean? She crossed her arms. "Is he one of your cronies?"

But then, that couldn't be right. Surely she might have crossed paths with George in another life.

"Not a crony, no." He looked away and raked a hand through his hair, causing it to stand in sandy spikes. "I'd rather not distress you by mentioning the association, but Padgett's sister is my former mistress."

At the word, a shiver brought goose bumps to her arms. "I see."

She shouldn't care. She most certainly shouldn't feel anything akin to jealousy. His skill in the bedroom, his clear relish for the female body, hadn't sprung from no-where.

Still, having his past lovers flung in her face cut surprisingly deep, and the cut was not a clean one. Like a dull knife, it tore into her chest, through flesh and bone and muscle to leave a ragged scar, alongside the scar Padgett had left.

She shouldn't let it affect her, shouldn't let it show. Beyond his vow to bring Jack home, George had made her no promises. He hadn't attempted to win her affections through false declarations. Good Lord, he had asked *her* to become his mistress not even a week ago. True, he'd also asked her to marry him, but that was only because he'd forgotten himself. He'd dissembled nothing.

Her own mind had betrayed her once again. It had allowed itself to construct yet another fantasy, one that permitted her to justify giving herself to another man.

No more.

She was going to get her son back, and from then on, she was through with men using her for their pleasure. *But you also took pleasure.* More than pleasure, it was paradise.

She cast the thought aside, thrust it from her mind the way God had cast Adam and Eve from Eden. She deserved it no more than they.

"I see," she repeated, firming her voice along with her chin. She could do this. She could hold herself apart. Eventually, the feelings he stirred in her heart would fade. Eventually, she'd forget she nearly let herself fall in love. "I do not care about your former mistresses or even your current one."

"There is no current one." His gaze bored into her.

Heat rushed up the back of her neck. "I want my son back," she said, ignoring the prickle of embarrassment. "If you know how to find him, I'd appreciate you telling me."

There. That sounded sufficiently cold. If nothing else, her family had taught her how to retreat behind a façade of manners.

"I suspect we'll find Jack in London," he replied stiffly. "I can take our family's carriage and have him back to you by tomorrow."

"You'll take the carriage? Oh, no. You're bringing me with you."

He didn't reply straightaway. Instead, he opened his

mouth a few times, as if he'd decided on the proper response, only to close his lips just as quickly.

She glared at him. "You cannot expect me to remain here alone like some simpering milksop."

His shoulders lifted as he pulled in a long breath. "No, I suppose not. But I must warn you. I'm taking you to my former mistress's house."

Dear Lord, could it get any worse? If he still had his mistress's direction, not much time could have passed since he'd ended the liaison. In fact, she still must be inhabiting the quarters he'd provided for her. She'd still be occupying the bed where he'd visited her.

Isabelle closed her eyes against a vision of some voluptuous beauty writhing beneath his expert touch. Her stomach plummeted to somewhere in the vicinity of her feet. Did this former mistress know George referred to her as such or did the woman anticipate his return to Town?

And now such a woman had Jack.

Trust me. Yes, George had begged for her trust until she'd given in. She'd trusted Padgett as well, only to watch him abandon her the moment she'd given him what he wanted. Well, George had secured her surrender, along with her trust.

Her heart lurched in her chest, on the verge of shattering into a thousand shards. No. No, no, and no. She would get her son back, she would retain her heart, and she would move on from this episode.

Alone.

By late afternoon, the carriage clattered through the streets of Mayfair. The rumble of the wheels echoed in George's ears, the noise unnaturally loud as if it were trying to compensate for the stony silence in the cab. If Isabelle was angry with him now, how much colder would her fury become once she confronted the reality of Lucy?

Above all, he'd wanted to avoid introducing the two, but he couldn't in good conscience keep Isabelle from her boy.

Damn scruples, always getting him into difficulties. Why couldn't he lay aside the inconvenient things and do as he pleased? Why must he involve himself?

Across from him, Isabelle stared out the window at the parade of fashionable dwellings. With every passing jostle of the carriage, with every start and stop as they penetrated the heart of what had once been her world, she erected another layer of chill about herself. A pearl constructed of ice, perhaps, but ice made a brittle buffer. One solid blow would shatter the shield.

At last they shuddered to a halt at Lucy's Bedford Street townhouse, an address outside Mayfair proper, but close enough for the other residents to be wealthy tradesmen. Walls of pale sandstone fronted the street from behind wrought-iron grillwork. It looked respectable if not completely fashionable. A prosperous merchant might choose such a dwelling. The rent on the place was certainly dear enough to line the landlord's pockets thickly.

Isabelle peered at the wrought-iron fencing that separated the building from the pavement. The house was a great deal larger, more comfortable and more richly decorated than her house in the village. Christ, what thoughts might be running through her head?

She deserved far better than even this. She certainly grew up with better, and yet she endured worse without complaint.

The carriage rocked as the coachman leapt from the box to let the steps down. George alit first and offered his hand. She pressed her lips into a line and barely touched him as she stepped onto the pavement.

"Six years since I've been to Town," she murmured. "Six years, and when I come back, it's to pay a call on a courtesan." She shook out her faded gray skirts. "And I'm dressed no better than a servant."

She might have made such a comment sound rancorous. Lord only knew Lucy would have in Isabelle's place. But Isabelle sounded merely embarrassed and a touch sad. A wash of pink colored her cheeks.

"Would you rather wait in the carriage?" George ventured. God, let her say yes. Lucy would take one look at Isabelle and leap straight for the jugular.

"If I meant to wait, I'd have stayed behind in Kent." Her reply was cold, yes, but she'd once again retreated behind her shield of ice. Let her remain there for now. She was going to need all the protection she could get.

He mounted the stairs and let the knocker fall once, firmly. Presently, the door creaked open.

"Miss Padgett ain't receiving callers, unless—" Lucy's maid broke off midsentence, and her eyes went round. "Oh, dear."

George arched a brow in a practiced affectation of boredom. "Indeed."

"She told me ye wouldn't be back, sir. Called ye all manner of names, she did."

"I imagine she did." He inspected his nails. "However—"

"Does this mean ye've changed yer mind?" Impertinent as her mistress, this one. Small wonder she couldn't find a more respectable employer.

"I mean to call on Miss Padgett, and before you claim she's not at home, shall I remind you who hired you for this position?" Not only hired her, but overlooked a suspect character reference.

"That ye did, sir." Any other maid would have smiled and blushed. Bessie looked him straight in the eye, her cheeks retaining their habitual sallow tinge.

"Glad you remembered." He made to step past her.

"Ye can't go in there, sir," Bessie said in a rush.

"Why?" He drummed his fingers against a marble statue of a cherub just beyond the threshold. The devil? When had Lucy acquired this monstrosity? More importantly, who had received the bill? "Is she entertaining another gentleman?"

Lucy finding another protector would be an absolute godsend. Only how long would she keep him once her belly started growing round?

"Ye might say that, sir, yes."

He might say that? "Yes, well, I suppose I'm a gentleman only in a manner of speaking. Now let me pass."

"Mr. Upperton." Damn it, Isabelle sounded as outraged as any number of society's sticklers who might have caught their only daughter alone with a notorious rake. Or him, for that matter, although he made a point of avoiding fresh-faced chits. "If my son has been exposed to . . . to improper carryings on, I shall never—" She broke off and looked away.

No doubt she'd been about to say she'd never forgive him, only she'd remembered Jack's disappearance was not George's fault. No matter, she had plenty of other reasons not to forgive him.

He turned to her. "I'm sure Jack's safe and sound."

Lucy possessed a catty streak, but surely she wouldn't harm an innocent, if rambunctious, boy.

"I shall see that for myself." Isabelle pushed past him, past a shocked Bessie, and on into the foyer.

"What is the meaning—" Damn. All the commotion must have drawn Lucy from wherever she'd been hiding. "Who are you, and what do you mean, simply walking in off the street?" Lucy's voice dripped with hauteur.

George stepped into the foyer to find the two women sizing each other up.

Lucy's upper lip curled as she eyed Isabelle's garments.

"The servants' entrance is below, but you may as well move on. I'm not looking for staff at present."

Isabelle peered down her nose at the other woman. "Where have you hidden my son?"

If the two were in competition for disdain, George wouldn't be sure where to place his wager.

"What makes you think I want anything to do with a common brat?"

"That's enough, Lucy." George advanced across the parquet.

"You." Lucy went white beneath the generous layer of rouge on her cheeks. "My goodness, haven't you come down in the world."

He ignored the gibe. "We know you've got Jack. Your brother signed the ransom note." A lie, but what did that matter when one dealt with kidnappers and charlatans? "We've simply decided to change the conditions of the exchange." *Thump, thump, thump.* His boots struck the floor in an even rhythm, and with every thud, Lucy's complexion resembled chalk a bit more. "Do you know what they do with kidnappers? I wonder what a year or two in Newgate would do for your looks."

"This was not my scheme," Lucy protested. "It was all Roger's."

"Then you know where the boy is."

Instead of replying, Lucy touched the back of her hand to her forehead, heaved a great sigh and crumpled to the floor, as smoothly as any Covent Garden actress.

Isabelle looked pointedly from the silk-swathed heap on the floor to George. "How convenient."

"She always did have an impeccable sense of timing." He tried to smile but feared he'd managed no better than a grimace.

Bessie tiptoed to her mistress, as if afraid of waking her. "P'rhaps the herb woman knows what to do."

"Don't be ridiculous," George said. "She's feigning. A good slap—"

"Herb woman?" Isabelle sounded impossibly hopeful. What were the chances?

Bessie nodded. "Ma'am heard about her in the village and had her brought in. Funny name. Not Bingham or Bingley or anything ye'd expect."

"Biggles?"

"Yes, that's it."

Isabelle stretched out a trembling hand. "And Jack's here? Where? I beg you, take me to him."

Bessie caught her lower lip between her teeth. "I'm afraid he's a bit poorly."

Just as Lucy had done earlier, Isabelle went white, only the effect was entirely different. That expression of terror set George's heart pounding. It ignited an urge in him to go to her, take her in his arms and protect her from all the world's ills. If only she'd allow the gesture.

"What's the matter with him?" Her voice shook along with her limbs. "He's never ill. Oh, take me to him."

"He's above stairs." Bessie pointed with her chin. "He'll be fine in a day or two. Ma'am thought to keep him quiet with sweets. He's just had a few too many."

Isabelle strode toward the staircase. "Thank heavens she thought to search out Biggles then."

Bessie followed in her wake. "Oh, ma'am didn't bring in Biggles for your boy. She wanted someone knowledgeable about . . ." The maid cast a quick glance at George and whispered something in Isabelle's ear. He caught something about restoring female regularity. "Wanted to make sure she didn't drop a brat."

Between school and his boxing club, George had received more than his fair share of punches to the gut. Bessie's declaration felt strikingly similar—a heavy blow that tore the air from his lungs, followed by the burning of trying to get his breath back. He ought to be relieved that she wasn't going to saddle him with the responsibility of a child, and part of him was quite happy to learn he wouldn't be supporting Lucy's babe for the next twenty or so years.

Another part of him wanted to smash something, preferably something fussy and fragile like the god-awful statue of a cherub that now adorned the foyer.

Instead, he knelt on the floor, reined in his temper and tapped Lucy's cheek. She opened her eyes immediately. Naturally. She'd been feigning her swoon.

"Were you planning on notifying me of your change in circumstance any time soon?" he asked through gritted teeth. "Or were you going to see how long you could get away with duping me?"

She pushed herself upright but at the same time shrunk away. Good. He'd never stoop to hitting a female, but let her worry. "This wasn't my scheme. It was all Roger's. All of it."

"But you stood to profit from going along with it, didn't you?" He leaned forward. His angry side had seized him in an unbreakable grip. "Didn't you?"

"Naturally," she said as calmly as if she were choosing a new gown at the modiste's. *Naturally, I'll have the silk. Mr. Upperton is footing the bill.*

"Naturally," he spat back. "You don't do anything unless there's a profit to be had."

She shrugged. "Business is business."

"My business with you is through. I expect you to have vacated the premises by the end of the week."

"End of the week? How am I to find a new protector so quickly?"

He raked his gaze down her body. To think, at one time he'd found her attractive. Now he only saw vulgarity. "I'm sure you'll manage. You were a good enough fuck."

"And I suppose you'll have installed my replacement by Friday." She nodded at the ceiling. "I do hope you plan on dressing her better."

"Or perhaps you'll be fortunate to find a dupe wealthy enough to take over the lease on this place. You won't even have to move."

"Is she a good fuck?"

If she were a man, he'd be beating her to a bloody pulp by now. No. No, he couldn't stoop to such a level. Verbally, perhaps, but physically? Never. He clenched his fists to stop himself from taking her by the bodice and hauling her upright to slam her against the wall.

"Not that it's any of your affair, but I haven't fucked her." It wasn't even a lie. He'd taken Isabelle to his bed, but what had transpired there was nothing like his encounters with Lucy or any of his previous mistresses. With Isabelle, he'd transcended the earthy physicality of a mere swiving.

She pushed herself to her feet. "I don't believe you."

"I'm tired of this topic." Their endless darts at each other were leading nowhere. "Why don't you tell me where your brother is so I can be done with the lot of you?"

He expected more gibes, considering the way he'd emerged from his last encounter. Although that ape hadn't really been Padgett, had he?

Instead, she turned away to run her finger across the rim of a porcelain vase. No doubt assessing its value. "He's gone out."

"Convenient, that." George stood. "And when do you expect him back?"

She considered a mother-of-pearl snuffbox. This townhouse would most likely be presented to its next tenant minus all its portable valuables. "He doesn't often trouble me with such details."

"No, of course he wouldn't." He paused for a beat.

Like a knock-out punch, verbal sparring was all about timing. "Tell me, have I ever actually seen your brother?"

"What on earth are you on about?"

"Oh, just a hunch. That man who tried to knock my block off. You must recall. You showed him such sisterly concern. Or was your concern of a baser nature?"

"Why you—" Lucy's bosom heaved, and her fist clenched about that damned snuffbox. "How dare you? You know *nothing*."

"Methinks the lady doth protest too much." He studied his nails. "That ape tried to beat my brains out, you see, but he didn't actually succeed. So you might as well admit it. You've set me up."

"All right, but this was not my idea. Roger didn't want to take the chance you'd recognize him since he was to attend the same party as you. So he hired a thug."

"Ah yes, the truth will out in the end. Now I've only to wait for him to come back so I can return the favor. He'll have to come back by tomorrow morning at the latest. He was to bring Jack back to Kent, after all."

"You cannot simply invite yourself to stay."

He snatched the snuffbox from her hand and replaced it on the console. "It's my house. I've paid for its use. I can stay here if I have a mind."

"You're staying? Here?" Isabelle spoke from halfway down the stairs, cold contempt lacing her words. In her arms, she hefted a decidedly green-looking Jack. Biggles trailed behind her.

"Only until I've finished my business with her brother." He climbed to meet her and extended his arms to take the boy.

She tightened her grip. "I mean to return to Kent as soon as possible. I wish nothing more to do with this place."

George went rigid as an icy chill blasted through his

belly. He hadn't mistaken her tone. It was distant and imperious, the same as her demeanor this entire trip to Town. *Nothing more to do with this place* might well mean *nothing more to do with you.*

No. He would not let her go so easily. He could settle his score with Padgett later, but he refused to let Isabelle go home with matters still unresolved between them. "You cannot return now. It's too dangerous after dark."

"I will not stay here."

"I should say not." Biggles sniffed. "I can't say ye've much taste when it comes to lightskirts."

"Lightskirts?" Lucy shrieked. "How dare you?"

George ignored the outburst and trained his gaze on Isabelle. *Look at me. See.* "I'll take you to my family's townhouse." Before she could voice any protest about propriety, he added, "There's no one in residence but the servants with my mother and sisters still at Shoreford. You can travel on to Kent in the morning."

He backed away from the stairs to give them room to pass. "We'll be leaving now," he added to Lucy. "If your brother decides he would like to collect his ransom, I shall be delighted to receive him."

He'd pay, all right. He'd pay in jabs and uppercuts. And if the coward should try to talk his way out of the situation, George wouldn't stand for it. He'd go in swinging and let his fury for Isabelle's sake fuel his blows.

CHAPTER TWENTY-ONE

ISABELLE BRUSHED the hair back from her son's forehead. Jack stirred on crisp bed linens, but his eyes remained closed. His skin was cool but dry, a sign he'd soon be back to his usual impish self, a handful of a child, and she'd have to find a way to keep him in her sights.

"He'll be fine," Biggles had reassured her, but Isabelle was just as happy to see the evidence for herself.

Thank God. Thank God, her boy would be full of the devil once more when things could have been so much worse. From all appearances, Lucy hadn't exposed Jack to anything scandalous. George's former mistress had spent the past few days ignoring the boy as much as possible, and when Jack insisted on making his presence known, she'd plied him with sweets to keep him quiet. Isabelle must concentrate on that reality, and not think about what might have been—or the disgust that rolled through her belly whenever she thought of George with that woman.

A knock sounded on the door. She knew who it was before answering. Biggles wouldn't stand on ceremony, and Isabelle had asked nothing of the servants.

Blast it all, she didn't want to face George. Why had he insisted on bringing her to his family's townhouse when surely the servants would talk? His family would still learn of her presence once they returned home—if not sooner. He'd left the house party without notifying

anybody. Surely they'd ask questions on his return to
Shoreford.

And she might be partway home by now. The sooner
she was rid of George, the sooner she might start to
forget—both the pleasure they'd shared and what she'd
learned today about his true character.

"Isabelle," came his voice, muffled by the thick plank
of wood, "I know you're in there."

Heaving a sigh, she crossed the heavy carpet to the
door. Six years had passed since her footsteps had known
this sort of cushioning. Six years of unforgiving wood
and ill-fitting shoes. She pushed the thoughts aside as
mere childish complaints. She'd adjusted, and she could
stay that way.

She opened the door a crack. "Keep your voice down.
Jack's gone to sleep."

"Good." He'd had a chance to bathe, shave, and
change. He stood before her now, expression composed
and closed, dressed in a black topcoat, deep green waistcoat and starched cravat of all things. Eveningwear—
velvet and brocade no less—as if he were planning on
going out. "We might speak plainly then. You never gave
me an answer this morning."

Goodness. The proposal. After all that had transpired today, he was concerned over a blasted proposal
made out of duty to assuage a guilty conscience. Only
until this afternoon, she hadn't known just how guilty.
"I was about to refuse you."

"Refuse? Even after you've had time to consider?"

She wanted to shut the door in his face. No, she
wanted to slam it, but he'd only bang away and insist
she speak. To avoid disturbing her son, she crossed the
threshold and closed the door behind her. "The answer
is no, now more than ever."

He opened his mouth. Heavens, and he thought to

argue? Time to forestall him. "Tell me, did you propose to your mistress?"

He shook his head slightly as if he hadn't heard properly. "Propose to Lucy? Why in God's name would I do that?"

"She was expecting, wasn't she?" Isabelle drummed her fingers against her thigh. "Well, wasn't she?"

"Yes, but—"

"So let me see if I understand this correctly." She meted her words carefully, a difficult proposition when his blindness made her want to scream. How could he not see how Lucy's circumstances paralleled hers? "You propose to me on the chance I may be in a delicate condition, while another woman *is* carrying your child?"

"It's not the same. She was a mistress. She knew to take precautions."

"How is that any different? We both served the same purpose."

"No." He pinched the bridge of his nose. "No, you didn't. Don't even think of comparing yourself to that harpy."

"Harpy, is it? She was carrying your child."

"She never intended to see it through." He reached for her, and she backed up against the door. "You heard her maid. She brought in Biggles to get rid of it."

Biggles, yes. If Lucy spent so little as a day in the village, she'd have had a chance to hear of Biggles's reputation. "And you'd never have learned otherwise, if you hadn't come to Town today."

He pushed out an annoyed breath and glanced down the corridor for a few seconds. "Because Lucy was trying to get all the blunt out of me she could."

Right, then. If he refused to see, she had no choice but to spell it out for him. "That does not change the fact that you knew she was with child and you abandoned

her. That makes you no better than Padgett. I cannot
marry a man who would do that."

THE gaming hell stank of cheroot and brandy, those essentially masculine scents according to his sister, but cutting through that reek was the sharper stench of unwashed
bodies perfumed with desperation. George wove his way
between hazard tables, their baize-covered tops faded
and worn with use, where disheveled bucks wasted their
allowances on one roll of the dice.

Through the murk, he spotted his quarry at the very
back—a group of younger men, well dressed, seated at
a faro table. Potential pigeons, they.

What passed for a footman in a place like this, a
grubby man dressed in fraying homespun, emerged to
offer him a bottle of brandy. Ah, the advantages of being
known. George waved the man away. He wanted all his
faculties about him tonight.

Besides, if he gave into the temptation to drink, he'd
let down his guard and think about Isabelle. He'd recall
the way she'd impugned his character, and if he did
that, he might have to face the truth of what she'd said.

In her place rose the memory of a portrait—Julia and
Revelstoke staring into each other's eyes as if the world
began and ended there. For some reason, the look of
adoration on Julia's face made his throat thicken. After
his cock-up, Isabelle would never turn a similar expression on him.

Damn it all to hell if he didn't wish for that very thing,
even if it meant making an idiot of himself and gazing
back like some love-struck calf. Hellfire and damnation
if he wasn't the biggest, bloody, sodding idiot of them
all. He'd let himself fall in love and never realized it
until it was too late.

He shook off the thought along with the emotion.

The only truth he intended to face tonight was some judicious wagering at faro until he convinced a pigeon to take him on at a more easily manipulated game. Winning at piquet relied more on a player's skill than the pure chance of the faro table. If he was careful with the contents of his purse, he could multiply the amount several fold. He could win enough to pay Summersby's debts along with his own. Now that Isabelle had cast him aside, it was time he take up his quest to restore a friend's dignity, and perhaps, along with it, some of his own.

Alert to any sudden movement, he approached the group at the back of the room. One could never be too cautious in a place where strong drink and deep play formed an explosive combination. He carried a knife in his boot just in case, as much for the denizens of the hell as for the footpads who lurked without. By all appearances, these players were dandies. Their piled, pomaded hair and superfine topcoats reeked of money. Just as his did.

"Evening, gentlemen." Evening. What a joke. The time was going on two in the morning. "Might I join your table?"

One of the players pushed back a half-finished drink and looked George up and down. Assessing his worth, no doubt. He'd dressed just as carefully as the man who surveyed him. In a velvet topcoat with no less than three watch fobs dangling from his brocade waistcoat, he'd out-fopped these young men. To make his welcome certain, he withdrew his purse from inside his topcoat and hefted it. The sovereigns inside clinked against one another.

The man gave his crony a nudge and nodded. So much the better. Let them think George an easy mark. He took a seat and extended a hand. "Name's Upperton, by the way." He glanced from one face to the next. The other three were younger than he, but the man to his right looked vaguely familiar. "Didn't you attend Eton?"

"Why yes. The name's Matthews."

George reached into his purse and exchanged several guineas for chips. Just a few for now. He needed to save the bulk of his funds for later, when he lured one of them into a private game. "Thought I'd seen you somewhere."

Matthews reached out and moved his pile of chips to the king of spades. One glance at the case-keeper confirmed George's suspicion that the wager was an odd one. Three of the four kings had already been played. Either the man was in over his head or he was feigning his misunderstanding of the game.

"And your friends?" George prompted. He offered his hand round the table, collecting names: Andrews, Williams, and Roberts—men in want of proper family names, and not just superfluous first names vaguely disguised.

"They went up to Harrow," Matthews said. "Padgett, too."

"Padgett?" George shifted back in his chair and the damned thing nearly toppled over. It wasn't possible. It simply wasn't possible. George's luck was never this good. Of all the gaming hells in London, he'd just happened on Padgett by accident. If he'd set out to look for the idiot, he'd have spent a week or more in the search. "Is he here?"

Roberts grinned. "He's stepped upstairs for a moment."

Upstairs where the whores plied their trade pleasuring their customers out of their winnings. "Only a moment? Surely he's more of a man than that."

"He's already been gone awhile," Williams said.

George nodded, careful not to let his eagerness show.

Beneath the movement, the chair quivered. Damned cheap thing. No doubt it had seen use as a weapon a time or two, the encounters with one hard head and another weakening it further. "Seems a waste of valuable time, when you might be winning."

"How do you know Padgett?" Matthews asked. "He hasn't been back in England very long. Lived on the continent for the last few years, he did."

"We still had the chance to meet here and there." He kept his gaze trained on the dealer. "Are you planning on laying a wager?"

If George could manage to place a few poorly thought-out bets the same way Matthews had, he stood a chance of drawing one of them in. Anything, as long as he didn't wear out his welcome before Padgett reappeared.

The third time he lost, he gave a self-deprecating laugh. "Looks as if I'm out of practice. Whist always was more my game."

The thought of playing whist dredged up memories of inventing a two-handed version with Isabelle. He chased the image away, but not before an odd pang struck through his gut. Damn it all, he needed to concentrate more than ever, because once he'd won enough blunt and once he'd settled accounts with Padgett, he'd be well and truly quit of Isabelle.

Then he could set about the long and winding path that would lead to him forgetting her. Eventually. In another few decades.

Not surprisingly, none of the others took the hint and suggested a change of game. They could play whist for high stakes at any *ton* function, after all. But he must take care not to lose too much more, or he'd dig himself a hole he'd have difficulty clambering out of. In fact, best to sit the next turn out. "I bar this bet."

"Sorry for the delay, boys," rang out a cheery voice

behind George's back. "The lady simply wasn't satisfied with only one go."

George went rigid in his seat, and his chair swayed ominously. Yes, that voice, that intonation, that particular means of expression that suggested wild flourishes of a lace-cuffed hand. The man he'd met in Kent as Leach, but who was actually Lucy's brother. Jack's father.

George pivoted in his seat, nearly upsetting the beleaguered chair, to make certain. He called Miss Abercrombie's portrait to mind—the broad idiot's grin, the ace peeking out of his sleeve. He understood the symbolism of that card now. Padgett wasn't a cheat at cards, per se, but he was a charlatan.

George shot to his feet, mimicking that portrait grin. He'd never been one to seek out confrontation, but oh, how he was looking forward to this one, played out on his terms. He'd imagined meeting Jack's father and happily throttling the bastard, but now he had a much more satisfying plan. If he played this just right, he could ruin the man, just as the idiot had ruined Isabelle.

"Evening there." He thrust out a hand. "George Upperton. And your name?"

Padgett stepped back and looked George up and down. His smile stretched to a near grimace. "Good God, what are you doing here?"

"Playing faro with my pal Matthews here. Poorly, if you must know. The others have been telling me the oddest stories. Seems they're here with a man named Padgett. But you wouldn't know him, would you?"

Padgett's grin faded, and he lowered his voice. "Might I have a word with you in private?"

George resumed his seat, planting his feet to keep the chair from swaying. "I'm sure whatever you have to say you can say in front of the others."

The others were eyeing George and the newcomer the way a glutton might size up a ceiling-high trifle.

"What did you say your name was again?" George added.

"Padgett." He spat the name as if it were a curse, which in George's opinion was the most appropriate way to pronounce it.

"Care to join us?" George spread his chips out over several cards. Time to start employing a different strategy. "I have to admit this is the strangest coincidence." He ignored Padgett for now and addressed Matthews. "I've just come up from a house party in Kent. One of the guests looked exactly like Padgett here. Same height, same face, same voice. An identical twin, I'd swear to it."

Williams nudged at Padgett with his elbow. "Roger, you never said you had a twin."

"No, just a sister," added Roberts.

And what would the others say if George revealed that said sister had serviced him in bed for the past six months? "Oh, this man couldn't have been Padgett's brother. He told us his name was Reginald Leach."

"Leach?" Matthews paused in the middle of stacking his chips.

"Yes," George said, "that was the name. Have you ever heard anything more ridiculous? At any rate, this Leach fellow liked to listen to himself talk. Nothing like our friend Padgett here. You're awfully quiet, you know. Are you certain you feel up to a few turns?"

"Perhaps he's exhausted himself," said Matthews.

The others chuckled.

"Why don't you shut your gob and place the next wager?" Padgett growled. "Or are you afraid of running up more debts? Seems I've heard a thing or two about you."

"I'd be happy to match any wager you'd care to make. We could go one on one." George casually pulled a pack of cards from his topcoat and handed it to Matthews for inspection. "Piquet if you like."

George's words brimmed with bravado, but he didn't care. He knew enough unsavory details about the man sitting across the table. He could rattle Padgett with a well-placed barb. All lay in the timing, just like in the boxing ring. He only needed that one fleeting instant when his opponent dropped his guard and *bang*—he'd sneak in with his signature left hook. So what if, in this case, that hook was verbal?

"How do I know you're good for it?" Padgett sneered.

"I'm more worried if *you're* good for it. You see, I played against Leach last week."

"Wait a moment," Andrews broke in. "Who the hell is this Leach person?"

"God only knows. The name sounds made up if you ask me." George gave the cards a final shuffle. "Shall we get down to business, gentlemen? Why don't we begin with the amount of that marker?"

GEORGE held on to his final card, knowing it would beat anything Padgett held. That was the beauty of piquet. A reckless player could give away the contents of his hand in the declaration phase, making him that much easier to beat.

Padgett scowled across a mountain of chips. The final hand, and enough lay on the table to buy off Redditch and more, just the way George had planned.

"Go on," Padgett said. "Finish me."

George allowed himself a grin. "Perhaps I'd rather savor the moment."

"Why? You know you've won."

Not only won but taken all the tricks this hand—a *capot*. The victory ought to have elated him. In one turn of the cards, his debts would be cleared, along with Summersby's, but he'd let his opponent make off with the entire pot if it meant he could have Isabelle.

He nudged a stack of chips worth at least a hundred in Padgett's direction. "How about I give you a chance to earn back some of your losses before I turn the final card?"

Padgett rounded brandy-bleary eyes. "Why in God's name would you do that?"

"I want answers." George slammed his final card face-down on the table. "Why did you abandon Isabelle?"

Padgett's glance flitted from side to side—checking his friends' reaction. The others sat in rapt silence, riveted to the proceedings. With each verbal salvo, their heads bobbed back and forth as if they were tracking the progress of a cricket ball. With such captive witnesses, at least no one would later accuse George of cheating.

"I didn't know she was in a delicate condition."

George snatched a chip from Padgett's stack. "Oh, come now. You knew to contact her before you made off with her boy."

"I didn't *know* at first."

"Isabelle said you disappeared right after you seduced her."

"I had my reasons." Padgett eyed his chips, as if he were afraid George might deprive him of a few more. "Bad enough I ruined her. Only I didn't run far enough before her father's cronies caught up to me and told me of the rest of it, that I'd left her with child. He wanted restitution."

"So you ran on instead of doing the right thing."

"Good God, man. Do you know what sort the Earl of Redditch is?" Padgett had long since dropped his jovial manner and replaced it with a sort of grim desperation. George had seen similar expressions on Summersby's face. "Of course I ran. Thought he couldn't touch me on the continent. As it was, it took him a while to find me."

"Then why come back?"

"I came up with a scheme to beat the bastard at his

own game." Padgett stretched his lips into a semblance of a smile that was as far from his usual grin as a skull's leer. "Instead of me paying, it would be him paying me to keep quiet about his daughter."

George tamped down an upsurge of rage. "And you had to involve the child in that?"

"The boy was a means to get Redditch's attention. Isabelle couldn't pay, but Redditch could. Not that it matters anymore, does it?"

God in heaven, what an idiotic risk to take. As much care as the man had shown his daughter, he wouldn't have given a fig for the child. No, Redditch was cold enough to leave them all to rot.

Game over. He flipped the final card, stood, and seized Padgett by the lapels. "So just like that you were willing to ruin her all over again?"

Padgett rolled his shoulders free of George's grip. "She was already ruined. What's it to you?"

Roberts and Matthews stood, but George pushed past that negligible barrier. He rounded the table, reared back a fist and smashed it into Padgett's face. His nose crunched beneath George's knuckles, his head snapped back and his chair overturned. The heavy table beckoned. How George would love to upend that, as well, but not at the expense of his hard-won gains.

"You're no more than a pathetic coward," he growled over Padgett's inert form.

He scooped up his winnings and stalked to the wicket to exchange his chips for blunt. With every clunk of his Hessians on the floor, his anger drained away, as the echo of his last words replayed in his mind. *Pathetic coward.* George might as well have aimed those words at himself.

* * *

THE Upperton carriage rattled to a halt in the middle of the dusty street. After hours of sitting still, Jack squirmed out of Isabelle's embrace, no doubt eager to run the kinks from his legs. No sooner were the steps lowered than Jack bounded free.

"You're to stay near the house," Isabelle scolded as she alit.

"Aw, Mama."

"He's spent days cooped up with naught to do but eat," Biggles reminded her. "Let him run."

"He can run all he likes in the garden." She would never let him out of her sight again.

Biggles laid a fleshy hand on her shoulder. "Ye won't hold him forever."

Isabelle knew. God, she knew. But for the next few days, she would fly into a panic every time the boy left her line of sight.

"Come in the house." Biggles gave her a comforting squeeze. "I'll start a fire and make ye some tea."

Isabelle paused on the threshold. Biggles had stepped over a cream-colored rectangle of paper lying on the floor. She picked it up. A quality calling card, such as she used to possess. A shiver snaked down her spine, and she turned the card over. Her father's name and title marched across the vellum in stark black ink, so thick the letters were raised. A summons. Her father was calling her home, so many years after he'd turned her out. But why?

"Wot's all this then?"

She looked up sharply, but Biggles's gaze was fixed not on her, but in the corner near the hearth.

Isabelle had cleared away the remains of the scandalous picnic she and George had shared, but the basket still stood in the corner next to the fireplace. The sight brought back a spate of now painful memories, but she refused to dwell on them. "I was sent a few gifts from the manor. There's chocolate. Perhaps we can make a pot for Jack."

Biggles lowered her brows into a scowl. "That boy's had more than his fill of sweets. He'd be certain to refuse after all the bellyache he's endured."

That pronouncement was nearly as painful as any memory of George her brain might conjure. The thoughtfulness of Julia's gift had touched her deeply. The idea of finally providing her boy with an indulgence had delighted her, and now even that chance had been ripped away. Lucy had got there first and spoiled the treat for Jack. Now Isabelle was deprived of even the small joy of watching her son's eyes widen with relish the first time he felt the velvet glide of chocolate on his tongue.

"Damn the woman," she muttered, folding her fingers about her father's card.

Crouched before the hearth, Biggles glanced over her shoulder. "Wot's this now?"

"That . . . that . . ." Isabelle couldn't bring herself to voice the name, nor could she come up with an adequate identifier to describe her.

Biggles, however, cottoned on. "That strumpet? She is to be sure, but such talk is beneath ye."

Well Isabelle knew it. She didn't even think of her cousin in those terms, but Lucy . . . Lucy had stolen her boy, and George . . . No, no, she must not think of him. George had never been hers. He never would be.

You could have had him. You could have said yes.

Perhaps, but at what price? Best she never found out.

"Do ye want to talk about what happened while I was away?"

"I let a man charm me again." That much was safe. That much she could admit to without dwelling on what might have been. "You'd think I'd have learned better after the first time."

"Men are meant to charm women, and we as women are inclined to fall. It's the way of things."

Isabelle stared while Biggles poked at her nascent fire. "You were never so foolish."

"Foolish?" Biggles reached for the kettle. "P'rhaps. But lucky, too. I was never caught."

Of course she wasn't, and if she had found herself with child, she knew just what to take to restore her courses.

"Ye wouldn't be wanting some pennyroyal with your tea, would ye?"

"No." The reply was automatic. More the fool her, perhaps, if she actually was expecting George's child, but she could no more expunge the seed than she could Jack. She looked up to find Biggles watching her closely. She held the other woman's gaze and repeated the reply. "No."

"Have ye fallen for the man, then?"

Isabelle closed her eyes against Biggles's continued scrutiny. "It does not matter. I've no claim on him, whatever else happens. If I bear his child, he'll never know."

Biggles opened her mouth, but a rapping at the door cut off her reply.

"Lawks, give a body time t' get home," she muttered. "Must've had their noses pushed t' the window awaitin' our arrival."

"Yes, and now they've come to see what they can dig up," Isabelle replied darkly.

Biggles pressed her lips into a line of assent and opened the door. "Why, Mrs. Weston."

The vicar's wife stood on the threshold, her expression collected, or perhaps a better term would be set.

Isabelle stood and fumbled immediately for her pocket. She'd carried Mrs. Cox's bundle of herbs on her for the better part of three days, although they might now be worse for wear after their dousing. "Is Peter ailing again?"

"I haven't come about Peter."

Mrs. Weston's tone carried an edge that sent a finger of warning creeping down Isabelle's spine. She'd heard that very tone of censure before—from her own family. "Then why have you come? We've only just arrived from retrieving my son."

"I am aware." The vicar's wife remained rooted firmly to the doorstep, as if the air in the cottage might somehow be tainted. Yet she craned her neck, and her gaze darted to the far corners of the room. "Rather a fancy conveyance. I trust it was well sprung."

So cool she was in her superiority, so composed. Isabelle's father had comported himself in the same manner—ever the gentleman, even when he turned his own daughter out of the house.

Biggles crossed her arms over her ample bosom. "Have ye come for a reason or are ye nosing for gossip?"

"It is my unfortunate duty on behalf of the parish to inform Miss Mears she is no longer welcome as a resident of this village."

"Wot's this now?"

Mrs. Weston went on as if Biggles hadn't said a word. "We were willing to tolerate one natural child. Anyone might make a mistake, but as long as the error is atoned for, as long as it is viewed with contriteness and a firm intention not to repeat the error, well . . ."

She waved a hand as if chasing off a fly. "What we will not tolerate is the kind of carryings-on that might lead to more bastards. Beyond the intolerable example set by such behavior, we see no need to give alms when such could be avoided through more rigid morality."

The ruffles on Biggles's mobcap shook as she drew herself up. "Such nerve ye have, goin' on about morality when Isabelle's been sick with worry over her boy. Have ye no heart? I'll warrant ye never lifted a finger to help her search."

"*My* son was ill."

"He wouldn't always be ill if ye made certain he ate properly. Spoiled little brat."

Isabelle should have reacted by now, but a numbness caused by the overwhelming emotions of the past few days encased her. She might as well be walking waist-high in icy water. No more. After losing her son, after Lucy, after George, after all the years she'd fought for acceptance in this place, she no longer felt the inclination to fight. Society had defeated her. Let it win.

She closed her fist about her father's card, and its thick edges cut into her palm. She did, after all, have a choice. "It's all right, Biggles. Jack and I will be gone in the morning."

CHAPTER TWENTY-TWO

REDDITCH'S BUTLER ushered George into a small parlor. The room was clearly not a place where the master would receive his most distinguished guests, but its polished woods, silk-upholstered furnishings, and embossed wallpaper made the space well enough appointed. An understated taste that screamed of blunt.

Lush carpeting muffled the sounds of his footfalls as he crossed to a painting. An ornate frame, edged in gilt, surrounded the portrait of a haughty-looking man in a white periwig, his cheeks rouged, his hand tucked into the breast of a teal blue coat. Lace cascaded from the subject's cuffs and throat. His free hand perched atop a walking stick.

George allowed himself a grim smile. Redditch was such a stickler for propriety, or at least the appearance of propriety, but this ancestor—"Nothing but a macaroni."

Footsteps echoed through the vast corridor beyond, and George turned, even though their rapid cadence indicated legs too short to belong to an adult.

Jack trotted into the room. "Thought I saw you."

George caught his breath. What the devil was Jack doing here? And in that garb? The boy was clothed in deep green breeches and waistcoat of the same velvet he'd spotted on the footmen. Livery. Redditch had turned his own grandson into a servant.

George knelt to bring himself on a level with the child. "Why have they got you all jumped up like that?"

Jack glanced down at his garments and scrunched his face into a scowl. "Eastwicke says I have to. I don't like it much. The coat itches, and the shoes pinch."

"And what have they got you doing in such dress?" George couldn't imagine a position fit for a lad his age. He was too small for the stables and had yet to develop the physical strength required of house servants.

"They're fixing to make me hall boy. Only Eastwicke says I'm to improve my manners and speech."

George shot to his feet and strode to the window. Hall boy! Fit for nothing better than to empty the servants' chamber pots and polish the master's boots. When he was a bit older, he might advance to lighting the kitchen fire. How could Isabelle allow it? How could she think this life was an improvement over their life in Kent?

"Do you like being hall boy?" He struggled to keep his tone casual.

"It's all right. I don't like the clothes, but Cook gives me all the beef I can eat."

Well, yes, at least he wasn't starving, but hall boy! "What does your mama have to say about your situation?"

Before Jack had a chance to reply, a voice sounded in the corridor. "That boy! Where has he got to now?"

That boy's eyes widened. "I've got to run."

He scampered from the room before George could say another word. Just as well. He wanted to smash something. He eyed the portrait of the dandy. "I ought to put you out of your misery."

Not that sending his fist through the canvas would make him feel any better. Or endear him to Redditch, for that matter. He must at least start this interview on a friendly note. Defacing the earl's ancestor hardly fit the bill.

And just where was Isabelle in this monstrosity of a townhouse? Did she even have a say in Jack's upbringing now that she'd returned to her family? Had they truly taken her in, or did she live like a servant as well?

He shook his head, as if that would clear out his thoughts of her. It was over. She couldn't forgive him. He must accept that and forget. Once he was quit of Redditch today, his last tie to her would be severed. And then he'd have no more reason to think of her, to lie in bed at night and dream of the sweet haven of her body.

More footsteps, heavier this time, announced another imminent arrival. George pressed his fingernails into his palm, the mild pain a reminder that he must maintain his *sang-froid*. The idea of Jack being treated like the lowest of servants sent his blood pounding through his veins in seething torrents.

But he'd cooled his heels for weeks waiting for Redditch to return to Town. He would achieve nothing if he got himself thrown out for insolence or, worse, violence.

"Yes, and what might I do for you?" Redditch possessed nothing of his daughter's ethereal beauty and delicate lines. Except for his lack of overly garish clothes, he bore a striking resemblance to the fop in the portrait, although his nose was longer and thinner. The better to look down on peons.

"Have we been introduced?" His tone matched his air, cold and distant. In sheer disdain, Isabelle was his equal. She'd uttered her final words to George with the same amount of frost.

"Did your man not give you my card?"

No response. Not even a blink of a steely gray eye.

"No matter, my lord. I've come on business."

Redditch hitched up his chin. "You have business with me?"

"In the name of Adrian Summersby, I do." George expected a reaction to that name, at the very least.

"Am I supposed to know who that is?"

Was the man made of ice? Even so, the heat of George's anger would be sufficient to melt the earl, and soon. His blood was ready to boil over.

"Am I to surmise from that question that you hound so many men to take their own lives, you can't even keep their names straight?" George reached into his pocket with a shaking hand and withdrew a heavy purse. "There's more where this came from, a down payment, if you will. I thought to give it to you to clear a friend's name."

Redditch looked him in the eye. "Do you enjoy tilting at windmills?"

"What the devil are you talking about?"

"You wish to restore the honor of a suicide." Redditch gave an ugly shout of laughter. "What next? You'll petition the church to give him a decent burial and the courts to restore his goods to his heirs?"

George let his chest expand with air, again and yet again, enough that the urge to hurl the purse at Redditch's head subsided. "Do you have any idea what it looks like when an old friend puts a pistol in his mouth and pulls the trigger? I do, thanks to you. It isn't pleasant."

Redditch's pasty cheeks took on a pinkish tinge. "You can't lay the blame at my feet if the man was too cowardly to face up to his obligations."

"He was desperate," George hissed. He wouldn't let himself shout, wouldn't give in to the need to grab this bastard by the lapels and pummel some sense into him. "Your lackeys hounded him until he saw no other way out. And for what? Filthy lucre. You don't look as if you're in any great need."

He flung a hand in the direction of the fop. "Good

Christ, you might sell a painting or two and make up the difference."

"Now see here—"

George hefted the purse. It weighed heavy in his palm, but surely not as heavy as Summersby's worries during those final days. Most definitely not as heavy as Jack's duties would weigh on him over the years.

Jack.

Only one of them was alive. Only one would have to endure this man's notion of justice and propriety. And Jack was so young. Years stretched ahead of the boy before he might extricate himself from this situation, if he ever did. George couldn't condemn a child to that. He'd had enough personal experience with a relative holding him back.

As for Summersby's widow, he had enough to ensure her care, as well.

"Yes, I see now." He closed his fingers about the bag of coins. "I've changed my mind. I'm not about to hand you as much as a pence for Summersby's debts. You can choke on them."

Redditch opened his mouth, no doubt to summon the butler, along with a bulky footman or two to convince him to leave.

"No matter what," George said before Redditch could call out, "Summersby isn't coming back, and there's the living to consider. I'm going to put these funds into a trust—in the name of your grandson."

The pink in the earl's cheeks turned to two ugly red blotches. "I have no grandson," he roared.

"I can see how you prefer to deny him, since you're currently treating him as your hall boy."

"You know *nothing* of my family. Nothing!"

"I reckon you have your daughter spirited away somewhere as well. Perhaps I'll find her in the scullery."

"Eastwicke!"

"You might want to reconsider before summoning your toughs. I know a great deal about your family's scandals, a great deal I'm sure you'd rather keep quiet." George turned the purse in his hand. "I'm sure I've got enough here to print pamphlets."

The butler loomed in the doorway. "You called, sir?"

"An error on my part. I do not require anything." Redditch waited until Eastwicke had returned to his designated circle of hell before continuing. "If you print pamphlets, I shall sue for libel."

"One problem with that, my lord." George permitted himself a smile. "It isn't libel if it's true."

"How dare you threaten me?"

"I'd prefer not, if we can come to an understanding. I'd much rather spend this blunt on something worthy, such as arranging a place for Jack at Eton."

"Eton?" Redditch laughed. "More windmills, is it? Eton does not admit bastards."

"Harrow then. Never fear, I shall find a public school that will admit him."

"He will never be admitted into polite society, no matter if he has the education for it. In fact, once he gets to school, the other boys will remind him of his origins daily."

George nodded. How well he knew the machinations of English public schools. He'd survived and so would Jack. "I plan on ensuring he has the proper tutors. Both in Latin and boxing."

A snuffle just outside the morning room set Isabelle's senses on alert. She set aside her dusting cloth and turned toward the sound. Jack lurked in the corridor beyond. The look in his downturned eyes screamed guilt.

That boy, always wandering off. "What are you doing

here?" she asked. "You know Eastwicke won't approve if you're not at your post."

"Don't care what he thinks." His response was hard and sullen.

"You *must* have a care for his good opinion." How many times in the past weeks had she repeated this dictum? "It's how you'll retain your position so you can earn your keep like a grown man."

"I don't want to earn my keep here anymore." He advanced a few steps into the room. "I want to go back and live with Biggles."

Isabelle crossed her arms over her dark gray bodice and tapped her fingers against her elbow. Jack's dissatisfaction with their current living arrangement was hardly a new thing, but the past few days had passed without complaint. She'd thought he was getting used to it. Finally.

"Did Eastwicke have words with you again?"

Lower lip caught between his teeth, Jack shook his head.

A glance down the corridor showed no butler or footman bearing down on them. Perhaps she had time to convince him to return to his post. She knelt and put an arm about his shoulder. He jerked beneath her touch, the movement not evasive. No, it was more of a wince. He held his right hand hidden behind his back. How odd.

"Do you have something for me?" she asked carefully.

Another shake of his head.

"What are you hiding then?" Her gut told her it wasn't anything good.

On his refusal to reply, she reached for his arm. Stubborn to the last, he held himself stiff. When she finally managed to coax his hand into view, her breath rushed out in a gasp. Angry, red welts lined a rapidly swelling palm.

"Did Eastwicke do this?" She resorted to a whisper in order to keep her voice steady. No sense in upsetting the boy any further. She was upset enough for them both.

He nodded, and she pulled him into a full embrace. The backs of her eyes burned, and her fingers trembled against her son's coarse hair. Blast it all to the devil. Eastwicke, that overblown oaf. She wouldn't stand for it. Jack may have no more standing in this house than the lowest servants, but she wouldn't step aside and allow him to be mistreated.

"We'll see about this," she said, the words as much a promise to herself as an affirmation to her son. "I'll have a word with Father, and we'll see."

She released Jack and scrambled to her feet, pressing her palms along her skirts without thought. She'd no reason to smooth such weeds, but she still retained enough pride to face her father with her chin held high.

He tugged at her apron. "Mama?"

"What is it, dear?"

"I wasn't at my post."

"Yes." She ruffled his hair. "And you're still not."

"But, Mama, George is here."

"George?" What on earth? Her pulse kicked up a notch. "You mean Mr. Upperton."

"Yes, George." Heavens, Jack sounded so hopeful, as if George might rescue him again. "It's why I wasn't at my post. Eastwicke showed him in, and I had to make sure."

Her heart leapt into her throat. She pressed her fingertips to the notch at the base of her neck, as if that might persuade it to calm its rapid beat. She could not hope for a rescue this time. What could he possibly want here? Blast it all, she shouldn't care. She wouldn't let herself. She'd never get over the hurt if she couldn't control her reaction to the mere thought of his presence.

She'd do this. George or no, she'd face her father and tell him in no uncertain terms what she would not tolerate.

She sent Jack back to his post and strode down the corridor, failing to stem the barrage of memories. George stumbling from the waves with Jack in his arms. Wandering in from the garden at Shoreford to catch him at the piano. Ducking into the gamesman's cottage to escape a sudden downpour. George laying her out on her kitchen table to prove to her the ecstasy possible between a man and woman.

The glare of cold steel he'd turned on his mistress. Yes, she must keep that image foremost in her mind. The rest was nothing but distraction.

Exceedingly pleasant distraction, but distraction nonetheless.

The sound of raised voices emanating from one of the smaller parlors brought her up short. Gracious, what could they be arguing over? Something about pamphlets and decent people and society's opinion, but the words jumbled in her mind. Then she heard mention of her son's name.

Of course. George knew Jack was here. They'd seen each other.

Shame billowed through her. George had seen how low she'd stooped to ensure a roof over their heads and decent food in their bellies. Jack's belly, especially.

No more. She refused to put up with the humiliation of seeing her boy polish boots. Somehow she'd find a better way, but not here. Squaring her shoulders, she stepped into the doorway.

George stood less than a foot away from the familiar figure of her father. The two men glared at each other. George's hand curled into a fist at his side, and his shoulders heaved with rapid breaths. Handsome as ever, he seemed to swell to fill the space of the room.

Distraction. She blinked the image away.

"What is it you want?" her father demanded.

George turned his head toward the door. He met her gaze and held it. A glimmer of longing passed through the gray depths of his eyes. How she wanted to shutter her lids against that expression, but it compelled her to bear witness, as if it had a will of its own. *This is my naked emotion, and you* shall *see it. You shall.*

Good Lord, she couldn't imagine a man wearing such an open expression—unless he was in love. The force of his feeling speared her through the chest and arrowed deep into her gut until her knees threatened to buckle.

But then his eyes flicked down her body. Heat flooded her face. Dear God, he was staring at her serviceable rag of a dress, so out of place in this fashionable townhouse. He'd never seen her bedecked in finery, but it had never mattered until now.

He turned to her father. "What I want most is not in your power to grant me."

Her father pivoted, following the direction of George's gaze. "Not now, Isabelle."

"It may as well be now." The anger seething behind George's words pulled their attention back to him. "I didn't think I could possibly form a lower opinion of you. This interview is over."

Before Isabelle could interject, before her father could react, George hauled back a fist and delivered a devastating blow to the older man's jaw. Father's head jerked back before he crumpled to the floor.

George pushed past her without a word of acknowledgment. His booted feet echoed down the corridor, the thuds growing fainter as he neared the foyer. Just like that, he was once again gone from her life. Only this time, she hadn't sent him away.

Her father raised himself on his elbow and shook his head like a dog emerging from a pond.

Some deeply engrained sense of filial duty pressed her forward. "Are you all right?"

Her father probed at a reddening knot just behind his chin. "My teeth seem to be all in their proper places." He lowered his hand and eyed her closely. "And what is he to you?"

"Nothing." Isabelle swallowed and cast a swift glance over her shoulder, as if somehow George might reappear to put the lie to her reply. "What on earth would give you the idea I had any connection to him?"

"He said he wants to send your boy to Eton."

She backed up a step. "What?"

"You heard me. He wants to send that boy to Eton of all places. Where would he get such a notion if he wasn't the boy's real father?"

"He is most certainly not Jack's father." If only. "I told you years ago who Jack's father was. I didn't lie about that." She wasn't sure how she managed to spit out that reply. Her throat had gone oddly tight.

Jack at Eton. She couldn't fathom such an idea. How generous of George, but at the same time how presumptuous. As if he could blithely waltz in and take her son from her. The nerve!

"Jack. Such a common name."

Isabelle ignored the gibe. She'd purposely chosen the name for its commonness. When her son was born, she'd wanted nothing to do with the polite society that had spurned her—that spurned her yet.

"I came to see you about Jack, as it happens. I won't tolerate Eastwicke's treatment of him."

Her father pushed to his feet. "I knew it. You can't stand by and let him learn his place. If you coddle him—"

"Eastwicke beat his hand with a stick," Isabelle shouted over him. Manners be damned. "How do you expect him to perform his duties with a sore hand? I will not tolerate it. In fact, I've come to a decision. As of this moment, Jack is no longer in your employ."

"You shall not leave. I forbid it."

Right. She'd expected as much. He'd only called her home to ensure she caused the family no more embarrassment. Doubtless Emily had told him where he could find his wayward daughter. "You cannot stop me. I shall pack our things, and we'll be gone within the hour."

As to where they would go after that, somehow she'd find the means to take Jack back to Kent. If Mrs. Weston insisted on barring her from the village, she'd appeal to Julia's sense of fairness. But before she left Mayfair, she had a call to pay.

CHAPTER TWENTY-THREE

IT WAS over. George slumped in his study, fingering the brandy decanter. He might have been halfway through it by now—in celebration, naturally—but the mere thought of drink turned his stomach. In the end, he'd accomplished nothing. Redditch wasn't about to change his ways, and Isabelle . . .

A discreet cough cut into his thoughts. "George, I think you'd better come to the foyer."

He glanced up to find Henrietta standing before him. How had she entered his inner sanctum so soundlessly? "What now?"

His mood had not improved a whit since his return from Redditch's. Seeing Jack—seeing Isabelle—treated like servants in what should have been their home. Good Christ! Although he shouldn't be surprised. Redditch was a right bastard.

"Come."

He lowered his brows. Henrietta seemed rather breathless, but why should she be breathless on his account?

"Quickly, before Sanders puts them off."

"Puts who off?"

"Just come," his sister repeated.

He heaved himself to his feet. His right hand still throbbed dully from its impact with Redditch's jaw. The damned idiot's thickness of skull apparently extended as far as his mandible.

He followed his sister to the foyer, where Sanders blocked his view of the entrance. "I really must insist, Miss—"

Miss? What the devil? "I say," George interjected, "what's the matter here?"

Sanders turned. "I've tried to explain to this woman you are not at home, but she refuses—" A small figure darting past him cut him off abruptly. "Ho there."

"Good day, George." Yes, a small figure—small, blond, and very familiar.

Jack. He might have known. At least the lad was no longer clad in livery. And if Jack was here, Isabelle couldn't be far behind. God, he was in no temper to face either of them. "That will be all, Sanders."

Gait stiff and insulted, the butler took himself off, and Isabelle stepped into the foyer. "Forgive the intrusion, but—"

George swept his gaze over her. She still wore the shabby gray gown, and her bonnet wasn't in much better condition. No wonder Sanders refused to let her in. She held a bulging satchel in one hand, a satchel that may well have contained all her worldly possessions. With a six-year-old boy in tow, she looked every inch the beggar.

But why turn up on his doorstep when she'd made it quite clear she wanted no more to do with him?

"Why have you come?" He refused to observe the niceties, not after the confrontation with her father, and not with her.

"We're going to have a talk, you and I." Apparently she wasn't about to observe the niceties, either. Not if her tone was any indication. She might have addressed her son in such a manner after she'd caught him shirking his chores and sneaking off to the beach.

"You can come into the front parlor." At least he could

do Redditch one better and show her to a proper receiving room. He led the way, aware of the slightly shabby air that hung about his family's townhouse. The Uppertons might inhabit Mayfair, the same as the Marshalls, but the difference in their fortunes showed in the fading wallpaper, the thinner carpeting and the loosening threads on the furnishings.

"Perhaps your sister would take Jack to the kitchens?" Isabelle suggested.

At such a scandalous suggestion, Henrietta pressed her fingers to her lips. "What would Mama say if she knew I'd left you alone?"

"Mama's opinion be damned. And she won't say a word, because she won't find out about this." George eyed his sister. "Will she?"

"You know I wouldn't mention a thing, but the servants . . . Sanders is sure to tell."

"If he does, I'll see him dismissed. Be sure he knows that—if he hasn't already overheard. Now take Jack to the kitchen and give him anything he wants. Whatever his mother has to discuss with me shouldn't take long."

George waited until Henrietta had marched the boy toward the stairs leading below before asking his next question. "Where are you going?" He pointed his chin at the satchel.

She opened her mouth and closed it. "I shouldn't tell you."

"Why not? You're here. Clearly you feel you have business with me."

"Yes, and that business is the reason I oughtn't to tell you." She paused in the midst of removing her bonnet. A tousle of blond curls cascaded to her shoulders. "What are your designs on Jack?"

He rubbed tingling fingers together. How well he recalled the texture of those curls. What he wouldn't give to feel them once more sifting through his hands. Something squeezed the air from his lungs. His damned heart, hang it all. "Who says I have any?"

She stepped closer, and a line formed above the bridge of her nose. "My father. He says you want to send Jack to Eton."

"I might have mentioned that, yes." He crossed his arms and set his hip against the back of a chair. "Public school, at any rate, if Eton won't admit him."

The line above her nose deepened into a full-on scowl. "You've no right. He's my son. You've no claim on him."

"I hadn't meant to stake a claim. Only . . ." How to explain this? "I thought I'd give the lad a chance."

"A chance?"

"Yes, at a better life. You can't tell me you approve of him living as a servant in his own grandfather's house."

"Of course, I don't. It's why I left."

"Left? You should never have gone back in the first place. Good God, your own father, treating you as a servant as well." He stopped short at the realization he'd come close to shouting those final words. He could get through this interview without creating a scene.

To Isabelle's credit, she did not flinch in the face of his anger. If anything, she drew herself up even further. "I received a summons."

George tamped down an irritating wave of admiration. There was no longer any point to it. "A summons? After he turned you out? And you obeyed?"

"Yes." She cupped a hand over her mouth and looked past his shoulder for a few moments. "I didn't want to go back there," she whispered. "I just . . . I didn't feel I had a choice. Mrs. Weston was waiting for me when I returned to Kent. She informed me that Jack and I were no longer welcome in the village."

"After all you did for her son when he was ill?" A burning in his gut flamed upward, threatening to cloud his vision with red. "And your own was missing? The—"

He cut himself off before he voiced his true opinion of the vicar's wife.

"She felt I was a poor moral influence due to my recent activities." Isabelle looked hard at him.

Yes, they'd been seen. No doubt Mrs. Weston had noted George spending the night at the cottage. Another sin to lay at his doorstep.

"Returning to Father meant a roof over our heads and decent food in Jack's belly," she went on. "And Father wanted me back, even if I could not go into society."

"And why, after all the time he left you to fend for yourself?" How much easier to concentrate on Redditch's shortcomings, rather than his own.

"He didn't know where I'd gone. I'm positive Emily informed him of my whereabouts." She paused to swallow, no doubt reigning in some heightened emotion of her own. "He turned me out in a fit of anger when he learned I was expecting Jack. I suspect if he'd stopped to think, he'd have wanted to keep me closer. So I didn't embarrass the family, you see."

"Embarrass, yes." God, could his opinion of her father sink any lower? "Odd way he has of showing it, treating you like a servant."

"What point in wearing nice gowns when no one would see me and the old ones would serve?" The words seemed to catch in her throat. "And I thought Jack would accept his lot more easily if I set an example."

"His lot, his lot." George drummed his fingers against the back of the chair to stave off an upwelling of sympathy. How well he knew her pride. How it must have pained her to return as the prodigal daughter and witness the ill treatment of her son. But he couldn't afford such feelings where Isabelle was concerned. She'd already cost him his heart. "And so you accept that? You won't try to do better for him?"

"No, I won't accept it." She swiped at the corner of her eye. "Not when they beat his hands raw for disobedience. It's why I left."

"You didn't imagine things might come to that?" Cold of him, such a comment, but if he didn't maintain some sort of barrier between them, the dam of his emotions would burst, just as it nearly had in front of Redditch.

As it was, she'd witnessed his raw feeling when their eyes met. For that instant, he'd been unable to maintain his façade of indifference. If he wasn't careful, it would happen again—he'd be open and vulnerable.

Once more, she drew herself up. "I had hoped Eastwicke would take Jack's parentage into consideration."

"Seems he did, only the wrong parent."

She glared at him. "I did not come here to discuss this matter with you."

"Ah, now we've come to it. Why did you come here?"

"I've told you. I do not wish you to send him to Eton."

"Why?"

"Because I will not be beholden to you."

There went her damnable pride again. "Would you allow it as an apology?"

"Apology? For what?"

"I used you poorly in Kent. I should have shown greater restraint and greater discretion. I have no excuse. I simply could not help myself." The appearance of aloofness was beginning to wear thin. He gripped the back of the chair, his fingers tightening until they ached.

"You owe me nothing."

"Would you say the same if I'd got you with child?" He breathed in and asked the real question that plagued him. "*Have* I got you with child?"

"No."

He felt as if he were once more in the waters of the Channel, grasping for Jack. Cold, desperate. An unex-

pected sensation rose up on a wave to engulf him, surprisingly akin to disappointment. But why should he be
disappointed? He ought to rejoice. He'd never wanted a
connection with a woman beyond the carnal.

Only Isabelle was different. He wanted her in his life,
in his future, along with whatever entanglements that
entailed. A home. Jack. Their children. His heir.

"Well, that's . . ." That was what? A relief?

In a sense, yes, because he did not want to saddle her
with another child when she was struggling to make
ends meet with the first one.

Good? God, that was callous, even for his façade. It
also was most emphatically not good, and that thought
scared the hell out of him.

"It's for the best," he supplied.

She turned toward the door.

"Is that all you came for?" He didn't think he'd managed to keep the hope out of his voice.

She eyed him warily from over her shoulder. "I came
to tell you that I did not want you sending my son to
Eton. I've done so."

God, the imperiousness of her tone. Once again, he
recognized her relationship to Redditch. Yes, she'd
grown up commanding servants and expecting unques-
tioned obedience.

"You would deny him a chance at a better life?"

"I do not wish you to take him from me."

"I never said I'd do that." He reached into his morning coat and withdrew the purse with which he'd sought
to settle accounts with her father. The coins clinked
against one another. "I only wished to provide."

She stared at the pouch, and he could practically see
her calculating how much meat the sum might fetch, how
many yards of fabric for new clothes, how many months'
rent on a house. Practical considerations. In her circumstances, they all came before Jack's education.

"If you prefer," he said to break the silence, "I'll just give this to you to spend as you see fit."

She choked, and the noise sounded suspiciously like a sob. A moment later, she composed her features into strict lines. "You cannot buy me."

"I do not wish to."

"Then, pray, what is it you want?" The same question her father had asked not an hour since.

She already knew the answer, he was sure, if not consciously then in her heart. He'd been unable to mask his stark yearning earlier when he'd met her gaze.

"Do you want my plain answer?" Part of him prayed she'd decline. For if he bared his heart to her, she might still refuse him.

He scanned her expression for any hint of her mind-set. Her lower lip disappeared between her teeth, and a bolt of need shot through him as he recalled its plump pliancy moving beneath his mouth.

At the same time, hope blossomed within him. If she was just as hesitant, it might mean her feelings mirrored his. That she, too, feared the sting of rejection.

"All right." Her response was deceptively casual, but it carried an edge that proclaimed his answer mattered and mattered deeply.

"I want you to marry me."

"You've asked before. I turned you down."

Responding with a clever turn of phrase—with just the right witticism—had always come so easily. So why, now that it signified, could he not find the right words? But that was the whole problem. His response to her *signified* more than anything ever had. If he mucked this up, it was over. Last chance. No pressure. None at all. God, he'd rather sit down on a stage before the entire *ton*, the king included, and play a concerto.

"It's different now." He held himself rigid against the back of the chair. "I'm not asking you out of a sense of obligation. I'm asking because, ever since I met you, I cannot keep you from my thoughts. You . . . you are like the music inside me. As much as I may wish to, I cannot excise it. It is part of me."

"Do you wish to excise me then?"

"No." The hell with it all. She might yet reject him, but he could no longer hold himself from her. He strode across the room and grasped her by the upper arms. "I'd sooner cut out my own heart."

A tear leaked from the corner of her eye and traced a path down her cheekbone. Damn. He'd never been able to stand firm in the face of her tears. He raised a hand to take a droplet onto his fingertip.

Her face crumpled, and she fell against him. He settled her into an embrace, just shy of crushing.

"Isabelle?" He smoothed his palm down her spine from her neck to her waist and back. Her unique scent of lavender and woman tickled his nostrils, and he marveled at how well her petite form molded to him. No other female had ever fit so well.

She pressed her face to the front of his waistcoat, trembling, but her hands remained at her sides.

"Isabelle." He eased his palms to her shoulders, gently, and then slid them farther until they cradled her face. He searched her gaze, her expression, her stance for answers and read only confusion. "Don't you have an answer for me?"

She cast her glance downward, and he steeled himself for her rejection. She'd never get past the way he treated Lucy, and he couldn't blame her. He'd been an utter scoundrel over that situation, no better than Padgett. No excuse he could make would ever change that.

He dropped his arms and stepped back. Her lack of response felt like a kick in the gut. Several kicks, in fact. It was as if the entire sixth form back at school had decided to have a go at him, one after the other, while the rest held him down. "I understand. Please. Take the money. I will send along the rest as soon as you give me your direction, but I'll not deliver it in person. You need not see me again."

Somehow, somehow he would get past this moment. Maybe in a year or two, he'd find it within himself to satisfy his mother and marry some chit, the more brainless the better. Anything, as long as she was the complete opposite of Isabelle.

He'd certainly never find her equal.

But who was he fooling? He'd never get over her. She truly was as deeply engrained in his heart as the music.

"I couldn't help myself, you know," he said, as much to fill the void left by her silence, as anything. "Falling for you was as simple as breathing. Lucy and I . . ." God, why was he bringing this up? He was only driving the final nail into his coffin. "I know there's nothing I can say to excuse my actions in your eyes. She's a courtesan. She understood it was business. For her as much as for me. I'm not proud to admit that, but I would never have touched her again. I would have provided."

Provided. It sounded so damned sterile and disconnected. Empty. In no way did such a word relate to his sentiments where Isabelle was concerned. He'd already dug himself six feet deep, but with every word he added, he felt as if he were only going deeper. He might make it clear to China before he was through.

"I know." God help her for that admission, but she couldn't hold back the words any more than she could have stopped the blood coursing through her veins, any more than she could stop his earlier statement from echoing through her mind.

I'd sooner cut out my own heart. How the truth had rung through those few syllables.

"I—what?"

"I know. I know you would have provided." She gestured toward the pouch full of money. That burgeoning sack represented everything to her, freedom and choice both. "You're ready to press all of that on me. I shouldn't take it, but I can't stop thinking what sort of start it would give us."

"Then take it and go. I'll not darken your lives any further." Pain and resignation laced his reply.

She closed her fingers about the pouch of coins and pushed it back toward him. "I cannot accept this."

"It is a gift, and I would give you more." Expression closed off, he bit out the words. "I would give you all you deserved, everything your family has taken from you. If you would have me, I would give you all of myself."

The backs of her eyes stung, and a knot formed in her throat. As much as experience had taught her to erect a barrier about her emotions, nothing was strong enough to stem the tide that rose in her now. She couldn't do this to him, couldn't stand to see him hurt any longer. The man made mistakes, yes, but he had stood by her at a time when almost no one else had. He still stood by her, no matter what she decided. The choice was hers.

And his arms about her just now—nothing had felt more right.

"I don't wish for your coin. Save it for someone more deserving." Her vision clouded, and she raised her eyes to the ceiling until it cleared. "I've also used you ill. When you sent me home after we found Jack. And just now. And I never thanked you for all your help in bringing my son back to me."

She leaned forward, intent on kissing his cheek, but George met her halfway. He claimed her mouth, conquered it fully. His arms wrapped about her, and crushed her body to his. Thank goodness for the support because her knees refused to hold her up any longer. She clung to his shoulders for dear life, until at last he relented. By then he'd left her gasping. His breath released in a warm rush into her mouth, his life mingling with hers. As it should.

When he pulled away, a light of hope shone in his eyes, a light that made her heart swell in reply until it bruised her ribs.

"You'll pardon me," he whispered. "I was never one for poetry or pretty words. So I'll say it plain. I love you. I never expected to say such a thing to any woman, ever, but you are not just any woman. Might your response give me hope that one day you'll feel the same?"

She pressed trembling fingers to her lips. Never since her downfall had she expected to hear those words from a man. "Not one day. Now."

"Then I shall ask you for the last time. Will you marry me?"

The only reply she could possibly give him was her lips on his, her body to his, an anticipation of a far deeper surrender. After that, no further words were necessary.

EPILOGUE

Two months later

ISABELLE FLOATED through the long, gentle fall from the heights, eased back to earth by George's kiss. She snuggled into his embrace, rubbing her cheek through the rasp of his chest hair. Beneath her ear, his heartbeat slowed.

Very unfashionable of them to share a bed every night, but if fashion meant spending the long, dark hours apart, she'd happily call herself rustic and move on.

The bed was wide, the mattress thick, the sheets crisp beneath her naked body. Overlaying the clean scent of rich cottons and wood polish was the musk of their joining.

George stirred beneath her, dipping his head to brush a kiss to her hairline before inching himself upright.

"Mmmm, must you leave just yet?" she murmured.

The rumble of his laughter vibrated through her. "Not even married two months and already you've become a sluggard?"

How her life had changed in those two months. Polite society, naturally, would never accept her back as one of their own, but Isabelle didn't need them. Not as long as she had George and his circle of friends. Sophia and Julia, their husbands and extended family had gathered round them in support on her wedding day. Even George's mother was coming around, helped, no doubt, by a long conversation held behind closed doors between mother and son. Isabelle had not been privy to the content of that discussion, but her mother-in-law had emerged from George's study white-faced, tight lipped, and apparently chastened.

Isabelle pushed herself up on an elbow, swiping a handful of curls from her eyes. "I'm normally up before you are."

"Correction, my dear. You climb out of bed before I do, but you're never up first."

She gasped. Had he just insinuated . . . He had.

"Rogue," she said through a smile before dissolving into a girlish giggle. How unlike her, but George never failed to lighten her heart.

He rose from the bed, the morning sunlight gilding his naked skin, and thrust his arms through the sleeves of a green velvet banyan. "A pity to have to say so, but you may want to cover yourself."

She stretched herself across the mattress, languid and satisfied, smiling as his gaze traced her form. "You cannot be concerned I'll shock the maid."

"The maid? Hardly. But have you forgotten what day it is?"

"Day? Oh!" She groped for her chemise, hastily discarded the night before.

He was right, of course. Jack might come bursting into the bedchamber at any moment, already dressed and demanding they hurry through breakfast. George had promised to take the boy back to Kent to visit Revelstoke. But the real reason George had declared a holiday from tutors and lessons and most especially mathematics was their plan to pick out a pony. Riding lessons in Hyde Park were soon to become a feature of Jack's upbringing, all in preparation for the day they'd send him off to school.

At the thought, Isabelle ducked her head. Once he was away at school, she'd have to accept not seeing him for weeks at a time. She'd have to settle for letters, but knowing Jack's fondness for writing, those would be scarce as hen's teeth, as Biggles would say. A few years yet remained, but she suspected they'd fly by as quickly as Jack's first six years. Biggles was constantly remarking on the phenomenon.

"Here now." George tipped up her chin. "You're not going broody on me again, are you?"

"A little," she admitted. "Before I know it, my boy will be grown and gone."

"He's only six."

"Six and far too wise for his age." She twisted her hands in the cotton of her chemise. "I feel like it was only yesterday he learned to walk, and I had to keep a constant watch so he wouldn't toddle into the fire. Now you want to put him up on a horse?"

"A pony." He ran his palms down the backs of her arms. "Best he learn while he's young so he doesn't end up like me."

"How's that?"

"Unable to cope with the Buttercups of the world."

She wasn't sure who Buttercup was, beyond surmising one form of equine or another, but she refused to let that question distract her. "You'll have him galloping about, jumping five-foot fences."

"If he has a mind to, I'm not sure how you'll stop him."

She swatted at him. "You are not helping. You're supposed to tell me it'll be all right and not frighten me half to death."

He caught her by the waist and pulled her close. "It'll be all right, five-foot fences and all. If I wasn't positive Jack was about to burst in here, I'd take you back to bed."

"And how would that help?"

He grinned, a woman's downfall wrought in a simple stretch of his lips. It was her downfall, certainly, her personal undoing because she never saw the expression outside their private chambers. It was her exclusive domain and never failed to turn her knees wobbly.

"I should be insulted, having to explain this, but the temptation to demonstrate is too great." He pulled her flush with his body and pressed his lips just beneath her ear. "Pay close attention now. These are the proper uses of conjugal relations."

He nipped at her earlobe. "Distraction. You can't worry if I drive the thoughts from your mind."

"Mmmm." The tactic was working already and all too well. Heavens, one would think he hadn't been near her in a week the way her body responded.

"Seduction." With his tongue, he blazed a trail along her neck. "You're far more open to suggestion in this state."

"Suggestion?" she breathed, tipping her head back. "What can you possibly ask of me now?"

He chuckled against her throat, and the vibrations rippled through her awakening body. "Give me time to think on it, and I'll come up with all manner of ideas. But now you're distracting me, darling, and we can't have that."

He skimmed a hand up her waist to cover her breast. Her nipple hardened into his palm. The hard length of his erection pressed into her belly. She'd only just had him, and she wanted more.

"Last use—gestation."

"Gestation?" How had he guessed? She was only just beginning to suspect herself.

"If I give you another child, you'll be too occupied to worry about Jack so much."

"Rather I'll have two to worry about, but I suppose we'll find out for ourselves in a few months."

He set his hands on her shoulders and pulled back to study her. "Really?"

"I'm more certain with every day that passes."

A different sort of smile spread across his features. Not devious, not promising pleasure, but in its own way just as seductive. This was his face etched into the contours of joy so pure it sent a pang through her midsection. Not heat, but an answering contentment that pulled at her own lips until her cheeks ached.

"If your son is anything like you," she said lightly, "I believe I'll run more than the usual course of worrying."

His smile did not falter. "You can always pray for a daughter."

"Whether it's a boy or a girl, I want you to promise me something."

"Anything." So unreserved, that one word. She really could ask anything of him, and he'd do all within his power to give it.

"If your child shows a talent for music, you will not deny it."

"That will be a very easy promise to keep." He slipped his hands to her cheeks, framing her face before he brushed his lips against hers. "No child of mine shall be forced to hide his true nature."

Warmth bubbled inside her. A vow, just as he'd made when Jack was missing, just as he'd made on their wedding day. "Then I shall worry somewhat less."

"Only somewhat?"

"There's always the chance he'll want boxing lessons."

George's grin turned wolfish. "Or lessons in seduction."

She attempted a scowl, but she wasn't certain how well she succeeded. Her lips wanted to mirror his. "I'm afraid I'll have to draw the line there."

"He won't need them. If he takes after his father, those things will come naturally."

"Scoundrel!" She swatted at his shoulder and tried to duck away from his embrace, but he caught her about the waist. She squealed as he spun her back against him, his lips seeking hers. The clatter of youthful footsteps echoed through the corridor, announcing their imminent interruption.

George pulled out of the kiss but kept his palms planted firmly against her back. "I'm afraid we'll have to pick up this discussion later, if you're amenable."

She rested her head on his shoulder, savoring the last few seconds of peace. "Always."

ACKNOWLEDGMENTS

Without a great deal of help and occasional nagging, this book would still be a figment of my imagination (or, to paraphrase a girl I knew in high school, I might be a figment of this book's imagination). I owe a debt of thanks, as well as possibly chocolate and wine to the following:

To my critique partners, Caryl, Kathleen, Wendy, Tessy, Renee, Sam, Averil, and Deborah—without you, this book would be riddled with confusion, errors, repeated words, and extra spaces all over the place.

To Marian, Matan, Lizzie, Clemence, and Carina for being the best cheerleaders ever.

To Tracy Brogan for her help and suggestions on the first draft.

To the Lalalas once again for your continued support and occasional ass-kicking.

To Anne Barton, Valerie Bowman, Erin Knightley, and Sara Ramsey, thank you for being there and putting up with my occasional freak-outs. Thanks even more for understanding.

To the Dashing Duchesses for general awesomeness.

To my chapter-mates, both local and strictly online—the Ottawa Romance Writers Association, Hearts Through History Romance Writers, and the Beau Monde—thank you for all your help, whether or not you knew it at the time.

To all the readers who bought my debut and who have continued to support my writing by purchasing this book. I hope you liked George's story.

To Sara Megibow for her perpetual enthusiasm, advice, and support.

To Junessa Viloria for talking me through revisions and helping me to realize I can fix things the easy way.

To my husband and daughters, because, nope, the house still isn't clean. Why can't I be like my characters and employ servants?

Read on for a preview of Ashlyn Macnamara's

A MOST SCANDALOUS PROPOSAL

Available from Ballantine Books

CHAPTER ONE

April 1816, London

William Ludlowe wagers five thousand pounds that Miss Julia St. Claire will become the next Countess of Clivesden.

Benedict Revelstoke reread the lines in White's infamous betting book. What the devil? His fingers constricted about the quill, just shy of crushing it. Right. He'd been about to sign on his friend's wager. Some idiocy, no doubt—hardly worth the bother now.

The book's most recent inscription was scrawled, for all the world to see, in gold ink, no less. How fitting. Gold ink for Ludlowe, whom many of the *ton*'s ladies dubbed their golden boy. The man's lack of a title did nothing to diminish their opinion.

Upperton nudged him. "What's the matter? Your feet coming over icy all the sudden?"

Lead blocks would be more accurate, but Benedict was not about to admit to that. He laid the quill aside and jabbed a finger at the heavy vellum page. "Have you seen this?"

The page darkened as his oldest friend peered over his shoulder. "Clivesden? Thought he was married. Ludlowe's a jumped-up bacon brain. And what's Miss Julia got to do with either of them?"

"I've no idea, but I intend to find out." He released a breath between clenched teeth. "Appalling how so-called gentlemen will lay bets on young ladies of good reputation."

"Young ladies in general or Miss Julia in particular?"

Ignoring the gibe, Benedict turned on his heel and strode down the steps to the pavement. A glance at his pocket watch told him it was ten minutes past eleven, still early by the *ton*'s standards. That was something. At least he knew where he'd find Julia at such an hour.

He sighed at the prospect of dodging a passel of marriage-minded misses. But he'd be damned before he let some idiot besmirch her reputation.

JULIA stiffened her arms, but her dance partner refused to take the hint. Dash it, he held her too close for propriety's sake. Hang propriety—on that last turn, he'd actually tightened his grip so much her breasts grazed the front of his tailcoat. Too close for her comfort. So she did what any self-respecting young lady would do and trod on his toes.

"I do beg your pardon, my lord." The lie slid easily from her lips.

Lord Chuddleigh's smile faded, and his grip slackened along with his jowls. "Not at all."

Thankfully, the final notes of the waltz rose to the high ceiling of Lady Posselthwaite's ballroom a moment later, and Julia backed out of her partner's greedy embrace, stopping short when her skirt brushed against a dancer to her rear. "If you'll excuse me."

Chuddleigh eyed her up and down, before his red-rimmed gaze halted at a spot several inches below her chin. "Are you engaged for the next set?"

What could he be thinking? The roué. He was forty if he was a day, and a strong hint of brandy surrounded him like a cloud.

Julia made a show of consulting her dance card. "No.

I actually find I'm rather exhausted," she added before he could ask her for the next dance.

"It's the crowd. Dreadful crush as it is every year, of course. Perhaps a turn on the terrace?"

Drat. The man was relentless. Julia cast a swift glance about the ballroom. Unfortunately, Lord Chuddleigh was right about the crush. So many members of the *ton* packed into one spot, the men in starched linen and intricate cravats, the ladies in pastel ball gowns, it was a wonder anyone could move at all. Attendees wove past one another with polite smiles and quick *pardons,* intertwining like maypole dancers.

Convenient for Lord Chuddleigh, though, if he wanted an excuse to brush against her a bit more. Not that he had to expend much of an effort the way his paunch preceded him. She should never have agreed to the first set, but he'd seemed a safe enough choice when he asked. At his age and still unattached, she'd expected he wouldn't turn into a serious suitor.

Apparently, Chuddleigh had formed other ideas.

The crowd made it impossible to pick out a convenient means of escape. Her father was too occupied in the card room to concern himself with her dance partners. The ballroom—the marriage mart—that was her mother's exclusive domain. Papa was all too happy to leave Mama with the responsibility of landing wealthy, titled husbands for Julia and her sister, while he gambled to increase the family's meager earnings. Alas, for Mama aimed high in the hopes of giving her daughters what she had never had—social standing and influence.

In short, power. But such power came at the price of keeping up with fashion and maintaining a house in Town.

"I think a lemonade would be quite sufficient," she finally replied with a weak smile.

Lord Chuddleigh pressed thick lips together but acquiesced with a nod. "Do not move from that spot. I shall return anon."

The moment he disappeared behind Lady Whitby's bright orange turban, Julia elbowed her way in the opposite direction. She'd left her older sister amid a group of twittering hopefuls in their first season. With any luck, Julia could use them and their mamas as a shield against any further unwelcome advances.

She discovered Sophia next to a potted palm, deep in conversation with the dowager Countess of Epperley. Between the plant's fronds and the matron's ostrich plumes, Sophia was well camouflaged.

On Julia's approach, the dowager snapped a lorgnette to her face and eyed her from her sleek, honey-colored coiffure to the tips of her silk-clad toes. A frown fit to curdle new milk indicated Julia had passed muster.

"Oh, Julia." A rosy glow suffused Sophia's normally pearl-white complexion.

Julia pasted on a smile, knowing she was in for at least half an hour's worth of gushing, and that was just in public. Depending on what time they made it home tonight, Sophia could easily chatter away the remaining hours before dawn in her ebullience.

As long as she didn't end up sobbing herself to sleep, as had happened all too often in the past. So full of affection, Sophia. If only she hadn't bestowed her heart on a man who only occasionally acknowledged her existence. On such evenings, the urge to pull her sister into a hug warred with the desire to give Sophia a stern talking-to.

Tonight, apparently, was one of those evenings.

"My lady," Sophia breathed, "you simply must repeat to my sister what you've just told me."

The dowager pursed her lips and subjected Julia to a second inspection, as if she might find evidence of Julia's unworthiness to hear the latest gossip. Defensively, Julia spread out her fan and held it in front of her bosom, before Lady Epperley concluded her gown revealed too much.

"There's no need to sound so pleased about it," the old woman huffed. "You young chits, you have no conception of the serious nature of events."

Julia cast a sidelong glance at her sister. Such high color in Sophia's cheeks was normally associated with only one person.

"Then I shall have to tell her myself," Sophia pronounced.

"You shall do no such thing." The dowager harrumphed, setting both her jowls and plumes a-shudder. "It's a perfect tragedy, I tell you. It must be announced with the appropriate solemnity. It isn't as if we were exchanging the latest *on-dit*."

"What's this about the latest *on-dit*?" growled a familiar voice.

Julia smiled warmly at her childhood companion. Thank goodness. Better Benedict than Chuddleigh turning up with the lemonade.

At his appearance, Sophia inclined her head.

"Ah, Revelstoke." Acknowledging Benedict with a nod, Julia suppressed a jolt of surprise. She'd become so used to seeing him in his scarlet uniform that his bearing in eveningwear and starched cravat startled her. By rights, he should have looked like any other man of the *ton,* but the black superfine of his coat, matched to his ebony hair, only served to set off his dark complexion and sparkling blue eyes.

Snap! The lorgnette put in a reappearance. The dowager's frown lines deepened as she inspected the new arrival. Her gaze lingered on his sharp cheekbones, square jaw, and shaggy waves of hair that hung nearly to his shoulders, too long to be fashionable.

Or, for that matter, respectable.

"In my day, a young lady would never dream of addressing a gentleman in such a familiar manner. Why, I never called my husband by anything other than his title in all the years of our marriage, even in the most intimate of settings."

Benedict's shoulder brushed against Julia's as he leaned close and whispered, "That was more than I needed to know about their marriage."

She ducked behind her fan to hide both her grin and the blush that suddenly heated her cheeks. And why should she blush over Benedict of all people? She'd experienced the warmth of his breath wafting just beneath her ear on any number of previous occasions. She ought to be long accustomed to his brand of cutting commentary.

The dowager let out another harrumph, raised her considerable chin, and sailed off in a cloud of ostrich feathers and plum-colored silk.

"I believe she overheard you," Julia said.

"Without a doubt. The old dragon just trod on my foot."

Sophia giggled into her fan.

He turned his gaze on Julia, and her heart gave an odd thump. Normally, when he had a chance to seek her out at these functions, it was for one of two reasons—to save her from overzealous suitors or to escape from the pack of society mamas and their daughters. They might pass an agreeable hour or two on the sidelines exchanging pithy observations on the *ton*'s foibles, laughing together as she tried to match him in wit.

In all the years of their friendship, she'd had occasion to witness many moods etched on his face. Rarely had he turned so serious an expression on her, and never this strange intensity. *Thump.* Another pang in her chest. And where was that coming from?

Rather than press her fan to the spot, she tapped his forearm. "What's happened?"

He opened his mouth to reply, but Sophia chose that moment to interrupt. "I suppose I'll have to tell the news myself."

Julia turned to her sister. She watched as Sophia's features suddenly bloomed with renewed excitement. Something else was amiss there. Julia craned her neck. Had William Ludlowe actually put in an appearance?

"What news?" Benedict leaned closer. "What's going on?"

As if on cue, a collective sigh passed through the room, emanating from the females in attendance. A late arrival stood between the plaster columns of the entrance, his tall form easily visible over the heads of lesser men. Waves of golden blond hair flowed neatly back from an even-featured face that set feminine hearts to racing all across the room. The snowy linen of his artfully tied cravat stood in stark contrast to the austere black of his eveningwear.

Elegantly coiffed heads tilted toward each other, and the twitter of conversation increased its pace, punctuated by giggles. Sophia's smile broadened, and her fan fluttered double time, while the rosy glow on her cheeks extended to her forehead. On Julia's other side, Benedict let out a groan.

An easy smile graced the newcomer's lips as he nodded to an acquaintance. His gaze glided over the room to alight almost immediately in Julia's corner. Sophia grasped her arm, and her fingers tightened until Julia was sure she'd be sporting bruises tomorrow.

"Oh," Sophia sighed. "He's coming this way. How do I look?"

Julia didn't spare her sister a glance. With her neat golden hair swept off her lovely face and an ice-blue gown that, despite its age, displayed her figure to its best advantage, Sophia set a standard of beauty to which most of the *haut ton* could only aspire. If not for their mother's humble origins and the hints of scandal surrounding their parents' marriage, she might have been declared an Incomparable in her first season. Still, she'd turned down enough offers of marriage to cause their father to pull out what little remained of his hair.

"You look perfect as always."

The ragged edges of Sophia's fan flapped so fast that the breeze cooled Julia's own skin.

Benedict tugged at her other arm. "Might I have a word? In private?"

Sophia's eyes went round. "Not now. You cannot just leave me here. What if I faint?"

Faint? In five seasons, Sophia had yet to succumb to that particular malady. "Do not be ridic—"

"Then Ludlowe can catch you." Benedict's response was clipped. His fingers curled about Julia's wrist. "I really must insist."

"What is the matter with you tonight?" Julia whispered to Benedict. "You're behaving so strangely, if I did not know better, I'd say you were foxed."

"Believe me, Julia, I'd like nothing better at the moment."

She stiffened at the use of her given name. They'd known each other so long, the address came naturally in private, but it was unlike him to forget himself in the middle of a ballroom.

"Oh, M-Mr. Ludlowe," Sophia breathed.

Julia turned her attention to the man before her. His smile might have bedazzled the dowager Countess of Epperley into forgetting her lorgnette—or snapping it out for a better view—but it had little effect on Julia.

"Good evening, ladies. Revelstoke," Ludlowe added with a nod in Benedict's direction. "My dear Miss Julia, I must say you look particularly enchanting this evening."

For a moment, she didn't react. She couldn't have

heard right. But then he reached for her hand as if it were his due. Belatedly, she disentangled her arm from Sophia's death grip and allowed him to brush his lips against the back of her glove.

"Mr. Ludlowe." She deliberately flattened her tone to coolness, hardly what anyone would term friendly.

After another moment, he dropped her hand to turn his considerable charm on Sophia. Julia could feel its effect radiating off her sister in the form of heat. A dazzling smile threatened to split Sophia's face in two.

"A pleasure, as always, Miss St. Claire."

If Sophia noticed that he paid her beauty no compliment, she hid it well. Dipping her head, she dropped into a curtsey. "My lord."

Julia's mouth dropped open. *My lord?* The evening was growing stranger by the minute.

Ludlowe's chuckle rumbled, low and smooth as hot chocolate, over their corner. Even the potted palm perked up. "Now, now, Miss St. Claire, let's not be overly hasty. Nothing's settled as of yet."

Beside her, Benedict held himself rigid, the tension seething in the air around him.

"What isn't settled?" Julia's question floated free before she could stop herself.

Ludlowe turned back to her. His smile would have melted butter. "You haven't heard of my good fortune then?"

"No, I haven't."

The fine lines on his forehead smoothed to solemnity. "It's quite boorish of me to refer to it as good fortune, actually. Do forgive me. My fortune is another family's tragedy, you see."

What on earth? She frowned, resting her fan against her bosom. "Oh dear."

"The Earl of Clivesden has met with an unfortunate accident. Horrific, really."

Foreboding settled over her. "Accident?"

"Poor man. He should never have ventured out on those winding Devonshire roads. Entire carriage tumbled off a cliff into the Channel. His young son was with him."

She pressed suddenly icy fingers to her lips. "How dreadful." At the same time, she noted Sophia's lack of reaction. This must be the news Lady Epperley had imparted to her sister, doubtless with the proper ceremony.

Benedict's lip curled. "I fail to see how such a tragedy might turn to anybody's advantage."

Ludlowe had the grace to avert his eyes. "There's an appalling lack of male issue in that line. They had to trace the family back four generations to find an heir."

"You'll forgive me," Benedict said, his words clipped to the point of rudeness, "but what's that got to do with you?"

Ludlowe sketched them a bow. "My great-grandfather was the third Earl of Clivesden's younger brother."

Benedict surged forward with such force and suddenness that Julia laid a restraining hand on his forearm. "*You?*" he snarled. "You're now Clivesden?"

Ludlowe's smile did not falter for an instant. "Not yet, but my claim is solid. I daresay the Lord Chancellor ought to accept it without delay."

"As long as the former earl's widow isn't in a delicate condition, you mean." Benedict seemed to be forcing the words through gritted teeth.

Julia slanted her eyes in his direction. What she could see of his neck above his cravat flushed red. Beneath her hand, the muscles in his arm had turned to steel. Why was he so upset over the circumstances? While tragic, to be certain, none of them had actually known Clivesden well.

Ludlowe's smile remained fixed. "Of course."

He stepped closer to Julia, and the muscles beneath her fingertips jerked.

"I had hoped to keep the news quiet a bit longer. I might have known gossip would foil my plans." He acknowledged Sophia with a nod, and she beamed at him from behind the protection of her fan.

"Ah well, *c'est la vie.*" Ludlowe shrugged. "I hadn't come over with the intention of discussing this matter. I was wondering if Miss Julia would care for the next dance."

If he hadn't been looking her in the eye, Julia would never have credited the notion. When Ludlowe turned up at a ball, he remained decidedly ensconced in the card room or on the sidelines. He chatted with the ladies, he flirted outrageously, he might disappear into the gardens for long stretches, but he rarely danced.

The lilting strains of violins in three-quarter time met her ears. Goodness. Ludlowe certainly never waltzed.

An expectant silence fell over the group, while the music swelled around them. She couldn't possibly, not with her sister standing right there, deflating a bit further with each joyous note. "I'm terribly sorry—"

"She promised the next set to me," Benedict said over her reply.

"I'm sure Sophia would be delighted," Julia added quickly. "That way, no one is disappointed."

Ludlowe hesitated a second too long before nodding. "Your servant. I must insist you save another dance for me later."

He didn't wait for her reply. Offering his arm to a glowing Sophia, he led her to join the whirling couples already on the dance floor.

Julia rounded on Benedict, who bent his left arm in invitation. "I believe this is our waltz."

She ignored him. "Are you planning to tell me what that was all about?"

He held her gaze, the breadth of his shoulders blocking the flickering light from the crystal chandeliers. That disturbing intensity still lit their depths. And where had it come from along with his, well, protectiveness? She pressed her lips into a line and shuffled her weight from one foot to the other.

"After this set. Meet me outside. For now, we'd better make a proper show of dancing. Just so no one is disappointed."

She took his arm, and he set off at such a clip that she stumbled after him through the crowd until they found a spot among the dancers.

"Why can't you tell me now?" she persisted. His brows lowered in disapproval, but she ignored the reaction. The waltz permitted conversation, after all.

He set a solid arm about her waist, seized her hand, and spun her into the first turn. "Not here. Not where others might overhear." He tipped his chin toward an orange turban swaying not far from them. "Lady Witless, for example."

At the nickname, Julia suppressed a laugh and tapped him on the shoulder with her fan. Benedict had so christened the old gossip two years ago when Lady Whitby's spiteful tongue had run her afoul of a few other matrons who had overheard her and arranged to knock her into the punch bowl. "Stop. You're terrible. By the by, what are you doing here tonight? I didn't even realize you were in Town."

"I only arrived two days ago. I came to have a look at some horses."

"Ah, of course. No wonder you haven't seen fit to call. What's more important than cattle?"

"Quite a few things, it turns out."

"Oh?"

But his gaze settled at some point beyond her. Well. Whatever was more important must have to do with this mysterious discussion he refused to have in the middle of the dance floor. He guided her through the steps of the dance with practiced ease until she felt as if she were hovering several inches above the floor. This was not dancing; it was floating. On every turn, her stomach tripped over itself.

It was nothing more than a waltz. Meaningless. The buoyancy that lifted her heels on every step had nothing to do with the hand planted at her waist, the fingers flexing into every pivot. Those strong fingers, calloused from the constant rubbing of reins, capable of controlling the most hot-blooded of horses, burned through the layers of her ball gown and stays. And his thighs, powerful from years in the saddle, brushed against hers through her skirts. She should not allow herself to think of such things. This was Benedict, steady and dependable, not one of her suitors.

Suppressing a sigh, she tried again. "I had no idea you danced so well. How is it we've never waltzed before?"

He winked. "You've never twisted my arm into it before."

"I twisted? As I recall, this was your idea."

"Perhaps I ought to have ideas a bit more often." His words slipped out easily.

For a moment, Julia was dumbfounded. That sounded rather roguish. "Who are you practicing for?"

"I beg your pardon?"

"You're practicing your flirting on me." Once again, she tapped him with her fan. "I shall not allow it unless you confess immediately who you intend to pursue."

He grinned maddeningly at her. "Then I suppose I shall have to remain woefully out of practice. A gentleman never tells. But if I remain forever a bachelor, I shall lay the blame at your feet."

Out of the corner of her eye, she caught a glimpse of Sophia dancing with Ludlowe. With their matched coloring, they turned heads all about the room. Sophia absolutely bloomed in his arms, the very portrait of an utterly smitten young woman.

Smitten indeed. Julia had vowed never to allow such tender feelings to overtake her. They made her anxious and edgy. Vulnerable. Her fingers curled about her fan until its delicate ribs threatened to snap. She'd witnessed too many others ensnared by what they termed love to aspire to anything more than a civilized, sensible union.

She concentrated on keeping up with Benedict. But for the occasions when he came home on leave, the past few years he'd spent with the cavalry had prevented her from enjoying his company at the *ton*'s events. To think she'd missed dancing such as this, when she hadn't even known it possible.

At long last, the music swelled toward the coda. He leaned down to mutter next to her ear, "I'll be out on the terrace in five minutes."

Heart still thudding, she slipped out of his arms, only to collide with something soft.

"Careful now." Lord Chuddleigh caught her in an enthusiastic grip.

Blast it all. She cast a glance about for Benedict, but the crowd had already swallowed him. Why couldn't he have said his piece now, rather than playing games? Surely, they could have found a quiet corner away from overzealous ears.

She pressed her fingers to her temple. "Your pardon, my lord. I'm afraid I'm not feeling at all well. If you'll excuse me."

With that, she wove her way through the crowd in the general direction of the ladies' retiring room. Just before stepping into the corridor, she glanced over her shoulder.

Fan a-flutter and rosy with excitement, Sophia still

chatted with Ludlowe. Thank the heavens. Perhaps something good would come out of this evening, after all.

Five minutes later, Julia found herself second-guessing that prediction. Benedict led her into a quiet corner of the garden far from prying eyes.

"I want you to stay away from Ludlowe," he said in a harsh voice and without preamble.

A shiver prickled along the back of her neck. Never once had he seen fit to give her orders, as if she were one of his men. In the darkness, half his face lay in shadow so that he appeared as some creature of the night.

Puzzled, she frowned. "But why does it matter? It's not as if he makes a habit of attending these things. He's made a career of avoiding marriage." Unfortunately for Sophia and her hopes.

"He's about to inherit an earldom. His priorities have changed."

"It hardly signifies. Besides, we've managed to arrange things so he's spending time with Sophia."

Benedict stepped closer to her and placed his hands on her upper arms. The heat of his palms permeated his gloves and seared into her bare skin.

"He hasn't got his sights set on Sophia. He's set them on you."